GINA'S
LITTLE SECRET

BY
JENNIFER TAYLOR

MILLS
BOON

DID YOU PURCHASE THIS BOOK WITHOUT A COVER?

If you did, you should be aware it is **stolen property** as it was reported *unsold and destroyed* by a retailer. Neither the author nor the publisher has received any payment for this book.

All the characters in this book have no existence outside the imagination of the author, and have no relation whatsoever to anyone bearing the same name or names. They are not even distantly inspired by any individual known or unknown to the author, and all the incidents are pure invention.

All Rights Reserved including the right of reproduction in whole or in part in any form. This edition is published by arrangement with Harlequin Enterprises II BV/S.à.r.l. The text of this publication or any part thereof may not be reproduced or transmitted in any form or by any means, electronic or mechanical, including photocopying, recording, storage in an information retrieval system, or otherwise, without the written permission of the publisher.

This book is sold subject to the condition that it shall not, by way of trade or otherwise, be lent, resold, hired out or otherwise circulated without the prior consent of the publisher in any form of binding or cover other than that in which it is published and without a similar condition including this condition being imposed on the subsequent purchaser.

® and TM are trademarks owned and used by the trademark owner and/or its licensee. Trademarks marked with ® are registered with the United Kingdom Patent Office and/or the Office for Harmonisation in the Internal Market and in other countries.

First published in Great Britain 2012
by Mills & Boon, an imprint of Harlequin (UK) Limited.
Harlequin (UK) Limited, Eton House, 18-24 Paradise Road,
Richmond, Surrey TW9 1SR

© Jennifer Taylor 2012

ISBN: 978 0 263 89153 9

Harlequin (UK) policy is to use papers that are natural, renewable and recyclable products and made from wood grown in sustainable forests. The logging and manufacturing process conform to the legal environmental regulations of the country of origin.

Printed and bound in Spain
by Blackprint CPI, Barcelona

Jennifer Taylor lives in the north-west of England, in a small village surrounded by some really beautiful countryside. She has written for several different Mills & Boon® series in the past, but it wasn't until she read her first Medical™ Romance that she truly found her niche. She was so captivated by these heart-warming stories that she set out to write them herself! When she's not writing, or doing research for her latest book, Jennifer's hobbies include reading, gardening, travel, and chatting to friends both on and off-line. She is always delighted to hear from readers, so do visit her website at www.jennifer-taylor.com

To Pam and Dudley, with love and thanks
for all your help and support.

CHAPTER ONE

4 p.m. 11 December

'THAT was ED on the phone. Bet you can't guess what they wanted?'

Sister Georgina Lee groaned as she looked up from the computer. 'Don't tell me—they want us to find yet *another* bed for yet *another* patient.'

'Got it in one!' Rosie James, their young student nurse, grinned. 'Give yourself a pat on the back.'

'I would do if I had the time to spare.' Gina's expression was wry as she glanced at the computer screen. 'It's the third time I've tried to fill in this order form. At this rate, we're going to run out of basic supplies.'

'It has been busy,' Rosie agreed. 'I had no idea that life on the acute assessment unit would be so hectic. I thought it would be a doddle, to be honest. Patients would be sent here for a couple of hours and then they'd either be moved to a ward or sent home.'

'That's what most folk believe if they haven't worked here.' Gina laughed, her slate-grey eyes filled with amusement. 'It's what I thought happened here too when I took this job. I soon discovered how wrong I was!'

'It must have been a shock,' Rosie suggested.

Gina shrugged. 'A bit, but I must admit that I enjoy the variety. If you work on a ward like Women's Surgical, for instance, then you know that your patients will be either preparing for an operation or recovering from one. In here, you never know what you're going to have to deal with. It certainly keeps you on your toes.'

'I suppose so, although I'm not sure I'd be able to cope with the pressure, long term,' Rosie admitted.

'It's not for everyone,' Gina said firmly, not wanting the younger woman to feel discouraged. She shot another glance at the screen and stood up. 'We'd better go and see if we can sort out a bed. Mr Walker in the end bay is supposed to be moving to Cardiology, so maybe we can sweet-talk them into taking him sooner than planned.'

Gina led the way, pausing en route to let the rest of the staff know that another admission was on the way. She smiled when her friend, Julie Grey, groaned. 'I know how you feel, Jules. We're bursting at the seams as it is. At this rate we'll soon be having to use the staff-room!'

'Either that or leave patients on trolleys in the corridor as used to happen in the past,' Julie said ruefully.

'Thank heavens those days are gone,' Gina retorted. 'The thought of any patient being abandoned like that makes my blood run cold.'

'We all hated it,' Julie assured her. 'This new unit might get crowded but it's a huge improvement on how things used to be.'

Gina left the staff to get on with their work and went to have a word with Frank Walker. He had been rushed in by ambulance at lunchtime complaining of chest pains. Subsequent tests had shown blockages to three of the main coronary arteries and the decision had been made to perform a bypass. Now Gina smiled as she stopped beside his bed.

'So how are you feeling now, Mr Walker?'

'So-so. The pain has eased off thanks to the medication, so that's a blessing.' He sighed. 'I suppose I've only got myself to blame. My wife's been nagging me for years to stop smoking and eat sensibly but I took no notice. I thought she was making a fuss about nothing.'

'It's hard to accept advice sometimes,' Gina said tactfully. 'Still, once you've had the bypass done, you'll feel a lot better.'

'Do you think so?' Frank looked worried. 'Oh, I know that young chap who came to see me was very dismissive, but you can't help worrying, can you? I mean, they have to stop your heart and everything.'

'Yes, they do, but they attach you to a special machine which takes over the jobs your heart and lungs would normally do,' Gina explained, wishing, not for the first time, that Miles Humphreys had a better bedside manner. An operation such as this might be routine to him but it certainly wasn't routine for the patient.

'So you think it's quite safe, do you, Sister?' Frank said anxiously. 'And that I should have it done?'

'I do. Although it's a major operation, it's performed frequently. And I know for a fact that the cardio team here at St Saviour's are highly skilled.' She patted Frank's hand. 'You'll be fine, I promise you.'

'Thank you.' Frank smiled at her. 'I feel much happier now. Shame that young doctor didn't take the time to reassure me like you've just done. You should give him a few tips on how to talk to his patients.'

Gina smiled although she didn't say anything.

Talking to Miles was something she was trying to avoid. Ever since he'd asked her out on a date and she'd refused, there'd been an atmosphere when he came into the ward. If only he would accept that there was nothing personal about her refusing his invitation.

She sighed as she went to phone the cardiology unit. The truth was she wasn't interested in Miles or any other man. She'd had her heart broken once and there was no way that she was going to risk it happening again, especially when it could impact on Lily. Making sure that her two-year-old daughter was safe and happy was all that mattered. There was no room in her life for a relationship.

Frank Walker had just been transferred to the cardiology unit when the porters arrived with their latest admission. Gina was in the office, making yet another attempt to get to grips with the paperwork, but she went out to meet them. Julie had already directed them to the end bay and they were manoeuvring the bed into place when Gina got there.

'So, who have we got?' she asked, unclipping the notes from the foot rail. She glanced at the patient's details. Name: Marco Andretti. Age: thirty-seven. Address: Villa Rosa, Florence, Italy. Just for a moment the full impact of what she was reading didn't hit her and then all of a sudden her heart began to pound. It had to be a mistake! It couldn't be her Marco....

Could it?

Gina took a deep breath as she forced herself to look at the man lying on the bed. His eyes were shut and the right side of his head was swathed in a thick white dressing but neither of those things mattered. As her eyes drank in the olive-tanned skin, the elegant nose, the chiselled jaw and sensuous curve of his mouth she felt panic assail her. It *was* Marco. There was no mistake about that!

'Gina? Hey, are you OK?'

Gina jumped when Julie tapped her on the arm. She knew there was no point claiming that she was fine because her friend wouldn't believe her. 'I...um...I feel a bit queasy, that's all. I expect I'm hungry.'

'Probably because you worked straight through your break.' Julie made flapping movements with her hands. 'Go on, scoot! You go and make yourself a cup of coffee. We can manage here, can't we, Rosie?'

'Well, if you're sure...' Gina turned away when the older woman nodded. Normally, she wouldn't have dreamt of leaving the staff to settle in a new patient without her being present, but this wasn't a normal situation, was it? A wave of hysterical laughter welled up inside her and she pressed her hand to her mouth as she made her way to the staffroom. Thankfully, there was nobody in there so she switched on the kettle then sank down on a chair as her legs suddenly gave way.

What twist of fate had brought Marco here to the very hospital where she worked? she wondered dizzily. It would be three years this Christmas since she had seen him last, three whole years since he had told her bluntly that he didn't envisage them ever having a future together. His expression had been so cold that any protests she might have made had remained unuttered. What would have been the point of trying to convince him that they'd had something special, something worth fighting for, when he obviously hadn't believed that himself? She couldn't have *made* him love her, definitely wouldn't have begged him to, so she had done what he had wanted and walked away.

Gina's heart was heavy as she recalled that terrible period in her life. She had wondered in the beginning if once she had gone, he might realise that he missed her more than he had thought; however, as the weeks had passed, and he had made no attempt to contact her, she had accepted how foolish she'd been to hope for that. Marco may have enjoyed making love to her. He may even have enjoyed spending time with her for a short while, but he had never needed her as a permanent part of his life.

It had been hard to face that fact but at least it had made it easier to decide what to do when Lily was born. But now Marco was here and Gina knew that his reappearance in her life would have repercussions. It was bound to. Marco was Lily's father. He had a daughter he knew nothing about.

CHAPTER TWO

'RIGHT, everything's sorted. One of the neuro team will be here shortly... Hello! Earth to Gina—are you receiving me?'

'What?' Gina jumped when Julie appeared in front of her. She took a quick breath, forcing the feeling of panic to retreat if not to actually disappear. The situation was way too volatile to hope that would happen.

'Sorry, I was miles away,' she said, getting up to spoon instant coffee into a couple of mugs. She added boiling water then reached for the sugar jar, deriving comfort from the familiar routine. Maybe that was the answer, she thought suddenly. Behave normally and Marco wouldn't suspect anything was wrong. After all, there was no reason to tell him about Lily, was there?

'Here, let me do that. I know I like my coffee sweet but three spoons of sugar is too much even for me!' Julie edged her aside, tipping the offending brew down the sink before starting again from scratch. She treated Gina to an old-fashioned look as she handed her a fresh mug of coffee. 'If I didn't know better, I'd say the sight of our dishy new patient has knocked you for six.'

'Rubbish!' Gina gave a sharp little laugh, anxious to stamp on that idea before it could take hold. The last thing she needed was people speculating. 'I'm just hungry, as I said. I didn't have time to eat anything before I came into work, so it's my own fault.'

'I've got some sandwiches left. Here you go.' Julie handed her a plastic container then leant against the work top while she drank her coffee.

'Thanks.' Gina forced herself to bite into one of the thick ham sandwiches even though the last thing she felt like doing was eating. Could she pull it off, make sure that Marco remained unaware of Lily's existence? After all, he would only be in AAU for a short while; he would either be moved to a ward or discharged depending on what treatment he required. There was no reason why she should bring up the subject of their daughter.

Pain speared through her and she hurriedly took another bite of the sandwich. Their daughter, the child they had conceived together. She had truly believed that they had been making love when it must have happened, but that wasn't how Marco had viewed it. It couldn't have been. It had just been sex for him, pure and simple, and the fact that it had resulted in a beautiful, healthy little girl was incidental.

'I've not dealt with a case like this before. It's one of those things you read about but rarely experience.'

Gina looked up when she realised that once again her thoughts had been running off at a tangent. 'What do you mean?'

'Amnesia. Hopefully, he'll recover his memory soon, but it must be really scary, not knowing who you are.'

'You're talking about Marco?' Gina queried, then flushed when Julie looked at her in surprise. 'That is his name, isn't it? I think that's what it said in his notes.'

'Yes, that's right. Marco Andretti. Apparently he's a

doctor, a trauma specialist, no less. I don't know if that makes it better or worse, do you?'

'I've no idea,' Gina replied, struggling to follow what her friend was saying. 'Are you telling me that he's lost his memory?'

'Hmm. Seems he had no idea who he was or where he was going when he was brought into ED. All the paramedics could tell them was that he was on his way from Heathrow when he was involved in an RTA.'

'So how did they find out his name?'

'One of the staff went through his pockets and found his passport—they got the details from that. They also found a letter confirming the time and date of an interview for the post of Head of Trauma care at the Southern Free. He must be pretty high up the ladder if he's being interviewed for a post like that.' Julie grimaced. 'Not that it helps very much at the moment. It must be awful for him, mustn't it? He's all on his own in a strange country and he hasn't got a clue who he is.'

'So what's going to happen next?' Gina asked, her head reeling from what she had learned. Marco had come to London to attend an interview? She had never imagined that he would leave Italy and the news threw her so that it was hard to concentrate when Julie continued.

'The police are going to try to contact his family. I expect he's married. I can't imagine a gorgeous hunk like him being single, can you? Hopefully, his wife will be able to fly over to be with him. One thing's certain, though—he's going to need a lot of support until he gets his memory back.'

Gina put the sandwich down after Julie left. Standing up, she went to the door. She could just see the end bay from where she stood although she couldn't see the man who was lying in the bed there. So Marco had lost his memory? He didn't remember who he was or anything about his life? She too had read about this kind of thing happening, but had never experienced it. Would he remember her? she wondered suddenly.

Her heart began to race. In one way it would be so much easier if he had forgotten about her, yet in another she couldn't bear to think that those few weeks they'd spent together might have been expunged from his mind forever. Even though it was crazy to feel like this, she knew she had to find out.

She closed the staffroom door and made her way back to the ward. Everything was starting to settle down now as the patients adjusted to the idea that they were in hospital. There was open visiting in AAU and there were a number of friends and relatives gathered around the beds, but even they seemed calmer. It was always a shock when a loved one was rushed into hospital and people reacted in many different ways to the stress.

Gina had learned to cope with it all, the anger, the fear, the questions. It was rare that anything fazed her but she had to admit that her nerves were jangling as she approached the end bay. Marco still had his eyes closed and didn't seem aware of her presence as she stood beside the bed, looking down at him. He had always been an extremely handsome man and nothing had changed in that respect. His body looked as lean and fit as ever beneath the thin hospital gown, his skin glowed with good health, his dark hair was lustrous and thick. Only the few strands of grey at his temples proved that time had passed, but even they did little to detract from his appeal.

Gina felt her stomach muscles clench as a wave of awareness rushed through her. Despite everything Marco had said and done three years ago, despite how much he had hurt her, she was still attracted to him!

Marco could feel the blood pounding inside his skull. He knew it was a result of the accident because the ED consultant had explained it to him. When the car he had been travelling in had collided with a lorry that had pulled out in front of them, he had hit his head and suffered a concussion. That accounted for the headache but did it really explain why he couldn't remember who he was or where he'd been going?

He opened his eyes, gripping hold of the rails at the sides of the bed when the room swam sickeningly. Taking a deep breath, he forced the nausea to subside and focused on his surroundings. White walls, blue curtains, a familiar smell of antiseptic, which all added up to his being in hospital. He knew where he was. He also knew that it was somewhere he was used to being, too.

Marco frowned as he tried to make sense of that idea. Had he been ill recently, so ill that he had needed a prolonged stay in hospital? He didn't think so. Apart from the headache, he felt quite well, not like someone who was recovering from an illness. So if he hadn't been a patient, had he worked in a hospital in some capacity?

That idea seemed much more fitting. He closed his eyes again as he let it seep into his consciousness. He worked in a hospital? Yes, that was right. He knew instinctively it was true. And yet there was something odd about being here, something not related to the fact that normally he wouldn't be lying in bed…

It was the voices, he realised with a start. Or, more

accurately, the fact that they were speaking English. Although he understood what was being said, he knew that English wasn't his first language. What was?

'Dr Andretti. Can you hear me?'

Marco's eyes shot open when a quiet voice spoke beside him. Turning his head, he saw a nurse standing beside the bed. She was small and blonde, her hair caught back at the nape of her neck with a dark blue ribbon that matched the blue of her uniform. Marco felt something stir inside him, something that felt almost like recognition. He had the strangest feeling that he had seen her before, but before he could work out where, she spoke again.

'How do you feel?'

Her voice was soft, husky, and Marco felt a ripple of awareness run through him. The low, sweet tone of her voice was oddly soothing as it flowed along his taut nerves. For the first time since he had regained consciousness in the back of the ambulance he didn't feel afraid.

'I am not sure.' His own voice sounded rough and he paused while he tried to work some moisture into his mouth. The nurse must have realised his dilemma because she reached for the jug and filled a glass with water. Bending, she slid her hand beneath his head and raised it a fraction while she held the glass to his lips.

'Take a sip of this,' she instructed, tilting the glass so that a trickle of cool water slid between his lips.

Marco swallowed greedily, frowning when she took the glass away, and she smiled faintly, her grey eyes filled with understanding. 'You'll be sick if you drink too much. You can have another sip in a moment.'

She gently removed her hand and he felt a wave of

disappointment wash over him that owed nothing to the fact that he'd been deprived of the water. Why should it have felt so good to have her touch him like that? he wondered. And why did he want her to touch him again?

He watched as she placed the glass on the bedside cabinet, studying the gentle curve of her cheek, the sweeping length of her lashes, the upward tilt of her small nose. She was extremely pretty in a very English way with that fine, pale skin and those delicate features. Everything about her was refined, feminine, and he found it very appealing. He realised with a start that he was attracted to her, even though she was very different in appearance from Francesca.

The memory slid into his mind without any warning. He remembered who Francesca was, how she had looked...*everything*! Pain lanced through him and he closed his eyes, wondering if he could bear to go through the agony all over again. If this was what it felt like to get his memory back, he would rather forget!

Gina frowned as she looked down at Marco. His eyes were tightly shut and his hands were clenched into fists. Bending, she felt for his pulse, concerned in case he had taken a sudden turn for the worse. Head injuries were notoriously difficult to treat and it wasn't unknown for a patient's condition to deteriorate in the blink of an eye.

The thought sent a shaft of fear scudding through her. Gina's fingers tightened around his wrist as she counted the life-giving beats. Julie should have put him on a monitor, she thought as she made a rapid calculation. He needed his blood pressure checked and his oxygen saturation levels monitored. You really couldn't take any chances with an injury like this.

His eyes suddenly opened and she felt her own blood

pressure zoom several notches up the scale when she found herself staring into their golden-brown depths. Was that recognition she could see in his gaze? Had Marco remembered who she was? The thought scared her and she let his hand drop back onto the bed, afraid that her touch would be the catalyst to make him regain his memory. She didn't want that to happen until she had worked out what she should do about Lily!

'I'd be happier if you were on a monitor,' she said hurriedly, ashamed that she could think that way. It must be terrible for Marco to lose his memory and she should be doing everything she could to help him…

Everything except telling him about Lily and how the little girl had been conceived, a small voice whispered inside her head.

'Just lie there and try to relax while I fetch it,' she instructed as calmly as she could. She hurried away, afraid that he would realise something was wrong if she lingered. There was a spare monitor outside the office so she went to fetch it then hesitated, unsure if she should go back at that moment. Although she wanted him to recover his memory, maybe it would be better if she steered clear. He would be going up to Neurology soon and once he left AAU that would be the last she needed to see of him. When Rosie appeared, she called her over.

'Can you set this up in the end bay for Dr Andretti? I want you to keep an eye on him, too. Don't let him go to sleep. We need to check there's nothing brewing.'

'But ED said he was OK,' Rosie protested. 'He's had a CT scan and it was clear.'

'That may be so, but it isn't unknown for a bleed to

develop later,' Gina said sharply. 'That's why he's been sent here, so we can monitor what's happening.'

'Oh, I see. Sorry. I just assumed he was here because of losing his memory.' Rosie looked so downcast that Gina instantly regretted being so brusque with her.

'That's certainly one of the reasons why he was sent to us, I imagine. Hopefully, someone from the neuro team will be here soon. I'll give them a call and see what's happening. But in the meantime, we'll apply both belt and braces, i.e. put him on a monitor *and* do fifteen-minute obs.'

'I understand.' Rosie perked up a bit. She grinned as she manoeuvred the monitor out of the corner. 'Not that it's any hardship to keep an eye on him, mind. He's definitely fit, *despite* his age!'

Gina laughed as the young nurse hurried away. Anyone would think that Marco was in his dotage if they heard that, whereas from what she had seen, he was in his prime. Her heart gave a little jolt at the thought and she hurried into the office to phone Neurology. They promised to send someone down within the hour so she had to leave it at that. There were other patients who needed her attention, after all; she couldn't devote herself solely to Marco's care even if she wanted to, which she didn't.

She squared her shoulders. Marco had made his feelings perfectly clear three years ago and even though he may have lost his memory, she doubted if he had changed his mind. She hadn't figured in his life back then and she wouldn't figure in it now, with or without Lily.

CHAPTER THREE

By the time the neuro registrar arrived, Marco was feeling decidedly out of sorts. It seemed that every time he closed his eyes that young nurse would appear and start talking to him. He was sick and tired of her shrill little voice buzzing in his ears like a demented wasp. Why hadn't that other nurse come back, he thought impatiently, the one who had spoken to him so gently? He could put up with her disturbing him very easily.

He frowned as once again a memory tried to surface only to disappear the moment he attempted to capture it. He was more convinced than ever that he had met her before, but if that were the case then why hadn't she said something? His head ached even more as he tried to work it out but it was just too difficult. Hopefully, it would all come back to him in time, all the good memories as well as the bad, like those about Francesca.

Sadness welled up inside him and he closed his eyes, afraid that in his present state he would do something unforgivable like cry. After Francesca had died, he hadn't cried, hadn't been able to. He had been too numb at first, too eaten up by grief later to give vent to his emotions. Over the years it had become increasingly important that he shouldn't break down. He had needed to remain strong if he was to stick to his decision never to allow himself to fall in love again. There had been just that one time he had wavered, when he had realised that he was letting himself feel things he shouldn't...

'Dr Andretti? I'm Steven Pierce, the neuro registrar. Sorry about the delay but it's been like a madhouse today.'

The memory melted away and Marco's eyes shot open. He stared at the man standing beside the bed then let his gaze move to the woman beside him. So she was back, was she? She had deigned to spare him some time now that her colleague had decided to pay him a visit?

Marco's irritation levels shot up several notches and he glared at the younger man. 'About time too. Is it normal practice to leave a patient suffering from a head trauma in a busy ward like this?' His gaze skimmed around the room, taking stock of the patients and their visitors, and his expression was frosty when he looked at the nurse. 'The noise level in here is appalling, Sister. If I was in charge of this department then you can be sure that it would be run along very different lines.'

'But you aren't in charge, are you, Dr Andretti?'

Her voice was still soft, but there was a coolness about it that stung and Marco's frown deepened. However, before he could say anything else the younger doctor intervened.

'Unfortunately, AAU is one of the busiest departments in the hospital. We think we have a tough time on the wards, but I don't know how the staff here copes with all the comings and goings.'

Marco inclined his head, acknowledging the rebuke and the justification for it. He had been rude and there was no excuse for that. 'Of course. I apologise if my comments caused offence, Sister. *Mi scusi.*'

'There is nothing to apologise for.'

Her tone was still chilly and he felt a prickle of disappointment nibble away at his irritation. For some reason he couldn't explain, he didn't want her to be so distant with him. The thought surprised him so that it was a moment before he realised the registrar was speaking again.

'I noticed that you spoke Italian just now, Dr Andretti. Obviously, some aspects of your life are starting to return.'

'Si,' he concurred slowly. 'I realised earlier that English wasn't my first language, but it is only now that I know Italian is.'

Steven Pierce nodded. 'It's a start. You will probably find that bits and pieces come back to you in no particular order. You'll recall one event and not recall something else that happened at the same time.'

'You think it is retrograde amnesia,' Marco queried.

'Yes, more than likely. Most people with amnesia suffer a gap in their memory that extends backwards from the onset of the disorder. When you hit your head during the accident that was the start and now you're finding it difficult to recall what went on before then.' Steven smiled. 'However, the fact that you are able to diagnose your own condition is another indication that your memory is starting to return.'

'Bene. It is not pleasant to not know who you are and what has happened to you,' Marco admitted. He glanced at the nurse and felt surprise run through him when he saw the alarm on her face. It was obvious that some-

thing was troubling her even though she was doing her best to disguise it.

She must have sensed he was looking at her because she glanced round and he saw the colour run up her face before she turned away, busying herself with re-arranging the water jug and glass. Marco knew that it was merely an excuse to avoid looking at him and felt more perplexed than ever. It was on the tip of his tongue to ask her what was wrong when the younger man continued.

'I'd like to move you to the neuro unit so we can run some tests, but unfortunately we're short of beds right now.' He turned to the nurse. 'I'm afraid Dr Andretti will have to stay here for tonight, Gina. Sorry about that.'

'It's fine. Don't worry about it.'

She summoned a smile but Marco could tell how strained it was even if the other man didn't appear to notice. He listened without interrupting while the registrar explained that he would like Marco to be kept under observation. If he was honest, his attention was focused more on Gina than on the plans for his ongoing care.

Marco shivered as he silently repeated the name. Once again there was that flash of recognition, the feeling that he had met her before. He tried to force the fog from his brain but it wouldn't lift. Was he imagining it? Was his brain trying to compensate for its lack of memories by creating new ones?

As a doctor, he knew it was possible. False memories could be implanted in a person's mind; it was a proven fact. But why would he want to do such a thing? Surely

he wasn't so desperate to ease his loneliness that he
would choose to latch onto a total stranger?

That was another memory, the fact that he was lonely.
Marco let it settle in his mind then dismissed it as he
did every single time. He wouldn't allow himself to
wish for more than he had. He'd had everything a man
could have dreamed of once and lost it. He couldn't and
wouldn't go through that agony again.

His heart began to pound as he looked at the woman
standing beside the bed. Maybe he couldn't recall where
they had met but he knew—*he just knew*—that they
had! In that second he realised how vital it was that he
regain his memory as quickly as possible. He had to
find out why Gina was pretending not to know him.

The evening wore on, bringing with it the usual mix
of the mundane and high drama. Gina had worked on
AAU for almost two years and had seen it all before,
but that night seemed very different from all the others. She was so conscious of Marco's presence that her
senses seemed acutely heightened. The noise level *was*
extremely high; the number of visitors per bed *did* need
reducing; waiting times *were* too long—people needed
to be seen by a specialist far sooner than was currently
happening.

She sent Julie off to clear the ward of excess visitors.
Two per bed was the designated limit and she intended
to stick to that. While Julie was doing that, she phoned
all the departments that were supposed to be sending
someone down to see a patient, refusing to accept the
usual excuse that they were short of staff. As she politely reminded them, AAU was for acute cases only. It
wasn't an overflow for the various wards. She had just

finished when she heard a monitor beeping and Rosie came rushing into the office.

'The man in bed seven can't breathe!' the student gabbled at her.

'Have you put him on oxygen?' Gina asked, getting up. She didn't say anything when Rosie shook her head. She would run through the emergency procedures again with her later, after they had dealt with this crisis. Hurrying into the ward, she picked up the oxygen mask and swiftly fitted it over the patient's nose and mouth. 'Just try to breathe normally, Mr Jackson. That's it, nice and steady now. Good. You're doing great.'

She checked the monitor, noting that his pulse rate was much faster than it should have been and that his blood pressure was too low. Philip Jackson was forty-four years old and had been admitted via ED after complaining of being short of breath. His symptoms had disappeared since he had been on the unit and Miles Humphreys had concluded that the man had suffered nothing more serious than a panic attack. Miles had overruled her suggestion that Philip should remain there overnight for monitoring and had discharged him. Philip had actually been waiting for his wife to collect him when this had happened.

Gina bit back a sigh as she turned to Rosie. Miles wasn't going to be happy about being proved wrong. 'Can you ask the switchboard to page Dr Humphreys, please?'

She picked up the patient's notes as Rosie hurried away. The best way of dealing with Miles, she had found, was to be totally clued up about every aspect of a case. There was nothing of any significance in the notes that ED had made so she delved further into the file, frowning when she discovered that Philip Jackson had undergone surgery to repair a hernia three months earlier. It hadn't been included in the patient's recent history, but could it have a bearing on his present condition?

Miles arrived a few minutes later. Gina's heart sank when she saw him striding down the ward because she knew he was going to give her a hard time. Why wouldn't he just accept that she didn't want to go out with him? You couldn't *make* someone want to be with you, as she knew from experience. Unbidden her gaze went to Marco and she felt heat flow through her when she discovered that he was watching her. She hurriedly turned away, forcing herself to concentrate as Miles demanded to know what had happened.

'Mr Jackson has had difficulty breathing again.' She kept her gaze on the patient but she could feel Marco's eyes boring into her back. Had he remembered who she was? she wondered sickly. It was obvious that his memory was starting to return, so it could happen any time. What was she going to say if he asked her about her life? Could she simply ignore Lily's existence, pretend that she didn't have a daughter?

'I asked you a question, Sister. If it isn't too much to expect then I would like an answer.'

The sarcasm in Miles's voice cut through her musings and Gina jumped. 'I'm sorry, what did you say?'

Miles's expression darkened. 'I asked if any of the staff were present when the patient started to complain of shortness of breath.'

'No,' she replied truthfully. 'Rosie came to fetch me when the monitor started beeping.'

'I see. It appears that things are getting rather slack

around here. If you'd been keeping a closer eye on your patients, Sister Lee, this might not have happened.'

Gina forbore to say anything. She knew that Miles would love it if she argued with him. The fact that he had discharged Philip Jackson didn't matter, it seemed. She waited silently while Miles examined him. Although Philip was responding to the oxygen, his blood pressure was still low. He also complained of having a pain in his chest which was worse every time he breathed.

'Keep him on oxygen for now and we'll see how he goes,' Miles instructed after he'd finished. 'I'm still not convinced it isn't another panic attack.'

'According to his notes, Mr Jackson had surgery to repair a hernia almost three months ago,' Gina pointed out levelly. 'Could that have any bearing on what's been happening recently?'

'Certainly not.' Miles's tone was scathing. 'If there was a problem following surgery, it would have shown up before now. I suggest you stick to nursing the patients, Sister, and leave the diagnoses to those of us who are qualified to make them.'

Gina's face flamed. It was galling to be spoken to that way. The visitors at the next bed had obviously heard what Miles had said because she could see the sympathy on their faces. However, before she could say anything another voice cut in.

'Sister has raised a valid point. It is an established fact that a pulmonary embolism can occur up to three months following surgery.'

Gina swung round, her eyes widening when she saw the grim expression on Marco's face. He wasn't looking at her, however; he was staring at Miles. His deeply accented tones were icy as he continued.

'I suggest you send the patient for a scan to rule out that possibility.'

A rush of heat ran up Miles's neck. 'I assure you that there is no need for you to get involved, Mr...um...' Miles stopped, obviously at a disadvantage because he didn't know Marco's name.

'Andretti. *Dr* Andretti,' Gina told him, placing just enough emphasis on Marco's title that Miles couldn't fail to notice it. 'Dr Andretti is an expert on trauma care,' she added sweetly.

'Oh, I see.' If anything, Miles went even redder. 'Thank you, Dr Andretti. Rest assured that I shall bear your advice in mind,' he blustered.

Marco's expression didn't soften. 'You would be better off sending the patient to Radiology rather than waste time thinking about it. If it is a pulmonary embolism then time is of the essence.'

'I...ahem...yes, of course.' Miles hurriedly scribbled an instruction to that effect and thrust it into Gina's hands. 'See that Mr Jackson is sent for a scan immediately, Sister.'

'Of course,' Gina murmured as Miles hurried away. She told Philip Jackson that she would arrange for a porter to take him and moved away from the bed, pausing as she drew level with Marco. She wasn't sure why he had stood up for her, but she had to admit that it felt good to know that he had. She forced that foolish thought aside as she smiled politely at him. 'Thank you, Dr Andretti. I appreciated your help just now.'

'Prego!' He shrugged, drawing her attention to the solid width of his shoulders beneath the thin hospital gown. Although there wasn't an ounce of spare flesh

on him, he had a leanly muscular physique that looked impressive in or out of clothes.

The thought was more than she could deal with and she started to move away, only to stop when he caught hold of her hand. Gina could feel the light pressure of his fingers on her skin and a wave of longing suddenly shot through her. It had been three years since she had felt his touch, three years since any man had touched her, because she'd not had another relationship since. Maybe that explained why it felt as though there was fire, not blood, running through her veins.

'I was happy to help…Gina.' His gaze held hers fast and she felt her heart rate increase when she saw the question in his eyes. In that second she knew that he had recognised her and panic rose up inside her.

'Look, Marco, this really isn't the time or the place to discuss what happened between us,' she said urgently.

'No? Then when would be a good time?'

His tone was even so it was impossible to guess what he was thinking. Gina struggled to regain her control. She still hadn't made up her mind if she intended to tell him about Lily. When she had first found out that she was pregnant, she had decided to contact him. After all, he'd had a right to know that he was to be a father, although she'd planned to make it clear that she didn't expect anything from him. However, when she had failed to contact him by phone and the letter she had sent to his home had been returned, un-opened, she had changed her mind.

Marco had made it abundantly clear that he wasn't interested in anything she had to tell him. To her mind, he had forfeited any rights he'd had and she wouldn't contact him again. However, that had been before he had reappeared in her life. Even though she loathed the idea, it made a difference. It was hard to know what to do, although one thing was certain: until she had made up her mind, she needed to stay calm.

'I don't know. The last thing I want is people talking, so maybe it would be better if we left things as they are until you're discharged.' She gave a sharp little laugh, hearing the strain it held and praying that Marco couldn't hear it. 'That's assuming we have anything to talk about. After all, it's not as though we parted the best of friends.'

CHAPTER FOUR

1 a.m. 12 December

MARCO couldn't sleep. It wasn't just the fact that he wasn't used to being surrounded by so many people that had kept him awake, but what Gina had said: *It's not as though we parted the best of friends.*

It didn't take a genius to work out that they must have had a relationship, but what sort exactly? The obvious answer was that they'd had an affair, but although there were gaps in his memory, he remembered enough to know that he didn't normally indulge in affairs. The thought of moving from one woman to the next purely for sexual gratification was anathema to him, but if that were the case, it meant that Gina must have played a very different role in his life.

He closed his eyes, wishing he could recall what had gone on between them. Oh, he could remember all sorts of things now: where he had worked for the past few years—six months in Australia followed by two years in the USA. He also remembered why he had come to England—he had been head-hunted by one of London's top teaching hospitals. He should have been attending an interview for the post that very day, in fact. He would have to contact them and explain why he wasn't able to make it, although that didn't seem nearly as important as this. Why couldn't he remember what Gina had meant to him? All he knew was what she had told him, that their parting had been less than amicable. Hell!

Marco swore softly as he tossed back the bedclothes. Thankfully, his headache had gone and apart from the swelling above his right ear, there were few physical mementoes of the accident. If he could only fill in these gaps in his memory, he would be fine and definitely well enough to leave here. Quite frankly he'd had enough of being a patient!

His mouth compressed as he made his way down the ward. He knew the two nurses had gone for their break because he had seen them leave. It meant that Gina was on her own, so it would be the ideal time to talk to her. He frowned as he stopped outside the office because he still didn't understand why she had been so reluctant to admit that she knew him. Obviously something serious must have happened between them in the past and he wouldn't rest until he found out what it was.

The thought spurred him on. He didn't bother knocking before he opened the door. Gina was sitting at the desk and he saw the surprise on her face when she glanced up.

'You were quick,' she began then trailed off when she saw him.

Marco saw the colour drain from her face and the fact that he had no idea what he had done to cause her to react that way angered him. His tone was harsher than he had intended it to be. 'I need to know what you meant when you said that we hadn't parted the best of friends.'

'And as I also said, this isn't the time or the place to discuss it.' She stood up abruptly. 'Now, if you wouldn't mind returning to your bed, I have work to do.'

She took a couple of steps towards him, obviously intending to usher him from the room, but he stood his ground. Drawing himself up to his full six feet he stared haughtily down at her. 'I am not going anywhere until you explain what is going on. It's obvious from what you said that we have met before, so why did you choose not say anything sooner?'

She turned away, taking her time as she sat down. Marco could tell that she was struggling to gather her composure and was more perplexed than ever. Even if they'd had an affair, this was the twenty-first century and most young women would take it in their stride. So what was she so afraid of?

'I thought it best if I didn't say anything.'

Her voice was so low that he wondered if he had misheard her and frowned. 'Best? How? I don't understand.'

'Because...well, because they always say that it's better if people remember things for themselves.' She took a quick breath and hurried on. 'If I'd told you everything I know about you then you'd never be sure if you'd remembered the details yourself or if I'd planted them in your mind, would you?'

It made sense, so much sense that Marco hesitated. It could very well explain why she had been so reluctant to acknowledge him and yet he had a gut feeling that there was more to it than that. A lot more, too.

'I see. So it was purely a desire to help me that kept you quiet,' he said smoothly.

'I... Yes, that's right.' A little colour touched her

cheeks as she reached for her pen. 'I'm glad you understand that it was in your best interests that I said nothing, Dr Andretti.'

'And how about your interests, Gina? Was it in your best interests that you remain silent, I wonder?'

He knew he'd scored a hit when he saw her face pale but, oddly, it didn't give him any pleasure. To know that something must have happened in the past to make her so afraid of him was very hard to take. His tone was gentler when he continued, less confrontational. 'Look, Gina, I don't want to cause trouble. Not for you or for me. I just want to fill in as many of the blanks as possible.'

He shrugged, aware that it wasn't usual for him to admit to any feelings of weakness. Normally he preferred to keep his emotions under wraps but he needed to draw her out, if he could. 'I cannot begin to explain how terrifying it is not to be able to recall what has happened in your life. Even though I now remember quite a lot, there are many questions that still need answering.'

'What sort of questions?' she asked, and he frowned when he heard the tremor in her voice. It was obvious that she was under a great deal of strain and he hated to think that he was adding to the pressure on her, but he needed to find out all he could about this situation.

'I don't know!' he declared in sudden frustration. 'When you forget so much about your life, everything becomes a question. What do I enjoy doing when I'm not working, for instance? Where did I go for my last holiday? I can't answer either of those things!' He ran his hands through his hair, wishing he could physically force the memories to surface, and winced when his fingers encountered the tender spot above his ear.

'Sit down.' Gina was around the desk in a trice. She steered him towards a chair then went to the filing cabinet and switched on the kettle sitting on the top. 'I'll make you a cup of coffee. It's only instant, I'm afraid. Sorry. I know you dislike it but it's all we have.'

'That is exactly what I mean.' Marco sighed when she glanced round. 'I didn't know that I dislike instant coffee because I didn't remember.'

The ghost of a smile touched her mouth. 'Maybe I shouldn't have said anything then you wouldn't have been disappointed.'

Marco laughed. 'Ignorance is bliss—isn't that a saying you have in this country?'

'Yes, it is.' Her smile faded abruptly as she picked up the jar of coffee. 'Sometimes it's better to live in ignorance.'

Marco had no idea what to say to that. He knew instinctively that she wasn't referring to his loss of memory and it puzzled him. What did she know that she didn't want anyone to find out?

His breath caught as he watched her pour boiling water into the mugs because he realised that he needed to amend that question. What did Gina know that she didn't want *him* finding out?

Gina placed the cups on the desk and sat down. She could feel herself trembling and took a deep breath. At some point during the past few minutes she had reached a decision. She wasn't going to tell Marco about Lily. Maybe she would regret it later but she would worry about it then. Right now, it seemed more important that she keep her daughter's existence a secret from him.

At the moment Lily was a happy and well-adjusted little girl. Gina had taken great care to ensure that the child enjoyed a stable home life. One of the reasons why she had ruled out having another relationship was because of the effect it could have on Lily. She had seen it happen to friends' children. New partners arrived on the scene and the family's dynamics had to alter accordingly. She didn't want that for Lily, didn't want her daughter to grow up surrounded by people who came and went in her life. She wanted Lily to have security.

If she told Marco about Lily, there was no knowing what he would do. Maybe he would be indifferent to the fact that he had a daughter but, more worryingly, he might want to play a role in the child's life, at least for a while. She couldn't bear to think that Lily might grow attached to him only to be let down at some point in the future. As she knew to her cost Marco could very easily change his mind.

Thoughts rushed through her head until she felt dizzy. She took a sip of her coffee, hoping it would steady her. If she was to stop Marco learning about Lily's existence then she would need to be extremely careful about what she said.

'How did we meet?'

She looked up when he spoke, feeling her heart jerk when she saw the way he was watching her so intently. He had always been very astute and she mustn't make the mistake of underestimating him. Although she hated to talk about the past, she knew it would be better to tell him the truth—as far as she could.

'I flew over to Florence to collect a patient you'd

been treating,' she answered, pleased to hear that her voice held no trace of the nervousness she felt.

'I see.' He frowned. 'Obviously, you weren't working here at the time.'

'I worked for a company that repatriates clients to the UK when they're taken ill abroad.' She shrugged. 'The gentleman I was due to collect had suffered a stroke. It was supposed to be quite straightforward. I'd collect him from the hospital and accompany him back to England. Unfortunately, he suffered a second stroke shortly before I arrived and you decided that he wasn't fit to fly.'

'So what happened then? Did you return to England?'

Gina heard the curiosity in his voice and realised there was no point prevaricating. 'No. The patient's family asked if I would stay while he was in hospital. He was on his own and they felt it would help if he had someone with him.' She shrugged. 'The family offered to pay my salary and the firm I worked for agreed to let me take some leave, so I said yes.'

'For how long?' Marco demanded.

'Six weeks.'

His brows rose. 'That seems an excessive amount of time to me. Surely your patient was fit to travel before then?'

This was the difficult bit, the part she didn't want to explain. 'Sadly, the patient died a week later.'

'But you didn't go home?'

She shook her head.

'Why not?'

'I'd never visited Florence before and it seemed like the perfect opportunity to see something of the city and surrounding area.'

'So you stayed to do some sightseeing?' His tone was flat and she couldn't blame it for the shiver that passed through her. It took every scrap of composure she could muster to answer.

'Yes.' She stood up, making a great show of checking her watch. 'I'm sorry but I really do need to get on.'

'Of course.' He stood up as well, looking so big and male as he towered over that her heart beat all the harder. 'Will you just answer me one final question, Gina?'

'If I can.'

'Did you also stay on in Florence because of me?'

Gina bit her lip. She could lie, of course, but she knew him well enough to guess that he would see through it. Tipping back her head, she looked him in the eyes. 'Yes, I did. Now, if that's all…'

She walked around the desk, steeling herself as she passed him. How she ached to touch him, to lay her hand on his arm and tell him the rest, that she had stayed because she had fallen in love with him, had thought he had loved her too, but what was the point? No doubt Marco would remember it all in time, remember those few glorious weeks they'd had before he had realised that he had no longer wanted her, although his memory of what had happened must be very different from hers. Tears pricked her eyes and she turned away. She refused to let him see her cry, refused to let him take away her dignity as well as everything else!

'I am sorry, Gina, so very sorry that I can't remember.'

The regret in his voice was almost too much. Somehow she made it out of the door but it was hard to hold onto her composure. When Julie came back from her break, she told her she was going to the canteen and hurriedly departed. And as the lift swept her up to the top floor, the tears that she had held at bay trickled down her cheeks.

She had loved Marco so much! Loved him with her heart, her soul and every scrap of her being, but it hadn't been enough. Not for him. He had taken her love and tossed it back in her face and there was no way that she would risk that happening again.

Gina took a deep breath as the lift came to a halt. Whatever she and Marco had had was over. What she needed to focus on now was Lily—the one good thing to have come out of the whole terrible experience. So long as Lily was safe and happy, nothing else mattered.

If he had hoped that talking to Gina would set his mind at rest, Marco was disappointed. He spent the night thinking about what he had learned or, more importantly, what he hadn't. He sensed that Gina was keeping something from him and had no idea how he could find out what it was. Maybe he should wait until his memory returned of its own accord and go from there?

He sighed. He had no idea how long it would be before he could remember everything that had happened and he wasn't sure if he could wait. It was obvious that Gina wasn't going to tell him anything else, so if he was to find out what she was keeping from him then he would have to start digging for the information himself. And to do that, he needed to get out of here. When Steven Pierce arrived shortly after eight a.m. Marco could barely contain his impatience.

'Good morning, Dr Andretti. How are you feeling today?' Steven enquired as he lifted Marco's chart off the end of the bed. The night staff had gone off duty by then and there was another nurse with him who introduced herself as Sister Thomas. Marco found himself wishing that it was Gina standing there, Gina with her soothing voice, her gentle manner, her beautiful smile. The world always seemed a much nicer place when Gina was around.

The thought slid into his head and he knew that it had occurred to him before. There was a familiarity about it that resonated deep inside him. Marco took a quick breath, feeling little waves of panic rippling along his veins. Gina had meant something to him in the past, something more than he would have expected if they'd had a casual affair. And the fact that any woman could have had this effect on him after Francesca stunned him.

'Dr Andretti?'

'Scusi.' Marco hurriedly marshalled his thoughts when he realised that Steven was waiting for him to answer. 'I am feeling a lot better this morning, thank you.'

'Good. That's what we like to hear, isn't it, Sister?'

'Indeed, Doctor.'

Marco tried not to wince when the woman spoke. She had a particularly irritating voice, rather nasal and high-pitched, completely different from Gina's low, sweet tones… He stamped down hard on that thought, forcing himself to concentrate as Steven asked him a series of questions aimed, Marco suspected, at checking how much of his memory had returned.

'That's excellent,' the registrar concluded. 'You obviously recall a lot more today than you did yesterday. Most people suffering from retrograde amnesia find that the gap in their memory continues to shrink over a period of time. I'm hoping that is what will happen with you.'

'Do you have any idea how long it will be before I remember everything?' Marco demanded. Maybe he would feel easier if he knew that in a week's time, say, he would remember all about him and Gina. What was so frustrating was the fact that he had no idea when the details of their relationship would come back to him.

'Sadly, that's a question I can't answer. It could be hours or it could be months.' Steven's tone was sombre. 'To be perfectly frank, Dr Andretti, your memory might never come back completely. It's one of the hardest things anyone who has suffered from amnesia has to live with, the feeling that there may be something he or she can't remember. All I can advise you to do is to take it one step at a time and see what happens.'

Marco knew that it was good advice, advice he, himself, would have given a patient. However, it was very different being on the receiving end. 'Surely there is something you can do to speed up the process!'

'I'm afraid not.' Steven looked a little taken aback by his vehemence. 'Rest and relaxation are what will help most at the moment. That's why I've arranged for you to be transferred to a private room. You should find it more peaceful there.'

'No.' Marco shook his head. 'I have no intention of remaining here. I feel perfectly fine, quite well enough to leave.'

'Oh, I really don't think that is a good idea,' Steven began, but Marco held up his hand.

'I have made my decision. Physically, I am fit enough to leave, do you agree?'

'Well, yes,' Steven conceded.

'*Bene*. So the only problem I have is my inability to remember everything that has happened in the past and as you have just told me, Dr Pierce, there is no knowing how long it will be before that issue resolves itself.' He shrugged. 'I cannot remain here indefinitely.'

'I appreciate that, Dr Andretti. However, a couple more days could make a huge difference,' Steven insisted. 'With rest and relaxation, maybe some counselling, we could achieve a real breakthrough.'

'I can rest at my hotel,' Marco assured him, knowing the younger man had his best interests at heart. That thought reminded him of what Gina had said and he knew that no matter what else happened, he had to get to the bottom of this mystery. If he and Gina had been more than simply lovers, he needed to know!

The thought sent a rush of heat coursing through him and he cleared his throat, stunned by the speed of his response. Although Gina was a beautiful woman, he had met other equally beautiful women over the past few years and had never reacted this strongly. What was it about her that seemed to touch him on so many levels? he wondered. He had no idea but he couldn't deny that she affected him deeply.

'I appreciate your concern, Dr Pierce, but I assure you that I know what I'm doing,' he said, forcing himself to focus on the issue at hand. 'I shall leave this morning and go to my hotel.'

'Do you remember where you're staying?' Steven put in quickly.

Marco named the hotel and smiled wryly. 'I stay there whenever I'm in London, as I recall.'

'I see.' Steven looked resigned. 'Obviously, I can't

keep you here against your will, but I do hope you'll be sensible, Dr Andretti. If you experience any problems, please get in touch with us immediately.'

'I shall.' Marco smiled as he held out his hand. 'Thank you for everything. You have been extremely kind.'

'Just doing my job,' Steven assured him, shaking hands.

Marco didn't waste a single moment after the other man left. He drew the curtains around the bed and got dressed. His clothes looked decidedly worse for wear but as he didn't have anything else, he put them on. He had no idea what had happened to his luggage. It was probably still in the back of the hire car, but that was the least of his worries. How long would it be before he remembered what had happened between him and Gina? A day? A week? A month? A year?

He shook his head. He couldn't wait that long. He had to persuade her to tell him the truth, but it wasn't going to be easy. All he could do was try to gain her trust—if he could. Something warned him that getting Gina to trust him was going to be an uphill struggle.

CHAPTER FIVE

12 December

GINA was dreading going into work that night in case Marco was still there. Although he should have been transferred by now, it depended on whether a bed had been found for him. It was a relief when she discovered that the end bay was occupied by another patient. At least she wouldn't have to field any more awkward questions that night, although she wasn't foolish enough to think it would be the end of the matter. Marco obviously suspected something was wrong and she knew him well enough to know that he wouldn't simply give up.

Panic assailed her at the thought of the harm it could cause if he found out about Lily. If only she could predict how he would react, it would be so much easier, but that was something she couldn't do. She had no idea if he would be thrilled or furious to learn he had a daughter, and no idea at all how he would feel about it in the long term. As she knew from experience, Marco could blow hot one minute and cold the next, and there was no way that Lily was going to be subjected to his mood swings.

Gina's heart was heavy as she set to work. It wasn't

in her nature to be deceitful, but she had to do what she believed was best for Lily. Rosie was working again that night so they made a start on the obs. Julie was supposed to be on duty as well but there was no sign of her. Gina knew they wouldn't be able to manage with a member of staff short and went into the office to phone the nursing manager to see if she could provide cover. She had just picked up the phone when Julie came rushing in.

'Sorry! My car broke down and I had to leave it in the street and walk the rest of the way.' Julie looked worried as she unravelled her scarf. 'I hope it won't cost a fortune to get it fixed. With Christmas just around the corner, money's really tight.'

'Fingers crossed it will be something minor,' Gina said sympathetically. Julie had three teenage children and Gina knew how hard she and her husband worked to pay all the bills.

'Fingers *and* toes,' Julie agreed, grimacing. 'Right, so what needs doing first? Obs?'

'Please. It's not quite as hectic as last night but we're still pretty full. Go and put your coat away and then we'll finish the obs. Bearing in mind that it's Friday, I'm sure business will pick up soon.'

'Bound to,' Julie replied cheerfully. 'By the way, is that dishy Italian doctor still with us? It would be nice to have a stunner like him to look at instead of the usual Friday night drunks.'

Gina dredged up a smile. 'You're out of luck, I'm afraid. There's another patient in the end bay so I assume he's been moved to Neurology.'

'Pity. I could have done with a pick-me-up after the evening I've had.'

Julie laughed as she hurried away. Gina sighed as she went to check on Rosie. She didn't want to keep thinking about Marco but it was impossible not to do so. It was the uncertainty that was worst of all, the fact that she had no idea what he would do next. Would he seek her out and try to get more information out of her about their past?

The thought made her stomach churn. Every time she spoke to him, she ran the risk of saying something revealing, and it was worrying to know how easily she could trip up. Quite frankly, it would suit her fine if she never had to see Marco Andretti again!

Marco spent the day resting in his hotel room. Despite his claims, he felt far weaker than he had expected when he had left the hospital. It was a relief when the porter showed him to his room.

He tipped the man and asked him to send up a pot of coffee. Although there were coffee-making facilities in the room, he couldn't face another cup of instant brew. Gina was right—he did hate it—and the fact that she remembered such a minor detail seemed to highlight this problem he had. They must have been very close if she knew his likes and dislikes, so why couldn't he remember what had gone on between them?

He sighed wearily because there was no answer to that question. Stripping off his clothes, he went into the bathroom and took a shower. Wrapping himself in one of the thick towelling robes hanging behind the door, he went back to the bedroom and phoned housekeeping. By the time the waiter arrived with his coffee, he had arranged for his suit to be dry cleaned and half a dozen white shirts and assorted underwear to be delivered to his room. At least he would have some clean clothes to wear while he waited for his suitcase to turn up, he thought as he poured himself a cup of the fragrant brew, automatically inhaling the aroma of freshly ground beans...

Gina used to laugh at him whenever he did that, he thought suddenly. She used to tease him about being addicted to the smell of coffee. He could picture them now sitting in their favourite café overlooking the River Arno. Her slate-grey eyes were dancing with amusement, her cheeks pink from the heat in the café. It was winter and everyone was bundled up in scarves and hats. Gina didn't have a scarf so he had given her his; the dark grey mohair was the perfect foil for her blonde hair. She looked so beautiful as she sat there laughing at him that he couldn't help himself. He simply leaned across the table and kissed her.

Marco shuddered as the image melted away. The memory had been so clear that he could feel his lips tingling from the contact with hers. Gina had told him that it had been three years since they had met, yet it felt as though it was mere seconds since he had kissed her, felt the warm urgency of her mouth as she had kissed him back.

He stood up abruptly, not proof against how it made him feel to discover that Gina had felt something for him, too. At the back of his mind he had been hoping they had merely had a fling, out of character for him, granted, but perfectly acceptable between two consenting adults. However, that theory had been shot right out of the water. He wouldn't have felt this intensely when he had kissed her if she'd been just someone he had slept with; she wouldn't have responded so passionately if he had been a one-night stand.

Marco went to the window and stared out. There was no point trying to pretend that their relationship had been no more than a fleeting affair. It had been much more than that.

'Her blood alcohol reading is 450 milligrams per 100 millilitres. According to her friends, she only had a couple of glasses of wine, too.' The ED nurse rolled his eyes. 'Call me a cynic but somehow I don't think that's true, do you?'

'Not from the look of it.' Gina looked sadly down at the girl lying on the bed. Katie Morris was seventeen years old and a student at sixth-form college. She had been out celebrating the end of term with a group of friends but had carried the celebrations too far. She had been brought into ED after collapsing in the street and subsequently been moved to AAU. She would need careful monitoring with that level of alcohol in her system.

'Thanks, Terry, we'll take it from here. Have her parents been informed, do you know?' Gina asked.

'A message was left on their answering-machine requesting that they contact the hospital,' Terry informed her. 'Not heard anything yet, though.'

'Hopefully, they'll get in touch soon,' Gina replied, deftly attaching the girl to one of their monitors. She did Katie's obs, noting down her BP, sats and pulse rate on the chart. The teenager was still unconscious and likely to remain that way after the amount of alcohol she had consumed. Sadly, far too many youngsters failed to understand that alcohol taken in such quantities caused acute poisoning and could prove fatal.

Gina made sure the girl was comfortable. She had just finished when Julie came to tell her there was a phone call for her. She hurried into the office and picked up the receiver. 'Sister Lee speaking. How may I help you?'

'Gina, it's Marco.'

The shock of hearing his voice stunned her into silence. There was a brief pause before he continued and she couldn't fail to hear the impatience in his voice. 'Did you hear what I said? It's Marco.'

'I…um…I thought you were on the neurology unit.' It took every scrap of willpower to reply calmly when her heart was racing. Why was he phoning her? What did he want? Surely he hadn't found out about Lily, had he? The questions tumbled around inside her head, so that she missed what he said and had to ask him to repeat it.

'I said that I discharged myself this morning,' he repeated, his deep voice grating. 'There was no point in my staying in hospital. If I am to recover my memory then I need to find out all I can. That is why I have to talk to you.'

'I'm sorry but I can't talk now,' she said, hurriedly. 'I'm far too busy.'

'I appreciate that, which is why I am phoning to set up a time and a place when we can meet.'

Gina's heart sank. The last thing she wanted was to meet him. 'I really can't see the point. I've told you everything I can, Dr Andretti.'

'Have you indeed?' His tone was silky yet there was no mistaking the scepticism it held.

'Yes,' she retorted. 'Now, I'm very sorry but I really don't have the time right now...'

'I have remembered, Gina.'

Gina paused uncertainly. 'Remembered?'

'*Si.* Oh, I can't recall everything that happened between us but I know that we were close at one point.' His voice dropped and she shivered when she felt the richly accented tones stroking along her nerves. 'We were lovers, weren't we?'

'I...' She had to stop and swallow to unlock the knot in her throat. She was tempted to deny the allegation but what was the point if Marco had remembered? 'Yes, we were.'

'I thought so. I remembered us being in a café overlooking the River Arno. It was a cold day and you were wearing my scarf. *Si?*'

Heat flowed through her as she instantly recalled the occasion. Marco had managed to wangle some time off work and they had spent the afternoon strolling through the city. It had been bitterly cold, the river shimmering steel-grey under a wintry sky, but it hadn't mattered. Just being with Marco, feeling his hand clasped around hers as they had strolled along the busy streets, had filled her with warmth and happiness. And when they had stopped for coffee and he had leaned across the table and kissed her, she had known her life would never be the same again. That was the moment when she had realised that she was in love with him, the moment when it had felt that all her dreams were about to come true.

Pain seared through her. It was all she could do not to cry out but she couldn't afford to let him know how much he had hurt her. If she could pass off their relationship as little more than a brief affair then he would stop digging for information and Lily would be safe. 'I can't say that I remember it in particular, but I'm sure it happened if you say it did.'

'Of course.' His tone was as unrevealing as hers had been so Gina couldn't explain why she knew that he was disappointed by her answer. Surely he hadn't wanted her to remember that kiss, had he?

The thought was both poignant and foolish. She brushed it aside, knowing how stupid it was. Marco had been perfectly clear when he had broken up with her, so what was the point of harking back to the past?

'I'm pleased that your memory is coming back, but I really cannot see what I can do to help. Yes, we were lovers at one point but I haven't seen you since we split up. I have no knowledge whatsoever of what's happened in your life in the past three years.'

'The past three years are probably what I remember best,' he informed her. 'I remember where I worked as well as the people I worked with—all the details like that.'

'Then you're obviously on the way to making a full recovery.' Gina knew that she had to wind up the conversation. The more she said, the greater the risk that something might slip out. 'All I can do is wish you well. I hope that everything works out for you, Dr Andretti.'

'Marco.'

'Pardon?'

'My name is Marco. Bearing in mind that we have been so intimate with each other, I find it rather ridiculous that you insist on being so formal.'

There was a teasing note in his voice that immediately stirred her senses. Although Marco gave the appearance of being a very serious person, he had a wicked sense of humour and had loved to tease her.

The thought sent another little stab of pain through her heart but she ignored it. She refused to look back, refused to go down the path of 'what if'. Marco hadn't wanted her three years ago and he didn't want her now. 'Marco,' she echoed, allowing a touch of weariness to creep into her voice.

'*Bene*. Now we are making progress. Let us hope that we can continue to do so, Gina.'

'I have no idea what you mean by that. I have just explained that I can't tell you anything else that might help. We had an affair. It lasted six weeks and when it was over I returned to England. That's it. There's nothing to add.'

'Are you sure?' His tone was calm. There was no hint of threat in it yet all of a sudden she felt scared, really scared.

'Of course I am! Now I'm sorry but I have to go. Goodbye, Dr….Marco. I hope everything works out for you.'

She dropped the phone back onto its rest. It was obvious that Marco suspected something, but what? She wished she knew because maybe then she would have known how to deal with the situation. Knowing Marco, he wouldn't be content to leave things as they were. He would seek her out again, press her for more information, and each time he did so the risk of him finding out about Lily would intensify.

She needed to get away, she decided. Go someplace where he couldn't find her and that way Lily would be safe. However, it wasn't that easy to up and leave. She would need to find somewhere to live, another job so she could support them, and then there was the problem of childcare. Lily was happy with the childminder Gina had found to look after her while she was at work. Not all childminders were prepared to care for children whose parents worked shifts and she had been lucky to find Amy. Running away would entail as many problems as staying and facing Marco, it seemed.

All of a sudden Gina felt torn in two. Lily could be badly hurt if she stayed, yet she could be equally hurt if she was taken away from everything and everyone she knew.

CHAPTER SIX

GINA had the following four days off so once she finished work she collected Lily and took her home to the small basement flat they shared. With its tiny living room and minuscule kitchen, it wasn't exactly luxurious living, but she had done her best to brighten up the place by hanging lots of colourful prints on the walls.

She had also partitioned off a corner of the bedroom so the little girl had her own space complete with a child-sized bed. They were comfortable enough, although she was very aware that they would have to move when Lily grew bigger. Still, that was something to worry about in the future. At the present time she had other matters on her mind.

She gave Lily a drink then helped her build a tower out of some wooden blocks. Lily had a nap after her lunch and usually Gina tried to snatch an hour's sleep then. By the time Lily was tucked up, Gina's eyelids were drooping so she lay down on the couch. However, the minute she closed her eyes it all came rushing back: Marco and his questions and what she had—and hadn't—told him. Should she have told him the truth? Had she been right to withhold such an important piece of information from him? Was it fair to Lily not to tell her that Marco was her father?

By the time Lily woke up, Gina felt dreadful. The combination of tiredness and guilt had left her feeling wrung out. If this was how she felt after just a couple of days of covering up her secret, how much worse would she feel in a week or so's time? Surely telling Marco the truth couldn't be any worse than this?

Just for a second she wavered before her resolve stiffened. This had nothing to do with how *she* felt and everything to do with how it could affect Lily. No matter how hard it was, it would be a mistake to tell Marco about his daughter.

Marco spent the following week wondering what to do. His memory was returning rapidly and he now had a fairly comprehensive picture of what his life had been like. However, the one memory he yearned to recall continued to elude him.

Apart from a few tantalising flashes, his relationship with Gina was still a blank and the worst thing was knowing it could remain that way if she refused to tell him what had really happened. It was obvious that she was scared of him and he had no idea why. Maybe he couldn't remember everything he'd ever done, but he knew enough to be sure that he would never harm a woman physically.

He sighed. Rationally, he knew that he should stop worrying about Gina. So they'd had an affair and it had ended badly—so what? He should accept it and move on, but it was proving impossible to do so. There was just something about her that drew him, something that made him unable to dismiss her from his thoughts. He needed to uncover the truth about their relationship. Although he had shied away from the idea of falling in love again after Francesca had died, he only had to recall how he had kissed Gina in that café to know that he had felt something for her.

Had he been in love with her? Was he even capable of loving a woman again?

He couldn't answer either of those questions but in his heart he knew that the rest of his life could depend on what he did now and it scared him to realise that Gina could hold the key to his future.

Gina was on days when she went back into work. AAU was as busy as ever and the morning flew past; before she knew it, it was time for lunch. She decided to go to the canteen and headed for the lift. She was just about to step inside when she heard someone calling her and looked round to see Marco striding towards her.

Her heart sank. She really didn't want to talk to him, but what choice did she have? She couldn't afford to do anything that would arouse his suspicions even more. She pinned a polite smile to her lips as he came closer. 'This is a surprise. I didn't expect to see you here.'

'I have an appointment,' he replied evenly.

He waited for her to step into the lift, pressing the button for the fifth floor once she had selected her destination, and Gina frowned. The fifth floor was home to the administration department and she couldn't help wondering what business he had up there. She was on the point of asking him when she thought better of it. It would be safer if she didn't show any interest in his affairs.

'Has it been a busy day?' he enquired as the lift carried them up.

'It always is.'

'It can't help that you're carrying a number of vacancies at the moment, though. That must put added pressure on the staff.'

Gina frowned, unsure where he had gleaned that information. 'It does. One of our registrars is off sick and won't be back for another month, and our consultant retired at the end of October. They did hire a replacement, but he pulled out. They've advertised the post again, but it could take a while to find someone suitable.'

'Good staff are difficult to find,' he agreed. He glanced round when the lift came to a halt. 'Ah, my floor, I think. Enjoy your lunch.'

'Thank you,' Gina murmured. She put out her hand to stop the doors from closing as she peered after him, trying to see where he was going, but he rounded a corner and disappeared from sight. She sighed as she continued her journey. She should just be glad that he hadn't tried to cross-examine her. Maybe his interest in her was waning?

The thought should have been a comfort yet she couldn't help feeling deflated. She had expected Marco to give her a much harder time in his desire to uncover the past but it appeared he was no longer interested.

Had he already recalled what had happened? she wondered suddenly. And now he had remembered their affair and his reasons for ending it, there was no need to question her any more? So far as he was concerned that was the end of the matter.

Just for a second she experienced an overwhelming sense of guilt at not telling him about Lily before she dismissed it. It was far better that Marco didn't know about their daughter. He could go back to Italy and get on with his life while she and Lily got on with theirs. There was no reason why they should see one another again.

CHAPTER SEVEN

February

IT HAD taken Marco far longer than he had expected to finalise the details. First there had been the necessary checks to ensure that he was fit to do the job. Then, once he'd overcome that hurdle, there had been the usual contractual delays. Now, however, as he stared up at the grey concrete façade of the hospital, he found himself wondering if he had been mad to make such a life-changing decision.

He *never* did things on a whim. He *always* weighed up the pros and cons beforehand, yet here he was, about to jump in at the deep end, and for what? To solve a mystery that might not even exist? To find answers to questions that might not need to be asked? Hell!

His mouth thinned as he pushed open the door. He knew there would be a reception committee waiting to greet him on the fifth floor but strode straight past the lifts. He didn't want thanks for taking on the post of locum consultant in charge of AAU when there had been nothing altruistic about his decision. He had done it for one reason and one reason alone: he needed to know what had happened between him and Gina to make her so wary of him.

AAU was busy when he arrived. He paused in the doorway, feeling his heart jolt when he spotted Gina standing near the window. She was talking to an elderly female patient and didn't appear to have noticed him so he had time to take stock.

Marco felt his blood quicken as he studied the delicate line of her profile. Her skin was so fine that it appeared almost translucent in the pale morning light filtering through the glass, the rose-pink blush that tinted her cheeks making his fingers suddenly itch to touch it. Her skin would feel like the inside of a rose petal, he thought wonderingly, so soft and smooth, so warm and velvety.

A shudder ran through him and he took a deep breath, knowing that he couldn't afford to let his emotions run away with him. In the past few weeks he had found it increasingly hard to keep them under control. Maybe it was the fact that he still couldn't remember this affair he'd had with Gina that had upset his emotional balance—he didn't know. But where once he could have buried his feelings, now they seemed to lie just beneath the surface, ready to erupt at the least excuse.

She suddenly looked up and he stiffened when their eyes met. Just for a moment her expression was blank before he saw her lips part in a tiny gasp. This was the moment he had been anticipating for weeks, yet all of a sudden he wasn't sure what to do. Should he go to her or let her come to him?

The decision was taken from him when someone rudely elbowed him aside. Marco swung round, his annoyance fading when he saw the anxious face of the porter who was pushing a trolley bearing a small child into the ward.

'Sorry, mate, but this is an emergency,' the man muttered, hurrying past him. There was a nurse with him and she had to run to keep up as the porter propelled the trolley towards an empty bay.

'Chloe Daniels, aged seven. She arrested when we were halfway along the corridor,' the nurse explained. She squeezed the ambubag she had placed over the child's nose and mouth. 'Can someone give me a hand, please?'

Marco reacted instinctively. Crossing the room in a couple of strides, he bent over the child. 'Why was she admitted?' he demanded as he checked for a pulse.

'Suspected concussion. She fell off a garden wall and banged her head. Her mum didn't see it happen and wasn't sure if Chloe had passed out, so she's being kept in for monitoring.' The nurse looked uncertainly at him. 'I'm sorry but who are you exactly?'

'Dr Andretti,' Marco replied shortly, hoping she wasn't going to ask for proof of his identity. He should have collected his ID tag after meeting the reception committee, but as he had avoided that pleasure he had nothing to back up his claim…unless Gina would vouch for him.

He glanced round when she appeared, doing his best to behave like the professional he was. Never in the whole of his working life had he allowed his personal feelings to intrude on his work, yet they were in danger of doing so now. 'Sister Lee knows who I am,' he replied tersely, not appreciating the fact that he was behaving so out of character. 'I am sure she will vouch for me. Won't you, Sister?'

'Yes. I know Dr Andretti,' she replied in a tight little voice.

Marco shot her a quick glance before he returned his attention to the child but it was enough to tell him how shocked she was to see him. She looked as though the bottom had dropped out of her world and the thought touched an already raw nerve. Come what may, he *had* to get to the bottom of this mystery!

Gina could feel ripples of shock spreading through her body. She had no idea what Marco was doing there…

She gasped. There had been rumours flying around for weeks that someone had been appointed to the consultant's post, but the powers-that-be had neither confirmed nor denied them. Everyone had put it down to the fact that they hadn't wished to suffer any further embarrassment if the new appointee decided to pull out, but maybe there was another explanation. Maybe Marco had asked them to withhold the information for his own reasons?

The thought that those reasons might have something to do with her made her stomach churn with nerves but she fought to control them. Positioning herself beside the bed, she glanced at Marco. 'I'll start chest compressions.'

'*Si.*'

He stepped aside as she began pressing lightly on the little girl's chest. The method for resuscitating a child was the same as for an adult; the only difference was the amount of pressure needed. Too much force and ribs could be cracked so she took extra care, working in sync with the ED nurse who was maintaining the child's breathing.

'*Un momento.*'

Gina stopped as Marco bent over the child. He checked the pulse in her neck, his long fingers with their olive-toned skin looking dark against the little girl's flesh.

'*Bene!* We have a pulse. Put her on a monitor and let us see how she goes. Has she had a CT scan?'

'Yes, Dr Andretti.' The nurse produced a hand-held computer and showed him the results of the scan. 'Dr Humphreys checked it and said it was clear.'

Marco scrolled through the images. He frowned as he studied one particular frame. 'There is a hairline fracture on the right side of her head. It is difficult to see, but it is definitely there. See.'

He showed the screen to Gina, pointing out the area in question, but it still took her a moment to see what he was referring to. 'There does appear to be a very fine fracture,' she agreed finally.

'I want another scan. We need to see if there is a bleed in the area. That would explain why she arrested.' Marco was all business as he rapped out instructions. 'Can you get onto Theatre and inform them that I may need to operate? Where are her parents?'

'Her mum went outside to phone the grandmother,' the ED nurse explained. 'She should be along any moment.'

'Good. I'll leave it to you to ensure the relevant forms are signed so the operation can go ahead if need be, Sister.'

'Of course, Dr Andretti.'

Gina didn't waste time querying how and why he had the right to set things in motion. The explanations would come later, although there didn't seem much to explain. Her heart sank as she went to the office and put through a call requesting a second scan. It appeared that Marco was indeed their new consultant and it didn't take a genius to work out why he had decided to take the post. The thought of what he might uncover made her knees go weak. She knew that if he found out about Lily it would be even worse now. He would be furious that she hadn't told him sooner, when she'd had the chance to do so.

The thought of facing his wrath on top of everything else was almost too much. Gina could barely concentrate as she contacted Theatre and informed them that Dr Andretti would probably require a slot shortly. Naturally, that triggered a whole host of questions as to who Dr Andretti was, where he had worked previously, and whether he seemed a bit more clued-up than their previous consultant had been.

Gina pleaded pressure of work to wriggle out of divulging anything more than the basics—that he was Italian and seemed extremely competent. However, she knew the questions would be coming thick and fast as everyone tried to find out all they could about their new boss and not just about his working methods either. His private life was bound to attract a great deal of interest, too.

What would *Marco* tell them? she wondered as she hung up. Would he mention her, admit that they'd had an affair?

She hoped not because it would make her situation even more precarious. All it would take was for some bright spark to do the maths, work out that Lily must be his daughter, and that would be it—her secret would be out. She groaned in dismay. Why in heaven's name had Marco decided to pursue this?

'Swab, please.'

Marco waited while the blood was swabbed away. So far the operation to relieve the pressure on little Chloe's brain had gone quite smoothly. He had made a burr hole through which the blood had been drained away. He was confident that the child would make a full recovery and nodded in satisfaction as he placed a dressing over the wound.

'*Bene.* Thank you, everyone. It is always good to work with a skilled team.'

A collective sigh of relief greeted that statement. As Marco exited Theatre a short time later, he heard the hum of conversation break out. No doubt they were discussing him, he thought as he headed for the changing room. It was always an uncertain time for staff when they met their new boss and in this case it must be doubly difficult for them. They didn't know him so they were bound to have concerns. Hopefully, he had convinced them that he knew what he was doing, although, realistically, it would take time for them to accept him. Maybe Gina would put in a good word for him, he mused as he switched on the shower, then realised how foolish it was to hope for that. From the expression on her face when she had seen him that morning, it was doubtful if she would have anything good to say about him!

It was an unsettling thought. Marco tried not to dwell on it as he changed back into his clothes. Gina was with a patient when he returned to the unit so he waited until

she had finished and called her over. 'I need a word with
Chloe's mother. Is there a room I can use?'

'Yes. It's through here.' Gina showed him into a
small but comfortable sitting room, with twin sofas
set either side of a coffee table.

Marco nodded. 'This is fine. Are both her parents
here, do you know?'

'I'm not sure. Ruth—that's the nurse who accompa-
nied her from ED—only mentioned her mother.'

'In that case, I would like you to stay while I speak
to her.' He shrugged when Gina looked at him in surprise. 'She might feel more at ease with another woman
present.'

'Oh. Well, yes, of course I'll stay. Do you want me
to fetch her in now?'

'*Si*. Chloe will be leaving Recovery shortly. I am
sure her mother will be anxious to be there when she
returns.'

Marco smiled pleasantly but Gina didn't respond as
she left the room. He sighed, wondering how he was
going to approach the task of gaining her trust. It was
going to be an uphill battle from the look of it but he
intended to keep on until he wore down her defences
and convinced her that he wasn't going to hurt her in
any way.

He frowned when it struck him that he couldn't guar-
antee that she wouldn't get hurt. As he knew nothing
about what lay behind her fear of him, he couldn't make
such a promise. It worried him that he might end up
doing something to cause her even more distress but
what choice did he have?

If he gave up now, he might never find out this secret she was keeping from him. Although he had been

passed as fit to work, there were still a few blank spots in his memory. The specialist he had seen had been pragmatic: he might remember everything eventually and he might not. Maybe he could live with the thought that he had forgotten the odd minor detail, but he couldn't live with not knowing about his relationship with Gina. It was far too important, even though he wasn't sure why.

Marco tried to put that thought aside when Gina appeared with Chloe's mother. 'Mrs Daniels, I'm Dr Andretti. I operated on your daughter.'

He shook hands then ushered her towards one of the sofas. Gina sat down as well, her expression betraying very little as she waited for him to speak, yet he sensed her inner turmoil. It made him feel guilty to know that he was the cause of it, too. He cleared his throat, refusing to allow himself to be sidetracked.

'First of all I want to say that the operation went very smoothly. I am confident that it has resolved the problem.'

'Thank heavens!' Donna Daniels seemed to crumple in her seat. Marco could see tears in her eyes and smiled sympathetically.

'I know it must have been a very worrying time for you, Mrs Daniels, but I am sure that Chloe will be fine. She will need a few days to get over the operation so she will be transferred to the children's ward once she leaves Recovery. She may have a headache for a few days but that will pass and I am not anticipating any long-term problems.'

'Thank you, Doctor. I can't tell you how relieved I am to hear that.' Donna sighed shakily. 'I still don't know how it happened. Chloe was playing in the garden while

I got ready to take her to school. She was only on her own for a couple of minutes but when I went out, she was lying on the ground...'

She broke off and gulped, obviously distraught at the thought of her daughter coming to harm. Marco watched as Gina leant over and squeezed her hand.

'It isn't your fault, Donna. You can't watch a child every minute of the day.'

'Maybe not but I should have realised she might try to climb up that wall at some point!'

'If it wasn't a wall then it would be something else.' Gina smiled, her slate-grey eyes filled with compassion, and Marco felt the strangest emotion rise up inside him. He was jealous, he realised in amazement. Jealous at the thought of her sparing all that emotion for someone else when he wanted it for himself.

The thought shocked him so that it was an effort to focus on the conversation. He had never experienced jealousy before, not even for Francesca, and the realisation was like a knife being thrust through his ribs. He had loved Francesca yet he had never felt this way about *her*!

'Children always manage to do the one thing you never expect. It's as though they have some kind of sixth-sense that makes them home in on danger. Why, only the other day I found my daughter perched on a chair, attempting to reach a vase that I'd put out of her way. Another second and she'd have got it *and* probably dropped it, too!'

The two women laughed but Marco didn't join in. He couldn't because he didn't have enough breath to spare. *Gina had a daughter?* Was it true? Or was it something she had made up to console the other woman?

He stared at her and saw the dawning horror on her face when she realised why he was looking at her. In that second he knew that he had uncovered her secret, found out what she had been keeping from him. What he didn't understand, though, was why she had been so determined to keep the child's existence from him.

He took a deep breath, his head reeling. He may have solved one mystery but now, it appeared, he needed to solve another.

CHAPTER EIGHT

GINA could barely contain her panic as Marco brought the meeting to an end. How could she have been so stupid as to say that? It had been such a simple slip, yet it could cause untold damage. Fortunately there was no opportunity for him to say anything with the other woman there, but she knew that he would have questions later.

Could she lie if he asked her how old Lily was? Add on a couple of years to her daughter's age, perhaps? It would put him off the scent but could she live with herself if she deliberately misled him? She felt guilty enough without adding that to her score sheet.

'If there is anything else you want to ask me, please, don't hesitate, Mrs Daniels. Although Chloe will be moving to the children's ward, as the surgeon who operated on her, I shall still take an interest in her on-going care.'

'Thank you, Doctor. You've been very kind.' Donna grimaced. 'And it's Miss Daniels, actually. Chloe's dad didn't want anything to do with me when I told him I was pregnant. He's never even seen her, in fact.'

'That's a huge shame.'

Marco didn't say anything more so Gina couldn't tell if the comment had been merely a politeness or a genuine expression of regret. She sighed as she ushered Donna from the room. What did it matter how he felt about Donna's situation? He was bound to feel differently when it came to his own child, wasn't he?

The thought nagged away at her as the morning wore on. Marco called all the staff into the office during a quiet period and formally introduced himself. He gave them a brief summary of his career to date and Gina was surprised to discover that he'd been working overseas for the past few years. She had never expected him to leave Italy, but it appeared he had worked in Australia and the United States. Even though he downplayed his achievements, no one was left in any doubt that he knew his stuff. As Miles Humphreys sourly remarked when they trooped out of the office, the hospital's board must have thought all their birthdays and Christmases had come together when Marco had applied for the post.

That comment gave rise to a great deal of speculation as to why someone of his calibre would choose to relocate to the less salubrious areas of London. Gina managed to avoid giving a direct answer when her opinion was sought, murmuring something about everyone needing a change of scene. The fact that she had a very good idea why Marco had taken the job wasn't something she intended to share. However, it was added pressure on top of the worry about her slip-up that morning. By the time lunchtime arrived her head was aching from thinking about it.

She'd brought a packed lunch and decided to eat it outside in the hope that the fresh air would do her good. It would also mean that there would be less chance of her running into Marco—a definite inducement.

It was rather chilly outside but Gina found a sheltered spot. There were several other members of staff about, although thankfully nobody attempted to join her. She had just finished her sandwiches when she heard footsteps and looked up to see Marco striding towards her. He stopped when he reached the bench, his face betraying very little as he looked down at her.

'So here you are. I wondered where you had got to when I couldn't find you in the canteen.'

Gina gave a little shrug. 'I felt like some fresh air.'

'Ah, I see. So you weren't trying to avoid me? *Bene*. That makes me feel so much better.'

His tone was silky but she still flushed. Bending, she dug into her bag and found the apple she had brought with her, taking her time as she wiped the skin with a paper tissue. However, if she had harboured any hopes that he would take the hint and leave, she was disappointed.

He sat down beside her, tipping back his head so that the sun's rays fell on his face. 'It is good to feel the sun on your skin, *si*?'

'Mmm.' Gina bit into the apple, using that as an excuse not to answer. If she didn't encourage him, maybe he would give up, she reasoned.

They sat in silence while she ate. Gina could feel her nerves humming with tension as the seconds ticked past. At any moment she expected him to start asking questions and the prospect was almost worse than it actually happening. In the end, she couldn't stand the suspense any longer. She turned and glared at him.

'What do you want, Marco? I don't know what game you're playing but whatever it is, it won't work.'

'Why do you think that I am playing games?' His tone was still smooth but there was an undercurrent to it that sent a prickle of alarm racing through her.

'Because I can't think of a single reason why you

would choose to relocate to this area of London apart from it being some sort of…of *stupid* game!'

'That is not true.' He turned to look at her, his brown eyes holding hers fast. 'I came here to solve a problem.'

'What problem? And how can your being here solve anything?'

'Because it was the only way I could think of to get to the bottom of what happened between us, Gina.' His voice dropped, the rich tones sending a flurry of heat through her veins. 'I need to remember you and me, and what we had.'

'Why? It's history, Marco. What's the point of raking up something that is dead and buried?'

'But is it, Gina? Is it really dead and buried? Or is there still something there, some feelings that refuse to be confined to the past?' He shook his head and she could see the bewilderment in his eyes. 'That's what haunts me. This feeling that what we had isn't over, that it should never have ended in the first place.'

Gina felt tears burn her eyes and blinked them away. How she had longed to hear him say those very words at one time, but not now. It was too late for them to go back and too late for them to try again when it could have such a huge impact on Lily.

'That's not what you said when we broke up.' She laughed harshly, whipping up her anger to help her stay strong. 'I can't remember exactly how you phrased it, but I do know you left me in no doubt that you didn't envisage us having a future together.'

'And what about you, Gina? Was that how you felt?' He reached for her hand, his fingers closing firmly around hers. 'Were you sorry we parted? Did you try to make me see sense? Did you want us to stay together? Maybe I shouldn't ask those questions but I need to know.' He lifted her hand and placed it flat against his chest so that she could feel his heart beating beneath her palm. 'I need to know in here that I did the right thing. For both of us.'

Gina took a deep breath. If she told him the truth, that she would have walked over hot coals if it had meant they could be together, it would invite more questions. Yet if she lied and told him that she was glad they had parted, it would feel as though she was renouncing the most important decision she had ever made. The reason why she had refused to consider a termination was because she had been carrying Marco's child. Nothing would have induced her to harm it when she had loved him so much.

'What happened three years ago, Marco, happened. Yes, I was upset but I got over it.' She gave a little shrug. 'So in a way that proves you were right to call a halt when you did.'

Marco couldn't believe the pain he felt when she said that. He realised in a sudden flash of insight how much he had been hoping for a different response. He had wanted her to admit that she had loved him, that she had wished they could have stayed together; that she would have done anything to have made it come true. He had wanted to hear all that and more. How odd.

'I see,' he said, struggling to deal with the thought. 'It appears that everything worked out for the best, then, that both of us were happy with the outcome.'

'Yes.'

There was a hesitancy in her voice that made him look sharply at her. 'Are you sure about that, Gina?'

'Of course I'm sure. Look, Marco, I understand why this is so important to you.'

'You do?' It was his turn to sound hesitant and he saw her grimace.

'Yes. Losing your memory must have been awful for you. You're bound to want to know the ins and outs of everything that happened in your life. It's only natural.'

Was she right? Was it the fact that he couldn't fill in this gap with any degree of certainty that troubled him? Most of the blanks he could fill in at a guess. A half-remembered conversation could make sense once he reasoned it out, a snippet of a scene could be brought to a logical conclusion. But this was different. He couldn't apply logic to second-guess his emotions.

'Maybe you're right.' He summoned a smile, knowing that he wasn't going to achieve anything more by pushing her.

'I am.'

There was such naked relief in her voice that his senses immediately went on the alert. He realised all of a sudden that he still hadn't broached the subject that now concerned him most of all: her daughter. He placed his hand on her arm when she went to get up. 'If it is true that you believe our affair came to a timely end, Gina, why do I have this feeling that you are afraid of me?'

'Afraid?'

'*Si*. It's the reason why I decided to remain in London. I had the strangest feeling that you were scared of me.'

'That's ridiculous! Why on earth would I be scared of you?'

'I don't know. Maybe it has something to do with your daughter.' Marco knew he was right when he saw her blanch. What he didn't understand was why she was so afraid of him finding out about the child. 'I can tell I'm right,' he began, determined to get to the bottom of the mystery. 'I just need to know why…'

He broke off when he heard a child's excited voice calling 'Mummy'. The next second a little girl appeared and flung herself at Gina.

'What are *you* doing here?' she exclaimed as she swung the child into her arms.

'She insisted on coming to find you, I'm afraid.'

Marco automatically rose when a woman came to join them. She had two young boys with her, obviously twins, but he barely registered them. His attention was focused on the child, on Gina's daughter. With her blonde hair and delicate features the little girl was the image of Gina…apart from her eyes.

Marco could feel the blood pounding inside his skull as he stared at the child. He had seen eyes that colour before; in fact, he saw them every single morning when he stood in front of the mirror, shaving. They were the exact colour of his, a deep golden-brown.

The pressure inside his head seemed to intensify as the memories suddenly came rushing back, memories of him and Gina, and the time they had spent together in Florence. He remembered it all—how he had felt, how afraid he'd been when he had realised that he was falling in love with her. It was all there inside his head, a jumble of conflicting emotions that would have been more than enough to contend with, but there was something else he now had to deal with, something even more mind-blowing.

He shuddered, feeling the shock reaching deep inside him. Was it possible that Gina's daughter was his daughter too?

CHAPTER NINE

GINA'S heart was pounding as she set Lily down on her feet. How long would it take Marco to work out that Lily was his daughter? He only had to look at her to see that she had his eyes so it shouldn't take him long. If he asked her directly if Lily was his child then she would have to tell him the truth; she couldn't not, couldn't lie about something so important.

'This is a lovely surprise, but what are you doing here?' she asked, hearing the strain in her voice. She shot a wary look at Marco but he wasn't looking at her. He was staring at Lily and she knew—she just knew!—that he had worked it out.

'Charlie fell off the swing and cut his knee. It was quite deep so I brought him into ED,' Amy, the child-minder, explained. 'He's ended up with three stitches plus a sticker for being such a brave boy.'

'Wow, you are brave,' Gina agreed when the little boy proudly showed her his sticker.

Amy laughed. 'He and Alfie have a collection of stickers on the wall at home. There's hardly a week goes by without one or other of them hurting them-selves! Anyway, as soon as Lily knew we were com-ing to the hospital, she insisted on seeing you.' Amy glanced from her to Marco and grimaced. 'Sorry. We didn't mean to interrupt.'

'You aren't,' Gina assured her quickly. She introduced Marco, ignoring the speculative look on Amy's face. Whatever her friend was thinking was way off beam! There was nothing going on between her and Marco, or nothing like that, at least.

'We'd better let you get on,' Amy said finally, taking hold of Lily's hand. 'Come on, you lot, it's time we went home.'

Gina gave Lily a kiss and waved them off, wishing that she could go with them. Given the choice, she would take Lily home, lock the door and stay there until all this blew over, only it wasn't going to happen. Marco wasn't going to let her escape without telling him the truth, and her heart quaked at the thought.

'We need to talk,' he said flatly, then stopped when his pager beeped. Unhooking it from his belt, he checked the display. 'I am needed in ED,' he said, cancelling the message with an impatient stab of his finger.

Gina nodded, not trusting herself to speak. She couldn't tell him like this, couldn't blurt out that, yes, he was a father and not have time to tell him anything else, like why she had kept Lily's existence a secret. She needed to explain her reasons, convince him that although he might be right to blame her, he must never blame Lily. Her daughter was the innocent victim in all of this, the one who could get hurt the most.

In the end, Marco didn't utter another word. Swinging round on his heel, he strode back up the path. Gina sank back down onto the bench, her whole body trembling as reaction set in. She had no idea what would happen next but he wouldn't let the matter rest here.

Would he demand to see Lily once it was confirmed that she was his daughter? Or would he be less interested in the child than in the fact that he had solved the mystery that had brought him back here? The truth was that she didn't know how he would react. They had never discussed having children so she had no idea if he hoped to have some of his own one day.

In fact, now that she thought about it, she had no idea if he already *had* a child, maybe more than one, a family even. Their affair had been so brief and so intense that they hadn't delved into each other's pasts. Just being together had been enough and whatever had gone before hadn't mattered. Or so she had thought. Now, however, she found herself wondering if the reason why Marco hadn't asked about her past or told her about his was because he hadn't been interested. She had been merely an eager and willing bedmate, nothing more.

Marco finished conferring with the young F1 doctor from ED and bade her a brisk goodbye. His opposite number from ED was in a meeting, which was why he had been paged. On his recommendation, the motorcyclist would be on his way to Theatre shortly. His diagnosis, that the rapid fall in the man's blood pressure was the result of internal bleeding, had proved correct: a ruptured spleen was to blame.

He had led the younger doctor through his diagnosis a step at a time, making sure she knew what to look for the next time. He had always enjoyed the mentoring side of his job and normally derived a great deal of satisfaction from it. However, all he could think about was Gina and her daughter.

Was the child his? Was it possible that their brief li-

aison had resulted in the one thing he had assumed he
would never have after Francesca died? As he made his
way to AAU he realised that he had to find out the truth
before he did anything. There was no point building up
his hopes when it might not be true. He couldn't face
the disappointment. And even if it did turn out that he
was the child's father, as he suspected, it wouldn't be
plain sailing; there would be many obstacles to overcome, the biggest one being Gina. The fact that she had
chosen not to tell him about their daughter was a good
indication of how she felt.

Marco's mouth compressed as he entered the ward.
Gina was with a patient. She glanced round when he
approached the bed and he could see the fear in her eyes
and it annoyed him. What did she think he was going
to do? Kidnap the child and make off with her?

'I would like a word with you, Sister, after you've
finished here,' he said quietly, nodding politely to the
young man lying on the bed.

'I could be a while yet, Dr Andretti.'

'There is no rush. I shall wait in the office until you
are free. There are some calls I need to make.'

He walked away, unwilling to give her the chance
to think up any more excuses. If it was up to her, they
would never have this conversation, but he refused to
let her off the hook that easily. If the child was his, he
needed to know!

Gina delayed as long as she could until she couldn't
think of anything else that needed doing. She made
her way to the office, her footsteps dragging as she approached the door. She knew what Marco was going to
say and knew what her answer must be but that didn't
make it any easier. Once she told him the truth about

Lily there could be no going back. It was the thought of what would happen that worried her, the fear of the repercussions the next few minutes might have. She couldn't bear to think that Lily might suffer in any way.

The thought gave her a much-needed boost and she pushed open the door. Marco was on the phone and he glanced up when she appeared. Just for a second his eyes met hers and she felt shock course through her when she saw the apprehension they held. Marco was worried about what she would say? Why? Because he knew that Lily was his and hated the idea of having a child or, rather, having a child with *her*?

The thought was so painful that she flinched and she saw him frown. He curtly ended the conversation and replaced the receiver in its rest. His voice was harsh when he spoke, the richly accented tones grating in a way she had never heard before.

'There is no point dragging this out, Gina. We both know what I want to ask you, so is it true? Am I the father of your child?'

'Yes.' Her voice came out as little more than a croak and she cleared her throat. 'Yes. You are Lily's father.'

'Lily.' He repeated the name as though he was testing it out and that surprised her. Given the circumstances, she wouldn't have expected him to pay any heed to her daughter's name, but obviously it meant something to him. 'Why did you decide to call her Lily?'

'Because I like the name and it seemed to suit her,' she explained, wondering why she felt so touched by his reaction. 'She was so tiny and so perfect when she was born—just like a little flower.'

'I see.' He stood up and walked to the window, his

back towards her so that she couldn't see his face. 'It is a very pretty name.'

'I...I'm glad you like it.' Gina knew it was ridiculous to say that. What difference would it have made if he had hated Lily's name? And yet she couldn't deny how good it felt to know that she had done something he approved of.

'I do. I like it very much. Given the choice, I may even have chosen it for her myself, but I never had that choice, did I?' He swung round and she saw the anger that blazed in his eyes. 'You decided that I didn't have the right to help you choose our daughter's name or anything else!'

'I did what I thought was best,' she replied hoarsely, stunned by the speed of the onslaught.

'And that makes it right, does it?' His voice was laced with contempt. 'You decided not to tell me that you were pregnant with my child because you deemed it the *best* thing to do?'

'I did try to tell you! I tried to phone you and even wrote you a letter.'

'Really?'

'Yes, really.' She glared at him. 'When I couldn't reach you by phone and my letter was returned, I realised that you weren't interested.'

'Did it never occur to you that I might not have received your calls or your letter?'

'No, it didn't. As far as I knew, you were still in Florence. I had no idea that you'd moved away to work.'

'You could have found out, though. Someone at the hospital could have told you where I was, if you'd asked.' He smiled thinly. 'But you didn't ask, did you,

Gina? You were more than happy to let me live in ignorance of the fact that I was to be a father.'

'Yes, I was.' She stood up straighter, refusing to let him see how much it hurt to have him speak to her that way. 'You'd made your feelings very clear when we broke up, Marco. Although I was going to tell you that I was pregnant, I had no intention of asking you for anything.' She shrugged. 'Maybe I could have tracked you down if I'd tried harder but I did what I thought was in everyone's best interests.'

'How? How can it be in my best interest not to know that I have a child? How can it be in Lily's best interest to grow up not knowing her father? You must forgive me if I appear particularly stupid, Gina, but I fail to see how anyone could benefit from your lies except you.'

'Me?'

'Si.' He gave a very expressive shrug. 'We'd had an affair and gone our separate ways. When you found out you were pregnant, I imagine it came as a shock. After all, we had taken precautions. A child was never on the agenda and yet there you were, expecting my baby.

'I imagine you thought about having a termination but in the end decided not to go through with it for whatever reasons. However, deciding that you wanted to keep the baby didn't mean that you wanted me to be involved. I was well out of the picture by then. You had probably moved on to someone else, so why muddy the waters?'

'It wasn't like that!'

'Then what was it like? Come on, Gina, I'm longing to hear why you decided to cut me out of our child's life.'

Gina opened her mouth to reply but just then there

was a knock on the door and Julie appeared. She shot a wary glance at them and it was obvious that she had sensed the tension.

'Sorry, but the woman in bay three is kicking up a fuss. She's threatening to discharge herself if she isn't moved to a ward.'

'I'll have a word with her,' Gina said quickly. She glanced at Marco. 'Is that all, Dr Andretti?'

'For now.' Marco strode around the desk. He paused as he drew level with her. 'We shall continue this conversation later.' He stormed out of his office without a backward glance.

It sounded distinctly like a threat and obviously appeared that way to Julie because her mouth dropped open. 'What on earth is going on?' she demanded. 'How have you managed to get into our Italian stallion's bad books so quickly?'

'Don't ask,' Gina replied grimly as she made her way to the ward. She managed to calm down the patient but it was worrying to know that the situation was impacting on her work. If she and Marco were to continue this discussion, it would need to be outside working hours.

The thought wasn't exactly comforting. Given the choice, she would have avoided going anywhere near him again that day, but she didn't have a choice. She would have to arrange to meet him on neutral ground, find out what he wanted, and proceed from there. If Amy would mind Lily that evening, maybe they could sort something out. One thing was certain: the sooner she knew what his intentions were with regard to Lily, the happier she would be.

Marco knew that he had allowed his emotions to get the better of him and hated the thought that he appeared to have so little control. Normally, he viewed each and every problem in the same calm and rational fashion, but he was unable to do that in this instance. Not only had he remembered what Gina had meant to him but he'd found out that he was a father! It was no wonder that his emotions were in turmoil.

He sighed. He needed to calm down and think about what he had learned before he did anything. It was just that Gina's claim to have withheld the fact that he had a daughter had been in his best interests had annoyed him intensely. It took two people to create a child and two people to raise it. Gina must really hate him to have deprived him of all knowledge of his child.

It was incredibly painful to face that fact, especially when he recalled the way she had felt at one time. Gina had been in love with him but he had destroyed any feelings she'd had for him when he had ended their relationship. The thought nagged away at him as the afternoon wore on and he was glad that he was kept busy, monitoring both AAU and ED. When five o'clock arrived, he decided to go up to the admin. department to collect his ID and all the other paperwork he was lacking. He had just summoned the lift when he heard someone calling his name and glanced round to see Gina hurrying towards him.

She got right to the point. 'It's obvious that we need to talk, Marco, so I suggest we meet tonight and try to sort things out.'

'That seems like a good idea to me,' he agreed, wondering if this was really an olive branch or another attempt to sideline him. He sighed inwardly. They would get nowhere if he approached the matter with such a cynical attitude. 'Where do you suggest we meet? I'm afraid I don't know very many places in this part of London.'

'Maybe it would better if we met somewhere more central,' she said with a frown that made her brow pucker in the most adorable way.

Marco was hard-pressed not to reach out and smooth away the tiny furrows but he knew it would be a mistake to blur the boundaries. He had to behave as impersonally as she was, treat this as a business matter and nothing more. 'How about my apartment, then? It's central and there's a tube station five minutes away.'

'I'm not sure if that's a good idea,' she began, then stopped when his brows rose. A wash of colour ran up her face as she glared at him. 'Your apartment will be fine. Shall we make it seven o'clock?'

'Seven is fine with me,' he replied evenly. Was she worried about what might happen if she came to his flat? he wondered. Afraid that their business discussion might turn into something else? Pictures of them lying naked together in his bed suddenly flooded his head and he had to breathe deeply before he continued.

'Use the entry phone and I'll buzz you in. My apartment is on the fifteenth floor so you'll need to take the lift. I'll wait for you in the hallway.'

'Fine.'

He told her the address then stepped into the lift. Gina had already disappeared before the doors closed and he sighed. It was obvious that she didn't view the coming meeting with any enthusiasm. As far as she was concerned, it was a necessary evil. Maybe he should feel the same but there was no escaping the fact that he was looking forward to seeing her that night and not just because he wanted to learn more about his daughter.

Unbidden the image of them lying together in his bed came rushing back and he groaned. It wasn't a memory from the past he was recalling; that would have been just about acceptable. What he was seeing now hadn't happened. He knew that because the bed they were lying in was the bed in his apartment, not the one at the Villa Rosa that they had shared. These images in his head were projections into the future, something he *wanted* to happen.

Just admitting it worried him. Marco knew that if he made love to Gina now it would be different, that *he* would feel differently. Three years ago he had still been grieving for Francesca, still felt angry about losing her, but the accident had changed things and now he had come to terms with what had happened. When… *if*…he made love to Gina again it would be without the shadow of Francesca hanging over him. He would be free of all restraints, free to follow his heart. Free to get hurt. Only this time the pain would be even worse because he had more to lose: Gina *and* his daughter.

CHAPTER TEN

IT WAS a few minutes after seven when Gina arrived at the building where Marco rented an apartment. She pressed the entry button then glanced around. This part of London was one of the most expensive in terms of property. She knew that the rent on an apartment in this area would be as much as her monthly salary. Marco must be extremely well off if he could afford to live in such an exclusive location.

'*Si?*'

She swung round when she heard his voice coming through the speaker. 'It's me,' she said shortly, wondering why the thought unsettled her. The difference in their lifestyles had never bothered her before. She had stayed at his home in Florence and was well aware of how beautiful the villa was with its antique furniture and air of restrained luxury. She had never really thought about it before, but for some reason the contrast between how she and Marco lived suddenly made her feel uneasy.

'*Bene.* I shall unlock the door. Cross the reception area and use the right-hand lift. It stops outside my apartment.'

Gina did as she was told and a few minutes later

stepped out into a smartly decorated hallway. Marco was waiting for her and he smiled politely as he ushered her towards one of the doors that opened onto that floor.

'This way,' he said, placing his hand lightly at the small of her back as he guided her inside.

Gina stepped away from him as soon as they were in the apartment, making a great production out of unbuttoning her coat to avoid having him touch her again. Maybe it was nerves but her skin seemed to be tingling in the strangest way where his hand had rested.

'Let me take that for you.'

He took her coat and hung it up in the closet beside the front door then led the way to the sitting room. Gina gasped when she was confronted by the most spectacular view. One entire wall was made of glass and the view across the river towards the Houses of Parliament was stunning.

'The view is the reason why I decided to take this apartment,' he said softly beside her. 'It is magnificent. *Si?*'

'It is.'

She moved away when she felt her skin break out in tingles again. Crossing the room, she sat down on one of the two huge chocolate-brown leather sofas that formed an L-shape in the centre of the room. Her whole flat would fit into this one room with space to spare, she thought wryly.

'I rented the place fully furnished,' Marco told her as he sat down on the other sofa. He shrugged as he reached for the glass cafetière standing on the coffee table. 'It is a little bare for my taste but as I shall only be living here for a limited time, I can put up with it.'

'So you're not planning on staying in England,' she said quickly.

'I wasn't. My contract is for six months. Although there is an option to extend it, I was planning on returning to Italy at the end of that time.' He poured coffee into two china mugs. 'However, that was before I found out about Lily. Obviously that changes things.'

Gina bit her lip, unsure what to say. Assuring Marco that he shouldn't change his plans because of their daughter might cause him to dig in his heels and do just that. It was going to be difficult enough to cope with having him around for six whole months, but if it was for longer... Well!

The thought of their lives being entwined for many years to come wasn't something she had considered before. However, if he insisted on playing a role in Lily's life then he would play a major role in her life too. She picked up her cup, determined to control the panic that flowed through her. She would deal with his presence in her life if she had to; she really would!

'I assume from your silence that you aren't happy at the thought of me changing my plans because of our daughter.' He shrugged when she glanced up. 'I am sorry if you feel that way, Gina, because it will make life more difficult for all of us.'

'There is no way that I will allow you to upset Lily!'

'And there is no way that I wish to do so.' His tone was so sharp that she flinched. He leant forward and she could see the determination on his face. 'Upsetting *our* daughter isn't part of my plan. I am just as anxious as you are that Lily shouldn't suffer in any way from all of this.'

Gina knew she should have been reassured but she

resented the fact that he thought he had a claim on her precious child. She and Lily had managed perfectly well without him so far and they would have continued to do so if fate hadn't brought him into their lives.

'In that case, the best thing you can do is to leave.' She stared back at him, wishing she had a magic wand to make him disappear. She didn't want him upsetting Lily. She didn't want him upsetting *her*.

The thought that Marco still possessed the power to disturb her wasn't one she welcomed and she glared at him. 'Lily is perfectly happy the way she is. However, if you insist on involving yourself in her life then it's bound to unsettle her.'

'That's your opinion and it seems to me that you have a rather jaundiced view of me, Gina.'

His tone was even but she could hear the underlying hurt it held and couldn't help feeling a little guilty. Maybe he genuinely believed that it was right to involve himself in their child's life but how long would he continue to feel like that? His interest in Lily would probably wane as quickly as it had arisen and she would be left trying to console a disappointed little girl. The thought helped her harden her heart.

'If I have a jaundiced view of you, Marco, it's all down to past experience. I hate to say this, but you don't have a good track record when it comes to being dependable. In fact, I've never met anyone who blows hot and cold as quickly as you do.'

'Hot and cold? I'm sorry but I am not sure what you mean.'

He leant forward, his brown eyes holding hers fast. Gina felt her breath catch when she found herself trapped by his searching gaze. It had been a long time since he had looked at her with such intensity, as though her every thought mattered to him, she thought wonderingly.

'Gina?' He prompted her to answer and she jumped.

'I...I meant that you seem to change your mind on a whim. One minute you appear to be very keen on something and the next it's the last thing you want anything to do with.'

'Something or *someone*?' he put in quietly.

She shrugged. 'If you want the truth, yes. One minute we seemed to be as close as two people could be and the next you didn't want anything to do with me. Is it any wonder that I don't trust you when it comes to Lily?'

Marco wasn't sure how to answer. How could he explain why he had chosen to break up with her without revealing too much? Would it be wise to admit that he had been on the brink of falling in love with her and that the thought had terrified him when he had sensed that she wouldn't want to hear it?

He stared at her for a long moment, letting his eyes drink in the delicate beauty of her face. It wasn't just that her features were so perfect, but the inner sweetness beneath the outer beauty. Gina was everything a man could want and he had given her up because he had been afraid of getting hurt. He took a deep breath, aware that the problem hadn't changed. He was still afraid, especially as he had even more to lose this time.

'There's nothing I can say apart from promising you that I will never let Lily down.' He cleared his throat, aware that his emotions were far too near the surface. 'Just because we split up, it doesn't mean that I will reject Lily. She's my daughter and I swear on my life that

I shall do everything possible to make sure she is safe and happy if you will let me.'

Gina didn't say a word as she stared down at her hands. He could tell how difficult it was for her and the thought of what she must be going through was too much. Leaning forward, he laid his hand over hers, willing her to believe him.

'I mean it, Gina. You really can trust me this time. I promise you.'

'It's easy to say that now but you could change your mind.' She removed her hands from his grasp. 'The time may come when it isn't convenient to have a child around.'

'Convenient?' He frowned, hiding his chagrin at the way she had drawn away. She had made it plain that she didn't want him to touch her and it stung to know how she felt when he felt so very differently.

He clamped down on the re-run of those images he'd had earlier in the day, the ones that involved him and Gina in his bed, and forced himself to focus on what she had said. So what if she never slept with him again; what did it matter? He would survive as he had survived in the three years since they had parted. 'Why should having a child cause me any inconvenience?'

'Because a lot of women wouldn't be happy at the thought of their husband or lover having a child from a previous relationship.'

It took a second for him to grasp her meaning and a few more before he could work out what to reply. Maybe it was silly but did he really want to admit that there had been no other women in his life since they had parted? 'That isn't an issue, I assure you.'

'Maybe not at the moment but who knows what will

happen in the future?' She shrugged. 'You could meet someone and find that you neither want nor have the time to spend with Lily. It happens, believe me.'

'It won't happen in this instance,' he insisted.

'If you say so.'

It was obvious that she didn't believe him and he knew that he had to convince her he was telling the truth if they were to get anywhere at all. 'Yes, I do. I am not interested in having a relationship with another woman, Gina. I never was interested even when I met you.'

'I see. Well, that answers one question.' Her eyes glistened with tears as she stood up. 'I always did wonder why you got involved with me and now I know. You just wanted someone you could have sex with and I fitted the bill.' She gave a bitter little laugh. 'Thanks for that, Marco. I'm under no illusions now!'

She snatched her bag off the couch and headed for the door but there was no way he would let her go thinking that. He hurried after her, catching hold of her arm to bring her to a halt. 'Wait! That wasn't what I meant. You got it all wrong.'

'I don't think so. Now, if I can have my coat…' She turned towards the wall, searching for the concealed catch that unlocked the closet door.

Marco reached past her and opened the door, lifting out her coat, although he didn't give it to her. 'You've got it wrong, Gina,' he repeated. 'It was never just sex. You must know that.'

'Oh, please! Spare me the platitudes. Why not call a spade a spade and be done with it?'

He smiled faintly although there was nothing amusing about the situation. To know that she was hurting this much was almost more than he could bear. 'I assume we aren't discussing gardening implements, *si*? In that case, if you want the truth, that's what I am giving you.'

He turned her to face him, feeling her resistance in the stiffness of her body. 'It was never just sex between us. It was far more than that.' He cupped her chin with his hand so that she was forced to look at him. 'What I felt for you, Gina, was so much more than sex that I was terrified. That's why I broke up with you. Because I was afraid.'

'Afraid? Of what? What could you possibly have been afraid of?'

Her voice echoed with disbelief and hurt, and he couldn't bear it. Bending, he placed his mouth over hers and kissed her, a kiss that held a plea for understanding. Maybe he was making a mistake but he needed to convince her that he was telling the truth: she needed to believe it!

He drew back, seeing the shock that shimmered in her eyes, yet it was the fact that he could also see the awareness they held too that was the biggest surprise of all. Gina had been stirred by his kiss, even enjoyed it, and the thought made him feel ten feet tall.

'Of getting hurt again.' He paused, battling to contain his emotions because this wasn't the time to get carried away. He needed to be honest with her and hope that it would help him gain her trust with regard to Lily. 'Like I'd been hurt when I lost Francesca.'

Gina could hear a rushing in her head. It was so loud that it blotted out everything else. She could see Marco speaking to her but she couldn't hear what he was saying. When he led her back into the sitting room and sat her down, she didn't protest.

She had never expected him to kiss her and certainly never expected to feel that familiar surge of desire rise up inside her. However, the moment his lips had claimed hers, she had been transported back to the days when he had been her whole world and she had thought she'd been his, only that hadn't been true. It couldn't have been, not when he had spoken about another woman in such a way.

'Here, drink this.'

He pushed a glass into her hand and she obediently took a sip of the liquid then coughed when the spirit hit the back of her throat. He took the glass from her and went to pat her on the back but she moved out of his way. She couldn't bear to feel his hands on her. She had a feeling that she might break down and that was the last thing she could afford to do. It appeared the situation was worse than she had imagined. Now there was another woman to add to the equation, a woman who, apparently, had meant everything to him. It took all her courage to ask the question but she needed to know.

'Who exactly is Francesca?'

He glanced down at the glass he was holding and when he looked up there was a bleakness about his expression that made her heart ache. 'Francesca is…was my wife.'

CHAPTER ELEVEN

'YOUR wife!'

Marco saw the shock on Gina's face. He took a deep breath, knowing that he had to get this over with as quickly as possible. '*Si*. She died four years ago.'

'*Died*? But how? Why?'

She stopped, obviously equally stunned by this new revelation, and he sighed, aware that he wasn't handling things very well. 'It was a tragic accident. Francesca was out shopping and a car swerved to avoid a child who ran into the road. It mounted the pavement and knocked Francesca down.'

He paused, waiting for the familiar rush of pain he always felt whenever he spoke about what had happened and yet, oddly, all he felt was sadness at such a cruel waste of a life. He cleared his throat. 'There was nothing anyone could do. Francesca was crushed against a wall and she was killed outright.'

'How awful! I don't know what to say…' She tailed off, biting her lip as she struggled to find some words of comfort to offer him.

'There is nothing anyone can say, Gina. It was a terrible accident, the sort of thing you read about in the newspapers and never imagine will happen to someone you know.'

'You must have been devastated.'

'I was. I couldn't believe it at first. I kept expecting to wake up and find that it had been some sort of awful dream. It took me a long time to accept that Francesca wasn't coming back.'

'It must have been so hard for you, Marco.' Tears shimmered in her eyes as she reached out and touched his hand.

'It was.'

He turned his hand over, his fingers closing around hers, feeling the jolt of awareness that shot through him when his skin made contact with hers. That he was capable of feeling like that when they were discussing such a terrible period in his life shocked him. It was difficult to concentrate but he knew that he had to tell her everything in the hope that it would help.

'It was the sheer unexpectedness of what happened that was the worst thing of all. If Francesca had been ill, I would have had time to prepare myself, but with an accident like that…' He stopped, not trusting himself to continue. His emotions were already raw and it would take very little to let all the shock and horror he had kept bottled up pour out. Whilst it might be healing for him, it wouldn't help Gina. She had enough to deal with without him burdening her with this.

'It was a very difficult time,' he said finally, 'but I had my work and that helped me get through it.'

'I'm glad, but still…'

She paused, obviously expecting him to say something else, but he stayed silent. This wasn't a bid for her sympathy but a chance to explain his actions. Maybe then she would understand why he had felt the need to end their affair, accept that it hadn't been a lack of feeling that had driven him to do so but, rather, the fear of feeling too much.

His heart began to race as he recalled how desperate he had felt three years ago. He had been on the brink of falling in love with Gina and he'd been terrified of what it could mean. That was why he had pushed her away, because he'd been afraid of getting hurt again if anything happened to her.

What if he started to feel that way again? he wondered. What would he do then? How could he walk away when they had a child to consider?

Marco stood up, feeling his stomach churning as he went over to the window. He couldn't turn his back on his daughter. He couldn't and wouldn't abandon her, yet the more involved he became with Lily, the more involved he would become with Gina. Somehow he had to take control of the situation, minimise the damage it could cause for all of them. As long as he recognised his own vulnerability, he would cope. He had to.

He sat down again, deliberately removing any trace of emotion from his voice. 'Whilst what I've told you obviously had a bearing on what happened three years ago, we need to focus on the future now. I meant what I said about wanting to be involved in Lily's life, Gina. Maybe you find it hard to believe but it's true. Our daughter's welfare is my only concern from now on.'

Gina knew that he was waiting for her to say something and struggled to find the right words. He sounded so composed and she envied him that. She took a quick breath, trying not to think about what he had said about his reasons for ending their relationship…

He must have really felt something for you if he'd

been afraid to let matters continue, a small voice whispered inside her head.

She closed her mind to that tantalising thought, determined that it wasn't going to distract her. It was Lily's future at stake now and nothing was more important than that. 'I hope you mean that, Marco. I hope it isn't just…well, a reaction to finding out that you have a child.'

'A reaction? I'm not sure what you mean.'

'Obviously, it was a shock to learn that you have a daughter. It's understandable if you feel you're responsible for Lily in the first rush of enthusiasm. However, I understand if you have second thoughts.'

'I shall not have second thoughts.' His face closed up as he stared coldly back at her. 'If the child is mine, there is no question that I intend to be involved in her life.'

'*If* Lily is yours? That implies you have doubts. Do you, Marco?'

Gina wasn't sure why she felt so hurt. After all, it was only natural that he would want to be sure that Lily was his child. In fact, it could work to her advantage because he would be less keen to play an active role in Lily's life if he doubted his paternity. And yet the thought that he might think she would lie about something so important stung.

'No. I don't have any doubts whatsoever.' His gaze was level. 'If you say that Lily is my child then I believe you.'

It was the affirmation she wanted and yet she found herself pushing him for more. 'Even though I failed to tell you about her?'

He shrugged. 'They are two separate issues. Whilst

I still believe you could have tried harder to contact me,
I don't believe you would try to pass off another man's
child as mine. Lily is my daughter, isn't she?'

He challenged her to deny it but there was no way
that Gina would make matters worse by doing that.
'Yes, she's your child, Marco. There is no question
about that.'

'*Bene.* Now all we need to decide is when I can see
her. Obviously, I don't want to wait. I've lost enough
time as it is, so I suggest we arrange to meet this weekend. You can bring Lily here or I can come to your
home.'

'This weekend! But that's just a few days away. It's
far too soon to see her this weekend.'

'That is your view, Gina. My view is that the sooner
I meet her, the sooner we shall get to know one another.'
His tone was unyielding. 'I realise that it will be hard
for the little one to understand who I am at first. I assume you haven't mentioned me to her—isn't that so?'

Gina nodded, wondering if he could tell how guilty
she felt. She hadn't told Lily about him because there'd
seemed no point. They weren't going to see him so
there had been no reason to confuse Lily by telling her
about a father she would never meet. It had seemed so
sensible before and yet she felt awful for deliberately
cutting him out of her daughter's life.

'I thought not. In that case, I suggest we don't confuse her by telling her who I am to begin with. Let her
get used to me and then, when she has accepted me as
part of her life, we can tell her that I'm her daddy.'

It made sense, although she was surprised that he
was willing to wait. She had assumed that he would
want to rush in, claim Lily as his own and make a fuss

about being her father. It made her wonder if she had misjudged him and that if she had done so with regard to this then perhaps she had misjudged him in other matters too.

The thought was more than a little unsettling. Gina forced it to the back of her mind. 'That seems the most sensible thing to do,' she agreed. Marco might be keen to take on his new role as a father but it didn't mean he was interested in resuming his old role in her life. Their affair was over and he had made that clear. The fact that they had a child was the only thing that united them now.

'I'm glad you agree.' He suddenly smiled. 'It appears that we can work together if we try, doesn't it?'

'So it seems.' Gina shrugged, hoping he couldn't tell how on edge she felt. She should be pleased they had managed to reach an amicable solution, and she was. However, she couldn't deny that part of her hated to think that the only thing which bound them now was Lily.

'*Bene*. Now all that is left to do is to arrange a time and a place where we can meet. Where do you suggest?'

Marco was all business. If he felt even a flicker of regret that their affair was well and truly relegated to the past, it didn't show, Gina thought, then wondered why it bothered her so much. She forced herself to emulate his businesslike tone so that he wouldn't have any inkling of how confused she felt.

'I suggest we go to the park. It will be less formal that way and Lily won't feel so daunted about meeting a stranger.'

Marco's lips compressed at the word 'stranger' but

he didn't challenge her. 'If that's what you feel is best then that is what we shall do.'

They agreed to meet in Hyde Park at eleven on the Saturday morning then Gina stood up. 'I'll have to go. Lily is usually in bed by now and I need to get her home.'

'Who's minding her tonight?' he asked, holding her coat so she could slip her arms into the sleeves.

'Amy,' Gina replied, struggling to get the coat on as quickly as possible. She knew it was silly but just feeling him there, behind her, made her feel all keyed up. She shoved her hand down the left sleeve, grimacing when her watch strap snagged on a loose thread in the lining. She tried to work it free but it was well and truly stuck. Marco frowned as he peered over her shoulder.

'What's the matter?'

'My watch has caught on a thread,' she said, trying to force her hand down the sleeve.

'Careful! You will rip the lining.' He stepped in front of her and took hold of her arm so he could slide his hand inside the sleeve. 'Ah, yes, I can feel it now.'

He inched his hand further up the sleeve and Gina felt her breath catch. By necessity they were standing so close that she could smell the tang of soap that came off his skin, feel the heat of his body, and it was such a heady mix that all her senses suddenly went on the alert. It was sheer torture to feel his fingers smoothing over her skin and not respond. Even though there was nothing overtly sexual about his actions, she could feel desire pooling in the pit of her stomach, feel every nerve ending quivering with anticipation…

'Ah! That seems to have solved the problem.'

He removed his hand and stepped back. Gina blinked

as all the emotions that had been building up inside her
suddenly drained away. She took a quick breath as she
pushed her hand out of the sleeve. She didn't want to
make love with him. It was the last thing she wanted!

'Thank you.' She hurried into the hall, reaching for
the catch to open the door, but he was ahead of her.

'I can tell that you're in a hurry so I won't keep you,'
he said as he opened the door for her. 'Thank you for
coming tonight, Gina, and for being so reasonable. It
has helped to set my mind at rest.'

'I'm not sure I understand what you mean,' she said,
frowning up at him.

'I was worried in case our past relationship would
make it impossible for us to work together.' His voice
dropped, the richly accented tones sounding more pro-
nounced than ever as he continued. 'I know I hurt you
and I am truly sorry about that. But I hope you understand now why I couldn't allow our relationship to continue.'

'Because you were afraid of getting hurt again.' She
took a quick breath, knowing it was foolish to ask but
unable to resist. 'And could that have happened, Marco?
Was I really such a threat to you?'

'Yes.' He kissed her gently on the cheek and his eyes
were very dark when he drew back. 'I knew you had
the power to turn my life upside down and that is the
one thing I shall never risk. I don't want to fall in love
again, Gina. I refuse to allow it to happen. I just hope
that we can move on and become friends as well as good
parents to our daughter.'

'Ye-yes, of course.' Gina managed to smile before
she swung round and hurried out of the door. She summoned the lift, praying it wouldn't take long to arrive.

When Marco bade her goodbye she somehow managed to respond. Within seconds she was exiting the building and hurrying along the street but realised that she was heading in the wrong direction.

She retraced her steps, averting her eyes as she passed the apartment block. No doubt Marco was congratulating himself that everything had been sorted out with so little fuss. He was determined not to get emotionally involved, or at least not with her.

Gina felt a wave of pain wash over her. Although he claimed that he had been on the verge of falling in love with her, was it true? She had loved him so much that nothing could have persuaded her to give him up, neither bad memories nor fear of what the future held. Her love for him had transcended everything else; he had been all that had mattered. But he hadn't felt that way, had he?

He had examined his feelings, decided that he wasn't prepared to risk getting hurt, and acted accordingly. It made her wonder if he really understood what love was all about. Not that it mattered now, of course. Not when he had made it clear that their relationship was going to be strictly that of friends and parents.

She took a steadying breath. She had to accept that she and Marco were never going to be lovers.

CHAPTER TWELVE

MARCO spent a restless evening after Gina left. Although he was relieved that they had managed to sort things out so satisfactorily, he couldn't rid himself of the feeling that he had made a mess of things. He went over what had happened a dozen times or more but he couldn't pinpoint what was causing him to feel so edgy. It was just a feeling he had that he had said something to upset her and it worried him.

Maybe he would ask her in the morning if everything was all right, he mused as he got into bed. And maybe he wouldn't, he decided as he switched off the light. If they were to stick to their roles as parents and friends, it would be better not to introduce any other issues into the equation.

AAU was frantically busy when he arrived the following morning. He was surprised to discover that many of the patients who had been due to be transferred were still on the unit, including little Chloe Daniels. He waited until Gina had finished dealing with a new admission and called her into the office.

'What's going on? Why are so many of yesterday's patients still here? Chloe Daniels should have gone straight to Paediatrics after she left Recovery.'

'There's a problem in Paeds as well as in Women's Surgical. Water's been leaking from the storage tanks on the roof and it's brought down part of the ceiling on that floor. Some patients have been transferred to other hospitals, but they decided not to move Chloe as she'd just had surgery and sent her back to us.'

'I see.' Marco frowned as he considered how this would affect them. 'How long will it be before everything is back to normal?'

'No one seems to know.' Gina sighed. 'If it's just a matter of clearing up and replacing the ceiling then it could be a week, but if the damage is more serious it will take longer.'

'And in the meantime we're going to be pushed for space. Are there any side rooms that can be made available?'

'There's two beds in the high dependency unit which we can use. And there's another in the room we use for any patients requiring barrier nursing. That's it, though.'

'So that makes three plus any that become available throughout the day,' he concluded.

Although it was annoying to know that they would be put under extra pressure, it was a relief to turn his attention to a less personal problem. It had taken him a long time to fall asleep and when he had, his dreams had been filled with images of Gina. It was as though now he had remembered their affair, his memory was more acute than ever. He could recall in vivid detail every day he had spent with her: each hour, each minute, each second. It had been such a magical time that it was hard to believe he'd had the strength to let go.

He hastily dismissed that thought, knowing how dangerous it was. 'I want you to ring round all the wards and make it clear that we won't be able to keep patients here once they have been referred to a consultant.'

'They're not going to be happy,' Gina warned him.

'Probably not but there is nothing we can do about it. We need to free up beds for those who require urgent treatment. In other words, we have to get back to basics and make sure the department is used for acute admissions only. I noticed yesterday that some cases don't fall into that category. I'll have a word with Tom Petty, the ED consultant, and make sure he's aware of the problems we're facing. If we work together, we should be able to find a solution.'

Gina nodded, trying not to think about the other problem Marco had been so keen to find a solution to. She sighed as she followed him out of the office. She had spent the best part of the night thinking about what had happened in his apartment. Even when he had admitted how devastated he had been after his wife had died, he had still remained in control. Add to that the way he had been able to rationalise his feelings for her and it all added up to a man who rarely allowed himself to be led by his emotions.

Was that a good or a bad thing with regard to Lily? she wondered. Would he be able to detach himself as easily from his own child? Her biggest fear was that Lily would grow attached to him only to be let down at some point. Marco may have managed to allay her fears the previous evening but during the night they had come flooding back. She wouldn't allow him to break Lily's heart as he had broken hers!

'Marco, just a moment,' she said hurriedly as he went to walk away. She felt her pulse quicken when he turned and tried to ignore the rush of blood that ran through her veins. The fact that she was so aware of him didn't matter. It was the damage he could cause to her precious daughter that was important.

'About Saturday and you meeting Lily, I don't think it's a good idea after all. I think we should wait a couple of weeks. It will give me time to prepare her and, more importantly, give *you* time to think about what you're doing.' She gave a little shrug when he didn't say anything. 'There's no point jumping in, feet first, and then regretting it.'

'So you still think that I shall have second thoughts.'

'I think it's extremely likely given your track record.'

'What happened between us has no bearing whatsoever on my relationship with our daughter.'

'In that case, it doesn't matter if you meet Lily this weekend or next.'

'It matters to me.' He stepped closer, his eyes holding hers fast. 'And it matters to Lily as well. The longer it takes before I meet her, the harder it will be to establish a relationship. So if you're planning on not turning up on Saturday, I suggest you think really hard about what you are doing. I don't want to fight with you, Gina, but I will if you try to stop me seeing my child. Understand?'

He didn't wait for a reply. Gina took a shaky breath as he strode away. He had sounded so angry that it made her wonder how she had ever imagined they could work together.

'Hey, are you OK? You've not had another run-in with the gorgeous Marco, have you?'

Gina jumped when Julie tapped her on the arm. She dredged up a smile. 'Just a minor difference of opinion.'

'Hmm, interesting.' Julie grinned at her. 'There's definitely a vibe when you two are together. I'm not the only one who's noticed it either. Still, they say that love and hate are two sides of the same coin, don't they?'

'Rubbish! It's just a clash of personalities. I'm sure things will even out once Dr Andretti gets used to our way of doing things.'

'Pity!' Julie heaved an exaggerated sigh. 'Here was I thinking that you had finally met a man who pushes your buttons. You're too young to be on your own, Gina. You need love, romance, *sex*!'

Gina laughed. 'I shall bear that in mind. However, you can strike Marco off the list. Been there, done that and thrown away the T-shirt, thank you.'

'What! Did I hear you right?' Julie gaped at her. 'Are you saying that you two were an item once?'

Gina could have bitten off her tongue. The last thing she needed was for folk to start gossiping. 'That's a bit strong. I met him a while ago in Italy. We went out a few times and that was it. I came back to England and didn't see him again until he was brought in after that accident.'

'You never said anything,' Julie pointed out, and Gina sighed.

'No, I didn't. I know what the grapevine is like in this place and I didn't want everyone making something out of nothing. Marco was just someone I dated, so I hope you won't say anything to the others.'

'My lips are sealed.' Julie fastened an imaginary zip across her mouth. 'I won't say a word, except that I think you might be wrong about him being just some-one you went out with. There's obviously something going on between you two. OK, so maybe things didn't go too well in the past, but who knows what could hap-pen in the future, eh?'

Julie winked at her then hurried off to answer a patient's bell. Gina went into the ward and made a list of all the patients who had been referred to other departments. Phoning round took some time and Marco hadn't returned by the time she finished. Whether he was still consulting with Tom Petty in ED, she didn't know and didn't care, she assured herself. Where Marco went and what he did wasn't her concern except when it impacted on Lily. And she had no intention of allowing him to bully her round to his way of thinking. If she decided something wasn't right for her daughter, she would stick to her guns and he could either like it or lump it!

Saturday dawned bright and clear. As Marco stepped out of the shower, he could feel anticipation bubbling inside him. Meeting Lily today was going to be a life-changing experience.

He had always wanted a family, although since Francesca had died, he had never really thought about it. However, now that it was fait accompli, so to speak, he realised how important it was to him. He was excited by the prospect and it could only have been better if he and Gina had been able to provide Lily with a proper home. Children needed both a mother and father, preferably living under the same roof.

He sighed because the likelihood of that happening was nil. Apart from the fact that he had no intention of getting involved with Gina, she would never agree to it. He had really hurt her and although she might be able to accept what he had done eventually, she wasn't there yet. She was still hurt, still angry with him, and it meant that he would have to tread very carefully.

Setting up home together wasn't on the cards even for Lily's sake.

It was just gone ten when he arrived at the park and there were already a lot of people about. He strolled along beside the Serpentine, checking his watch frequently so he wouldn't be late. At ten minutes to eleven he headed over to the children's playground, feeling his pulse quicken when he spotted Gina sitting on a bench. At least she had come, he thought as he went to join her.

'*Buon giorno*, Gina. How are you today?'

She turned to look at him and he could see the wariness in her eyes. 'Fine.'

She didn't ask how he was, didn't seem keen to make conversation, in fact, and he sighed. 'We shall get nowhere if you insist on treating me like some kind of pariah. Children are very astute and Lily will soon notice that something is wrong. It isn't fair that you should colour her view of me before I've had a chance to get to know her.'

Heat rushed up her cheeks as she glared at him. 'I have no intention of colouring her view of you! I just need you to understand that once you start this, you can't suddenly change your mind. If this isn't what you really want, Marco…'

'Mummy! Look!'

They both turned when a small voice interrupted them. Marco felt a lump come to his throat as his gaze settled on the little girl. Her blonde hair was caught up into a ponytail, a bright pink bobble that matched her T-shirt holding it in place. She was wearing denim jeans with a pair of miniature trainers on her feet. Marco felt his heart catch when it struck him that if he and Gina had never met then Lily wouldn't be here.

'Here.'

Lily held out her hand and Marco saw that she had a buttercup clutched in her fist. Tears welled into his eyes as he gently took it from her.

'Is this for me, *tesoro*?' he asked, his voice thickening with emotion. *'Grazie.'*

Lily stared at him for a moment then suddenly turned and ran over to the slide. Marco watched as she climbed the steps. He was overwhelmed by what had happened and didn't know how to react. This was his child, his flesh and blood, and meeting her affected him in a way he had never expected.

'She loves the slide and will spend hours on it if you let her,' Gina said quietly beside him.

Marco knew that she had seen his tears yet, oddly, it didn't embarrass him. 'She's beautiful, isn't she? So perfect...' He tailed off, unable to put into words the awe he felt that they had created this precious human being.

'She is but, then, I expect I'm biased.'

She laughed but there was a wobbly note in her voice that told him she was touched by his reaction. Hearing it seemed to release even more emotions inside him and he sighed.

'I never expected to feel so overwhelmed. It's hard to get my head round the idea that if we hadn't met Lily wouldn't be here.' He turned to her. 'Thank you, Gina. I know how inadequate that is, but thank you from the bottom of my heart for giving me something so wonderful and so precious.'

CHAPTER THIRTEEN

IT WAS a magical day. Whether it was Marco's obvious delight in his daughter, or the fact that Lily seemed to accept him without question, Gina wasn't sure, but the day went so well that even her fears were allayed. As they made their way to the café for lunch, she found herself thinking that maybe everything would turn out all right after all. If Marco continued to show this amount of interest in his daughter then surely there was nothing to fear?

'Shall we sit here?' Marco put his hand under her elbow and guided her towards a table near the window.

Gina shivered when she felt the warmth of his fingers on her skin. She bent down to lift Lily out of her pram, glad of the excuse to break the contact. Even though Marco had responded far more favourably than she had expected, it wasn't a reason to allow her emotions to run riot. He would have to do an awful lot more before he cast his spell over her as he had so obviously cast it over their daughter!

The thought sent a shiver down her spine. Gina knew it would be a mistake to go down that route. She fixed a polite smile to her mouth as she turned to him, deeming it safer to stick to practicalities. 'Lily will need a high chair. There's one over there if you wouldn't mind fetching it.'

'Of course.' He bent and tickled the little girl under her chin, making her chuckle. 'One second, *tesoro*, and you shall have your very own seat, *si*?'

Gina sat down, glad of the few seconds' breathing space. Marco had already defined what his role was going to be and she mustn't forget that. The biggest mistake she could make would be to think he might become more to her than Lily's father.

It was a sobering thought but it did the trick. By the time he came back with the high chair, she had herself in hand. She started to rise so that she could strap Lily into the chair but Marco was ahead of her.

'May I do it? It will be good practice for me. I need some hands-on experience about the realities of being a father, don't you think?'

'Of course.'

Gina bit her lip as he lifted Lily off her lap. He swung the little girl above his head, buzzing her cheek with a kiss before he lowered her into the chair. Lily squealed with delight, obviously enjoying every second of the attention. The speed with which the child had accepted him surprised her. Normally, Lily was shy around people she didn't know but there was no hesitancy about her manner with Marco. Did she recognise him on some unconscious level? she wondered. Understand that he was her daddy? If anyone had suggest the idea, she would have dismissed it as nonsense, but having seen how Lily responded to him, it was hard to do so, and it made her feel incredibly guilty. She would have denied Lily the chance to meet Marco if he hadn't reappeared in her life.

'I think that is right.' Marco frowned as he studied the safety harness. 'I can see that I shall have to practise. These things are far more complicated than they appear.'

He gave her a broad smile and she felt her heart leap when she saw the amusement in his eyes. It was obvious that he was having just as much fun as Lily was and it was something she hadn't anticipated. Marco was usually so controlled that it surprised her he should take such delight in the simple task.

'I often think you need a degree to operate all the various pieces of equipment you buy when you have a child. Between the intricacies of unfolding pushchairs and the vagaries of safety harnesses, you need to be an engineer!' she observed lightly.

'Oh, dear. I didn't realise it was so complicated!'

He laughed, drawing the attention of two young women at the next table. Gina saw one of them say something to her friend and had a good idea what it was, not that she blamed her. With his dark Latin looks, Marco was enough to attract any woman's attention.

The thought stung even though she knew it shouldn't have done. She battened it down, knowing that she couldn't allow herself to feel jealous. Marco could date as many women as he liked and it had nothing to do with her! 'I'm sure you'll cope,' she said, doing her best to convince herself that she didn't care a jot what he did.

'And if I don't, I can ask you for help.'

His gaze was warm as it rested on her. Gina felt her heart begin to hammer and deliberately looked away. Picking up the menu, she scanned down the list of dishes on offer. Marco wasn't flirting with her—

he was just being friendly. However, it didn't feel like that…

'So what do you want to eat?' He leant over her shoulder so he could read the menu and her heart gave such a huge bounce that she gasped.

'Are you all right?' he asked in concern, bending so that he could look into her face, which only made matters worse.

'I…er…um…banged my knee on the table leg,' she murmured. 'Anyway, I think I'll have a chicken salad.'

'*Bene.* And Lily, what will she have?'

Marco ran a tanned finger down the menu until he reached the children's options. Gina bit her lip as she followed its progress. She mustn't think about all the times he had run his finger down her spine, the gentle touch setting alight every nerve-ending in its path. They were having a simple family lunch, not enjoying the precursor to an afternoon of seduction!

'Fish fingers, chips and peas,' she said quickly. She grimaced when he raised his brows. 'It's her favourite meal. She'd eat it every day if I let her.'

'In that case, fish fingers it is, although hopefully I can persuade her to try pasta one day.' He gave her another warm smile but she was prepared this time and smiled coolly back.

'You can try, although I'm not sure how much success you'll have. Like a lot of children, Lily is very determined when it comes to what she will eat.'

'And there is no point making an issue of it.' Marco nodded. 'You are right, Gina. The more we fuss, the more she will refuse to try new things. I shall remember that.'

He headed to the counter to place their order. Gina

shivered. Was it that unconscious use of the word 'we' that troubled her? He seemed to have taken it for granted that they would be enjoying many more outings like this in the future, but would it happen? Would he be content to spend his free time entertaining a small child when he could be doing something more exciting?

It was that same niggling doubt again and until she had laid it to rest, once and for all, she knew that she couldn't relax. She had to be on her guard around him for Lily's sake.

She bit her lip. She had to be on her guard for her own sake too.

By the time three o'clock arrived, it was obvious that Lily was flagging. After lunch, they had returned to the playground where she had played on all the equipment. Marco knew that the sound of her excited laughter was imprinted in his mind. It was one memory that no one could take away from him. In years to come he would look back on this day and know that it marked a milestone in his life.

He glanced at Gina because it wasn't just being with Lily that had made the day so special: it was the way Gina had reacted too. She had allowed him far more leeway than he had expected, letting him push Lily on the swing, spin her on the roundabout, do all the things that a proper father did, in fact. He was suddenly overcome with gratitude that she had made the occasion so easy for him. He turned to her, seeing the question in her eyes when he brought the pushchair to a halt.

'I just want to thank you, Gina, for being so kind. I know you have concerns but you haven't let them show.' He glanced at Lily, tenderness welling up inside him. 'I was wrong to accuse you of trying to colour the little one's view of me because you certainly haven't done that today.'

'I just want her to be happy. That's the only thing that concerns me, Marco.'

'I understand.' He bent and kissed her on the cheek, feeling his pulse leap when he felt the softness of her skin. It took a massive effort of will to draw back but he knew that he mustn't make the mistake of confusing the issue when everything seemed to be going so well. And letting Gina know that he desired her would be a mistake.

His breath caught as he was forced to acknowledge how strong his feelings for her were. He wanted her as much now as he had three years ago and it was scary to know that he felt the same after all this time. He straightened abruptly, forcing a note of lightness into his voice in the hope that it would disguise how he felt. He couldn't resume his affair with her. Even if she was willing, which was doubtful, he couldn't take the risk!

'I'd better let you get off home. From the look of this little one, she should sleep well tonight.'

'I'm sure she will.' Gina gave him a quick smile as they carried on. They reached Lancaster Gate, where she paused. 'We're going to catch the Tube so we'll say goodbye here. Thank you for lunch. It was very kind of you.'

'Thank you for agreeing to meet me,' he said formally. He bent and smiled at a sleepy Lily. '*Ciao, tesoro.* I shall see you again very soon.'

He brushed the child's cheek with his lips then stood up, feeling oddly bereft now that the time had come for them to part. It was on the tip of his tongue to suggest that they came back to his apartment and spend the evening there until he thought better of it. Lily was tired and no doubt Gina needed a breathing space after what must have started out as a stressful day.

'I hope we can do this again soon. I have enjoyed it, Gina. Very much indeed.'

'Lily enjoyed it too.' She gave him another quick smile then pushed the buggy out of the gate. She didn't look back as she hurried across the road and disappeared into the station.

Marco headed home, trying to rid himself of a vague sense of disappointment. So what if Gina hadn't given him any inkling if she had enjoyed the day? At least she hadn't ruled out the chance of it happening again and that was the main thing. He couldn't expect her to be enthusiastic about spending time with him after the way he had behaved three years ago, could he?

He sighed. She must be as wary of him as he was of her, although for very different reasons.

Gina had Monday and Tuesday off and didn't see Marco again until the middle of the following week. She had to admit that she was glad, too. Spending so much time with him had left her feeling very unsettled. Far too many times she found herself going over what had happened at the park. To an outsider, they must have appeared like a regular family—mum, dad, child. Whilst part of her relished the idea she knew it was dangerous to think of them that way. She and Marco *might* be Lily's parents but there was nothing binding them beyond that fact. Marco could disappear from their lives as swiftly as he had come, and she had to be prepared for that.

By the time she went into work, she was worn out from worrying about it all. She was on late that day and AAU was buzzing when she arrived. Sister Thomas did the hand-over, sighing in relief after she finished.

'Am I glad to be going home. It's always busy in here but the problem about finding beds has made it worse than ever.'

'What's the latest on the ceiling?' Gina asked. 'Do they know how long it will take to repair it?'

'From what I can gather there may be a problem with the actual roof. They've called in a team of structural engineers to check it.' Eileen Thomas grimaced as she picked up her bag. 'If it ends up that we need a new roof, heaven only knows how long it's going to take.'

Gina sighed as Eileen departed. If a new roof was needed then the staff in AAU could find themselves under extra pressure for months to come.

There was no time to dwell on that thought, however. A patient had been referred to them by his GP after complaining of severe stomach cramps. His name was Adam Sanderson, twenty-eight years old, and a painter and decorator by trade. She got him settled then asked Rosie which of the registrars was working that evening. Typically, it was Miles, so she had him paged then made a start on Adam's case history. According to what he told her, he had never had a day off sick until that week.

'Apart from the cramps, what other symptoms have you had?' she asked, noting everything down on the admission form.

'I've been sick a couple of times and I've had the runs, too,' he told her, looking embarrassed. 'My girl-friend said it was probably the curry we had the other night but I can't see it was that. I mean, I've had a dodgy curry before but I've never felt this rough!'

He groaned as he clutched his stomach. Gina smiled sympathetically. 'We'll give you something for the pain once the doctor has seen you… Here he is now, in fact.'

She stood up as Miles came striding down the ward. He didn't bother to greet her but just held out his hand for the notes. Gina bit her tongue to hold back the reprimand as she handed them to him. Why did Miles have to make such an issue out of the fact that she had refused to go out with him?

'I've seen junior nurses make a better job of taking a case history,' he said witheringly, studying what she had written.

Gina forbore to say anything, refusing to justify herself by explaining that she hadn't had time to take a detailed history yet. She waited while he examined Adam, palpating his abdomen and asking a series of questions. She could tell from the look on Miles's face after he had finished that he hadn't a clue what was wrong with the other man, although that didn't deter him. One thing Miles didn't lack was confidence in his own ability.

'I need bloods and a urine test too.' He made a note on the file then turned to leave but she stopped him.

'Mr Sanderson is in a lot of discomfort from the stomach cramps.'

'Five milligrams of morphine.' Miles barely glanced at her as he wrote out the instruction and signed it. 'Call me as soon as the bloods come back, if you can remember to do that, Sister.'

It was insulting to suggest she would forget. However, there was no way that she was prepared to get into an argument with him in front of a patient. 'Of course,' she said coldly, her tone making it clear how annoyed she felt.

Adam grimaced as Miles strode away. 'What's up with him? He did nothing but have a go at you from the time he arrived.'

'Probably had a bad day,' she said lightly, although the time was fast approaching when she would have to do something about Miles's attitude towards her. She couldn't allow him to carry on trying to undermine her in front of their patients.

Adam sighed. 'Tell me about it.'

Gina went to fetch the morphine, wondering how best to deal with the problem of Miles. Normally, the logical step would be to have it out with him, but she had a feeling that was what Miles was hoping for. He was spoiling for a row and the last thing she wanted was for it to develop into a full-scale war.

Maybe she should have a word with Marco and ask him to intervene, she thought as she unlocked the drugs cupboard. And maybe she wouldn't, she decided. Involving Marco in her affairs was something she was trying to avoid. Lily was the only link between them and she must never forget that.

Marco could feel his stomach churning as he entered AAU. Gina was working the late shift and he had to admit that he was looking forward to seeing her. It seemed ages since Saturday and he had missed her.

The thought brought him to a halt. He had missed Gina and there was no point denying it. It was as though those few hours they had spent together in the park had awoken all the old feelings he had tried so hard to banish. He'd been on the brink of falling in love with her three years ago; was he right back where he had been then?

The thought was too much to deal with. Marco drove it from his mind as he opened the office door. The room was empty so he headed into the ward, frowning when he failed to catch sight of her. When he spotted Julie, he called her over.

'Where's Gina? I thought she was working late today.'

'She is, although I'm not sure where she's gone, probably blowing off steam after her latest run-in with Miles.'

'What do you mean?' Marco demanded.

'Oh, nothing. I shouldn't have said anything.'

Julie hastily excused herself, but Marco had no intention of letting the matter drop. If there was a problem with his staff then he needed to know, especially if Gina was involved. He went back to the office and waited for her to arrive, which she did a few minutes later. He could tell at once that she was upset and was surprised by how protective he felt. If someone had upset her, they would have him to answer to!

'What is all this about you and Miles arguing?' he demanded, getting straight to the point.

She stopped dead when she saw him and he could tell that she was loath to explain what had been going on. However, there was no way that he was prepared to overlook what had been happening.

'Is there a problem about you and Miles working together?'

'Er…no. Of course not.' She picked up a lab report off the desk and turned to leave.

'And you are sure about that, Gina?'

'Of course I am.' She gave him a tight smile. 'I need to phone Miles and let him know the blood results are back for this patient.'

She hurried out of the door although she could just as easily have made the call from there. Marco frowned as he watched her leave. He couldn't force her to tell him what was wrong, but he hoped she would confide in him. If something was worrying her, he wanted to help. Maybe they could never be together as a couple but he cared about what happened to her.

He took a deep breath as the thought expanded. He cared about her far more than he wanted to and far more than he should.

CHAPTER FOURTEEN

GINA left a message on Miles's phone to tell him that Adam Sanderson's blood results were back then helped Julie do the obs. With patients coming and going at various times of the day and night, it was something that needed to be kept track of on an individual basis. Two patients were down for fifteen-minute obs, so they did them first then did the rest. They had just finished when Miles came storming into the unit and headed straight over to her.

'I thought I asked you to let me know as soon as Mr Sanderson's bloods came back, Sister Lee.'

'You did. I left a message on your phone about an hour ago,' she replied, determined to keep her cool.

'Really? Funny that I don't seem to have received it, isn't it?'

His tone was sceptical and she bristled. 'If you're insinuating that I am lying then you can stop right there. I tried your phone. It was engaged so I left a message. End of story.'

'Well, we only have your word for it, don't we? If you want my opinion, I'd say you're covering your back because once again you failed to do what you were supposed to do.'

His tone was harsh and Gina shivered. This had gone past the stage of sour grapes. Miles was turning this into a vendetta and if something wasn't done to stop him, heaven knew what would happen next. She drew him aside.

'I don't take kindly to being spoken to that way, Dr Humphreys, especially when there is no justification for it.' She stared into his angry eyes. 'This has all to do with the fact that I refused to go out with you, hasn't it? I'm sorry if I hurt your feelings but it wasn't personal. I don't date because I have neither the time nor the in-clination for a relationship.'

'Is everything all right?'

Gina spun round, feeling the colour run up her cheeks when she discovered that Marco was standing behind her. It was obvious that he had heard what she'd said and she was mortified. Did she really want him to know that she had avoided emotional entanglements since they had parted?

'Everything is fine, isn't that so, Dr Humphreys?' She turned to Miles, the look she gave him challeng-ing him to disagree.

'I…um…yes. If you'll excuse me.' Miles hurried away, obviously not wanting to continue the discus-sion in front of his boss either.

Marco frowned as he watched him leave. 'If Dr Humphreys is causing you a problem, Gina, I need to know.'

'It's a personal matter.' She turned to leave but he laid his hand on her arm.

'He is annoyed because you refused to go out with him?'

So he had overheard their conversation? Gina sighed.

'He asked me out a couple of months ago and won't accept that I'm not interested. I'm sure he'll get over it in time.'

'But in the interim he is making life difficult for you?'

She shrugged, neither agreeing nor disagreeing with the suggestion. Maybe Marco thought he was helping but she really and truly didn't want him involved in her affairs.

'Whilst I admire your discretion, Gina, I shall take a very dim view if the situation continues.' His tone was hard. 'If you two are at odds, it is going to affect the running of the department. I want this sorted out sooner rather than later. If you cannot resolve it yourself then I shall.'

He didn't give her a chance to reply as he walked away. Gina shook her head, feeling very much as though she had been run over by a steamroller. How dared he issue orders to her about her personal life?

She was about to follow him and tell him that in no uncertain terms only just at that moment Julie came hurrying over. A patient with suspected angina was experiencing chest pains again. Gina went to check on her and decided they needed the cardiothoracic reg. She asked Julie to have him paged then set about making the woman comfortable. By the time the registrar arrived and decided that an immediate bypass was necessary, there was no sign of Marco. It was after seven and no doubt he had gone home so she would need to have a word with him again.

She sighed as she headed for the canteen for her break. Marco might think he was helping but she didn't want him fighting her battles for her. She couldn't afford to rely on him when in a few months' time he would probably disappear from her life.

Marco couldn't believe how angry he felt. He'd had the overwhelming urge to punch Miles Humphreys on the nose when he had heard what he had said to Gina. He went into the consultants' lounge, intending to catch up on some of the more urgent paperwork, but he couldn't concentrate. So Gina wasn't interested in dating? She had turned down Miles's invitation but had she turned down many others too?

He frowned, wondering why the thought gave him such a buzz. It was nothing to do with him what she did and yet the thought of her going out with another man was anathema to him. He would be more than happy if she refused every single invitation that came her way!

There was no chance of him settling down to work while that thought ran riot. He made his way to the canteen in the hope that a cup of coffee would clear his head. He used the stairs, bypassing the fourth floor where all the damage had been caused. The corridor had been roped off and there were warning signs advising people to keep out. The hospital had been extended over the years with this new section housing Women's Surgical and Paediatrics. It meant that the damaged part of the building could be isolated from the rest.

The canteen was empty when Marco arrived. He bought a cup of indifferent coffee from the machine and took it over to a table by the window. From there, he could see London spread out below. It was raining again, a thin grey drizzle that leached the light from the sky, and all of a sudden he was overwhelmed with homesickness.

What was he doing here when he could be in Florence? He had filled in the gaps in his memory, discovered he had a child and met her, too. No one would blame him if at the end of his tenure he returned home…

The door opened and he froze when he saw Gina come in. No one apart from Gina, that was. She would blame him for doing exactly what she had foretold. He had let her down and she was only waiting for him to do the same to Lily. His head began to spin as the enormity of what was happening struck him. He couldn't leave, not now, not in six months' time. He wanted to be part of his daughter's life forever and it meant that, by default, he would be part of Gina's too. And it was that last thought which filled him with a mixture of excitement and dread.

He was no longer in control of his life. He was being swept along by a tide too strong for him to fight.

Gina bought herself a cup of tea then looked for somewhere to sit. The canteen was almost empty so she had plenty of choice but she paused when she saw Marco sitting by the window. There was no reason why she should join him and yet it seemed churlish to ignore him. She carried her cup across the room and stopped beside his table.

'Mind if I join you?'

'Please do.'

He stood up and politely pulled out a chair so she could sit down. He had always had exquisite manners, she thought as she got herself settled. It was one of the things she had loved about him, the fact that he had made her feel so special when they were out together—

opening doors for her, handing her into the car, treating her in a way she had never been treated before.

The thought wasn't one she wanted to dwell on and she hurriedly took out a packet of sandwiches from her bag. 'I thought you'd have gone home by now,' she said, deeming it safer to make conversation than allow her mind to run off at tangents.

'I was intending to catch up on some paperwork but it held no appeal.' He gave her a wry smile. 'Paperwork was the bane of my life when I was a junior doctor and it hasn't improved with age.'

'You could get one of the registrars to do it. That's what our last consultant did. He never wrote any notes himself.'

'So I believe.' His tone was dry. 'Maybe it would have been better if he had. There would have been less…confusion.'

Gina laughed wryly. 'True.' She offered him the packet. 'Would you like a sandwich?'

'Thank you but no. I shall make myself a meal when I get in.' He sat back in his chair. 'So who looks after Lily when you work late?'

'My childminder.' She saw his brows rise and explained. 'Amy was a nurse before she had her own family so she understands the problems of doing shift work. She baths Lily and pops her into her pyjamas so I can put her straight to bed when we get home.'

'It can't be easy balancing childcare and work.'

'It's a juggle, as any working mum will tell you, but we manage,' she said a shade defensively.

'I'm sure you do. It's obvious that Lily is a very happy and contented little girl.'

Gina smiled. 'She is.'

'Do you have any family who help you?'

'No. My mum died when I was fifteen and dad re-married a few years later while I was at university. He and his new wife moved to New Zealand so I see very little of him these days.'

'No sisters, brothers, aunts, cousins, etcetera?'

'No, just me, but that's fine. I have Lily and I don't need anyone else.'

'Not even a partner?'

Gina shrugged. 'I don't have time for a relationship. I'm too busy working and looking after Lily.'

'Which is why you turned down Miles's invitation?'

'I wouldn't have gone out with him even if I'd been looking for romance, which I'm not.'

'He's not your type?'

'No, not that I have a type, as you put it.' Gina broke the crust off the bread, hoping he wouldn't pursue the subject. What would she say if he asked her what sort of man she was attracted to?

'How about you?' she said quickly, terrified that she would say something stupid. Admitting that she wasn't interested in any man after going out with him would be a mistake.

'My parents are both dead and I, too, am an only child. Oh, there are lots of aunts and cousins but I see very little of them.' He shrugged. 'It isn't deliberate. We all lead busy lives and it's hard to find the time to meet. The only person I see regularly is Nonna—my maternal grandmother. She's very frail and a little con-fused these days, so she lives in a nursing home on the outskirts of Florence.'

'And there's no one special in your life?' she asked,

then could have bitten her tongue because it was the last thing she should have asked him.

'No one at all.' He glanced down at his cup and his eyes were very dark when he looked up again, so dark that it was impossible to tell what he was thinking. 'Apart from Lily, of course.'

Gina knew she should be relieved to hear him state once again his interest in their daughter and she was. However, she couldn't ignore the disappointment she felt that he hadn't added her to his list of special people. She cleared her throat, knowing how stupid she was being. 'I'm glad to hear it. I get the impression she thinks you are pretty special too.'

He smiled at that. 'I hope so. I hope that given time she will come to love me as much as I love her.'

'Love? Surely it's a bit premature to claim that you love her, Marco?'

'Not at all. The moment I set eyes on her my heart was filled with love.' He paused, seemingly loath to continue, before suddenly carrying on. 'Sometimes it happens that way, Gina. You realise that you love someone even though it's against your better judgement.'

'Has it happened to you before?' she whispered, her heart pounding.

'Si.'

'With Francesca?'

'No. Francesca and I knew each other when we were children. Our love grew over the years.' He reached across the table and touched her hand. 'It was different when I met you. I knew that I would fall in love with you if I let myself.'

'And it wasn't what you wanted?'

'No. I didn't want it to happen then and I don't want it to happen now.'

'So you've given up on love altogether?'

'It is safer this way. I couldn't go through the kind of pain I went through when Francesca died. It's better to be alone than risk that happening.'

Gina felt her eyes swim with tears at the bleakness of that statement. It seemed wrong that Marco should deny himself the chance of finding happiness again. Even though she wasn't looking for romance either, she hadn't ruled it out, especially if there was a chance that Marco might change his mind.

The thought made her see how precarious her position was. She knew that Marco didn't want to pick up where they had left off—he had been quite blunt about that! However, even knowing that didn't stop her wishing for the impossible, the happy ending she had been denied three years ago.

'I am sorry, Gina. I did not mean to upset you. You have a tender heart.' He stroked her hand, making her shiver when she felt the faintly abrasive touch of his thumb caressing her skin, and she hurriedly withdrew her hand.

'My mother always said I was a softie.' She summoned a smile, ignoring the tremor that ran through her. She couldn't afford to be so vulnerable around him. 'I would cry at the least little thing—a sad film on television, something I'd read in the newspaper—you name it.'

'As I said, you have a tender heart.'

He gave her a tight smile. Gina frowned when she realised that he looked upset. 'Is something wrong?'

'Of course not.' He pushed back his chair. 'I shall

have to make a start on that paperwork. *Ciao*, Gina. I hope the rest of the evening isn't too busy.'

He strode towards the door, not looking back as he left. Gina picked up her sandwich, wondering what had caused him to react that way. Had it been it something she'd said, but what?

She racked her brain but couldn't come up with an answer. Maybe Marco had remembered something, something to do with Francesca, and that was what had caused him to look so bleak for a moment. It must be very difficult for him to have to relive the past as he must have done when he'd recovered his memory. Losing the woman he had loved had obviously devastated his life. Although he claimed that he'd been on the brink of falling in love with *her*, it wasn't the same, was it? He had been able to stop himself taking that final step and he couldn't have done that if he had felt for her even a fraction of what he had felt for his wife.

Gina got up and threw the rest of her sandwiches in the bin. The fact had to be faced: even if Marco hadn't split up with her, she would only ever have been second best.

CHAPTER FIFTEEN

THE next few weeks flew past. As Marco settled into his job, he found to his surprise that he was enjoying it. Although the hospital wasn't as well equipped as the ones he had worked in recently, the calibre of the staff made up for it. He refused to dwell on the thought that it was working with Gina that was the best thing of all, however. There was no point getting fixated on that idea.

They spent several more days at the park and each time Lily seemed very receptive to him. She was a naturally sunny-natured child and Marco was enchanted by her. Although he'd had little contact with any children beyond work, he seemed to know instinctively how to relate to her and that gave him confidence.

The fact that Gina gave him a free hand also helped. She seemed to trust him to know how high to push Lily on the swing or to assess the risks of allowing her to climb unaided up the slide, and he appreciated that. However, if he did defer to her, she never made him feel lacking in any way. It was obvious that she was doing all she could to make the situation easy for them, or rather easy for *Lily*. He must never forget that Lily was her main concern.

That thought caused him more than one pang of regret, akin to how he had felt when she had confessed that she had always been soft-hearted. Although he called himself every kind of a fool, he wished that her tears that night had been for *him* and not just because of what he had told her. He knew it wasn't fair to want her to engage her emotions when he couldn't return them, but working together made it extremely difficult to distance himself. She was in his thoughts from the moment he got up to the time he went to bed, and beyond, as the erotic dreams he had about her each night would testify. His mind might want to reject her but his body had very different ideas!

They had arranged to meet on Sunday that week for either another trip to the park or to a local play centre if it was raining, so Marco was surprised when the phone rang just after eight on the Saturday night and discovered it was Gina. She got straight to the point.

'I'm afraid I'm going to have to cancel tomorrow's outing. Lily has chickenpox.'

'Oh, no!' he exclaimed, genuinely distressed by the thought. 'Is she very poorly?'

'She's hot and a bit fretful. I've given her liquid paracetamol for the temperature but I could really do with something to put on the spots to stop them itching.' She sighed. 'I've just got her settled, though, and I don't want to drag her out to the all-night chemist.'

'Certainly not. I shall get what you need and bring it round for you.'

'Oh, but I can't expect you to come all the way out here at this time of the night,' she protested.

'Why not?' Marco stamped down on a small spurt of irritation. 'I am her father and I want to be involved,

Gina. That means helping during the bad times as well as during the fun ones.'

There was a small pause while she considered that. 'Well, in that case thank you.'

She gave him a list of what she needed and hung up. Marco fetched his jacket and set off. There was an all-night pharmacy close by so he went there first and then, on impulse, popped into the supermarket and bought a Chinese meal for two that only needed heating in the microwave. No doubt Gina had been too busy since she had got in from work and hadn't had time to eat anything.

He took a taxi to her home, grimacing as he got out of the cab. It certainly wasn't the best of locations, but at least it seemed to be relatively quiet. He made his way down the basement steps and knocked on the door, smiling when Gina opened it. 'The cavalry has arrived. Here you are.'

He handed her the pharmacy bag, carrying the one from the supermarket inside and placing it on the table. Although the flat looked bright and cheerful, it seemed incredibly small for two people, to his mind, although he didn't say so. Gina didn't need him criticising her home when she had a sick child to care for. However, it made him realise that he needed to do something about the situation. If Gina would allow him, of course.

'I'll just go and check on Lily. I may be able to dab some of this calamine on the spots if I'm careful.'

Gina headed towards what was evidently the bedroom and he followed, pausing in the doorway because there didn't seem to be room for him as well in the confined space. One corner had been partitioned off to form a minute second bedroom and he could see

Lily tucked up in a child-sized bed. A toy box, some colourful cartoon prints on the wall and a small chest of drawers comprised the rest of the furnishings, and he was suddenly assailed by guilt. There he was living in that huge apartment all by himself while Gina and Lily were crammed into here!

'There isn't much room,' he said, unable to hold back the comment any longer.

'It's fine,' Gina assured him, tipping some calamine onto a pad of cotton wool. She gently dabbed it on Lily's face, murmuring soothingly when the little girl started to whimper. She dabbed at another couple of spots then grimaced. 'I'd better not risk doing any more. I'll wait until she wakes up. It should have helped, though. Thank you for bringing it over.'

It was obviously a hint that he should leave but he had no intention of going anywhere. How could he leave her to cope with a sick child on her own? 'There's some antihistamine syrup in the bag too—that will help control the itching.'

'Oh, right. Thank you.' She took out the package. 'Amy used that for the twins when they had it. It really helped.'

'Is that where Lily caught it, from the childminder's children?'

'I assume so.' She shrugged. 'By the time the twins' spots appeared Lily would have been infected so there was nothing I could do to prevent her getting it.'

'Better that she has it now rather than later.'

'Exactly.' She suddenly yawned and clapped her hand over her mouth. 'Oh, excuse me!'

'You're tired. You worked all day and I doubt if you've had any rest since you got in.'

'Lily has been a lot more demanding than normal,' she admitted, trying, unsuccessfully, to swallow another massive yawn. 'What I wouldn't give for a nice hot soak in the bath. It would wash away some of the cobwebs.'

'Then go and have one while Lily is asleep.'

'Oh, but I couldn't. I need to keep an eye on her...'

'Nonsense.' He placed his hands on her shoulders and propelled her towards the door of the miniscule bathroom, trying not to think about the state-of-the-art facilities back at his apartment. 'I shall look after Lily. You need some time for yourself, Gina. It could be a long night.'

'I don't expect you to look after her, Marco! She's my child, after all.'

'No, she is *our* child and that makes her my responsibility as well.' He gave her a gentle push, wondering when she would accept that his interest wasn't a passing thing. He was in it for the long haul and to his mind that meant for ever. He made his voice sound as reassuring as possible. 'I shall take good care of her, Gina. Trust me.'

Gina hesitated, not sure that she liked being told what to do. However, she had to admit that a bath could make the world if difference if she had to get up during the night.

'If you're sure,' she began, then tailed off when Marco's brows lifted in that deliciously sexy way that always made her insides feel as though they were melting into puddles of hot liquid. Swinging round, she hurried into the bathroom and locked the door, leaning back against it while she caught her breath. Stop it! she told herself sternly. This isn't the time to be having such lascivious thoughts.

Turning on the water, she filled the bath, adding a generous dollop of bubble bath so that foam frothed over the side as she slid into the water. She sighed luxuriously as she closed her eyes and let the heat soak into her tired limbs. She had no idea what Marco was doing because she couldn't hear a sound coming from the living room, and she didn't care. Maybe he was sitting quietly on the couch, waiting for her to finish.

The thought triggered another, far more erotic one. Gina bit her lip as she recalled the times she had come out of the bathroom at his villa to find him lying on the bed, waiting for her. He wouldn't say a word but would simply hold out his hand. Words hadn't been necessary. They had each known what would happen next, how he would pull her down beside him and strip off her damp towel. His eyes would travel the length of her body, drinking in each curve, each dip, each hollow, and if he had found any imperfections, he certainly hadn't let her see that. When his eyes had come back to hers they had been filled with desire, with need.

Gina groaned softly, recalling how sweet their love-making had been. Marco had been a wonderfully generous lover, taking care to ensure she had enjoyed it as much as he had done, and she had. He had raised her to heights she had never experienced before, made her feel things she had never felt for any man apart from him; made her feel things she would never feel again because it was only in his arms that she became truly alive.

Her heart caught painfully as she was forced to face

the truth. It was only when she was with Marco that she understood how it really felt to be a woman.

A soft tap at the door broke the spell. Gina opened her eyes, feeling an aching sense of loss seeping deep into her bones. No matter who came into her life in the future, she would never feel for him what she'd felt for Marco. 'Yes? Is it Lily? Is she all right?'

'She's fast asleep. I just wanted to know if you had eaten since you got home.'

'No. I haven't had time,' she told him, struggling to contain her emotions. She couldn't afford to indulge herself like this when it would make the situation all the more stressful. So far she and Marco had coped extremely well and the last thing she wanted was to ruin things. 'I'll get something later.'

'There is no need. I have brought some food with me. Ten minutes and it will be ready. *Si?*'

He obviously didn't expect a reply and she didn't give him one. She heard him walk towards the kitchen and a moment later heard the microwave ping open. Pulling the plug out of the bath, she wrapped a towel around her, wishing she had something more substantial to cover herself with as she hurried the short distance to the bedroom. There was a little too much bare thigh on show for comfort, not that Marco seemed upset by it when he glanced round, a small voice pointed out. In fact, he had looked rather interested.

Gina's teeth snapped together. Marco wasn't *interested*! She was just being silly.

Marco put the containers into the microwave then had to pause before he set the timer. He breathed in deeply, but the sight of Gina in that towel had had an unnerving effect. He closed his eyes but that only made matters worse. Now all he could see was the smooth, pale skin of her shoulders, her shapely thighs, the curve of her breasts thrusting against the damp fabric...

He swore under his breath and stabbed at the buttons on the microwave. He had to stop this. It was one thing to indulge his fantasies when he was alone in bed, but it was entirely different to do so here in Gina's home. She would be horrified if she had any idea what he was thinking!

By the time she appeared dressed in an all-concealing navy tracksuit, he had himself in hand. He turned when he heard her footsteps, battening down the fleeting thought that he much preferred her previous outfit. 'Good timing. This is just about ready. All I need now are plates and cutlery.'

'I'll get them.'

She inched past him to reach into the cupboard above the stove and he sucked in his breath when he felt her breasts brush his shoulder. He could tell from the brief contact that she wasn't wearing a bra and it was just the sort of thought his body needed to run riot again. Stepping back, he attempted to give her some room but the damage had been done. Every nerve now was on high alert, so that when she stood on tiptoe to reach the top shelf, causing the muscles in her shapely backside to tauten, he almost groaned out loud. How was he going to keep his hands to himself if he had to face this kind of temptation?

'Got them.' Gina smiled as she turned round. 'We'll use the good plates instead of the ones Lily and I usually use.' She placed a couple of china plates on the counter and turned back to the cupboard. 'I just need a couple of glasses now.'

'Let me get them for you,' Marco said hastily, unable to withstand much more. He took a couple of glasses off the shelf and placed them on the counter. 'Is that everything?'

'Apart from the cutlery. It's in the drawer under the sink.'

She went to get it but he shook his head. Opening the drawer, he took out the cutlery and handed it to her. 'I'll serve the food if you would lay the table.'

'Of course.'

She shot him a puzzled look as she headed towards the window where a small table had been placed in the bay. Marco's mouth tightened as he lifted the hot dishes out of the microwave. Had she sensed something was amiss? He hoped not but if she had then he would do his best to set her mind at rest. The last thing he wanted was for her to think he was coming onto her!

By the time he took the plates over to the table, he felt more in control. Gina looked up when he placed a plate in front of her and smiled. 'That smells delicious. What is it?'

'Chicken Foo Yung is what it said on the carton.' He went back for the wine and unscrewed the top of the bottle. 'I'm not sure if this goes with it or not, but we can only try.'

He reached over to fill her glass but she stopped him. 'I'm not sure if I should. Lily could wake up and I don't want to risk not hearing her.'

'Half a glass should be fine, surely,' he said quietly, leaving the final decision to her.

'All right, then. Just half a glass.'

Marco poured her some wine then poured some for

himself. Lifting the glass to his lips, he took a sip. 'It's not great, but not as bad as I feared.'

She took a small swallow of the pale liquid. 'It tastes fine to me but then I'm not exactly a connoisseur. I can't even remember the last time I had a glass of wine with my meal.'

She took another sip then picked up her fork, obviously relishing the simple meal. Unlike so many women, she didn't toy with her food: she enjoyed it. He had always found the way she had savoured all the new tastes he had introduced her to incredibly sexy, in fact, and it was just as erotically stimulating now, he realised.

Marco forked up a mouthful of chicken, trying to keep his mind from setting off down that track. He was here to help her and he must remember that. They ate in silence for several minutes before she gave a small sigh.

'This is a real treat. Just being able to sit here and enjoy the food is such a lovely change. Don't get me wrong—Lily is very good—but it's usually a question of grabbing a mouthful in between helping her. Thank you, Marco, for thinking of it.'

'It is my pleasure, *cara*.' The endearment slid out before he thought about it and he felt heat invade him when he saw her stiffen. It had felt as natural as breathing to call her that and it wasn't the most settling of thoughts in the circumstances.

They finished their meal, making desultory conversation, mainly, he suspected, because she felt uncomfortable with the silence. Was she recalling other meals they had shared when the food had been merely a precursor to a whole lot more?

He longed to know the answer and yet at the same time feared it. To know that she was as aware of him as he was of her would be too difficult to deal with. The trouble was that his mind wanted him to remain detached while the rest of him wanted the exact opposite.

It made him wonder which part would win. Would he be able to conquer this attraction he felt for her or would he be forced to give in? And if he did, where would it end? He may have been able to stop himself falling in love with her three years ago but he knew in his heart that he wouldn't be able to stop it now.

He took a deep breath. If he gave in, there would be absolutely nothing he could do to save himself.

CHAPTER SIXTEEN

GINA wasn't sure if the tension was all in her mind. On the surface, Marco seemed to be behaving as he normally did as they discussed a range of topics mainly centred on work. So why did she have the feeling that his thoughts were a long way away from the vagaries of the National Health Service?

She stood up abruptly, refusing to create problems where none might exist. 'How about coffee? I don't know about you but I could do with a cup.'

'Thank you, that would be nice.'

His tone was as bland as the smile he gave her. Gina knew she should have been reassured yet she wasn't. Marco was masking his feelings, deliberately hiding them from her, and the thought was more disturbing than it should be. Picking up their plates, she took them to the sink then filled the kettle, wondering how soon she could bring the evening to a close. As soon as they had drunk their coffee, she decided, she would make it clear that she expected him to leave.

She made the coffee and placed the cafetière on the table in front of the couch. 'We may as well sit here to drink it. It's more comfortable than those hard chairs.'

Marco walked over to the couch and sat down, leaving her to either sit next to him or perch on the stool. She opted for the stool, preferring the discomfort to sitting beside him. The couch wasn't very large and each time they moved, their arms would touch. A shiver ran through her and she hurriedly busied herself with serving the coffee.

'I hope this is all right for you,' she said, handing him a cup. 'It's only the supermarket's own brand, I'm afraid.'

'After the stuff that comes out of that machine in the canteen, it will taste like nectar,' he observed wryly.

Gina laughed, relieved to be distracted from her unruly thoughts. 'It *is* awful, isn't it? Everyone has complained but the management claim it's less expensive to use a machine than employ someone to make tea and coffee.'

'They haven't factored in staff morale, obviously.' He laughed deeply. 'There would be far fewer absences if there was some decent coffee available.'

'Probably,' she agreed, trying to control the sudden fluttering in her stomach. How she wished she wasn't so aware of him that even the sound of his laughter immediately drew a response from her. She stood up abruptly, needing a moment's respite from the torment. 'I'd better check on Lily again.'

The little girl was fast asleep. Gina smoothed back her hair and straightened the quilt but that took only a moment and she needed more time to collect herself. She glanced round when she heard a sound behind her, feeling the fluttering intensify when she realised that Marco had followed her. In the dim glow from the nightlight he looked so big and vitally male that she couldn't fail to be aroused and it was the last thing she needed.

It took her all her time to remain where she was as he came over to the bed.

'How is she?' He laid a gentle hand on Lily's forehead and frowned. 'She feels rather hot.'

'The paracetamol liquid I gave her earlier should bring her temperature down,' she assured him.

'Of course it will. *Mi scusi.* I did not mean to imply that you were not looking after her properly, Gina.'

'I know you didn't.'

She eased past him, anxious to make some space between them. The close confines of the room were doing nothing to help the situation, she thought dizzily as she breathed in the scent of his aftershave, something spicy and wholly masculine that stirred her senses all the more. Her foot suddenly caught on the edge of the toy box and she cried out in alarm when she felt herself pitch forward.

'Careful!' All of a sudden Marco was there, his hand gripping her arm as he saved her from falling. He set her back on her feet then looked into her face. 'Are you all right? You have not hurt yourself?'

'No, I'm fine. I just tripped over the edge of the toy box,' she explained, her heart pounding although whether from the fall or his nearness she wasn't sure. She summoned a wobbly smile. 'I should look where I'm going.'

'There is not much room…' He shrugged eloquently, his broad shoulders rising beneath the thin silk shirt he was wearing.

Gina felt a frisson of raw need run through her when she felt the solid wall of his chest brush against her nipples. It wasn't intentional on his part; they were simply standing so close that the moment he moved, his body made contact with hers. However, the effect was just as devastating as if it had been planned.

'Gina.' Her name was part groan, part plea as it emerged from his throat. It touched a chord inside her, one that she might not have responded to otherwise. He sounded as though he, too, was fighting his feelings and she knew how that felt. She really did!

Her eyes lifted to his and she knew that she was right when she saw the expression they held. He was looking at her with such hunger that there could be no mistake about what he wanted. Marco wanted her. He wanted her as a man wanted a woman he found deeply attractive and all of a sudden she knew it was what she wanted too.

'Marco.'

She said his name, softly and without inflection, and saw his eyes darken as he realised what she was doing. This had to be a decision they both made; neither must coerce the other and then have regrets. When his hand lifted to her cheek, she stood quite still, feeling the faintly abrasive touch of his fingertips skimming the line of her jaw, the curve of her cheekbone, the fullness of her lips. She had the feeling that he was relearning the shape and feel of her all over again and knew that it was something he needed to do. He had forgotten such a lot; had he forgotten this as well?

'Your skin is so soft,' he whispered, his fingers stroking and caressing her. 'I always thought it felt like velvet…'

He broke off, his hand stilling as the thought settled into his consciousness, another memory returned. When his fingers moved on, gliding down her throat, she could feel the tremor in them and knew that it had affected him deeply to realise that he had wanted her this much once before.

His hand slid down her throat until it came to the zip on her jacket and could go no further. Gina didn't move, leaving it to him to decide if he should go further. She knew what she wanted and he had to do the same.

His hand reached for the zip at last and she held her breath. She hadn't bothered with underwear after her bath and suddenly wished she had. When he started to run the zipper down its track, she bit her lip. It had been a long time since Marco had seen her naked and she'd had Lily since. Her body had changed as a woman's body did after she'd borne a child.

'You are so beautiful, *cara*. So much a woman.'

His tone was hoarse and she shuddered when she heard the emotion it held. There wasn't a doubt in her mind that he was telling her the truth as he parted the edges of her jacket and looked at her. Maybe her body had changed but he liked what he saw, and that was all she had needed to know.

She lifted her face, letting him see what she wanted not with words but by expression, and heard him groan. Bending, he covered her mouth with his, his lips drawing a response from her that she was more than willing to give. The kiss ran on and on and Gina knew that he was as helpless as she was to stop it. They needed this kiss, needed to feast on each other's lips to slake just a bit of this hunger they both felt.

'Dio mio!' Marco drew back at last although he didn't let her go. Gina could feel the tremor that was running through his body, a wire-taut tension that was mirrored by the tension inside her. Nobody could have kissed or

been kissed like that without being stirred to the very depths of their soul.

'I didn't realise…'

He tailed off, either unable or unwilling to put his feelings into words, but he didn't need to. She understood how he felt because she felt the same. She always had done. Whenever Marco had kissed her, she had felt raw and shaken, alive in a way she had never been before. Had Marco felt that way three years ago or was this a new experience for him? She had no idea and wouldn't ask him either. Whichever answer he gave would only create problems.

Her heart lurched at the thought that maybe he was more attracted to her now than he had been in the past, but she refused to dwell on it. He had been unequivocal when he had told her that he would never get involved in a relationship again and it would be foolish to hope he might change his mind. She had to accept that this was all they had, this rawness of desire, this need that burned within them. It might not be what she had hoped for once but it was enough for now. It had to be.

She wound her arms around his neck and drew his head down so that she could kiss him. Marco had loved it when she had instigated their lovemaking in the past and it was obvious that he appreciated it now. His lips immediately parted, allowing her free licence as she deepened the kiss, her tongue sliding inside the warm, coffee-flavoured recesses of his mouth to mate with his. When he pulled her closer so that she could feel the rigid tautness of his erection pressing into her, she smiled. It was the response she had wanted, the one she had expected, too.

'So you think it is funny that I want you this much,'

he said softly in her ear, his hips moving against hers so that she gasped.

'I think it's…sweet,' she said, struggling to control the rush of desire that shot through her.

'Sweet?' His tone said what he thought of that adjective and she laughed, loving the fact that she could make him rise with her teasing. *'Sweet!'*

'Hmm. I mean, I think it's really nice that you're so keen…'

She didn't get the chance to finish as he swung her up into his arms and carried her into the living room. He deposited her on the couch and smiled wolfishly at her. 'Oh, I am keen, *tesoro*. I think you can take that as read.'

He knelt beside her, parting the front of her jacket so that he could stroke her breasts. Gina shivered when she felt the pads of his thumbs edging ever closer to her nipples. She could feel them peaking in anticipation but each time she thought he would touch her there, his hands moved away, his thumbs tracing lazy circles on her skin until she felt she would explode with need.

'Marco, please,' she murmured, arching her back.

'Please what, my darling? Please stop? Please continue? Just tell me what it is you want and I shall do my best to oblige like the *sweet* man I am.'

Gina knew he was teasing her and it was a revelation. Although they'd had fun together in the past, making love had been a far more serious business. Marco hadn't teased her like this then and it was oddly disturbing to be on the receiving end of it now. She frowned, unsure what to make of this new side of him, and he paused.

'What is it, Gina? Is something wrong?'

'No…well, I'm not sure.' She bit her lip, uncertain if she should say anything.

'Tell me.' He bent and kissed her on the mouth, a kiss that was filled with reassurance. 'I don't want there to be any more secrets between us.'

She knew it was a gentle reminder of the biggest secret that she had kept from him—Lily—and flushed. 'There won't be. It's just that when we were together three years ago, you were different, Marco, less…playful.'

'*Si?*' He frowned this time. 'You mean when we made love?'

'Exactly. You never teased me like this. You were far more serious…' She broke off and shrugged. 'It was just different.'

'Maybe because I was different.' He cupped her cheek and his expression was grave. 'I felt guilty about wanting another woman, Gina, so maybe that was why making love to you was such a serious matter.'

'And you don't feel guilty now?' she whispered.

'No. Not that way at least.' He looked into her eyes. 'I shall feel incredibly guilty, though, if I cause you any distress, so think long and hard about what we are doing, *amata*. Is this what you really want when I can't make you any promises for the future?'

Marco held his breath as he waited for her answer. He wanted her so much that it hurt, wanted to bury himself inside her softness, feel himself enveloped by her sweetness, but if it wasn't what she truly wanted then he would stop. Maybe he shouldn't have allowed things to progress this far but he had and now he would have to deal with the consequences—whatever they were.

His heart lurched at the thought that there would be

consequences from this night but before he could have second thoughts, Gina's hand lifted. She touched his face, her fingers brushing his cheek, and once again there was that flash of memory, the knowledge deep inside that she had done the same thing before.

'But I do want this, Marco. I want us to make love for many reasons. Maybe it will help to lay a few ghosts from the past. I'm not sure. But what I am sure about is that I want it to happen.'

It was the affirmation he needed and yet still he hesitated. She talked about laying ghosts but would it? Or would it merely create more problems, make it harder for them to be parents to Lily? They had coped so well these past weeks, worked in surprising harmony, but such a massive shift in their relationship could alter everything.

All of a sudden Marco didn't know which way to turn. He wanted her so much he ached. And yet making love with her could open the way to all sorts of complications he wasn't sure he could face. It would take so little, so very little, to fall in love with her and then what would he do? Even if she reciprocated his feelings—and there was no saying that she would after the way he had hurt her—could he imagine living on a knife-edge, always fearing that something dreadful would happen to ruin his happiness?

The old fears came rushing back and he knew that he couldn't do it. He couldn't take the risk of loving her and losing her—his heart wouldn't withstand that kind of grief again.

He drew back, knowing that once he made this decision he would have to stick to it. He couldn't toy with her emotions, couldn't blow hot one minute and cold

the next, as she had put it. Either they moved their relationship forward and became lovers or they stayed as
they were: Lily's parents and friends. Nothing more.

'I'm sorry, Gina,' he said, his voice sounding rough
when it emerged from his throat. 'I should never have
allowed the situation to reach this point.'

'It wasn't solely your decision, Marco.'

He winced when he heard the hurt in her voice even
though she did her best to disguise it. The last thing he
wanted was to hurt her and yet once again he had done
so. 'No. It wasn't. And don't think I'm not flattered by
the fact that you want me, Gina, because I am. It's more
than I expected after the way I treated you and far more
than I deserve. I just think it would be a mistake to...
confuse the issue.'

'If that's how you feel, I'm sure you're right.'

She zipped up her jacket and Marco felt his heart
ache at the finality of the action. Just for a second he
was tempted to tell her he had changed his mind but
he managed to bite back the words. He couldn't allow
desire to rule his head as well as his heart.

The thought that his heart was already engaged was
disturbing. He knew that he needed time to come to
terms with what was happening. Maybe he'd been able to
pull back from the brink of falling in love three years
ago, but it would be far harder to do so now. Gina wasn't
just the woman he wanted; she was the mother of his
child. And that made her even more special in his eyes,
even more desirable. He stood up abruptly. 'I'd better
go.'

'Of course.' She followed his lead, masking her feelings as she saw him to the door. 'Thank you for bringing those things for Lily. I appreciate it.'

'Don't mention it.' His tone was as polite as hers was, which was surprising bearing in mind that inside he was seething with frustration. How he wished he could think of something to say that would make them both feel better but the right words—if there were any *right* words in a situation like this—escaped him. All he could do was pretend that nothing had happened, that a few minutes ago they hadn't been on the verge of making love.

A spasm of need shot through his body and he reached blindly for the latch. 'I hope Lily doesn't keep you up all night,' he said thickly, glancing over his shoulder. Gina was standing behind him and for a second her expression was unguarded. His heart ached when he saw the pain in her eyes because he knew he was responsible for putting it there.

'We'll be fine.' She pinned a smile to her lips and the sheer bravery of the action touched him on many levels. 'Sleepless nights are par for the course when you're a mum.'

'I'm sure they are.' Marco longed to say that they should be par for the course when you were a father too but that would have been pushing things too far. He couldn't offer to stay and help her look after their daughter, not when he couldn't trust himself around her. He opened the door and then paused, needing a salve for his conscience. 'If there's anything else you need, just let me know and I'll bring it over.'

'Thank you but I have everything now.'

She started to close the door, making it clear that she wanted him to leave. Marco knew that he should go rather than prolong the agony and yet he found himself lingering.

'You will call me if there's a problem, won't you?'

'There won't be any problems, Marco. It's chicken-pox, that's all. Lily will be right as rain in a few days' time.' She edged the door across and he knew that he couldn't drag it out any longer.

'*Bene.* I shall phone you in the morning to see how she is, if that is all right with you?'

'Of course.'

A last smile and then the door closed, leaving him on one side and her on the other. Marco sucked in a huge breath of cool night air, hoping it would help him put what had happened into some kind of perspective. As he walked up the basement steps, he ran back over everything that had happened since Gina had phoned him: his dash to the pharmacy; his insistence that she should have a bath; dinner; the near-fall in the bedroom.

It had been fine up till that point, a nice neat sequence of events that needed little explanation. However, what had happened after that was entirely different. Marco flagged down a passing taxi and gave the driver his address, his head feeling as though it would explode as he climbed into the back. There was nothing neat about his memories after that stumble. They were all jumbled up, a maelstrom of feelings and sensations: the softness of Gina's skin; the rounded firmness of her breasts; the heat inside him when he had pressed his body against hers.

He closed his eyes and let the erotic images seep deep into his consciousness. These were new memories, ones he wanted to store away so that he could retrieve them in the future when times were bleak. He knew how it felt to forget the important things and he didn't want to risk that happening again. If he couldn't have Gina then at the very least he could look back on this night and recall how good it had been to hold her in his arms and be held in hers. For those too-brief minutes he hadn't felt lonely. He had felt complete.

Gina managed to hold back her tears until the door closed but the moment the lock snapped shut they poured down her face. She went and sat down on the couch, thinking back over what had so nearly happened there. Marco had wanted her—she knew he had! However, his desire for her hadn't been enough in the end. Was it guilt that had stopped him making love to her, reluctance to betray the woman he had loved and lost?

It was the reason why he had ended their relationship before and it seemed the most likely explanation now. She knew she should accept that he would never get over Francesca, but she couldn't. The thought of him loving another woman to that extent was like having a knife plunged into her heart when she loved him so much.

She sat quite still as the thought settled deep into her mind. She loved Marco. Maybe it should have shocked her to face up to how she felt but it didn't. On some inner level she had been aware of her feelings for a while, but had not allowed herself to acknowledge them. Now it was a relief to face the truth.

She loved Marco and had never stopped loving him. Oh, she had been hurt and angry at the way he had treated her but not even that had been enough to destroy the love she felt for him. That was why she had been so eager to make love with him tonight. Not because she had wanted to lay some ghosts from the past but because she had wanted *him*.

Now she was ready to admit the truth, she could no longer pretend. She loved him with her whole heart and that made her vulnerable, but, worst of all, it made Lily vulnerable too. She couldn't allow herself to be ruled by her emotions where her precious child was concerned. She only needed to recall how swiftly Marco had changed his mind tonight to know how dangerous it would be.

She rubbed her hands over her face to wipe away her tears. Marco had wanted her tonight too, but he had changed his mind in the end. He couldn't be allowed to do the same to Lily.

CHAPTER SEVENTEEN

MARCO was aware that there had been a shift in Gina's attitude towards him. Although she was her usual courteous self in work, there was a new reserve about her. He knew what lay behind it and cursed himself for allowing his desire for her to get the better of him. The thought that he might have damaged their relationship was more than he could bear yet what could he do? If he apologised for almost making love to her, it could make the situation even worse.

It was all very frustrating and he found it difficult to put it out of his mind even while he was working. AAU was busier than ever, the ongoing repairs to the roof, causing everyone a headache. Patients were left on the unit long after they should have been moved to a ward. Consequently tempers became frayed as the staff dealt with the added pressure of overcrowding.

Marco tried to smooth things over as best he could, making endless phone calls to the various departments to chivvy them up. Although it wasn't his job, he found that if he phoned them personally there was a better chance of something being done. A request from the consultant carried more weight than a request from a member of the nursing staff.

He was about to make a couple more calls when he became aware of raised voices coming from the staff-room. It had been an exceptionally busy morning and he knew that everyone had been pushed way beyond their limits. He made a detour in that direction because the last thing they needed was the team at odds if they were to get through this stressful period. Pushing open the door, he came to a halt when he was confronted by the sight of Gina and Miles. It was immediately obvious they had been arguing.

'What's going on?' he demanded, looking from one to the other.

'Sister Lee was just trying to explain why she had failed to follow my instructions.' Miles turned to him. 'I specifically requested that a patient should be sent for a CT as soon as possible. However, Sister, in her infinite wisdom, decided it could wait. In the meantime, the patient suffered a bleed. It's in the lap of the gods now as to what happens but one thing is certain. If the patient dies, *she* is responsible!'

Miles pointed an accusing finger at Gina, who blanched. Marco came to a swift decision. 'I shall deal with this, Dr Humphreys. Can you bring me the patient's notes? I shall be in the office. Sister Lee, if you'd come with me, please.'

'I…um…the notes will have gone to Theatre,' Miles said hurriedly as Marco turned to leave, and he paused.

'In that case, please phone them and ask if we can borrow them. It shouldn't be a problem.'

Miles didn't look happy but quite frankly Marco didn't care. He led the way to the office with his heart sinking. It was a very serious accusation and could incur disciplinary charges if it was true. He sat down behind the desk and waved Gina towards the chair. 'I want to hear your version of what happened.'

She sat down and looked steadily back at him. 'My version? I don't have a version. All I can tell you is the truth. Dr Humphreys never requested that a CT scan should be done. His only instruction was that the patient should be placed on half-hourly obs.'

'Then why did he claim that he had requested a scan?' Marco queried.

'Probably because he knew he'd made a mistake and wanted to shift the blame away from himself,' she retorted. 'It's not the first time he's done that and it won't be the last, either.'

'I see. And is there anyone who can verify what you say?'

'No. The rest of the staff were attending to other patients. I was on my own, so it's my word against his.' She raised her chin. 'I am not lying. Miles never requested a CT scan.'

'Then it will show that in the patient's notes.' Marco looked up when Miles appeared. He held out his hand for the file, skimming through the notes which had been written since the woman had been admitted. He paused when he came to a section near the bottom of the page. 'It says here that you requested a CT scan at eleven-fifteen, Dr Humphreys. Is that correct?'

'Yes. It's written down there, plain to see.'

There was a triumphant note in Miles's voice that made Marco's hackles rise, although he didn't say anything. He read to the end of the report, which stated that the woman had been taken to Theatre to have a suspected subdural haematoma removed. 'Is there any news from Theatre?' he asked, glancing up.

'Not yet.' Miles sounded unbearably smug. 'However, I think those notes are conclusive, don't you? I did request a CT scan and Sister failed to carry out my instructions.'

'Thank you, Dr Humphreys.' Marco closed the file, refusing to be drawn into passing judgment even though it did appear as though Gina had made an error. 'That will be all for now. I shall speak to you later.' He waited until the younger man had left then handed her the file. 'Do you have anything to say about this, Gina?'

'No.' She stared at the notes in confusion. 'I don't know how that got there because the request certainly wasn't in the file before. Miles definitely didn't write it in these notes while I was with him.'

'You think he may have filled it in later, after he realised there was a problem with the patient?'

'I don't know... I mean, would he risk falsifying notes like that?' She looked up and he could see the worry in her eyes. 'All I know is that he never mentioned a scan to me.'

'I believe you, but I wish there was someone who could back up your story.' He shook his head. 'The fact that this instruction is in the file will carry a great deal of weight if it comes to a disciplinary hearing.'

'You think it could come to that?'

Marco sighed. 'If the patient doesn't pull through, then, yes, it could.'

'It would mean I'd get the blame.' She bit her lip and he could tell how upset she was. 'Even though I swear it wasn't my fault.'

'It could do. We shall have to hope that it won't come to that, but you need to be aware that you're in a very difficult position, Gina.'

'And Miles will do all he can to make sure that he remains blameless,' she observed bitterly.

There was nothing Marco could say to dispute that. From what he had seen Miles would do anything he could to wriggle out of admitting his mistakes and if that meant ruining Gina's career, so be it. When she excused herself he didn't try to stop her. They would have to wait and see how the patient fared before further steps were taken. However, he knew that if he had to choose sides that he would choose Gina's.

She wouldn't lie about something like this. It wasn't in her nature. However, even his support would carry very little weight if it came to an inquiry and the facts were presented. The thought of her being subjected to that kind of ordeal was more than he could bear. He might not be able to commit himself to a relationship but it didn't mean that he didn't care about her. On the contrary, he cared a lot. He cared so much that the thought of her getting hurt, hurt him even more.

The next twenty-four hours were a nightmare. The patient under question, Harriet Walters, was moved to ICU and the prognosis wasn't good. Gina tried not to let it worry her but it was impossible when Miles made a point of recounting his version of events to anyone who would listen. Whilst most believed she wasn't at fault, she was realistic enough to know that some would accept his story. When Harriet Walters died two days later and her family demanded an inquiry, Gina realised that she could be in a lot of trouble. The thought that she might lose her job over this was very hard to deal with. She had no idea how she would support herself and Lily if that happened.

The thought was constantly on her mind so that she found it difficult to sleep and woke each morning exhausted. It didn't help that Lily was still rather fretful thanks to the chickenpox. Gina felt as though she was struggling to keep on top of things and hated the fact that she seemed to have so little control over her life. However, when Marco offered to look after Lily to give her a break, she refused. Lily was her responsibility and it was up to her to look after her.

Marco had never felt so powerless in his life. He knew that Gina was worn out from trying to cope with Lily and the situation at work but she refused to let him help her. It made him see that whilst she might be willing to allow him access to Lily, she still didn't trust him. The fact that he hadn't helped his case the night they had almost made love was something he bitterly regretted. It would need drastic action to convince her that he was sincere about wanting to be a good father and there was just one way he could think of that might achieve that, even though he knew how risky it was.

He made arrangements to see Lily the following Saturday, determined that they were going to resolve the situation. It had been raining on and off all week so they met at a soft play centre in Camden. Marco was already there when Gina arrived and he couldn't help thinking how lovely she looked in a pair of trim-fitting jeans and a pale blue T-shirt, with her blonde hair falling softly around her face.

He forced the thought aside as he bent down to lift Lily out of her pushchair. He couldn't afford to let his emotions run riot. If his plan was to succeed then he needed to remain in control. '*Buon giorno, cara,*' he said, trying to calm his wildly hammering heart as he kissed the little girl on the cheek and thought about what he intended to say to Gina.

'Buon giorno.' Lily smiled as she proudly repeated the phrase and he laughed.

'What a clever girl you are!' He gave her a hug then watched as she ran off to play in the ball pit. He turned to Gina, smoothing his face into a suitably noncommittal expression so that she couldn't tell how on edge he felt. 'She is starting to learn the odd Italian phrase, I see.'

'She is. Children pick things up so quickly at this age. They're like sponges,' she said quietly, lifting her bag out of the pushchair before parking it against the wall.

'So they say, although it's the first time I've actually witnessed it,' he replied lightly, pulling out a chair for her. 'Another plus of being a parent, wouldn't you agree?'

She shrugged as she sat down. 'To counteract the minuses, you mean?'

'No, that wasn't what I meant,' he replied in exasperation. 'Why do you always put such a negative slant on whatever I say, Gina? Can't you accept that I am thrilled about being a father?'

'Because I find it hard to believe that you won't grow tired of the responsibility that comes with the title. Anyone can claim to be a father, Marco, but it takes a lifetime of commitment to prove you can do the job.'

'And you don't think I can make such a long-term commitment?'

'No. If you want the truth , I don't.'

She stared coolly back at him but underneath the calm mask he could sense her fear and it touched him.

All of a sudden he knew that he couldn't wait any longer. He couldn't bear to leave her worrying for a second longer than was necessary.

'Then maybe this will convince you.' Reaching out, he took hold of her hand. 'I want you to marry me, Gina.'

Just for a moment, Gina thought she must have misheard him. It was extremely noisy in the play centre with all the children running about after all. Her heart began to pound as she stared at him and read the expression on his face. It was true: Marco had asked her to marry him. It was what she had dreamed about three years ago, what she still wanted now, she realised with a sudden rush of joy. Marrying him, being with him, loving him and being loved by him was what she wanted more than anything!

She opened her mouth to tell him that, yes, she would marry him, that she could think of nothing she wanted more, when he carried on.

'It makes sense, doesn't it? If we get married then we'll be able to provide Lily with everything she needs.'

'You're asking me to marry you for Lily's sake?' she said hoarsely, feeling the pain scoring deep inside her. She didn't know why she should feel so hurt. Marco had made it clear many times that he wasn't interested in having a relationship with her, yet she had managed to forget that in the heat of the moment. The ache inside her seemed to intensify as he continued in the same pragmatic tone.

'Yes. If you marry me then you won't have to work—you can spend all your time with Lily. She'd also be able to live somewhere more suitable. Your flat is far too small for a growing child. There's hardly enough room for the two of you as it is. I can provide you with a house with a garden where she can play…'

'And you think that's all it takes to make a child happy, do you, Marco? A house and a garden?' She laughed scornfully, hiding her pain beneath a layer of contempt. She wouldn't let him see how devastated she felt, couldn't bear him to know how foolish she was. She had actually thought that he was asking her to marry him because he wanted to spend his life with *her*!

'No, but I am sure it helps. Children don't take kindly to being constantly uprooted. If we get married we can find a place where we can create a proper home for her, somewhere big enough to accommodate all her needs as she grows up.'

'And where do you suggest we do that? Here in London or in Italy? You seem to have everything worked out, Marco, so do tell me your plans.'

He frowned where he heard the edge in her voice. 'That is something we shall both have to decide. I am not proposing to ride roughshod over your wishes, if that's what you're implying. My sole concern is Lily and making sure that she has the very best start in life. It's obvious that you are a wonderful mother to her but I can give you both the security you need. You won't have to struggle to make ends meet any more.'

'So Lily gets a house with a garden and I get a free meal ticket for life? That's very generous, Marco.'

He stared arrogantly back at her. 'Providing for my child isn't an act of generosity.'

'No? Then I must be mistaken, obviously.' She stood up abruptly, unable to take any more. His cold-hearted proposal simply proved how little he really felt for her.

Marco was prepared to do the right thing by providing for his daughter, and marrying her was merely part of the deal. If he had come out and stated that he had no feelings for her, he couldn't have made his position any clearer.

'I'm sorry, Marco, but I shall have to refuse your generous offer. Lily and I manage very well as we are. We don't need your help, thank you.'

'I have rights, too, Gina. I am Lily's father and I intend to make sure that she is properly cared for.'

'Which she is. She always will be, too, with or without your help, and preferably the latter.'

'I warn you, Gina, that if you try to stop me seeing her then I shall fight you.'

He stood up as well, looking so big and arrogant as he uttered his threats that she felt sick. How could she have misjudged the situation so badly? How had she seriously thought that he wanted to marry her because he loved her? Everything he had done, from ending their relationship three years ago to walking away that night they had been on the verge of making love, proved how little he cared about her. It was her own foolish heart that had made her want to believe he had changed.

'That's up to you, of course. I just hope that you'll remember what's important in all of this. Lily is the one who could get hurt, not you or me. But if that's a risk you are prepared to take, I can't stop you. Now I think it's time we left.'

She didn't give him a chance to reply as she fetched Lily. The little girl wasn't happy about having her fun cut short but Gina hardened her heart to her daughter's tears. This was for Lily's benefit, after all. She couldn't risk her precious child getting hurt even more when Marco tired of his role as the doting father.

She strapped Lily into her pushchair, refusing to listen to the insidious little voice that was whispering in her ear that it would be less likely to happen if they were married. There was no way she was marrying Marco, under any circumstances!

CHAPTER EIGHTEEN

THE following week was one of the most difficult of Marco's life. It was worse even than waking up in the back of that ambulance to find that he had lost his memory. Gina refused to speak to him about anything that didn't concern work. The atmosphere in AAU whenever they were together was so bad, in fact, that he knew the rest of the staff had noticed it. He racked his brain to come up with a solution but there was nothing he could do.

Gina had taken his marriage proposal entirely the wrong way. He'd meant to help her, not hurt her, yet that was what he had succeeded in doing. If only he had admitted that it wasn't just for Lily's sake that he wanted them to together, he thought. Maybe he *had* tried to convince himself that it was a purely practical solution to their problems, but in his heart he knew there'd been other reasons why he had proposed marriage to her. He wanted to be with Gina every bit as much as he wanted to be a good father to Lily, and the thought terrified him, made him see how vulnerable he was. Gina had an even bigger hold on him now than she'd had three years ago.

If Marco had thought things couldn't get any worse,

he was mistaken. He was in the consultants' lounge when the phone rang. He picked up the receiver, surprised when an unfamiliar voice asked for him. His heart sank when the caller identified herself as the matron in charge of the nursing home where his grandmother lived. She briskly informed him that the old lady had pneumonia and was gravely ill. In the circumstances, he might wish to visit her.

Marco thanked her and hung up. He knew that he would never forgive himself if Nonna died without him being there, so he phoned round the airlines and managed to book himself a seat on a flight leaving that afternoon. Once he had informed the powers-that-be that he would need to take compassionate leave, he went to find Gina. Maybe she wouldn't be interested, but the very least he could do was to tell her that he would be away for a few days.

There was no sign of her on the unit and none of the staff seemed to know where she had gone either. He brushed aside Julie's offer to pass on a message and decided to phone her later instead. He certainly didn't want things to reach the point whereby they only communicated through a third party.

By the time he landed at Florence, it was already late but he phoned her mobile from the airport and left a message, briefly explaining what had happened when she failed to answer. Several times during the ensuing days he tried to contact her but without success. She was obviously screening his calls and it hurt to know that she didn't want to talk to him. He knew the situation couldn't continue and that he would have to do something about it when he returned to London. He wouldn't let her cut him out of his daughter's life. He couldn't bear it! He also couldn't bear the thought that she was cutting him out of her life too. Maybe it was a huge risk to allow himself to fall in love, he thought suddenly, but was it any worse than feeling like this, bereft and adrift?

Gina tried to keep everything normal for Lily's sake but it wasn't easy. The fact that Marco wasn't around should have helped but, strangely, it didn't. She missed him and there was no point denying it either.

It didn't help that Lily also seemed to miss him. When Gina suggested a visit to the park on the Saturday morning, the little girl eagerly demanded to know if Marco would be there. Gina gently explained that he'd had to go away but the ominous wobble to Lily's lower lip spoke volumes. It made her see that she couldn't cut him out of their lives, as she wanted to do. It wouldn't be fair to Lily. They would have to come to some sort of agreement to allow him access to their daughter, but that was all it would be—a civilised arrangement between two people for the benefit of their child. Marriage was strictly off the agenda!

Marco ended up staying almost a week in Florence as his grandmother fought off the effects of double pneumonia. Nobody expected her to pull through, himself included, but amazingly she defied all the odds. By the end of the week she was sitting up in bed, demanding her favourite food. He flew back to London early the following Friday and went straight into work and the first person he saw was Gina.

'Good morning,' he said, his heart leaping at the sight of her. He had missed her so much. She was such an important part of his life now that he simply couldn't imagine a future without her and didn't want to try. The thought shocked him so much that it was a moment before he realised that she was speaking. 'I'm sorry—what did you say?'

'I asked how your grandmother is.'

'I'm delighted to say that Nonna is much better.' He smiled at her. 'You obviously got my message, then?'

She shrugged. 'Yes.'

She didn't say anything else, certainly didn't explain why she had refused to answer his calls, and he didn't press her. The fact that she had bothered to enquire after his grandmother's health seemed a positive step and that was something to be grateful for.

'How's Lily?' he asked, following her to AAU.

'She's fine. Her spots have all gone now and she's back to her usual sunny self.'

'I missed her while I was away,' he said quietly.

She glanced at him and her expression softened. 'She missed you too, Marco. She was really disappointed when she found out you wouldn't be joining us at the park on Saturday.'

'Was she?' He put his hand on her arm and drew her to a halt. 'There has to be a way to work this out, Gina. I know I upset you the other day but I hope we can get past that—for Lily's sake.'

He knew he had said the wrong thing when her face immediately closed up. 'I'm sure we can reach some sort of agreement if we try. Now, if you'll excuse me, I need to get on.'

She hurried off down the ward, leaving him feeling more wretched than ever. He sighed as he headed to the consultants' lounge to find out what had been happening in his absence. If only he knew what Gina really wanted from him, it might help, but quite frankly he had no idea. Did she want him to be purely a father to their daughter or did she want more than that?

His heart leapt at the thought that she might want *him* before he battened it down. If he allowed himself to go down that route then he wouldn't be able to stop. Even now his mind was running riot, picturing how wonderful his life could be. He could have it all, a wife who loved him, a child they adored, the happily-ever-after that everyone dreamt of…

Until it all went wrong, of course.

Once again the old fears came rushing back and he knew that he couldn't do it. He was tempted, so tempted that it was agony not to follow his inclinations, yet the thought of going through all that pain again if anything happened was just too much. He couldn't bear it if he lost Gina as well.

Gina deliberately stayed out of Marco's way for the remainder of the morning. Maybe she was overreacting but did he have to constantly rub it in that he was only interested in their daughter? The thought played on her mind so that by the time she went to the canteen for lunch she had a headache brewing.

She took a couple of paracetamol then made her way back to AAU, using the stairs rather than the lift because she was early. She had just passed the barriers on the fourth floor when she heard someone shouting.

She stopped uncertainly, glancing along the empty corridor. Work on the roof had been put on hold while another structural report was prepared and there was nobody about. Had she imagined that noise or was there someone there?

She knew she had to check and slipped past the barriers. Huge metal props had been placed at intervals along the corridor to support the ceiling and she carefully skirted around them. She reached the door to the children's ward and peered inside but there was no sign of anyone so she carried on to Women's Surgical, gasping when she saw a teenage boy lying on the floor.

'What's happened?' she demanded, hurrying over to him.

'I tripped over and twisted my ankle.' He rubbed his eyes, obviously not wanting her to know that he had been crying. 'I think it's broken.'

'Let me have a look.' Gina knelt down and gently examined his ankle. 'It looks like it's broken to me, too. What are you doing here, though? Didn't you see the notices warning you to keep out?'

'I wanted to see what had happened to the roof,' he explained sheepishly, and she sighed.

'Well, you certainly got more than you bargained for.' She stood up. 'I'll have to phone for a porter. We'll need a wheelchair to get you out of here.'

Picking up the phone, she asked for a porter, briefly explaining what had happened, and went back to the boy. 'My name's Gina, by the way. What's yours?'

'Richard.'

'Nice to meet you, Richard, although I wish the circumstances had been different.' She smiled when he rolled his eyes. 'How come you're in the hospital in the first place? Are you visiting someone?'

'No, I'm here with my dad. I'm supposed to be shadowing him while he works—it's some stupid idea my school came up with—but it's so boring.' He shrugged. 'Dad told me about the roof, so I thought I'd check it out.'

'I see. And who's your dad?'

'Tom Petty. He works in ED. Do you know him?'

Gina nodded. 'Yes, I know Tom. I don't think he's going to be too impressed by having you for a patient, though.'

Richard was about to say something when all of a sudden there was a rumbling noise above them. Gina gasped when she looked up and saw that the metal prop they were sitting next to had started to shift out of place.

'Look out!' she cried as a section of the ceiling suddenly gave way.

She threw herself on top of the boy, shielding him as chunks of plaster rained down on them. Something hit her on the head and in the final second before everything went black she found herself wishing that she had told Marco she loved him. Maybe he wouldn't want to hear it but all of a sudden it seemed important that he should know the truth.

Marco was dealing with a new admission when he became aware of a commotion in the ward. He looked up, frowning when he saw Julie clap her hand over her mouth. It was obvious that something had happened so he quickly excused himself and went to see what was wrong.

'It's Gina.' There were tears in Julie's eyes as she turned to him. 'She's been hurt.'

'Hurt?'

'Yes. Another section of the roof has caved in and it

appears that Gina was there when it happened. They've managed to get her out and taken her to ED…'

Marco didn't wait to hear anything else. He'd heard more than enough as it was. Gina was hurt and he had to get to her! He ran out of AAU and straight along the corridor to ED. 'You've got Gina Lee in here. Where is she?' he demanded when he reached the nursing station.

'Resus,' the nurse replied, but she was speaking to fresh air. Marco had already gone.

He raced to Resus, his heart hammering as he pushed open the door. Only the most severely injured patients were treated in here and the thought that Gina fell into that category was more than he could bear. He scanned the room, oblivious to the startled looks he was attracting from the staff. He didn't care what anyone thought. He only cared about Gina. He needed to see her and make sure she was all right…

His gaze suddenly alighted on a figure lying on the end bed and his heart turned over when he realised it was her. She looked so small and defenceless as she lay there with all the various tubes and leads attached to her body. Marco felt a wave of ice-cold fear pass over him. It took every scrap of courage he could muster to cross the room.

'How is she?' he asked, staring down at her. Her eyes were closed and there was a huge purple bruise on her forehead but apart from that, she appeared uninjured.

'Not too bad,' Simon Rutherford, the senior registrar, replied cheerfully. 'A chunk of the ceiling hit her on the head so she may have a concussion. No fractures, though, and it doesn't appear that there are any internal injuries, although we can't rule them out just yet. All in all, I'd say she was extremely lucky. It's not every day that you have half a ton of ceiling fall on top of you and live to tell the tale!'

Simon moved away, leaving Marco alone with her. He reached for her hand, his own hand trembling as he raised it to his lips. He had been so scared, so terrified that he would lose her, and yet the worst thing of all had been the thought that he hadn't told her how much he loved her. He had been a coward, denying his feelings, turning his back on love because he'd been afraid, but he wouldn't make that mistake again.

'Marco?'

The sound of her voice brought his eyes winging to her face and he felt joy fill him when he saw the way she was looking at him. Bending, he kissed her on the mouth, feeling his joy intensify when she kissed him back. He drew back, knowing that she could see exactly how he felt but he didn't care. He was past lying to her or to himself. He loved her and he wanted her to know that.

'I love you, Gina,' he said simply.

'And I love you too, Marco.' She smiled into his eyes. 'There, I've said it, so if another chunk of ceiling drops on me then at least I've told you the truth.'

He laughed. 'You have and believe me it's the best thing I've heard for a very long time.'

'Is it? Are you sure about that?' Her gaze was searching and he sighed.

'Yes, I'm sure. It's taken me a long to admit how I feel but now that I have, I am not going to change my mind. I love you, *tesoro*, and I love the fact that you love me.'

'Good. It will make life a whole lot simpler, don't

you think?' She gave a little chuckle. 'This isn't how I imagined it would be when I told you.'

'Oh, so you were planning on making your confession *before* the accident happened?' He smiled at her. 'That sets my mind at rest.'

'It does?'

'Mmm. I was afraid the bump on your head might have had something to do with it.'

'It may have done,' she replied saucily. 'A bump on the head can cause a lot of strange things to happen to a person.'

'As I know from experience.' He dropped another kiss on her lips. 'If I hadn't had that bump on my head, I would never have met you again.'

'Do you think it was fate intervening?'

'I don't know. But whatever it was, I am truly grateful.' He pressed her hand against his heart. 'I found the love of my life and my daughter.'

'I'm sorry that I never tried harder to tell you about Lily,' she began, but he shushed her.

'No. That's all in the past and it doesn't matter now. You did what you thought was best and I don't blame you after the way I'd behaved. I was such a coward, Gina, and I shall always regret that. I missed out on three years of happiness because I was afraid of falling in love with you.'

'So it wasn't just because you didn't love me as much as Francesca?' she asked in a small voice, and he stared at her in surprise.

'No! That was never an issue. Oh, I loved Francesca, but my feelings for her have nothing to do with how I feel about you. I love you with every scrap of my being and all I want is to spend the rest of my life with you so I can prove it to you.'

'You don't have to prove anything to me, Marco.' Her eyes glistened with tears as she reached up to pull his head down so she could kiss him. 'I believe you because I love you, because I know you wouldn't lie to me about something as important as this.'

'I wouldn't.' They kissed hungrily, a kiss that would have lasted a lot longer if they hadn't been interrupted.

'Sorry to break things up, folks, but Gina is booked in for a scan.' Tom Petty grinned at them. 'You can resume what you were doing afterwards with my blessing. In fact, I shall personally find you some place private where you won't be interrupted. I owe you, Gina, for what you did for my son.'

Marco wasn't sure what Tom meant by that but didn't ask. No doubt Gina would explain it all to him later. He moved away from the bed as the porters arrived to take her to radiology. 'I'd better get back to AAU, I suppose. They'll be wondering where I've got to.'

'Oh, don't worry about that.' Tom grinned at him. 'No doubt the jungle drums will be spreading the news even as we speak.'

'The news?' Marco repeated.

'About you and Gina… I am right, aren't I? I mean, you two are an item?'

Marco laughed. 'If you mean are we together then, yes, we are.' He captured her hand and kissed it. 'We are very much together and intend to stay that way.'

'Good stuff! I love a happy ending.' Tom sketched them a wave and hurried off to deal with a new patient.

Marco turned to Gina. 'I'll be back as soon as I can, my darling. Promise.'

'I'm not going anywhere,' she replied, loving him with her eyes.

The porters took over then, wheeling her out of Resus. Marco followed although it felt as though his feet weren't touching the floor as he made his way to AAU. He was floating on Cloud Nine, hovering in his own little world, a world filled with love and happiness.

He pushed open the door, his head whirling with everything that had happened in the past half-hour. His life had changed completely. Now he had a future to look forward to, a whole new life that he had never dreamt he would have. He felt so lucky to have been given a second chance, knew that he would do everything possible to make sure that nothing went wrong, but he wouldn't waste the coming years, fearing what they held in store. He had wasted enough time doing that and now he intended to enjoy every second. He, Gina and Lily would create some wonderful new memories. Together.

EPILOGUE

FLORENCE lay serene and beautiful under a cloudless blue sky. It was the middle of June and the weather was perfect. Gina smiled as she stepped in front of the mirror and studied her reflection.

It was her wedding day and the dress she had chosen was everything she had dreamt it would be. Made from a length of antique cream lace that Marco's beloved grandmother had given her, it fell in soft folds to her ankles. It was a dream of a dress and she loved it, knew that Marco would love it too.

Happiness welled up inside her as she thought about what had happened in the past few months. She and Lily had moved out of their flat into Marco's apartment. Although Gina had been worried at first about how Lily would cope with the new arrangements she had settled in immediately. The little girl seemed to accept that Marco was part of their life now and obviously enjoyed being with him. Although they hadn't told her yet that he was her father, Gina was sure that Lily would take that in her stride too when the time came. There was already a bond between them, which was growing stronger with every day that passed.

Once the move had been accomplished they had arranged their wedding. When Marco had asked her if she would consider getting married in Florence so his grandmother could be there, she had agreed at once. She knew how important family was to Marco and wanted the day to be as special for him as it was for her.

Everything had gone surprisingly smoothly. Not even the fact that she had been summoned to appear at the board of inquiry the week before had spoiled things. She knew that she hadn't done anything wrong and in the event that had been proved when fresh evidence had been presented.

Engineers investigating the reason why the prop had failed had checked back through the CCTV footage on the days leading up to the accident and discovered that Miles had been in the vicinity. He had been asked to explain what he'd been doing there and eventually admitted that he had gone there to alter the notes he had retrieved from Theatre. He was currently suspended and it looked likely that he would be dismissed. Maybe Gina should have felt angry about the way Miles had tried to lay the blame on her but, quite frankly, it didn't seem to matter. She was going to marry the man she loved and nothing was more important than that!

A soft knock at the door made her turn and she smiled when she saw Marco come into the bedroom. They had decided to walk to the village church together. Maybe it wasn't traditional for the bride and groom to arrive together but after being apart for so long, every second they were apart seemed a waste. Now she felt a thrill run through her when he stopped and stared at her.

'You look beautiful, *cara*,' he said, his deep voice throbbing with a passion that made her shudder. He crossed the room and took her hand so that he could press a kiss against her palm. 'I cannot believe that in a short while you will be my wife.'

'Believe it, Marco, because it's going to happen!'

She reached up and kissed him softly on the lips, feeling the tremor that ran through him. Marco was unable to hide how he felt about her these days. Every touch, every kiss, drew a reaction from him as they did from her. It was proof she no longer needed of how much he loved her.

She stepped back and smiled at him. 'Is Lily all right?'

'She's fine, very excited about being a flower girl.' He laughed wryly. 'She's practising throwing her rose petals. I left Nonna in charge but I cannot see her stopping her. Lily can twist Nonna round her little finger, can't she? I only hope there are some petals left by the time we get to church!'

Gina laughed. 'We can only hope for the best.'

'It doesn't matter even if the basket is empty. Nothing is going to spoil today, is it?'

'No. It's going to be the best day of my life, Marco.'

'Mine too,' he murmured, bending so he could kiss her. 'But the most wonderful thing of all is knowing that we have a whole future to look forward to.'

Gina closed her eyes as she let the magic sweep her away. She was so lucky, lucky to have found Marco again, lucky to have his child, lucky to be loved by the man she adored. The future couldn't have been any better!

* * * * *

TAMING THE LONE DOC'S HEART

BY
LUCY CLARK

MILLS &
BOON

To Vikie & Luke,
Congratulations on finding your happily-ever-after!
Jer 33:11

DID YOU PURCHASE THIS BOOK WITHOUT A COVER?

If you did, you should be aware it is **stolen property** as it was reported *unsold and destroyed* by a retailer. Neither the author nor the publisher has received any payment for this book.

All the characters in this book have no existence outside the imagination of the author, and have no relation whatsoever to anyone bearing the same name or names. They are not even distantly inspired by any individual known or unknown to the author, and all the incidents are pure invention.

All Rights Reserved including the right of reproduction in whole or in part in any form. This edition is published by arrangement with Harlequin Enterprises II BV/S.à.r.l. The text of this publication or any part thereof may not be reproduced or transmitted in any form or by any means, electronic or mechanical, including photocopying, recording, storage in an information retrieval system, or otherwise, without the written permission of the publisher.

This book is sold subject to the condition that it shall not, by way of trade or otherwise, be lent, resold, hired out or otherwise circulated without the prior consent of the publisher in any form of binding or cover other than that in which it is published and without a similar condition including this condition being imposed on the subsequent purchaser.

® and TM are trademarks owned and used by the trademark owner and/or its licensee. Trademarks marked with ® are registered with the United Kingdom Patent Office and/or the Office for Harmonisation in the Internal Market and in other countries.

First published in Great Britain 2012
by Mills & Boon, an imprint of Harlequin (UK) Limited.
Harlequin (UK) Limited, Eton House, 18-24 Paradise Road,
Richmond, Surrey TW9 1SR

© Anne Clark & Peter Clark 2012

ISBN: 978 0 263 89153 9

Harlequin (UK) policy is to use papers that are natural, renewable and recyclable products and made from wood grown in sustainable forests. The logging and manufacturing process conform to the legal environmental regulations of the country of origin.

Printed and bound in Spain
by Blackprint CPI, Barcelona

Dear Reader

What a delight to be able to share with you the story of Lorelai and Woody. As authors, we always fall in love with our characters, and these two were no exception. Lorelai has such gumption, and I love the way she's firm but loving with headstrong three-year-old Hannah. Woody is tall and delicious—a man who loves life and is honourable in the way he lives up to high expectations.

We were fortunate enough to spend our Christmas vacation travelling through the Snowy Mountains of Australia. Even though it was during the height of the Australian summer, the weather in that part of the country changed frequently. One day we were sunburnt; the next day we had snow! It was delightfully inspiring.

We sincerely hope you enjoy reading about Lorelai and Woody, and accompanying them on their journey as together they find joy, hope and love.

Warmest regards

Lucy Clark

Lucy Clark is actually a husband-and-wife writing team. They enjoy taking holidays with their children, during which they discuss and develop new ideas for their books using the fantastic Australian scenery. They use their daily walks to talk over characterisation and fine details of the wonderful stories they produce, and are avid movie buffs. They live on the edge of a popular wine district in South Australia with their two children, and enjoy spending family time together at weekends.

PROLOGUE

'Woody?' Lorelai's breathing was erratic and she knew she had to control it. She gripped the phone tighter in her hand, channelling her frustration into the inanimate object.

'Lorelai? How did the meeting go?'

'There's been an accident. I need you.' She worked hard to keep the panic from her voice but knew she'd failed. She walked around to the rear of her car, which her father had parked on the shoulder closest to the mountain.

'What is it? What's happened?' There was a briskness to his words, the ever-present direct pitch of a surgeon switching his mind into 'action' mode. She'd never been more grateful that Woody had come to Oodnaminaby to visit his sister, Honey, especially as she could do with a skilled surgeon to help her.

'A car…drove through the barrier. He swerved then… just…went off the road. And…' Lorelai tried to control her wobbling voice. 'It's John.'

'John? Your husband?'

'Yes, and his *mistress* was in the car with him.' She retrieved her medical bag from the boot and slammed the lid shut. 'Dad and I were driving right behind them.

We saw the whole thing. I watched him lose control and veer off, smashing through the...' Her breathing had increased and she stopped, trying to slow herself down, to be calm and composed. If she was to be of any help, she needed to find her focus.

'Lorelai? Are you OK? You and your dad? You're both all right?'

'We're fine.' Lorelai walked quickly but carefully towards the broken guard rail, wanting to see what had happened but by the same token not wanting to know. 'Dad's controlling the traffic and calling the ambulance, fire rescue and police workers, as well as ordering the heavy machinery needed.' That's it, she told herself. Focus on the overall picture. Breathe. In, out. In, out.

'Right. Good. Glad you're both safe.' There was relief in his tone and she allowed his calm, deep tone to wash over her, helping to quell the rising panic. 'Where are you?'

Lorelai gave him directions and could hear him moving about in the background, the sounds of a small baby in the distance. *Her* baby. Her beautiful little girl who John hadn't wanted. He hadn't wanted to be a father. He hadn't wanted to be married to her any more. He'd chosen to be with his mistress and he'd wanted to get a divorce. Lorelai had agreed. She'd attended the meeting at the lawyers in Tumut, leaving Hannah in Woody's care, asking her father, BJ, to drive her to the appointment as she knew she might be too emotional to drive home.

Then, on the way back, she'd realised they had been driving behind John's car and it had been clear as he'd zoomed around the winding bends in the road that he hadn't been alone in the car, Lorelai often catching a glimpse of a woman sitting beside him. The woman who had stolen her husband.

She swallowed over her anger and pain as she carefully edged closer to the side of the road, which fell away down an embankment towards the lake.

'What about Hannah?' Lorelai asked Woody. 'If you come here, who's going to look—?'

'Hamilton's here. He's a responsible lad. I'll get him to mind your daughter. Honey and Edward are due back soon so I'm leaving a message for them.'

'OK. Hurry, Woody.'

'I'm on my way, Lorelai.' His words were strong, determined, dependable. 'Just…' He paused. 'Be careful, all right?'

'I will.' Lorelai nodded, drawing in the strength he was exuding down the phone. 'Thanks.' She disconnected the call, breathing deeply again, allowing a sense of calm to wash over her as she pushed her phone into the pocket of her jeans.

Reinforcements were on their way, her father was a trained State Emergency Services captain and together they'd be able to at least stabilise the situation. She'd attended emergencies before…but she'd never in her wildest dreams thought she'd have to treat her wayward husband and his mistress.

Unfortunately, with the winding roads along the great Snowy Mountains Highway in New South Wales, accidents like this were far too common. With all the back-up and emergency services on the way, surely that meant everything would be all right—wouldn't it?

She continued to work at steadying her heartbeat, telling herself this situation was no different from other emergencies of a similar nature. She put her bag at her feet, then wiped her perspiring hands down her jeans, but they didn't feel any drier. She closed her eyes for a moment, desperate to block out what was going to happen next, not wanting to face it but knowing she had to. When she opened her eyes again, nothing had changed. The car below still lay in a mangled heap before her. She picked up her bag and straightened her shoulders, knowing she could do this.

'Lore! Be careful. Don't touch the car at all,' her father called from above. Lorelai heeded her father's words and moved with care down the embankment towards the badly damaged car. She was still trying to come to terms with what she'd seen—John's car swerving through the barriers before tipping over the embankment.

What had John been thinking? Why had he been driving so fast? No. She didn't want an answer to that question right now. She couldn't think of all the terrible things John had done to her, of the pain he'd caused especially during the past few weeks. Right now he needed her help, her professional expertise…and so did his mistress.

Sliding on the dirt and stones beneath her shoes, Lorelai forced herself to slow down even more, watching where she was stepping otherwise she might twist her ankle and then she'd have one more obstacle to navigate. She picked her way through the shattered glass of the windscreen and when she eventually stood beside the car, which was almost on a forty-five degree angle towards the ground, the chassis of the car facing the sky, Lorelai gasped, covering her mouth with her hands as she looked at the man who was still legally her husband.

'Oh, John.' Her breathing was erratic and she shook her head, trying to keep her tears under control. She would do him no good if she lost the plot.

From what she could see, John was wedged tightly between the seat and the steering-wheel, slumped over, still held in firmly by the seat belt, a large red gash on his head oozing blood, his legs obscured from her view by the twisted metal of the car.

Knowing that until the car was secured, it could still shift, Lorelai stepped as close as she dared, calling his name, trying to keep the fear from her tone. He may have cheated on her, he may have rejected the baby she'd only given birth to a fortnight ago, he may have caused her immeasurable pain and heartache, but he didn't deserve to die. Not like this.

She reached forward and pressed two fingers to his carotid pulse, not surprised to find it weak but thready. 'Hold on, John.' She looked past him, to the passenger seat but, surprisingly, found it empty. She frowned. She knew for a fact that his mistress had been in the car because she'd seen the other woman laughing at John as they'd driven through the streets of Tumut. John, parading around the town with his new woman in tow, in front of people they'd known for years, in front of *her*. Had he honestly cared so little for their life together?

'Lore?' Her father's deep baritone pierced her distress and she stood to see where he was. 'Over here. Quickly,' BJ called, and Lorelai reluctantly left the unconscious John, knowing at this stage there was little she could do for him.

'Who's controlling the traffic?' she called as she made her way towards him

'Ike was passing by. He's a young cadet but he knows

his emergency protocols.' Her father was crouched next to something and as she drew closer, she realised it was the mistress.

'She's unconscious but she's breathing. How's John?'

'Bad. Trapped. Very bad.' She bit her tongue, trying to control her rising emotions. 'I can't…I can't see his legs, Dad.' Lorelai looked at her father, her voice wobbling on the last few words. BJ reassuringly put his hands onto her shoulders, looking into her eyes.

'There's nothing we can do for John at the moment, not until help arrives. We need to stabilise that car before I'll allow anyone near it. You understand, don't you, Lore? My first duty as an SES captain is to ensure the safety of all rescue workers.'

She nodded, the action small, her jaw clenched in an effort to control her emotions. 'I know, Dad.'

'For now, she…' he indicated the patient before them '…needs your help. Sweetheart,' BJ continued, 'I know this is difficult but you have to focus. You're a professional, Lorelai Rainbow. You're my daughter and it doesn't matter what either John or this woman—'

'Jean.' Lorelai swallowed. 'Her name is Jean.'

'Right. It doesn't matter what they've done to you, how they've hurt you, they don't deserve to die.'

Lorelai nodded, knowing her father spoke the truth. She closed her eyes and concentrated, drawing in a deep, calming breath, reminding herself that help would soon arrive, that Woody was on his way. She pushed aside her personal thoughts and pulled on her professionalism. She was a doctor. She'd taken an oath to uphold life and that was what she would do.

Opening her eyes, she nodded to her father and reached for her medical bag. 'As soon as Woody arrives, have him take a look at John,' she said, and knelt down beside the supine body of her patient. 'I have to be honest with you, Dad, even from my quick perusal and the feel of his pulse, I don't know if he'll—' She broke off, unable to say the words out loud. BJ nodded understandingly.

'You're strong, Lorelai. Stronger than you think, love.'

'You're the only man in the world who thinks so, Dad, and I love you for it.'

Twenty minutes later, all the back-up they'd requested had arrived, the SES firefighters had doused the overturned car with fire retardant and were starting to secure it with cables. BJ was organising and ordering whilst Woody was crouched down opposite her as they worked on continuing to stabilise Jean. At Lorelai's request, he'd taken a look at John but until the car was stable, BJ wasn't allowing anyone to get closer.

'I've just spoken to my sister,' he'd told her not long after he'd arrived. 'She and Edward are on their way here.'

Lorelai had sighed, pleased her two medical colleagues would be there soon. Right now, she needed all the help and support she could get. Edward was like a brother to her and Honey had become a very close friend in a very short time, so much so that it was Honey who had delivered Lorelai's baby.

As they worked together, Lorelai looked at Woody, amazed that when he'd first arrived on the scene, he hadn't demanded a report or behaved like all qualified general surgeons, in an arrogant and overbearing manner, taking charge of the case at hand. Instead, he'd assessed the situation for himself and then looked at her with admiration.

'You've done a great job of stabilising her, Lorelai.' His words were deep and calm.

She wasn't sure how he did it but just hearing his rich tone had somehow managed to sooth her frazzled nerves and settle her wayward thoughts. She was still worried about John and she was still trying to keep her professional focus as far as Jean was concerned but Woody's reassurance, his relaxed presence, as though he'd seen this sort of injury a thousand times before and knew exactly what to do, helped her to pause, draw in a cleansing breath and then slowly let it out.

'Jean's broken a lot of bones.' Woody shook his head as they finished carefully wrapping the fresh bandage around their patient's head. 'Carotid pulse is strong, which is a good sign, but with the facial lacerations she's sustained, she'll require skin grafts, plastic surgery and will be left with a multitude of scars.'

'You sound very sure of that.'

'I've seen it many times before, although on those other occasions I was usually in the jungles of Tarparnii or in Afghanistan. At least Jean has access to skilled surgeons and modern equipment.'

'You like to travel a lot, don't you?' Lorelai asked rhetorically as she performed Jean's observations again. Thankfully, with the arrival of the paramedics, they'd been able to insert an IV drip as Jean's blood pressure was still low.

'There's a big wide world out there. So much to see and do and learn,' Woody replied, although Lorelai was surprised to realise his words seemed rehearsed, as though he'd given that reply many times before. Why was that? She brushed the thought aside and concentrated on helping him to continue stabilising Jean.

'Honey said the longest you've ever stayed in one place was for two years.'

'She's right. I was thirteen years old and had fallen from a tree, landing on my back. I'd fractured my spine so spent a good deal of time in hospital. My parents couldn't give in to their wandering feet and had to stay put. It was strange, being in one place for such a long time.'

'Long time? Two years? Apart from medical school, I've lived my whole life in this very district.' She shook her head, quite bemused with his wanderlust.

'It seemed longer, especially when I was supine in traction. Not good for a teenage boy. However, I have to say being in hospital, watching the medical staff, the cleaners, the cooks, the maintenance staff, it brought to life this exciting new world. It was then I decided to become a doctor, so I guess it wasn't all bad.' He paused for a second and shook his head, clearing his thoughts of the past and focusing on the present. 'Jean's blood pressure is still low, even with the drip.'

'Internal bleeding?'

'Yes, although it can't be too bad as she's holding on.'

'She's voided, which is indicative of bladder rupture.'

'She'll need to go directly to surgery once she arrives in A and E. Will she go to Tumut or Canberra hospital?' he asked.

'She'll be taken to Tumut then airlifted to Canberra,' Lorelai supplied.

Woody nodded. 'I'll call a friend of mine who works there, let him know she's coming.' He looked down at

Jean and shook his head. 'She can't have been wearing her seat belt, hence why she was thrown so far from the car,' he continued. 'And given her head injuries, it's clear she went through the windscreen. Extremely dangerous to travel in a car without wearing a seat belt.'

'I had to pull several splinters of glass from her left eye. I've flushed it as best as I could but she'll need an eye surgeon to assess it,' Lorelai stated as Woody continued to wind the bandage over Jean's face, covering the pad Lorelai had placed over the woman's left eye. The cervical collar was protecting Jean's spine and they'd splinted her other limbs, Woody's clever and experienced hands moving quickly but cautiously so as not to create further complications.

'I think we're ready to get her out of here.' Woody took the walkie-talkie BJ had given him and radioed the paramedics. 'We're ready to transfer Jean.'

'Copy that,' came the reply, and soon the paramedics had Jean secured to the stretcher. Lorelai watched as they took Jean up the embankment to the waiting ambulance. Then, for the first time since her father had asked her to focus, Lorelai allowed her mind to drift towards the man who was still legally her husband. He may have cheated on her, he may have ripped her heart out, rejecting both her and their daughter, but he was still her husband.

On legs that were trembling as she stumbled over to where John was still trapped in the mangled car, Lorelai swallowed over the sudden dryness of her throat. Firefighters were attaching cables to the car and Woody had somehow crawled into the vehicle and was monitoring John closely.

She could hear voices around her, people talking and

calling instructions to each other, but they all seemed distant, far away. None of this seemed real. It was like a bad nightmare but she knew it wasn't one she could wake up from.

Lorelai swallowed. Everything around her slowed down, so much so that for a second everything seemed to stand still. She could hear no sounds, nothing except for the beating of her own heart pounding against her chest, the beat slightly faster than usual.

So much pain. So much anguish. Hot tears stung at her eyes. John was responsible for the pain in her chest, for the tears in her eyes, for the breaking of her heart. He'd destroyed her self-esteem, her self-confidence, he'd emotionally stripped her bare and then he'd discarded her like a broken toy.

But that didn't mean he deserved to die.

The blood continued to pound in her ears and with a rush of noise the world started to turn again. She knew the chances of John surviving this accident were slim and part of her wanted to leave so she didn't have to face the inevitable—watching her husband die, knowing there wasn't a thing she could do to save him—but she didn't want to go home alone. She needed someone with her. Someone with big strong arms who would hold and protect her. She didn't have anyone like that.

It was every doctor's worst nightmare when they were unable to save the life of a loved one. She'd seen John's legs, the way the twisted metal seemed to blend with his limbs as though he was one with the car. The fact he hadn't regained consciousness, that his pulse was weak, that… Lorelai stopped her thoughts, her heart hammering against her chest. She wasn't that strong.

Woody's voice came through on the walkie-talkie,

relaying John's latest set of vitals to BJ, who was at the top of the embankment, controlling the situation.

'It's not good,' she whispered into the wind. Logically, she knew it was hopeless to wish for John to survive. She wished she could change things, go back and fix her marriage, do whatever it took to keep her daughter's father alive, but she knew she couldn't. From Woody's last report, it was clear John's internal injuries were too extensive and he still hadn't regained consciousness.

The rescue teams were trying to get into position to cut John free but with the front of the car being so crushed, it was slow going…and time was something they didn't have on their side.

All she could think about was John and the sight of him hanging upside down, his legs obscured by the mangled metal. She really didn't want to be there when the verdict finally came, being told that John simply hadn't been strong enough to pull through—yet, still, she lacked the strength to go.

Then, almost as though she was dreaming, Edward, her surrogate brother, appeared as though from thin air. Edward, her friend. He'd know what to do. Edward always knew what to do and she trusted his judgement one hundred per cent.

'Lore?' He put his medical bag down and hugged her close.

'Oh, Edward.' Tears instantly flooded over the barriers she'd worked hard to erect. 'Edward, it's John.' She sobbed into his shoulder, her professional armour finally cracking. She had no idea how long she stood there, crying on his shoulder. It could have been seconds, it might have been hours. General time was irrelevant, especially as deep down inside, she knew she was waiting for TOD—time of death—to be called.

Edward eased her back a little and it was then, as she wiped her eyes, that she realised Woody was standing beside her.

'Come on, Lorelai. Let me take you home,' Woody offered, putting his hand on her shoulders. His touch was warm, gentle, comforting.

'Good idea. Go on up with Woody,' Edward agreed softly. 'Let him take you home. Honey and I will look after John.'

Lorelai looked at him, seeing the promise and the truth in his words. Edward had never let her down in the past and he wouldn't now. It helped to give her the strength to walk away. Edward knew John, whereas Honey had only met him once and Woody not at all. Knowing Edward was there, doing what he could to help John, lifted a heavy burden from Lorelai's shoulders and after a second of looking into his eyes, of seeing the reassurance there, she realised she could leave. Edward was family.

'OK.' She sniffed and nodded and once more wiped at the tears. She must look a sight! Glancing over at the twisted car, she took a shaky breath, said a silent goodbye, then slowly turned, allowing Woody to lead her away.

He held firmly to her hand as they walked up the embankment, ensuring she didn't slip over. They took it slowly, not wanting to rush on the loose dirt and gravel, but eventually they both made it to the top.

When they'd caught their breath, Lorelai stood to the side of the cordoned-off road and looked down at the car below. The rescue cables were in place to hold the car steady, to ensure it didn't slip any further, especially with Honey now inside the vehicle, doing her best to help John. Everyone was working hard, doing whatever they could to try and save John.

Woody's walkie-talkie crackled and hissed again in his pocket and a moment later Honey's clear tones came through.

'BJ?' Honey said, and a moment later Lorelai's father's voice crackled back.

'Honey?'

'Time of death…' Honey paused. 'Fifteen thirty-seven.'

Another moment of silence. 'Copy that,' BJ replied.

Woody looked at Lorelai but the expression on her face didn't change. 'Lorelai. I'm so sorry.' He put his arm around her shoulders. She didn't shrug him away, she didn't turn and face him, she just stopped and stared down at the car below.

Woody stood beside her, watching as all the workers stopped at Honey's news, just for a moment, out of respect. Then work started again but this time there was no need to rush. They weren't working against the clock any more.

'Goodbye, John.'

CHAPTER ONE

'Mummy! I finished.'

Hannah's words penetrated Lorelai's thoughts but not enough to make her move. Instead, she stood before her bathroom mirror, looking unseeingly at her reflection. For the first time ever she didn't want to go to work. If she'd been working at a large hospital, she could quite easily have called in sick and no one would have been any the wiser that she wasn't really sick at all.

However, she was a partner in the small GP practice in the small sub-alpine town of Oodnaminaby and any attempt to 'chuck a sickie' would result in over half the town knocking on her door to check she was all right and the other half cooking her a meal and offering to help in any way possible. It was what she loved most about her home town, the deeply caring nature the local residents had for each other—but on days like this, when she had to face something that seemed impossible, she wished for anonymity.

'It's not fair,' she told her reflection as she snapped out of her reverie and pulled the brush through her blonde locks. She didn't have the mental strength to cope with seeing her new locum again.

Woody Moon-Pie, just over three years ago, had been a shining light, guiding her through the darkest day of her life. She'd been feeling so flat, so useless after being carelessly discarded by her husband John. And not only had Woody provided medical support at the crash site but afterwards he'd made sure she and her daughter were well cared for.

He'd shown her support and compassion. He'd made her feel as though she was still a person of worth. He'd driven her home, reunited her with her daughter and then made sure she was safe throughout the evening. All she'd needed had been an anchor, someone to cling to during those first few horrific hours when her life had dramatically changed.

Woody had been attentive and kind, helping to restore her faith in the opposite sex, to let her see there were good men out there, men who weren't deceptive and negative. When she'd been at the darkest point in her life, Woody had shared his light with her and the memory of that night had made an enormous difference to her mental and emotional recovery.

It was why she'd often found herself thinking about him, wondering where he was, what he was doing and sometimes even dreaming about him.

The Woody of her dreams was every inch the hero, riding into town on his white horse, scooping her up into his arms and asking her where she had been all his life. It was a fantasy—nothing more—which was why she was incredibly embarrassed at the thought of facing the *real* Woody in just under half an hour.

The fact that Woody was starting work at the Oodnaminaby Family Medical Practice today was most definitely the reason why she'd been thinking about him a lot lately. While she kept telling herself that he meant nothing to her, that he was simply the brother of her best friend, who had played the part of knight in shining armour for one evening, she couldn't help the nervous apprehension she was feeling, knowing she'd be seeing him soon.

She was sure that during the past three years Woody hadn't even given her a second thought. Even the reason Woody was in Oodnaminaby wasn't anything to do with her. His sister, Honey, was five months pregnant and wanted to take a few months off work so she and her husband, Edward, could do some travelling before the birth of their baby. Woody had volunteered to come help out at the clinic for as long as was necessary and Lorelai was the one left to deal with the handsome surgeon.

'Mummy?' Hannah's voice rang out, tinged with a hint of impatience. When you were three and one quarter, you tended not to have a lot of patience.

'Coming,' Lorelai called back, and went to help her daughter off the toilet. 'I don't think it's fair that I have to put up with the stress of toilet training as well as dealing with Woody's enigmatic presence,' she grumbled to herself as she sorted Hannah out. Hannah's reply was to promptly put her arms around her mother's neck and press a big sloppy kiss to her cheek.

'I love you oodles and squoodles, Mummy,' Hannah remarked, before going to wash her hands. Lorelai stood for a moment, shaking her head in wonderment, a bright smile on her face.

'You always know the perfect thing to say to help Mummy,' she told her daughter. It didn't matter what the day would bring, she had Hannah, and therefore, everything else was immaterial.

* * *

'Is that coffee I smell?' Woody walked into his sister's kitchen, snagging a piece of toast that had just popped up.

'Hey. That was mine,' Honeysuckle Goldmark protested, and rubbed her pregnant belly. 'Think of your unborn niece or nephew. How could you? Mean uncle.'

Woody chuckled as he buttered the toast, accepting the cup of coffee his sister handed him. 'I promise to never steal food from your child—once he or she is born,' Woody promised. 'However, *your* food, big sister, is fair game.'

Honey swatted at him with a tea-towel but he quickly shifted out the way. 'Rotter,' she said.

'Are you teasing my pregnant wife?' Edward asked as he came in through the back door in his stockinged feet, his shoes left just outside the door. He undid his coat and took it off, hanging it over the back of a chair.

'No. I'm teasing my pregnant sister,' Woody returned, watching as his brother-in-law instantly crossed to Honey's side and kissed her on the lips before bending down and kissing her swollen abdomen. He couldn't be happier for his sister and to see her glowing with joy, it gave him hope. Maybe one day… Woody shook his head, stopping his thoughts from travelling in that particular direction. 'So, how's the weather this morning? Any snowfall overnight?'

'Only a light sprinkling,' Edward replied, wrapping his arms about his wife. 'It's more slushy out there now.'

'You two drive carefully,' Woody said, his tone holding a slight warning.

'And you be nice to Lorelai,' Honey retorted.

'What? Me? I'm always nice to everyone I meet, especially Lorelai. We really connected last time I was in town.' Perhaps a little too well, but he wasn't about to tell his sister that. Confessing something like that to Honey would only make her ask a lot of questions he was nowhere near ready to answer.

'The last time you were in town was possibly the worst time of her life.'

'And I was thoughtful and sensitive and supportive,' he pointed out.

'But you left without saying goodbye.' Edward's tone held no hint of teasing, his words soft and filled with meaning. Woody knew that although they weren't blood relations, Edward and his brothers looked upon Lorelai as the sister they'd never had. As such, they were all highly protective of her. 'She was upset about that.'

Woody tried to shrug his shoulders in a nonchalant way but didn't quite pull it off. Lorelai had been upset he hadn't said goodbye? But why? He knew he didn't mean anything to her and he'd also thought that after the horror she'd been through in facing her husband's death, the last person she'd want to have hanging around was the one who'd seen her at her worst—namely him.

'I was called back to Tarparnii so I thought it best to leave straight away.' He took another bite of his toast.

'Hmm.' Honey shook her head, watching him closely. 'So you've told me before but I can't help thinking there's more to it than that.' She sipped her herbal tea, glancing at the clock. 'Oh, help. Is that the time?' She put her cup down. 'We'd best get going,' she told Edward. 'Right after I go to the loo. The baby's jumping on my bladder.'

'Again?' Edward said with a smile on his face, as his wife quickly kissed her brother goodbye and then rushed from the room.

'I'd best be heading off, too. Don't want to be late for my first day on the job.' He finished his toast and coffee before stacking his dishes in the dishwasher. 'Have to keep in Lorelai's good books.'

'Yes, you do.' There was a protective tone in Edward's voice. 'Lore finally has her life back on track. The past three years haven't been easy but she's strong.'

'She always has been. Any doctor who can push aside personal feelings to provide emergency medical care to the woman who stole her husband is a permanent heroine in my books.' With a final nod towards his brother-in-law, Woody headed to the closet to collect his coat, scarf and gloves. 'Travel safe and stay in touch.'

'Will do,' Edward said with a wave.

As Woody stepped outside, the briskness of the morning surrounded him as he breathed in the cool air. After being acclimatised to the Tarparniian humidity, winter was something of a novelty. He blew steam with his mouth. 'Excellent.'

Just over three years ago when he'd arrived in Oodnaminaby for a one-week holiday with his sister—and to check out the man who had stolen his sister's heart—Woody had become quite familiar with the small sub-alpine town.

Back then it had been summer and he'd walked most of these streets before, having been invited out to dinner almost every night of his visit. When Honey and Edward had gone out of town for a few days, he'd filled in at the clinic and now he walked the same route towards the building situated in the small block of shops that was the hub of the town.

It was a lovely town and a place where he'd instantly felt at home. That had been odd for him given for the past few years he hadn't even called Australia home. His work had taken him to the pacific island nation of Tarparnii where he'd ended up staying far longer than he'd initially planned.

But that was long ago—another lifetime ago—and even though it had been almost four years since tragedy had struck his life, he was still finding it difficult to move forward. Being back in Oodnaminaby, filling in for Edward and Honey once more, was the diversion he'd been looking for. The only concern that had made him hesitate marginally when Honey had first asked him to locum for them had been Lorelai.

The last time he'd been in town there had been a strange sort of connection between them. He couldn't explain it and he certainly didn't understand it but often, during the past three years, when his world had, at times, seemed impossible to navigate, he'd thought of Lorelai. Her strength, her resolve, the way she'd slightly lift her chin, defiance in her baby-blue eyes. She had real gumption, something he'd always admired about her.

On a whim, he veered off course and headed down the street where Lorelai lived, secretly hoping he'd bump into her. He had no idea what time she left for the clinic, no idea where Hannah stayed whilst her mother was at work, no idea whether there was someone new in her life.

Over the years, whenever his sister had mentioned anything to do with Lorelai and Hannah, Woody had been attentive to every detail. However, he couldn't recall Honey mentioning a man in Lorelai's life. Why that should lighten his heart, he had no idea. He'd tried a deep, lasting relationship once before and it had ended in tragedy. He wasn't looking to go down that track again any time soon.

Still, there was no denying he felt something for Lorelai and he wasn't exactly sure why. However, he was in no position to follow through on any attraction he might feel for her. He had responsibilities elsewhere, people depending on him for their very survival, and it wasn't fair for him to ask any woman to endure that.

'Tum on, Mummy.'

Woody looked towards the sound of the cute little voice, watching as a little girl of about three came to the edge of the footpath and even though there were no cars out on this brisk morning, she stopped at the kerb and waited.

It was Hannah. Although he hadn't seen the child since she was a wee babe, the resemblance to her beautiful mother was unmistakeable, even though she was bundled up in her winter woollies. What a good girl she was, waiting for her mother. He could see she was wearing a pink coat, a purple and red scarf with matching gloves and beanie with little blonde curls peeking out between the collar of the coat and the edge of the beanie. He slowed his pace, watching intently as he drew closer to Lorelai's house.

'We be late for Tonnie's,' the child persisted, and for a moment Woody thought she might stamp her little foot with impatience. A smile lit his eyes at the defiance. Of course Lorelai's daughter would have as much strength, confidence and tenacity as her mother.

'I'm coming.'

At the sound of Lorelai's voice, Woody was surprised at the thrill of anticipation coursing through him. A moment later he heard a front door close. He held his breath, waiting, waiting for that first glimpse. A fraction of a second passed before he caught sight of the one woman who had often given him pause. He slowly exhaled as he watched her walk towards her daughter, his steps slowing down even further. She had her arms full, her coat all bunched up around her neck as though she hadn't yet found a second to settle the collar. A large handbag hung off one arm, the other held a purple and pink backpack, a red scarf and a set of keys.

Her blonde hair was loose, tumbling around her face but shining golden in the winter sun. It was shorter now than it had been the last time he'd seen her, the cool breeze teasing the ends as she helped Hannah to put on her backpack. Then she stood and started adjusting her coat collar, righting herself before looping the scarf around her neck and hefting her bag onto her shoulder.

It was only then she turned and saw him.

Woody's smile was instant and he was amazed that after all this time it didn't seem as though Lorelai had aged a single second. She still looked incredibly beautiful, even more so if that was at all possible. For one brief second his throat became thick with longing, his body filled with excitement at the vision of loveliness before him. He quickly squashed it and cleared his throat.

'Top of the mornin' to ya.' Woody brought his hand to his forehead in a loose salute, which ended in a wave. His smile was bright and welcoming, his eyes fixed on hers.

'Woody!' She couldn't help the blush that tinged her cheeks at seeing him again. The last time she'd seen him she'd been a mess, physically and emotionally. His bright smile also had the added effect of elevating her heart rate. She ignored it. Woody was here to help out, to work. He was a colleague. Nothing more. 'Hi.'

'Hi, yourself.' He grinned brightly, his teeth almost as white as the snow that had fallen last night. 'On your way to the clinic?'

'Er…yes, but…um, I have to drop Hannah at a friend's place first.'

'Hannah?' Woody opened his eyes wide as he came to stand beside them on the footpath. 'Good heavens.' He immediately crouched down so he was closer to Hannah's height. 'This can't possibly be baby Hannah. She's grown up so fast and she's three times as beautiful now as she was back then.'

'I *am* Hannah.' The little girl nodded enthusiastically and held up three fingers. 'I'm free and a quarter.'

'Wow. Three *and* a quarter. What a big girl you are.'

Hannah nodded again and Lorelai could see her daughter was quickly smitten with the man before her.

'Well, Hannah, my name is Woody.' He held out his gloved hand to her and with all the flourish of royalty Hannah placed her hand in his. Woody dutifully raised her gloved hand to his lips and kissed it. Hannah giggled at the gesture.

'You funny, Woody.'

'Thank you.' He glanced up at Lorelai. 'I do try to please my audience.' He was rewarded with one of Lorelai's dazzling, mind-blowing smiles for his efforts.

'I saw a photo of you,' Hannah told him, eager to keep his attention on her.

'Really? Where?'

'Aunty Honey showed me.'

'Ah. Of course she did.'

'You her little bruvver.' Hannah studied him for a

moment. 'But how come you so big, then? You bigger than Aunty Honey.'

Woody chuckled. 'That's right. I am her little big brother. Sometimes boys grow bigger than girls but Aunty Honey is much, much, *much* older than me.'

'By three years,' Lorelai announced, and shook her head. 'If Honey were here, she'd no doubt punch you in the arm.'

Woody stood and angled his shoulder towards her, pleased that his first meeting with Lorelai seemed to be progressing quite smoothly. 'You'd better do the honours, for Honey's sake if nothing else.'

Lorelai smiled and shook her head. 'Still the joker.' Even as she said the words she knew that was only one part of his personality she'd been enamoured with last time they'd met. Through the circumstances of her husband's death Lorelai had been privileged to witness a deeper, more personal side to Woody. However, it would do her well to forget about it and treat Woody as she treated all her surrogate brothers. Pretending he was just another member of the Goldmark clan should do well in controlling any frisson of awareness she might experience in his presence.

'We not allowed to hit people,' Hannah pointed out, and Woody instantly sobered and nodded.

'Quite right, too. I can see you're just as smart as your mother and every bit as lovely.' He glanced at Lorelai as he spoke, his gaze lingering on her for only a second but it was enough to reignite the slow burn Lorelai had been trying to douse all morning. She thought her knees might actually give way if he kept looking at her any longer and tried frantically to get her brain in gear.

'Uh…we need to keep going or we'll be late,' she

quickly interjected, needing to move, to shift, to do anything in order to put a bit of distance between herself and Woody.

'Late? This is Oodnaminaby, Lorelai. The place takes only fifteen minutes to walk around—and that's the circumference of the town! I know, I timed it last time I was here.' He smiled as he straightened up. 'I think you'll be fine.'

'We going to Tonnie's,' Hannah told him with a nod, before shaking her head. 'We tarn't be late.'

'Oh! Well, in that case, you're going to need a magic carpet to ride on.' Hannah's big blue eyes widened at Woody's words, as did her mother's.

'A what?' Lorelai asked, stunned and amazed at the way Hannah felt completely comfortable with Woody. Even though Woody had indeed known Hannah since she was a baby and even though he was Honey's brother, which brought with it a certain level of trust, Hannah had always been very cautious around strangers.

Woody laughed, then quickly bent down and scooped Hannah, backpack and all, off her feet and onto his shoulders. The little girl squealed with delight and clapped her hands before spreading her arms out wide. 'A magic carpet. Which way shall we fly today?' he asked, holding firmly to Hannah's legs before heading off down the street, leaving Lorelai to stare in stunned disbelief.

She watched as her daughter pretended to fly the 'magic carpet', the little girl no stranger to shoulder rides as Uncle Edward and grandpa BJ often gave her rides, teaching her how to balance properly without the need to clutch their heads.

As she followed them down the street, Lorelai wondered if Woody had chosen to walk down her street on purpose. There was a more direct route from Honey's and Edward's home to the clinic yet for some reason he'd walked down *her* street. Deep down she wondered whether he'd come this way in the hope that he might bump into her.

Ridiculous. She shook her head, pushing away the fanciful thought. Men like Woody Moon-Pie didn't fawn over women like her. He was a man of the world, always travelling, always heading off on a new adventure, while she was happy here, at her home, with her daughter.

Apart from when Woody had been here last, he hadn't been back to Oodnaminaby. He had kept in close contact with his sister, though, and Honey would often share the news with Lorelai.

'Woody's over in Afghanistan,' or, 'Woody's just returned from Japan,' or, 'Woody sent a postcard from Mozambique,' Honey would often announce. Sometimes there would be great stories to tell, especially of his escapades in Tarparnii—a place where he seemed to spend at least six months of the year—and Honey's eyes would be so alive with happiness that Lorelai found herself drawn in, wanting to hear about Woody's latest news. 'He called last night and told me about the most amazing thing that happened to him.' Then Honey would relate stories so wild and crazy and scary and downright funny that Lorelai was either gasping in shock or clutching her sides with laughter.

Woody was undoubtedly the most daring, exciting and incredibly sexy man Lorelai had ever met…and he'd seen her at her worst. Whenever she reflected on that night, she remembered it had been difficult for her to cry, difficult to think of what her future might hold, difficult to believe what was really happening. She'd felt incredibly numb, her mouth dry, her limbs heavy.

He'd helped her, there was no doubt about that. He'd been supportive, that wasn't in question either. He'd restored her faith in the opposite sex merely by being thoughtful and considerate but that was who he was. She was nothing special to him—just another person he'd helped through a terrible time.

Even when Honey had related stories about Woody's escapades, such as when he'd been part of the medical team to assist in the aftermath of a tsunami, and he'd carried two young children on his back whilst helping their mother to navigate the waist-deep waters…or when Honey had told her about Woody spending the night in a cave, keeping a badly injured teenage boy company while the rescue crews had figured out the safest way to extract their patient.

He was clearly good at all the knight-in-shining-armour stuff and was able to polish his breastplate quite often, going to different countries and helping out where needed. It meant she was nothing special to him, nothing more than one of his sister's closest friends, and anything else she might have read into that night, so long ago, was irrelevant to him working here now.

That point had been made abundantly clear to her when she'd woken, the morning after John's death, to find Woody had left. She'd heard Honey's voice coming from the kitchen so knew she wasn't alone in the house but when she'd enquired after Woody, Honey had told her that he'd had to leave.

It had taken Lorelai a while to realise he hadn't just left her house to go and shower and refresh himself, as she'd initially thought, but instead he'd left Oodnaminaby. That's when shame and embarrassment had zipped through her. Up until then, she'd thought they'd found some sort of connection, that in caring for her and Hannah, Woody had felt something deeper. With a thud she'd realised he'd just been doing his job and that she'd fallen victim to a reverse Florence Nightingale effect.

Woody had gone…returned to his life and hadn't been back in Oodnaminaby since… Until now.

Lorelai shook her head. She'd been foolish back then but she wouldn't be foolish now, not when she had Hannah to think about. Woody continued down the street, his steps sure and steadfast as he gave Hannah her magic carpet ride to Connie's house. Lorelai could hear Hannah chattering away, her sweet voice carrying easily through the crisp July morning.

It was one thing for Lorelai to be all silly, remembering the effects of Woody's natural charm, but it was quite another for him to use his charm on Hannah.

Allowing her daughter to form an attachment to the man who had no home, who was a drifter, who she doubted would ever want to settle down in one place for the rest of his life, would be disastrous.

Lorelai had made big mistakes in the romance department once before. Her marriage to John, she'd realised years later, had been nothing but a farce. He'd wanted a woman who was self-sufficient, who earned enough money for him to leech off and who lived close to his one true love—the snowfields. Skiing had been John's favourite thing to do and during winter he'd refused to work at his job as a demolition expert, preferring to live off the joint bank account Lorelai had set up when they'd married. She'd been fortunate that he hadn't had access to all her accounts, otherwise he would have left her with nothing.

During the past three years since his death, she'd come to realise what she'd been looking for had been stability, someone who would always be there for her and Hannah to rely on. Quite simply, with the way Woody had left three years ago and the way he seemed to travel the world, Lorelai knew he was the last person she should ever consider in a romantic light.

'He's just another brother type. That's all. Nothing special about him whatsoever.'

Yet even as she followed Woody and Hannah down the street, she knew she was fooling no one.

CHAPTER TWO

'Oh, he's just as lovely as I remember,' Ginny told Lorelai when the two of them met up in the kitchenette, the receptionist's cheeks tinged with pink as she spoke. 'And I think he's even more handsome than when he was here last time. Don't you think?'

'Uh…yes.' The last thing Lorelai wanted to do was to arouse any suspicions that she'd indulged in a bit of hero-worship where Woody was concerned, so thought it best simply to agree with Ginny, finish making her tea and head back to her consulting room. Just as she stepped into the corridor, she saw Woody come out from his room with Mrs Peterson in tow. He chatted patiently with the blushing seventy-three-year-old as she slowly manoeuvred her walking frame towards the waiting-room area.

'You're so right, young man. I *do* need to be looking after myself more. I'll look forward to your home visits and I promise to faithfully do my leg exercises. You'll see a big improvement when you come in three days' time.' Mrs Peterson nodded. 'Just you wait and see.'

Woody smiled at her. 'I'm looking forward to it as well.' He stopped by the empty reception desk as though only then realising Ginny wasn't there. 'Oh. Just a moment, Mrs Peterson. I'll see if I can loca—' He stopped as Ginny almost came sprinting down the corridor.

'I'm here. I'm here,' she called, having pushed past Lorelai so quickly Lorelai thought *Ginny* might break her hip. The receptionist had been a motherly figure to Lorelai for most of her life and it was odd to see her so flustered around Woody and his hypnotic good looks.

Not only did his handsome face set the female population of Ood a-twitter but his charming manner and easy humour had the ability to cause cheeks to flush and hearts to thump a bit faster. He would hold doors for his patients, helping them to their seats. He would make direct eye contact with them, listening intently to all they had to say. He would answer all questions quite patiently and provide answers that were couched in layman's terms so that people clearly understood what was happening.

Lorelai could quite see why every female in the town was flustered in his presence. Even *she*'d had trouble keeping herself under control during the past week since he'd arrived in town. Hannah had taken an instant shine to him, something that had caused Lorelai more than a moment of concern. Woody was only scheduled to be in town until Honey and Edward returned—whenever that might be. After their return, she had no doubt he'd pull his disappearing act again, heading off to goodness only knew where without a word of farewell to anyone.

That's what he'd done three years ago and even now Lorelai was surprised at how hurt she'd felt. Back then, with her state of mind being in total disarray, she'd thought she'd done something wrong to make Woody leave the way he had.

Now, having had years to think about it, she knew

his leaving had had nothing to do with her. She'd also realised what she'd felt for him that night had been nothing but gratitude. He'd stayed with her and Hannah, making sure they were safe during her darkest hours. For that she truly was grateful but that didn't mean she was going to let her daughter become so attached to Woody during this visit that she'd be heart-broken when he left.

'Almost ready to go?' Woody leaned against the wall in the corridor, facing Lorelai. 'Hello?' He waved a hand in front of her face. 'Lore? Are you in there?'

Lorelai moved her head back, only then realising she was still standing in the doorway of the kitchenette and he wasn't in the reception area any more but instead was right before her. 'Sorry,' she murmured, looking down at the tea in her mug, slightly embarrassed at being caught daydreaming. She searched her thoughts, trying to figure out what he'd asked her. 'Ah…house calls. That's right. I need to show you the ropes. Yes, I'll be ready in about ten minutes.' She sipped at her tea and then headed towards her consulting room. 'Just need to finalise things from today's clinic, grab the house-call files from Ginny and pack the medical bag.'

'I can do the last two. You get all caught up on your consulting notes and then we'll head off. I presume we're taking your car because it already knows the way?'

'Knows the way?'

'To where we're going.' Woody shook his head. 'Catch up, Lorelai.' Then, with a wink, he headed back out to Reception, no doubt to fluster Ginny further.

With a look he could set Lorelai's heart racing. With a wink he could make her knees turn to mush. With the sound of his deep laughter reverberating in her ears, he could make her entire body tingle with delight—*and* he was considerate. Lorelai wasn't sure just how she was supposed to keep her thoughts under control when her body was clearly reacting to him.

'Just another brother. He's just another brother,' she repeated as she headed into her clinic room. It was OK to think your brother was handsome, wasn't it? She certainly thought of the Goldmark boys as handsome but not her type. She could think of Woody in exactly the same, familial way.

Yet as she sat down to write up her notes, she found her thoughts returning to the way Woody smiled, the way he winked and the way he set her insides alight in a way that made her feel *anything* but sisterly towards him.

Half an hour later, after Lorelai had shown Woody the best way to attach the snow chains to the tyres of her car, they made their way towards Pleasing Valley, which was a small village not too far away from the snowfields but situated below the snowline. 'I'm sure I went to Pleasing Valley three years ago and it didn't take this long,' Woody commented after they'd been in the car for well over an hour.

'It's winter now. Everything takes twice as long as it does in summer. We can't get to Pleasing Valley through the hills. We have to go through Jindabyne and then head out.'

'I thought Honey said the Oodnaminaby practice usually shared house-call rotas with the doctors in Jindabyne, especially during the winter months?'

'We do. We combine with Jindabyne and Corryong

practices during winter as the influx in tourists and day-travellers to and from the snowfields tends to make things a little crazier than usual. With the extra patients, it can make it not only difficult to finish clinics on time but also to do house calls, and with an ever-increasing elderly population in these districts, we doctors need to be vigilant in our care for them. So we share the house-call roster and this week it's our turn.'

'What about if one of your patients contacts you and it's not your week?'

'Fair question. It's all circumstantial. You need to take into consideration who the patient is and whether or not it's better for them to see you rather than a different doctor. The weather is a big factor—is it snowing, raining, slushing? What's the medical complaint? Can it wait or is it urgent? And it also depends on what our own workload is like. Take today, for example. Afternoon clinic all finished by four o'clock. If there are any emergencies while we're doing these house calls, Ginny will send the patients to Tumut hospital, which, as you know, is about half an hour from Ood.'

'And Tumut's the closest hospital?'

'To us. There's a bigger hospital in Cooma and one in Corryong too but for the most part our patients either go to Tumut or, in very bad cases, are airlifted to Canberra. Tumut hospital mainly handles obstetrics, A and E and a few elective lists.' She was glad her vehicle was four-wheel-drive and switched on the windscreen wipers as snow began to fall.

'So there are no permanent surgical consultants there? Residents?'

'Not on a regular daily basis, no.' Lorelai glanced over at him. 'Why so many questions?'

Woody shrugged. 'Just trying to get a feel for the area. Goodness knows how long Honey and Edward will be away.' There was a hint of teasing humour in his words. 'You might be stuck with me far longer than you originally thought.' He chuckled, the rich sound washing over her. His tone was so deep and firm it almost vibrated through her, making her catch her breath.

Lorelai frowned, instantly annoyed with herself for being so receptive to him. It wasn't what she wanted. While she hoped Honey and Edward had a wonderful time on their travels, and while she knew they rightfully deserved the break given both of them worked hard in the Oodnaminaby Family Medical Practice, she couldn't help but wish them to return sooner rather than later. She focused her thoughts on driving, knowing it was safer than dwelling on the erratic way Woody seemed to affect her. He was looking out the window, almost mesmerised by the snow.

'This is glorious!' Woody remarked, and before she knew what he was doing, he'd wound down the window, put his head out and opened his mouth.

'What are you doing?' Lorelai asked, making sure she kept a clear watch on the road but glancing across at him from time to time. 'You look like a dog with your tongue hanging out like that.' To her chagrin, she couldn't help but laugh as he eventually pulled his head in and wound up the window. 'You're completely insane, Woody.'

'This is my first real time in the snow. This past week has been brilliant. I've been outside, making snow angels on the ground. I've had a snow-fight with some of the high-school kids in the town and even ran around my sister's back yard stark naked at midnight simply because I'd never before played in the snow in my birth-day suit.'

'Really?' Lorelai's eyes widened as images of Woody's tall, naked body running around in the snow in his sister's back yard came instantly to mind. The image was enough to distract her, but only for a split second. She shook her head, needing to clear her thoughts and concentrate on driving. 'You are certifiably crazy, Dr Moon-Pie.'

'Only compared to some,' he rationalised. 'Well, I've been living in hot or humid climates for most my life.'

'That's right. I remember Honey telling me the two of you were mainly raised in far north Queensland and the Northern Territory. Added to that, haven't you spent a lot of time in the jungles of Tarparnii?'

Woody paused for a moment, giving her a sideways glance. 'Honey told you about Tarparnii?' He seemed a little surprised.

'Sure. She would often tell me about your travels. She'd sit and show Hannah pictures of you in different places, or share the postcards you'd send. Everyone in the town knows about your travels.'

'My *travels*. Ah…right. Good.' He nodded and seemed to relax. 'Yes, I'm sure she's told everyone about my travels.'

'Why? What did you think she'd said?'

'Uh…nothing.' Woody shrugged but Lorelai sensed there was more to it.

'Honey's very proud of you, Woody, and after everyone in town met you, they'd always ask after you. Small towns are caring places.'

'That's what I like about them. They're like little communities. Everyone taking care of everyone else.'

'Is that what it's like in Tarparnii?'

'It is, actually.' His natural smile was back again and Lorelai wondered whether she'd imagined his moment of concern.

'How long *were* you in Tarparnii?' Her tone was filled with curiosity.

'Which time?' he asked, looking out the window. The snow had stopped falling but Lorelai still had the windscreen wipers on. Woody reached out his hand and flicked them off for her.

'How many times have you been?'

'Too many to count. The first time was almost ten years ago. I was a medical student, lending a helping hand and ready to save the world.' Woody shook his head. 'I was so green. My first day in a country in the grip of war and I had bullets whizzing past my head.'

'What? Really?'

'I kid you not. If it hadn't been for K'nai, my Tarparnese contact, I would have been dead. No more Woody-Gum Moon-Pie.' He was silent for a moment and Lorelai realised he was lost in thought. It was obvious, given the way he was highly reflective at the mention of Tarparnii, he'd undergone quite a few life-changing experiences there.

'I thought things had settled down there recently, that the fighting wasn't so bad.'

Woody nodded. 'There has been progress in the political arena and you're right, the fighting isn't so bad. That first trip was the exception, not the rule. I've never been shot at since.'

'Good to know.' Lorelai eased the car into a lower gear and started to drive down a steep descent, drawing closer to Pleasing Valley. 'I take it you have many friends there.'

'Yes. Many good and dear friends, both local and from around the world who are over there to help out. The plight of the country is becoming more well known and foreign aid is increasing, so that's good.'

'I remember seeing a documentary on Tarparnii a few years ago. It looks like a beautiful place.'

'It is. The most picturesque countryside. You'd love it, Dr Rainbow.' He smiled as they drove along. 'Do you realise,' he said a few minutes later, 'that your name is incredibly pretty? Lorelai Rainbow.'

Lorelai was a little stunned by his forthright words. 'Er…thanks.' She knew she probably shouldn't be surprised as he *was* Honey's brother and Honey was always open and honest. It stood to reason Woody would be the same.

'What's your middle name?'

'Emily. The same as Hannah's. We're both named after my mother.'

'Lorelai Emily Rainbow. Very pretty.' He angled his head to the side and watched her for a moment. Lorelai began to shift in her seat, starting to get a little uncomfortable with his gently scrutiny. 'Do you mind if I ask, why didn't you change your name when you married John?'

Lorelai blinked, taking a moment to mentally change gears. She'd been so interested in asking him questions, of hearing the love for Tarparnii in his voice, that for a second he'd thrown her when he'd mentioned John. 'Well…uh…professionally, my degree was in the name of Rainbow. I had intended to change my name, I'd even filled out the forms, but I'd never found the time to lodge them. Then I discovered I was pregnant and it was all I could do to keep up with work and morning sickness. And now, of course, it seems better that I didn't change my name.'

Woody cast her a worried glance. Great, the last thing she needed was his sympathy or concern. She really was glad she hadn't changed her name. In the end it had made things simpler.

Clearing her throat, she watched the road, keeping her tone light once more. 'Do you want to guess whether your sister is carrying a boy or a girl?'

Woody's smile instantly returned to his handsome face and Lorelai was both pleased and annoyed to feel that now familiar little fluttering of excitement in the pit of her stomach. She quickly dismissed the sensation as they started to discuss the various different old wives' tales in figuring out whether it was a boy or girl.

'Are you excited to be an uncle?' Lorelai slowed the car as she turned off the main road. They were almost at Pleasing Valley and although she knew these roads very well, it was still wise to take her time.

'I am. I intend to spoil the kid rotten, giving it lots of sweeties and loud noisy toys and then disappearing into the sunset to let my sister go quietly insane from the sugar-high, cymbal-banging toddler.'

Lorelai smiled. 'Well, please don't practise on my daughter.' She drove into the driveway of the first house and pulled on the handbrake. 'Hannah is noisy enough and spoilt by her uncles, aunts and grandfather as it is. She doesn't need any more.'

'You ruin all my fun,' he joked as she switched off the engine. Both of them climbing from the vehicle. Woody reached for the medical bag while Lorelai went to the rear of her car and took out a snow shovel. 'What are you doing?' he asked, standing there, watching her. Lorelai pointed to the mound of snow blocking the path to the house they were visiting.

'How do you expect to reach Mrs Maddison's front door? I'm not a fan of slipping on frozen snow and ice. Besides, with her recent hip replacement, Mrs Maddison can hardly do it.'

'So you not only provide elite medical care, you also work part time as a snow plough?'

'Only on patient driveways. I gave up doing main roads once I'd finished medical school,' she joked as Woody handed her the medical bag and took the snow shovel from her.

'Allow me.'

'It's OK, Woody. I'm quite capable of—'

'Shh. I'm being gallant,' he pointed out, and with that turned and shovelled the snow out the way. By the time he reached the door a few minutes later, he was nicely warm. 'Milady,' he said with a sweeping bow. 'Your patient awaits.'

Lorelai couldn't help but smile, enjoying the easy-going side of his personality. 'Why thank you, kind sir. You are most generous to have saved me from such a manual, bothersome task.'

Woody's eyes were brightened by the exercise, his cheeks tinged with pink, his lips curved into a smile revealing straight, white teeth. 'Anything for you, milady.' With that, he bowed again as Lorelai walked towards him, giggling at his silliness. She rang the doorbell and while they waited for Mrs Maddison, they both grinned goofily at each other.

Slowly their smiles started to slip as they simply

stood and stared. From the first moment she'd met Woody at a family dinner two weeks after Hannah had been born, she'd felt a tiny undercurrent of awareness towards him. Of course, back then she'd been in the throes of her own personal drama, with her husband not only refusing to have anything to do with Hannah but also wanting her to pay him far more than he deserved in their divorce. Still, when Woody had walked into her life and smiled at her for the first time, Lorelai had felt a stirring of attraction. That stirring was well and truly flowing between them right now, so many years later. What it all might mean she had absolutely no clue and wasn't even sure she wanted to find out.

At the rattling of the doorhandle, both Lorelai and Woody turned their attention to their patient on the other side. Woody was more than happy for the interruption as the way Lorelai had been looking at him made him feel highly uncomfortable. It wasn't the first time he'd experienced such a sensation when looking at his new colleague. It had happened three years ago when he'd first arrived in Oodnaminaby and been introduced to her.

She'd cradled Hannah in one arm, then held out her free hand to him as Honey had introduced them. The instant they'd touched, it was as though a spark of excitement had zipped through him and all from a simple handshake. When he'd looked down into Lorelai's face, he'd seen his own bewilderment mirrored in her reflection.

'Hello, Lorelai,' Mrs Maddison said as she opened the door, leaning on her walking frame for support. 'Oh, and, look, you've shovelled my walk. You shouldn't have worried, dear.'

'It was no trouble, Mrs Maddison,' Lorelai remarked as she headed into the lovely warm home. 'I brought a big, strapping young man along with me today. He made short work of the task.'

Mrs Maddison welcomed them into her home, Woody waiting patiently for Mrs Maddison to head back to her comfortable chair in the lounge room and watching her gait as she walked.

'How long ago did you have your hip replacement?' he asked.

'Almost eight weeks now,' she replied, and he could hear the pride in her voice. 'Aren't I walking well? Lorelai says I'm doing fabulous.'

'And you are,' Lorelai remarked as she disappeared into the kitchen. 'I'll pop the kettle on. Woody can entertain you.'

'Ooh, I'd like that,' Mrs Maddison said with a little giggle. Lorelai listened to the conversation going on in the other room as she prepared a tea-tray, finding some biscuits in the cupboard. She'd needed a bit of breathing space from Woody, especially after the look they'd just shared. She closed her eyes for a moment, unable to believe after all these years the attraction was still there, zinging between them, enticing them both to explore and to taste.

When they'd met three years ago, she'd thought it had only been her who had felt that instant tug of awareness. Then, as her life had been in turmoil, she'd locked the sensation up and put it into a secret cupboard in her mind, taking the memory out and dusting it off whenever she was struck with a sense of loneliness. Meeting Woody, experiencing that initial awareness, had boosted her ego but until just now she hadn't really known whether he truly felt it too.

Last week she'd thought her reaction to him had just been a mixture of excited nerves and past embarrassment. She'd watched him charm every woman he'd come into contact with, young and old, throughout the week. Even the men had taken to him, and she'd known that keeping her distance was the right thing to do. Professional. They would be colleagues and acquaintances and nothing more.

Until he'd looked into her eyes. Sharing that moment with him had been as though they'd both acknowledged the attraction openly. The realisation both scared and excited her. She knew Woody could be wonderful and charming and a little bit flirty but she also knew taking that flirtation seriously would only end in pain…and she'd been through enough pain. Somehow she'd have to put up barriers, to ward off the effects of his bright smiles and hypnotic eyes.

The kettle boiled, bringing her out of her reverie, and with a straight back and a firm resolve she carried the tea-tray through to the lounge room. The three of them sat around, politely drinking tea and nibbling on biscuits, before Lorelai whisked Mrs Maddison away to her room for a check-up.

Woody tidied up the dishes whilst waiting for the two women, washing the cups and saucers, drying the plates and finding out where everything went. He was looking at a photograph of Mrs Maddison when she'd been much younger, a Tarparniian man standing beside her, his arm about her small, slim shoulders, when the women walked back into the room.

'Ahh, that's my Ni'juk.' Mrs Maddison shifted her walker to come and stand beside him. She lifted a loving hand towards the frame, her frail fingers reaching out as though she desperately wanted time to rewind.

'He's Tarparniian,' Woody stated with a hint of incredulity as Lorelai sat down at the kitchen bench to write up her examination notes.

'Why, yes. Have you been to Tarparnii?' Mrs Maddison was intrigued.

'Many times. I have…' Woody stopped, a sad smile on his lips '…wonderful memories of the place.'

Lorelai stopped, pen poised as she heard a haunting wistfulness in Woody's tone. She turned to watch him.

'Ah, that sounds as though you fell in love.'

At these words Woody appeared momentarily startled but Mrs Maddison didn't notice. She was already back in the past, reminiscing.

'It was even more beautiful fifty years ago. That's when I met the man of my dreams. I was a journalist, you see, and went over there to report on that tiny country no one knew anything about. It took me three days to get there. No planes back then. Only boats. Ni'juk was my contact, my guide, and I knew as soon as he first took both my hands in his…' Mrs Maddison reached for Woody's hands and held both of his as she spoke. '…and moved them around in the little circle, which as you know is the way they greet people, I just knew… knew we would be together for ever.' Mrs Maddison sighed, a look of contentment on her tired features.

'A happy ending.' Woody's smile brightened, although Lorelai couldn't help but notice the smile didn't quite reach his eyes. She'd always known there was far

more to Woody than met the eye and here was her proof.
The question was, did she really want to find out what
lay beneath all his layers?

CHAPTER THREE

FOR the next two nights in a row, Lorelai dreamt about Woody. Every morning she'd wake up, feeling so at peace, so relaxed, and then as she lay in bed, trying to remember what she'd been dreaming about, it would all come flooding back in one great, big embarrassing rush.

In her dreams he would tenderly take her hand in his, he would caress her skin, he would smile at her in that way that instantly made her knees go weak. He'd draw her closer, brushing the backs of his fingers over her cheeks. He'd look down into her upturned face.

'Relax,' he'd whisper, then he'd press butterfly kisses to her cheeks, then her neck, giving her goose-bumps as he worked his way around to her collar bone. He'd lift his head, brush his thumb over her plump, parted lips before finally giving in to what they both wanted—and boy, oh, boy, did she want it.

'Stop it.' Lorelai opened her eyes and threw back the bed-covers, needing to be busy in order to control her wayward thoughts. Even during morning clinic she'd found herself daydreaming about what it would be like to feel his arms about her, her body pressed against his, the warmth between them building so high it was only right to let off steam.

She could no longer deny she was attracted to him. The other day when they'd stared at each other outside Mrs Maddison's house had been a clear give-away that…something was brewing between them. Of course, that didn't mean they had to act on it but even admitting to herself that she found Woody to be incredibly sexy was enough to rock her world.

Then again, acknowledging this physical desire she held towards him might be a good thing. It was all right for her to look, to appreciate the facts before her— namely that Woody Moon-Pie was an extremely handsome man. A physical attraction was something she could control. Now, if she developed *emotional* feelings towards him, well, then she'd be in real big trouble, but a physical attraction was easier to fight.

She'd been physically attracted to John and look where that marriage had ended up. She'd often wished she'd had better self-control, better judgement, better patience because if she had, perhaps her marriage to John would never have taken place. Although if it hadn't, she wouldn't have Hannah and that little girl had brought so much happiness and meaning into her life, there was no way she'd ever be without her.

Admitting she was attracted to Woody was one thing, following through on that attraction was a completely different matter and she had no intention of following through. He was in town for such a short period of time and then he'd return to his own life.

'Lore?' The door to her consulting room burst open and Ginny stood in the doorway, face flushed, tone urgent. 'Emergency. Treatment room. *Now!*'

Lorelai was up and out of her chair before the other woman had even finished talking. She rounded the desk and stalked across the room. 'Status?' She rushed towards the treatment room which was a room specifically set up to deal with emergencies such as this.

'Five-year-old boy. Not breathing. Face muscles swollen.'

'Sounds like an allergic reaction. Get Woody.' Lorelai entered the treatment room to find Woody pulling on a pair of gloves as the little boy's father placed his non-breathing child on the examination bed.

'Ritchie? I'm Woody.' He looked into the face of the terrified child as Lorelai came into the room. She grabbed a pair of gloves as Ginny ushered the parents to the side of the room, keeping them out of the way. 'This is Lorelai.' He smiled at the boy, his tone calm and controlled. 'We're going to take good care of you,' he said reassuringly.

'What happened?' Lorelai asked as both she and Woody assessed the situation, taking Ritchie's vital signs.

'Uh...we were at the club,' the father said hesitantly.

'Eating? At the Oodnaminaby tavern?' Woody confirmed.

'Y-yes.'

'He was eating his food and playing around,' the mother added. 'And...and swinging on his chair. And I...I got cross with him and, oh...oh...' She broke down and started to cry.

'What was he eating?' Woody asked, and glanced across at Lorelai, their gazes meeting for one split second, but during that brief moment it was clear they were both on the same page, their hands working completely in sync as they assessed and made judgements.

Woody was reaching for equipment just as it was on the tip of Lorelai's tongue to suggest it.

'We thought he was…choking…' the father continued as he consoled his wife.

'Not choking,' Lorelai supplied.

'Allergic reaction,' Woody finished.

'Angio-oedema around the mouth, pulse is dropping, bronchioles narrowing,' Lorelai continued. 'What was he eating?' She glanced over at the parents, the father blinking a few times as though trying to remember.

'Uh…nothing new. He had um…pasta with, uh… cheese. It came in a creamy sauce and he really liked it but he's eaten that sort of thing at home tons of times and this has *never* happened befo—'

'Did you order the adult portion? Not the pasta from the children's menu?' Lorelai asked.

The father frowned. 'Uh…yeah. How did you know?'

Woody already had the EpiPen in his hand, ready to administer the subcutaneous dose of adrenaline that would relieve the immediate threat of Ritchie going into anaphylactic shock.

'My guess is nuts. Spiros, he's the chef at the tavern, puts pine-nuts in the adult serving of creamy pasta. It's not in any of the children's menus.' She directed her comments to Woody but then glanced at the parents once more. 'Is Ritchie allergic to nuts?'

Woody administered the dose and within a matter of seconds the swelling surrounding Ritchie's airways started to decrease and he was no longer gasping for air.

The mother frowned. 'Not that we know. He doesn't usually eat much. Just pasta with cheese and breakfast cereal. We've taken him to a few nutritionists and they say that—'

'So he's never had anything nutty before?'

'Uh…no. Not that I know.' The mother's tone broke on her last few words and she started to sob against her husband's chest.

'Ginny, call the—'

'On it,' Ginny replied, and pulled her mobile phone from her pocket, calling to Tumut for an ambulance, knowing the practice's emergency procedures back to front.

'We want Ritchie to spend the night in Tumut hospital. It's just a precaution as he needs to be monitored for the next twenty-four hours,' Lorelai continued.

'Hospital? But we…we're supposed to be having ski lessons tomorrow,' the father said, and Lorelai felt her shackles begin to rise at the comment.

'Ski lessons?' Her tone was filled with stunned amazement. She looked at Woody and was surprised when she saw complete compassion for the parents reflected in his eyes. They also seemed to be calming *her* down and where she'd been about to deliver her speech about parents who didn't put the health of their children above their holiday activities, she stopped. Woody gave her a small smile before facing the parents.

'I'm sure if you call the place where you've booked your lessons, they'll be able to accommodate your change in plans. It's certainly a very stressful time for a parent, seeing their children like this…' He pointed to where Lorelai had covered Ritchie with a blanket in order to keep him warm and was hooking her stethoscope into her ears in order to check his breathing.

'Is this the first vacation you've had in a while?' he

asked Ritchie's father, who nodded mutely. 'Then congratulations on finding the time to head off on holidays with your family. Sometimes it's not easy to leave the office.'

'No.'

'When did you arrive in the district?'

'Last night.'

'Where have you travelled from?'

'Melbourne.'

Woody smiled. 'That's a lovely city.'

As he continued to speak to the parents, reassuring them and putting them at ease, Lorelai continued to monitor Ritchie, who was responding exceptionally well to the treatment. As Woody talked, she listened to that deep, soothing tone of his, relaxing and charming both mother and father so that when the ambulance arrived from Tumut, the entire family not only understood what was going to happen throughout the next twenty-four hours but somehow seemed closer as a family.

'How did you do that?' Lorelai asked as they stood outside the clinic, watching as the ambulance pulled away. Ritchie and his mother were safely ensconced in the ambulance, his father following behind in the car. The paramedics had turned the siren on for Ritchie's amusement as they drove away from town but had told him that as this wasn't an emergency transfer, they'd have to turn off the lights and siren when they reached the main road. Ritchie was more than happy with that.

'Do what?' Woody asked as he spread his arms wide and breathed in the fresh, crisp, wintry air, enjoying himself. They were at the bottom of the steps that led up to a colonnade where the small row of five businesses was situated—a doctor's surgery, a general store, a take-away, a post-office with banking facilities and a ski-hire and tackle shop. It was the hub of the bustling town that was Oodnaminaby, and Woody liked it. His sister had told him years ago that the town was a lovely place to live and he had to admit that being back here had felt akin to coming home.

It was an odd sensation given he'd never really had a proper home throughout his life. He looked at Lorelai, wondering what she was talking about, admiring the way the pale pink jumper she wore highlighted the blueness of her eyes. Her blonde hair was pulled back low on her neck with a rhinestone clip and he had to admit there was a certain classic style to her that was drawing him in. She was an incredibly beautiful woman and ever since he'd been back in town he'd found himself wanting to spend more time with her, wanting to get to know not only her but her daughter much better. For a man who usually tried to keep to the fringes of the places he worked at, it was a new and confusing sensation.

'Put people at ease so…easily.' She laughed as she tripped over her own words, the sound washing over him with delight. 'It doesn't matter whether it's a young child or a senior citizen, you seem to look right into their souls and you're able to relax them with a simple smile.' She shook her head.

Woody shrugged. 'I'm not sure I know what you're talking about. I'm just me.'

Lorelai rubbed her arms, pleased she'd worn her cashmere jumper and trousers today. It was silly to stand out in the wintry weather but for a moment she didn't feel like going back inside, even though there were patients waiting for both of them.

'You are, aren't you? Just you. Mr Relaxed. Mr Calm. Mr Easy Come, Easy Go.'

Woody's brow puckered for a moment but he smiled. 'I'm still not sure what you're talking about but I think it's a compliment so I'm going to say—thank you, Lore.'

Lorelai couldn't help the gasp that escaped her lips as they stood there in the cold, simply looking at each other. Woody's smile touched his eyes, making them twinkle. It was the way she'd dreamed about him looking at her, the exact image she'd been able to clearly recall that very morning. Of course, in her dream he'd stepped forward and reached for her hand before tugging her close and bringing his mouth agonisingly slowly to meet her own.

She licked her lips and swallowed over the sudden dryness in her throat. Woody's gaze flicked to encompass the action and she watched as the twinkle began to dim from his blue eyes, to be replaced with the hint of repressed desire. The atmosphere around them began to thicken and for a brief moment it was as though they were caught in their own little bubble in time.

The cold was forgotten. The patients inside the waiting room were forgotten. Nothing mattered except the way they made each other feel. It was odd and thrilling and strange and exciting all at the same time.

He breathed out, slowly and a little unsteadily, as though he was trying to hang onto his control. Part of her wanted him to let go, to unleash the tension she could feel emanating from him, to disregard their self-control and see where this moment might take them. The other part of her—the sane part—wanted to turn and run away, to put as much distance between herself and this man who was starting to really infiltrate her life.

Woody swallowed and her gaze followed the action before flicking to his eyes and then to his lips. Her heart was already starting to hammer wildly against her chest but when he took the smallest step towards her, it picked up its already frantic pace. Lorelai kept her gaze trained on his, her eyes wide as he tenderly reached for her hand. The touch of his warm skin on her cooling fingertips flooded her body with the sweetest tingles. She licked her lips again, unable to believe the same scene she'd dreamed about last night was actually playing out for real. If things continued on this path, it would mean that very soon Woody's lips would be pressed against hers. Was that what she wanted? She wasn't sure because right at this moment she didn't seem capable of coherent thought.

'Lore?'

As she continued to look into his eyes, she could see the same confusion and deep attraction she was also experiencing. It was the same way she'd felt when she'd first been introduced to him all those years ago and since that moment she'd felt this way towards him on several occasions. No wonder it was becoming increasingly difficult for her to control her thoughts and dreams where he was concerned. When he looked at her like this, as though she were the most beautiful, most intelligent, most cherished woman on the face of this earth, she had no idea how to respond.

As he rubbed his warm thumb and fingers over hers, her breathlessness seemed to increase. She licked her lips again and shook her head ever so slightly. 'Woody, I don't…' She couldn't finish the sentence as he edged even closer, the warmth from his body now surrounding her as the cool air puffed from her mouth, their little steam clouds mixing and blending in the air.

The tinkling of the bell above the practice door broke through their bubble, popping it instantly.

'There you two are.' Ginny called from the top of the steps. The instant they heard her voice, both of them stepped back, the moment dissipating along with the coolness from their breath. 'What are you doing out here?'

Lorelai tore her gaze from Woody's and headed up the steps. 'Nothing. Coming in now. Gee, it really is cold out here.'

'What? You're only just realising that?' Ginny asked, raising her eyebrows with interest. Lorelai ignored the comment. 'Anyway,' Ginny continued, 'Woody, there's a phone call for you. It's Pacific Medical Aid.'

Woody headed up the steps after Lorelai, a deep frown creasing his brow. He straightened his shoulders, as though a little uncomfortable, before pulling his mobile phone from his pocket and checking the display. Five missed calls, all from PMA. 'My phone must have been out of range.'

'It happens a lot here. Just was well they knew how to track you down. I'll put the call through to your clinic room,' Ginny said as the three of them headed inside. Lorelai watched Woody closely, noting the change in his posture, a slightly defensive stance. Did calls from PMA mean he'd be leaving Oodnaminaby sooner rather than later? Whatever it was, she hoped everything was all right because he didn't look all that happy.

Lorelai picked up a set of case notes from the desk and looked at the backlog of patients waiting for her due to the emergency. 'Plency.' She smiled at her patient. 'Come on through,' she said, and waited while the mother of four gathered up her children and shepherded them and herself through to Lorelai's clinic room. As Lorelai walked past Woody's room, the consulting-room door was closed and she could hear his deep, muted tones as he spoke on the phone.

At the back of her mind was the thought he might have to leave them sooner rather than later and while she'd been almost counting down the days until Honey and Edward returned so Woody could leave and her life could return to its normal pace, the sudden thought that he might need to leave sooner filled her with a sense of deep sadness mixed with a healthy dose of regret.

Throughout the rest of the day Lorelai only caught the faintest glimpses of Woody as they caught up on their patient lists. When she did pass him in the corridor, he would smile or nod politely as he continued with his work. Lorelai scanned his face for signs of stress or concern from the call from PMA but found nothing.

After the day was done and with Ginny having to leave early, Lorelai went into the kitchenette to tidy up and switch off the urn so everything was ready for tomorrow.

'Did you manage to catch up?' Woody's deep voice startled her and a cup she was drying slipped from her hands. Juggling it a bit, she managed to catch it. 'Sorry.' He smiled sheepishly. 'Didn't mean to startle you.'

'Uh…yes. I managed to catch up on my patient list. How about you?'

'Just, but only because Mr Sommerton cancelled.'

Lorelai raised her eyebrows. 'Mr Sommerton cancelled?'

'You seem surprised.'

She shrugged and continued putting the cups away. Woody walked over to the sink, picked up the cloth and started wiping the table as they talked. It was thoughtful and useful, exactly what one of the Goldmark men would have done. She knew she'd entered her marriage with rose-coloured glasses, expecting all men to be the same as those she'd been raised with, which was why she'd received such a shock to find that deep down inside John had been nothing like the men she knew. Woody, however, was showing her that she shouldn't tar every man with the same brush as John. He was a good man, a man of principle and honour, that much was evident simply from his actions. The knowledge warmed her heart, which was exactly what she didn't want. Glancing at him now, she could still feel the tingles where he'd touched her hand earlier in the day, and combined with the dreams and the way he seemed to be infiltrating every part of her life, she'd have to be stronger with the barriers she was almost desperate to erect.

'What's wrong?' Woody asked.

'Huh?'

'You're frowning.'

'I am?' Lorelai raised a hand to her forehead to check and realised he was right. 'Oh, I...uh...was just thinking we should add Mr Sommerton to the house-call list. He's a stickler for keeping his appointments so it might be best to check there isn't anything wrong that stopped him from coming today. The Jindabyne clinic is doing house calls this week so I'll make sure to call them in the morning.'

'You really care about your patients,' he stated. 'I like that.'

'That's what this practice is about.'

He nodded. 'That's how most of the PMA staff are. They're people who don't practise medicine for the money but for how they can be of service to others.' He returned the cloth to the sink and gave the area a final wipe before walking towards the door.

Now that he'd opened the conversation, Lorelai took the opportunity to make sure there were no drastic repercussions from his earlier phone call. 'By the way, is everything OK? With PMA, I mean.' When he gave her a blank look, she continued. 'The phone call you received earlier in the day?'

A guarded look entered his eyes. 'Oh, that. Yes. Everything's...fine.'

'You don't sound too sure.'

'Everything's fine.' The words came out a little too quickly and Lorelai was startled at his reaction. She hadn't meant to pry or to make him feel uncomfortable. 'They just had some questions regarding a village in Tarparnii,' he continued after a momentary pause, as though he was collecting his thoughts, deciding what to say and what to conceal. 'There were some things that required...clarification.'

'Oh. OK, then.' She forced a smile and nodded, even though she didn't understand at all. What she *did* know was that this room was starting to feel smaller, the two of them here, after hours, the clinic empty. She would have headed out but Woody blocked the doorway with his tall frame.

'I just thought you might have been called back into the field sooner rather than later, that's all.'

'No.' He shook his head for emphasis. 'I've told everyone that I'm here until my sister has had enough of travelling. This is the last opportunity she and Edward will have to be together, to see some new sights before the baby is born, and I'm going to support her in any way I can.' There was an edge, a vehemence to his words, as though he wasn't just saying this to her but to someone else. Perhaps it was the person who had called him earlier. 'I won't be leaving you in the lurch, Lorelai.'

There it was again, the hint of angry determination, as though he needed her to believe him.

'I never thought you would.'

He straightened his shoulders and exhaled slowly. 'I'm a man of my word.'

'Understood.'

'Good.' With a brisk nod, he turned on his heel and stalked from the room, leaving her standing there wondering what on earth had just happened.

That night, as Woody made himself some dinner, Honey and Edward's large home seemed even quieter than usual. He ate his dinner in silence, took a shower and then prowled around the different rooms, looking at the photographs on the walls, the Goldmark family portraits, the pictures Honey had added when she'd married Edward almost three years ago. His sister was happy. She'd found the place where she belonged, which was great for Honey as she'd been searching for so long.

But what about him? At the moment he felt so…disjointed and he'd never felt that way before.

He looked at the picture of himself, Honey, their parents and grandparents, which sat on the bookshelf. It had been taken at Honey's wedding—his whole family. It had been a good day. Throughout his childhood he'd been able to accept his parents for who they were, largely because Honey had been the one providing him with a stable influence. When he'd finished medical school and started his surgical rotation, he'd had the stable influence of hospital hierarchy to guide him. Even when he'd headed overseas to work in Tarparnii, he'd been governed by the rules and regulations set out by Pacific Medical Aid as well as the Tarparniian culture.

He'd met a wonderful woman, he'd married her, had had a child and for a brief time his life had felt complete. Then it had all been ripped apart, taken from him in a dramatic way, and at the time he hadn't thought he'd ever be able to move forward.

Woody walked to his satchel, which he'd left by the back door when he'd arrived home. He took out his laptop and switched it on, re-reading the emails sent from his mother-in-law, Nilly, via PMA. It was the only way she was able to contact him, to send information and updates on the village he'd previously called his home.

He hadn't replied to the emails because he'd simply been looking for a bit of time out. The pressures that had been placed on his shoulders after the tragedy that had struck his life had been something he'd never expected. For four years he'd carried the burden and he'd done it willingly, not wanting to let even more people down. Then today, because he hadn't answered his emails, PMA had tracked him down at the Oodnaminaby clinic, calling him with news that he'd need to return to his village for the *par'Mach* festival.

Woody closed the lid to his laptop and shut his eyes. Leaning back in his chair, he pushed his hands through his hair. After the tragedy he'd known what was expected of him and he'd carried that burden willingly. Yet somehow things had become incredibly complicated. His life had been calm, comfortable and controlled, and now he wasn't sure which way was up.

And it was all Lorelai's fault.

If only he'd been able to say no to Honey when she'd asked him to come and locum for her while she had a bit of a holiday, but he hadn't been able to. Honey had *always* been there for him throughout his entire life and he would always appreciate that. She was his sister. He'd known before he'd even set foot in Ood that being around Lorelai would be difficult. He'd often thought about her, often thought about that night when her husband had died and he'd watched over her and Hannah with infinite care. He'd felt her pain and he'd understood her loss. Support was what she'd needed and he'd done his best to provide it, but sitting there in a chair, holding her tiny baby girl in his arms as he'd watched Lorelai sleeping, her blonde hair splayed out over the pillowcase, her pretty features relaxed and at peace, Woody had felt such a deep stirring of emotion, of attachment, of need and longing that as soon as Honey had arrived the next morning, he'd hightailed it out of town.

Perhaps he'd overreacted. Perhaps leaving town so suddenly hadn't been the right decision to make, but in admitting to himself he'd had feelings for Lorelai he'd also realised he was emotionally ready to move forward with his life. After Kalenia's death, he'd never thought he'd ever be so deeply attracted to a woman again… and then he'd met Lorelai.

Since he'd returned to Oodnaminaby, he'd realised the sensations he'd felt towards Lorelai three years ago were still alive and kicking, and given the staring competitions they'd been having lately, the way their eyes seemed to meet and hold, both of them caught in such powerful sensations, the only natural course of action was to close the distance between them and press their mouths together in total surrender.

Woody closed his eyes as he relived the moment again, staring at her and having her look back at him as though she had been on the same page. The attraction between them was clear and he wished he could let nature take its course, but he couldn't.

He wasn't a free man. His own wants and desires needed to be shelved, to be put aside in favour of protecting others. Nilly was expecting an answer and rightly so. The *par'Mach* festival was a big deal, especially for his sisters-in-law and as head of the clan, his presence was required. As head of the clan, he would do his duty. As head of the clan, he would deny himself the happiness being around Lorelai afforded him.

His life wasn't here in Ood and it would be wrong of him to lead her on. He should pull back, put some distance between himself and Lorelai even though it was the last thing he wanted to do.

CHAPTER FOUR

THE following week, Lorelai was finishing up her clinic for the day when Ginny came in with a message.

'It's Martha. She's worried about Aidan. She thought he might have had a cold but last night he started vomiting and he's also had diarrhoea. She was going to take him to Tumut hospital but now, when she tries to move him, he says he's in too much pain. Her husband's out working at the ski resort and has both sets of snow chains in his car. She wanted to know if she should call the ambulance to her place or whether you wanted to come out and see him. Also, given the snowfall they had last night, she can't get a babysitter and all her kids are home.' Ginny looked up from the piece of paper she held in her hand where she'd quickly scribbled down some notes. 'So? What do you want to do?'

Lorelai thought for a moment. 'I think it's best if I head out to take a look. There has been a lot of bad gastro going around and chances are Aidan might actually feel better by tomorrow morning. I was on the phone to Tumut hospital earlier today and they said they've had a swag of admissions and the ambulances have been really busy. They've even airlifted two cases to Wagga Wagga Base hospital for further surgical treatment and one person was sent to Canberra for surgical intervention.'

'Well, Tumut is only a small thirty-four-bed hospital with a small operating theatre and no resident surgeon. They can't be expected to deal with mass emergencies,' Ginny rationalised. 'I'll call Martha back and tell her you'll head out.'

'I think that's the best alternative. The weather report said we'll be getting more snow this evening so the sooner I leave the better.' Lorelai checked the clock as she spoke. 'I'll pick up Hannah and take her with me. She can play with Martha's brood while I see to Aidan.'

'Do you think it might be appendicitis?' Ginny asked. 'She said it doesn't matter where she presses on his stomach, he says it hurts all over.'

Lorelai thought for a moment. 'There's a high possibility it could be that.'

'In that case, why not take me with you?' A deep voice spoke from the doorway and both women turned to see Woody lounging against the doorjamb.

Lorelai's breath caught and she fumbled with the papers in her hand, dropping her prescription pad and knocking over her coffee cup. Thankfully, it was empty. She quickly righted everything, looking down at her hands, willing them to obey the commands coming from her brain. Even just one brief glance at him had her all flustered. Though there'd been no repeat of their almost kiss of the previous week, that didn't mean her dreams hadn't been filled with images of her and Woody, kissing, touching and more. She'd made a vow to avoid him. Distance was definitely the only way to go.

'I couldn't help but overhear what Ginny was saying. How old is Aidan?'

'Uh…' Lorelai's mind was blank. Details? How was she supposed to recall details when his closeness turned her mind to mush?

'He's seventeen,' Ginny provided. 'He's Martha's eldest boy. She has seven children altogether, the youngest has just turned five.'

'Well if he's been having bad stomach pains, vomiting and diarrhoea then *I'm* your best bet. It might simply be a bad case of gastroenteritis but if it's not, if it's something more serious, it would be best if I came with you.' He nodded for emphasis. 'If the patient can't come to the general surgeon then, by golly, we'll take the general surgeon to the patient!' Woody thrust his arm triumphantly into the air as he spoke and Lorelai couldn't help but smile at his antics. He was handsome, clever and funny. If she had to pick any man to have a crush on, she was right to choose him. Then again, every woman in town had a crush on him so she guessed that made her normal and in no danger of taking those feelings further…except in her dreams.

'I'll go pack a medical bag with things I might need,' he finished before she could say another word, and disappeared as quickly and as quietly as he'd arrived.

'I guess that's it, then,' Ginny remarked, coming over to remove Lorelai's coffee cup from her desk. 'Go and get Hannah. I'll tidy up here while you go off gallivanting with the handsome surgeon.'

'I'm hardly gallivanting, Ginny. Besides, Woody is right. He would be Aidan's best bet. He doesn't know the way to Martha's farm otherwise he could go on his own. This is just a medical callout. Nothing more.'

Ginny grinned broadly and nodded. 'Sure. Of course it is.'

'Then why do you sound as though you don't believe me?'

'Oh, I do, darl, and I can see that you're not at all excited about spending some time stuck in the intimate confines of the car with Woody.'

'What? What are you talking about?' Lorelai fumbled with the paperwork in her hands once more. Ginny raised an eyebrow.

'You're not usually this flustered, Lorelai Rainbow. There's something going on between you two, don't forget I saw the way you two were standing outside last week—the heat could've melted all that fresh snow!'

'Shh.' Lorelai rushed around the desk and put her finger across Ginny's lips. The other woman stopped talking but smiled knowingly. Lorelai looked cautiously down the corridor, hoping Woody hadn't overheard them.

'It's about time you became interested in another man,' Ginny whispered when Lorelai had removed her hand. 'You couldn't do better. He's a lovely lad.'

Lorelai sighed and shook her head. 'He's about as stable as…as a three-legged chair!' She returned to her desk and gathered her haphazard bundle of papers together before thrusting them into her bag. 'So don't go thinking you can play matchmaker, all right?' She collected her keys. 'I just can't afford to make another mistake. I have Hannah to consider. *If* I ever decided to become involved with another man, or even marry again, it will be to someone who's going to be there for me, for Hannah—all the time. Not someone who spends their life gallivanting around overseas.'

'Woody does a lot of good with his overseas work.'

'And I'm not denying that and nor am I wanting him to give it up. I simply need someone I can depend upon.'

'Someone like Simon Arlington?' Ginny suggested. 'He's been sweet on you for years. Even before you married John.'

Lorelai didn't say anything but a frown marred her brow as she thought about Simon. He was a shy but sweet man, six years older than her, and had been working in the Jindabyne medical practice for the past seven years. Although they'd worked together on occasions, it was only recently that he'd asked her out in a social capacity. They'd had three dates over a period of six months and whilst they'd been nice, Lorelai had to confess he didn't set her heart aflame. All she needed was one second in Woody's company and she was a blazing inferno of rioting hormones!

'He's due back at the Jindabyne clinic next week, isn't he?' Ginny continued.

'Yes.'

'Such a nice man to rush home to Perth and care for his ailing mother. It's what every parent wants. Dependable children, and he'll make a dependable partner if that's what you're looking for. It's been...what? Three months since you last saw him?'

'Yes.' Lorelai put on her coat and scarf before wriggling her fingers into her gloves and reaching for her bag and keys.

'Have you been pining for him at all?'

Lorelai glared at Ginny. 'I know what you're trying to do.'

'And what's that, lovey?'

'To point out that as I haven't appeared to miss

Simon, I can't really be all that interested in him.'
Lorelai walked around her desk and stood in front of
Ginny, leaning over to kiss the woman's cheek, her
tone calm and controlled. 'I need to focus on Hannah,
on doing what's best for her future.'

'What about yours?' Ginny asked quietly, and placed
her hand on Lorelai's cheek. 'You deserve a world of
happiness after everything you've been through. If
Simon Arlington is the man to make you happy for the
rest of your life, then that's wonderful, darl, but I see
the way you look at Woody and I see the way Woody
looks at you.'

'Woody looks at me? How? What do you mean?' The
calmness momentarily disappeared.

Ginny's answer was to laugh and shake her head.
'Oh, you're definitely *not* interested in him. I can see
that.'

Lorelai closed her eyes for a moment, collecting her
thoughts and pulling herself together. 'I know you only
have my best interests at heart.' She sighed and opened
her eyes, determined to remain calm and controlled.
'Hannah is more important to me than my own love
life. If providing a stable and happy environment for her
means I deny myself a love life, then so be it. Hannah
comes first.'

Ginny nodded. 'You're probably right, darl. Now, off
with you.'

'Yes. Right.' Lorelai dug around in her coat pocket
for her car keys. 'Would you mind calling Connie and
tell her I'll be there directly to collect Hannah, please?
Then I'll come back and pick up Woody.'

'Right you are, lovey.'

As Lorelai walked to the car, she thought on Ginny's

words, realising she hadn't thought much about Simon while he'd been gone. In fact, she rarely thought about him when he was in the district. She shook her head as she drove the short distance to Connie's house.

During their three sporadic dates, Simon's behaviour had been exemplary and he'd never even made an attempt to kiss her. He would call her every few months, receive an update on the status of the Oodnaminaby clinic, give her an update on the Jindabyne side of things and ask after Hannah. Ginny was right. Simon was a nice, dependable man and he deserved better than her less than lukewarm attention.

'How much longer do you need to be away, Honey?' she muttered to herself as she headed up Connie's front path, being careful not to slip on the wet ground. She would just have to put up with Woody creating havoc within her life for a while longer. Then he would leave and she could find the neat, ordered, calm world that, up until two weeks ago, had been her life.

Within the hour, Lorelai was making her way out to Martha's place, which was situated on a farm between Oodnaminaby and the old village of Kiandra. The roads hadn't been too wet, the four-wheel-drive making short work of any slippery patches, and just before they'd turned off the main road, taking the gravel track that led to the family farm, Woody had volunteered to put the snow chains onto the tyres.

'You and Hannah stay nice and warm inside the car,' he'd instructed. 'Won't take me long.'

Lorelai had always known he was a gentleman from the night when John had died. She'd needed someone strong, someone to lean on, and Woody had been there for her. He'd shown her that chivalry wasn't dead and when he did little things like offering to put on the snow chains, it made her realise just how much she missed having someone to rely on.

'It's the little things that make the biggest difference,' her father always said, and Woody was proving him right. He'd shovelled the walk at Mrs Maddison's house, he'd put the chains on her tyres and when they arrived at Martha's house just as the sun was disappearing from the sky and snow covering the front garden, Woody collected Hannah from her car seat and carried her on his shoulders into the house, making the little girl giggle with delight. The sound warmed her heart and pierced it, all at the same time.

As soon as Lorelai entered the house, she carried the medical kit through to Aidan's bedroom, where the teenager was lying, curled up in his blankets. Woody was hard on her heels. 'I've left Hannah playing with Martha's children. She'll be fine with them.'

'Thanks,' Lorelai replied as she opened the bag and removed the stethoscope, noting that Woody seemed to genuinely care for her daughter, ensuring the child was safe.

Woody put his hand on the boy's forehead. 'He's burning up. Aidan? I'm Woody and of course you know Lorelai. We're here to help.'

'Pulse rate is elevated. Gurgling sounds in the abdomen. It's very tight and slightly distended. Just as well you packed a drip.'

'From what Ginny told me of the phone call, I came prepared for emergency surgery.' He pulled the equipment he needed from the bag as Lorelai asked a hovering Martha for a bowl of cool water and a face washer. 'The best way to lower Aidan's temperature is to sponge him down.' At his words, the anxious mother immediately headed off to do his bidding.

'This is definitely not gastro.' Lorelai said, happy and relieved Woody had decided to accompany her. If he hadn't, she'd be trying to figure out the best way to transport Aidan to Wagga Wagga Base hospital, which was the main hospital for rural surgical cases. She would have had to organise a plane or helicopter to come to the property to transfer the teenager but in this weather they wouldn't have been able to fly. Having Woody here, a trained general surgeon with all the equipment he needed, was Aidan's best chance of survival.

'I love teenagers who hang things from their ceilings.' Woody reached up and took down a large skull and crossbones home-made mobile Aidan had had floating around on his ceiling and looped the end of the bag of saline through the hook in the ceiling. 'Once, in Tarparnii, I was forced to operate in the middle of a jungle. I was literally surrounded by scrub and trees, the patient lying on a bed of dead leaves and twigs,' he related, and for a split second Lorelai wasn't sure whether he was talking to Aidan, trying to keep him alert, or to her. Either way, she was very interested in what he had to say.

'There was absolutely nowhere for me to hang a drip so I quickly lashed together a few sticks with a vine and stuck it in the ground, like a very tall cross. It wasn't all that strong and I was sure the twigs were going to break but thankfully they held long enough. I was able to repair the patient's large abdominal slash and suture him closed just as the twigs finally snapped. Thankfully by then help had arrived and we were able to move the patient back to a more sterile location.'

'Sounds so…full on,' Lorelai remarked as she drew up an injection of an anti-emetic to stop Aidan's vomiting.

'Hang in there, Aidan.' Woody finished inserting the drip and accepted the bowl of cold water from Martha, beckoning her into the room. 'Can you start cooling him down? Wipe his forehead, his face, around his neck. I need to gently feel his abdomen and then we can give him a mild anaesthetic.'

'What?' Martha was aghast but she continued to wipe her son down. 'What do you mean, anaesthetic? Isn't the ambulan—?'

'There's no time,' Lorelai interjected.

'I'm a general surgeon, Martha,' Woody reassured her. 'I've seen these symptoms so often, I know them by heart. Aidan has appendicitis and the sooner we remove it, the healthier he'll be. It won't be a full anaesthetic,' he continued as he carefully palpated Aidan's abdomen, both Lorelai and Martha wincing when the boy cried out in terrified pain. 'Symptoms are clear. Do you concur, Lore?'

'I do.'

'Good. Let's get started.' Woody reached into the medical bag and withdrew a vial and syringe.

'Midazolam?' Lorelai queried.

'By far the best option in this scenario. It's safe, easy to use, gives us enough time to operate and means Aidan doesn't need to recover from a general anaesthetic as well as everything else that's happened to him.' Woody quickly calculated the dose Aidan would require before administering it. It wasn't long before Aidan's face relaxed as he slipped into oblivion.

'Thanks, Martha.' Woody took the face washer from her then held both her hands in his and looked into her eyes. 'Would you mind getting some clean sheets for Aidan's bed and two large towels? I'll also need a bowl of warm soapy water in about half an hour's time.'

Lorelai watched as Martha nodded, responding to Woody's calm, controlled voice.

'Aidan's going to be just fine. In a few days he'll be back to his normal teenage self.' With a reassuring smile Woody let go of Martha's hands and the woman headed out of the room to do his bidding. Then he turned to Lorelai. 'Where's the bathroom? We need to scrub.'

They took it in turns to scrub their hands and by the time Lorelai returned and pulled on a pair of gloves and disposable apron Woody had packed into the bag, he'd already sterilised and draped Aidan's abdomen. A tall lamp, which ordinarily stood over Aidan's study desk, was shining brightly on the area, ready for operating.

'How are you feeling?' he asked Lorelai. 'Nervous? Worried? Calm?'

She shrugged her shoulders. 'Aidan requires an immediate appendectomy to avoid peritonitis,' she stated. 'I'm just glad you're here to do it.'

'Hmm, is that confidence in my ability or relief I hear in your voice?' he asked, taking the scalpel from its sterile packet. Lorelai looked at the instruments he'd set out on a sterile cloth on top of Aidan's desk and picked up the swabs, ready to assist him.

'Both.'

With a quick smile that almost made her knees buckle, Woody nodded. 'Then, Dr Rainbow, let us begin.' His incision was neat and precise and it was clear as his clever fingers worked that he really had performed this surgery many times before.

'I became so used to doing appendectomies via laparotomy that when I returned to a large teaching hospital I almost had to retrain myself to do it laparoscopically,' he remarked as he began suturing the layers closed.

Aidan's fever had broken and Lorelai had added a course of IV antibiotics to his drip to help guard against infection. She continued to watch Woody, her respect for his skill having increased rapidly during the past twenty minutes.

'Tarparnii seems to be a very special, very personal place for you, Woody.' Her words were clear yet soft and when his gaze flicked up to meet hers, she wasn't sure whether he was warning her the topic was off limits or whether he was surprised at her astute comment.

'It is and always will be.'

'Not that I'm wanting to pry…' she began, and was rewarded with a rich deep chuckle. 'What?' She stopped her flow of conversation.

'Nothing. It's just that any time a woman says "I'm not wanting to pry", it means they're *about* to pry.' Woody laughed again and reached for the prepared bandage, fixing it in place. A moment later he stepped back from Aidan's bed and pulled off his gloves and apron, balling them up and stowing them in a garbage bag. Lorelai followed suit and as they tidied up, he said calmly, 'If you want to know about my life in Tarparnii, just ask. I'll tell you want you want to know.' He spread his arms wide and almost knocked over the lamp. He switched it off and moved it away from the bed while Lorelai performed Aidan's observations.

She was a little annoyed at him for seeing through her intention and now that he was giving her permission to pry, she found she'd rather not know anything about him. 'It's fine,' she remarked, trying not to show him how huffy she felt. She continued clearing up, continued trying to ignore him, continued telling herself that keeping her distance meant not wanting to know about his past.

'Come on, Lore. Ask what's on your mind,' he cajoled as he moved past her to check the drip, noticing that she shrank away, desperate to ensure their bodies didn't accidentally touch. 'Did I like working and living in Tarparnii?' He asked the question himself. 'Yes. Did I meet people who became incredibly important to me? Yes. Did I fall in love and marry a Tarparnese girl?' His voice dipped as he spoke these last words and Lorelai instantly turned, lifting her gaze to his, surprised but almost desperate to hear his answer.

'Yes.' He paused, his gaze still intent on hers, the two of them caught in this moment in time, nothing else existing but the two of them. 'Did something bad happen to her?' The pain she could see reflected in his eyes was deep. She recognised it because it was pain she'd felt before. 'Yes.' His answer was barely a whisper. 'Do I like to talk about it?'

Lorelai gently shook her head from side to side before answering for him. 'No.'

CHAPTER FIVE

As SHE helped set the table for dinner, Martha insisting the three of them stay the night as it was too wet to head off now, Lorelai found herself watching the way Woody interacted with Hannah. The fact he'd been married, the fact his wife had been cruelly taken from him, made her look at him in a completely different light.

No longer did he seem to be such a drifter but instead a man who was keeping his mind occupied, keeping busy, moving around, doing anything and everything he could to stop his thoughts from dwelling on the pain and agony that went hand in hand with losing a loved one.

Lorelai had been eleven when her mother had passed away and even now, so many years later, there were days when the loss would encompass her so completely she found it difficult to breathe. She missed the wholesome hugs, the tender stroking of her hair, the reassuring smiles.

Thankfully, Edward's mother—Hannah—had happily taken on the role as surrogate mother, drawing Lorelai into the bonds of their family, treating her as her very own.

'I don't have a daughter,' Hannah had whispered a

few days after the funeral. They had been sitting on the seat in the lovely garden Hannah had made in her back yard, eleven-year-old Lorelai held securely on her lap as they'd watched a butterfly dance around the flowers. 'And your mother and I were always as close as sisters.' Hannah had tenderly stroked Lorelai's long blonde hair. 'Will you be my girl, Lorelai? We can go shopping in Tumut, we can sit and paint our toenails together, we can talk and talk and laugh at the boys. We can do all those girly things both of us used to do with your mum. What do you think?'

Lorelai remembered putting her arms around Hannah's neck, nodding emphatically before bursting into tears and burying her face against Hannah's neck. She'd never called her 'Mum', always 'Aunty Hannah' but the emotional bond between the two of them had grown rapidly from that day forward. Hannah had saved her, given a young girl the reassurance, the strength and the power to move forward with her life.

Then when Hannah and her husband Cameron had passed away during an avalanche not long after Lorelai's twentieth birthday, the grieving process had started all over again. Edward and his four brothers had grieved alongside her. Lorelai's father, BJ, had held them all together, binding them even closer as a family.

Years later, when she'd met John, Lorelai had yearned for the counsel of her mother or Hannah, desperate to know what she should do. John had been flattering and attentive, always making her feel as though she was truly special. Then, after their marriage, everything had changed. He would argue with her when she questioned him about all the times he didn't come home from the snowfields. He'd twist everything around to imply that it was all her fault, that she was paranoid, imagining things that weren't there. The man who had legally been her husband had ripped her heart out and tossed it carelessly aside.

She'd grieved for John, for the loss of his life. He'd been her husband but from the way Woody had spoken of his wife, it was clear that their marriage had been a loving one. That would have been a terrible tragedy for him to endure. A tragedy to make him keep on moving, keep on being busy so he didn't have to continually face the fact that she was gone. No wonder he'd known exactly what to say and do on the night John had died. *He'd* already been through it, the loss of a spouse.

Now she watched him, sitting on the sofa, a book open in front of him, children all around. They listened attentively as he read them a story, effectively keeping them out of Martha's way whilst she and Steven, the second oldest, continued with the meal preparations. The story he read was one about a mouse who tended to get into mischief, and this particular story was one of her daughter's favourites.

Hannah was sitting on her knees, jiggling with happy excitement as Woody read on. Her little hands clutched her chest in anticipation as Woody neared the end of the story. When he'd finished, Hannah giggled and clapped her hands, clearly delighted with the predicted outcome.

'Yay.' She climbed up onto his lap and put her arms around Woody's neck, hugging him close and pressing a quick kiss to his cheek. 'I lub that story.'

Woody seemed surprised at the action, the innocence of a child's kiss. He raised his hand and brushed his fingers lightly across his cheek before he smiled back at the little girl.

'Thank you for the kiss,' he said, and Lorelai could hear through his rich and honest tone that he really meant it.

Hannah kept her arms about his neck as the other children searched through their bookshelves for another story for Woody to read. Lorelai edged closer so she could hear what else was being said.

'You welcome.' Hannah smiled at him and Woody reached out to stroke his hand over her lovely blonde locks. A lump appeared in Lorelai's throat at his caring action and she quickly tried to swallow over it. 'I weally like that story,' Hannah told him again. 'It's my favouwite.'

'Mine, too,' he agreed. 'Aunty Honey used to read me that story when I was a little boy.'

'Weally?' Hannah's big blue eyes widened in surprise. 'Was you little?'

Woody's smile increased. 'Yes, I was. A very long time ago now, although Aunty Honey and your mother would probably say that I've never bothered to grow up.'

Another book was thrust in his direction and he accepted it with a smile, the children instantly settling down with looks of excited anticipation on their faces as they waited for him to begin.

The way the children so readily, so easily accepted Woody was a clear indication of his true personality. He was an extremely likeable man…a fact she was well aware of. He accommodated the children around him, ensuring everyone could see the pictures before he began reading.

'OK, kids,' Martha called a few minutes later as Lorelai still stood, spellbound by the man before her.

'Your father's home,' Martha continued. 'Which means it's dinnertime.'

A few of the children started to wriggle and complain, not wanting to leave the exciting world Woody was creating as he told the story. He started to read faster and a moment later, before Martha could come in and tell them *all* off, he finished the story.

'Quick.' He stood to his feet. 'You'd better go and wash your hands before your mother tells me off.'

'Nah, she wouldn't do that,' Riley, Martha's middle child said.

'I wouldn't be too sure,' Caitlin, his older sister, retorted as she headed towards the bathroom.

'I want more stories,' Hannah demanded. 'Not dinner.'

Woody picked her up and tapped his finger to her nose. 'Perhaps, if you're very good and eat all your dinner, we might be able to have a few more stories before bedtime.'

A cheer went up from all the children and Hannah quickly wriggled from his arms and raced along with the others to wash her hands in the bathroom. It wasn't until they'd all gone that Woody raised his arms above his head and stretched his cramped muscles. Lorelai watched the action from her vantage point in the shadows, eagerly drinking in the sight of his broad shoulders and firm muscles, her mouth going dry.

The shirt he was wearing rode up a little higher and the waistband of his denim jeans dipped a little lower, revealing a generous amount of rock-hard abdominals. Lorelai's gaze was drawn to the area, a small smattering of dark hair around his navel, his skin more tanned than she'd originally thought. She swallowed over the sudden dryness in her throat and unconsciously licked her lips at the perfect male specimen before her.

'See anything you like?' Woody asked a second later, and Lorelai instantly met his gaze. However, instead of seeing a teasing sort of censure, she received the message of reciprocated interest. He'd been well aware she'd been watching, and he'd clearly enjoyed every moment of her visual caresses. 'Should I turn the other way? Give you a different view?' he continued to tease, lowering his arms and gently twisting from side to side. All the time he was moving, his gaze held hers, and Lorelai couldn't help the blush that tinged her cheeks or the speechlessness that racked her mind.

'It's all right to look, Lore,' he said softly, seeing her discomfort increase. He moved to stand before her, his tone soft and intimate. 'You can even touch if you really want to.' Even though the light on this side of the room was dim, now that he was closer he could see the embarrassment on her beautiful upturned face. 'No need to feel self-conscious, Lore.'

'How can you even say that?' she blurted, quickly lowering her tone lest anyone should hear them. They'd come here to attend a sick teenager, not to flirt with each other.

'Easy. I like it when you look at me, Lorelai, especially when you look at me *like that*. Do you have any idea just how long it's been since I've felt the visual caress of a beautiful woman?'

'Uh…half a day?'

He smiled. 'No, and I'm not saying the women of Oodnaminaby aren't beautiful, just that they're never serious.'

'You are so conceited.'

'No, I'm not. I'm truthful. The last time I felt such a powerful and magnetic caress was about three months after I first met Kalenia.' His words were quiet yet filled with an intenseness that caught her off guard. The man standing before her was the same man who had cared for her on that fateful night. He had been serious yet protective and this time he was also a little flirty. She liked it.

'Kalenia?' Even as she said the foreign name, deep down Lorelai knew what his next words were going to be.

'My wife. I'm not the type of man to play the field, despite what you might think.'

'I don't think that…or at least I don't any more.'

'Thank you.'

'Was Kalenia receptive to your advances?'

Woody chuckled and leaned one hand on the wall behind her. Lorelai breathed in, her senses filled with the essence and scent of him. It was a heady combination, his spicy scent complemented by his warm nearness. She swallowed and tried hard not to lick her suddenly dry lips.

'Actually, no. She resisted my advances at first, telling me there was no way she'd ever marry an Australia *p'tak* like me.' He smiled at the memory. 'She was so clever and smart and pretty and full of life.' A hint of sadness tinged his words. 'Your strength and perseverance, the way you care for your patients and your daughter, your powerful and giving heart…' He nodded. 'You remind me a lot of her. The same inner qualities.'

He reached out and stroked the backs of his fingers down her cheek, leaning in a little closer, their breaths starting to mingle, the heat rising between them. 'Life has an…intriguing way of turning out, don't you think? Here we are, years later, both of us wary and scarred from our first marriages, unsure of ourselves, of protocol, given we've not been interested in anyone else for years, wondering what to do next.'

When he stood this close and spoke so openly, it was all she could do to keep her knees from buckling beneath her due to his enigmatic presence. She forced herself to close her eyes for a moment, just long enough to break the contact, to ensure the strong connection intensifying between them was severed before opening her eyes. The sights, sounds and delicious smells from the house around them started to permeate her mind, bringing her back to normal.

'What do we do next?' she reiterated, finding superhuman strength from somewhere in order to take a small step away from him. He was dangerous and he was definitely threatening her well-ordered life with his charisma, his chivalry and his charm. 'The answer to that question is very easy.'

'It is?'

'Yes. The next thing we do is…go and have some dinner.' With that, Lorelai turned sharply on her heel and walked away from him.

Throughout dinner, with Woody seated directly opposite her, it was difficult *not* to look at him—so she gave up trying to fight it. The fact that he was right in her line of sight wasn't her fault. Although she'd set the table, she hadn't decided where everyone would sit and, besides, she had Hannah beside her, sitting in the special booster seat, feeling very special and satisfied with herself. She ate up all her vegetables and five bites of meat.

'Good girl,' Lorelai praised as Hannah asked to be excused from the table, so she could go and play with the others. 'Not too long,' she told her daughter. 'It'll be bedtime soon.'

'But we don't have our beds,' she rationalised. 'Where we gonna sleep, Mummy?'

'You and I, possum, are going to sleep in the same bed.' Lorelai pointed to the sofa where Woody had previously been ensconced reading to the children.

'Where's Woody gonna sleep?' Hannah's wide eyes looked at the man who was fast becoming far too special to her.

'I'll be sleeping in Aidan's room,' he told Hannah. 'That way, I can look after Aidan throughout the night.'

'You don't have to do that,' Lorelai said quickly. 'I'm more than happy to take it in shifts. You can sleep in a bed and we won't have to disturb Riley and Darcy as they—'

'They'll be sleeping in a different room for tonight. I've already arranged everything with Martha and, besides…' He pointed to Hannah who was just climbing down from her booster seat to go and run after seven-year-old Ella and five-year-old little Martha. It was clear Hannah loved being around so many children. 'You have Hannah to worry about. Don't stress, Lore. Everything's going to be just fine,' he promised, but with the way she was starting to tremble with longing and hyperventilate with need each and every time he looked at her, she was beginning to wonder.

The next morning, Aidan was much improved.

'I still want him taken to Tumut hospital,' Woody told Aidan's parents. 'Even if it's just for one night. He needs to be monitored and also requires another course of IV antibiotics to guard against infection.'

'Does he really need to go? Can't you just give him more antibiotics here?' Martha asked, holding Aidan's hand tightly.

'Mum. It's OK,' Aidan tried to console her, a little embarrassed by his mother's fussing concern.

'He's right. We raised Aidan to be a fine young man. He'll be fine, love,' Neil told his wife, giving her a little wink. Woody couldn't help but smile, pleased to see a happy couple. They reminded him of his own parents who, while they most certainly had their own ideals and ways of doing things, were still very happily married after almost forty years.

'Well, all right. If you and Lorelai think that's best,' Martha agreed, then looked around as though she only realised then that Lorelai was nowhere to be seen.

'She's still sleeping,' Woody supplied. 'She seemed so wiped out last night.'

Martha nodded. 'I know she was worried about how Hannah would sleep in a different place so perhaps she didn't get much sleep at all.' She looked from Aidan back to Woody. 'I'll go and check on her.'

'No. It's all right.' Woody could see quite clearly that Martha wanted to stay with her son for as long as she could. 'I'll go. You stay and fuss over Aidan some more. I know he secretly loves it.' With a grin he left the room, not at all certain he was up to seeing Lorelai this early in the morning. He'd almost been thankful to monitor Aidan throughout the night as if he'd been able to sleep, there was no doubt in his mind that his dreams would have been about Lorelai.

As he neared the lounge room where Lorelai and

Hannah had been set up to sleep on the sofa bed, he heard the sound of sweet, soft giggles. He stopped just short of the doorway where he could quite clearly see the two Rainbow girls, lying on the sofa bed, Lorelai's arm around her daughter as they both looked up at the ceiling.

Lorelai pointed up. 'And look at that one, it looks just like a fluffy flower.'

Hannah giggled again and Woody closed his eyes at the sound, loving the innocence of laughter but at the same time feeling such a piercing in his heart for everything he'd missed. His own daughter, Ja'tenya, would have been almost four years old, had she lived. His beautiful, precious baby.

'It's not a flower, Mummy,' he heard Hannah contradict. 'It's a squashed beetle.'

'Beetle?' Lorelai's laughter joined her daughter's and the sensations passing through Woody changed from one of past sorrow to present awareness. Gone were the remnants of his past, to be replaced by the vision of the lovely Lorelai. How was it possible that his heart could pound out such an erratic rhythm whenever he was close to her?

The previous evening, when he'd stood close to her, his body warmed through and through from her visual caress, he'd found it exceedingly difficult not to haul her into his arms and cover her sweet, plump lips with his own. It wasn't the first time he'd thought, pondered, dreamed of kissing Lorelai and he accepted now that it wasn't going to be the last.

'Woody!' Hannah's delighted squeals brought him back to the present and he quickly advanced further into the room. Lorelai sat up amongst the covers and ran her hands self-consciously through her hair whilst Hannah bounced around the bed on her knees, clapping her hands with delight. 'We just looking at the clouds,' Hannah pointed out matter-of-factly.

Woody frowned in confusion but smiled at the little girl. 'What do you mean?' He glanced at the ceiling above them which was painted a lovely creamy sort of colour, not a cloud in sight. 'I can't see any clouds.'

'No, silly. The 'tend clouds.' Hannah rolled her eyes as though he were indeed quite thick. Woody instantly looked at Lorelai for some sort of translation.

'The clouds are pretend,' she said.

'See?' Hannah pointed to the ceiling. 'There's a monkey eating a banana. I like bananas.'

'Yes. Bananas are good,' he agreed.

'Some of the clouds we see are exceedingly specific,' Lorelai pointed out with a wide smile and stroked her hand lovingly over Hannah's hair.

'Have a look,' Hannah encouraged, and Woody came around the side of the sofa bed, kneeling down beside it before looking up at the ceiling to where Hannah pointed again. 'See? Now, that one is a elephant reading a book.'

'Oh, I see now,' he replied, and nodded. 'Good one. Oh, quick. Look over there.' He pointed to a different part of the ceiling. 'See? It's a jumping jelly-bean.'

Hannah giggled, then said quite seriously, 'I love jelly-beans.'

'Me, too,' Woody answered just as seriously, meeting Hannah's gaze. 'Did you have a good sleep, princess?'

Hannah nodded enthusiastically and looked at her mother, who seemed to be watching this exchange with quiet intent. 'I tuddled Mummy *all night*.' Hannah threw herself at her mother, Lorelai only just catching the child in time before receiving lots of quick pecking kisses from the three-year-old.

'Yes. We had a good sleep. How's Aidan? I'm presuming everything was all right last night otherwise you would have called me.'

'He's doing very well. I've already called Tumut hospital and they're sending an ambulance to come and collect him.'

'Great.' She was about to say more but Hannah obviously wasn't satisfied at the change in topic. She stood on the bed and held out her borrowed pink fairy nightie for Woody to inspect.

'Look at my fairy, Woody. She pretty.'

'She is. Just like you.' He winked, making Hannah giggle.

'And Mummy. Mummy's *weally* pretty, too.'

Woody turned to look at Lorelai, his gaze instantly turning serious. 'Yes. Yes, she is. Your mummy is *really* pretty, too.'

Lorelai met his gaze and found it impossible to look away. For a moment she didn't want to. She wanted to bask in the glory of a man who was openly expressing—albeit at the prompting of her daughter—that she was beautiful. It was something John had never done, not once in the entire time they'd been together. He'd never called her beautiful. He'd never just sat and stared, just looked at her, making her feel all warm and gooey inside, as Woody was doing now.

Her heart rate started to increase and her mouth went dry. She couldn't help it. Whenever Woody was around, her body would react with a powerful amount of awareness even though she'd spent a better part of the night lying awake, telling herself it was ridiculous for her to be flirting with the possibility of something romantic happening between herself and Woody. Even now, she longed for him to lean across, to close the distance between them and press his mouth to hers.

Woody nodded slowly. '*Really* pretty,' he echoed, as his gaze dipped to encompass her lips.

Hannah, distracted at hearing some of the other children playing down the hall, quickly scrambled from the bed and ran from the room, no doubt in search of a more appreciative audience. Within a split second the two adults found themselves alone…Lorelai sitting up amongst a mess of bedclothes whilst Woody knelt beside her, unable to look away.

'So…uh…why were you cloud-watching indoors?' His lips barely moved as he spoke but she watched the action closely, the way he formed the words, her sluggish mind taking a few seconds to process what he'd actually said.

'My mum had cancer. She was bedridden for quite some time and…uh…' Lorelai licked her lips and swallowed again, her throat dry, her heart still thumping out an erratic rhythm against her chest '…when I arrived home from school each day, I'd lie down next to her and even though she couldn't go outside, we'd…' She shrugged one shoulder.

'Cloud-watch,' they said in unison.

Woody nodded. 'That's a lovely story.'

Had he moved closer? He somehow seemed closer. She wasn't sure. When he was looking at her as though she were the most beautiful woman on the face of the earth, she wasn't sure of anything.

'Thanks.'

'Do you miss her?'

'Yes. I miss her. I miss Edward's parents. I miss everyone who's been taken from me, whether good or bad.' Her words were soft, barely a whisper, but she knew he'd heard.

In that one moment their hearts and minds connected and she found herself leaning closer towards him, no longer needing to speak words to convey what was on her mind. His eyes dipped to her mouth once again and she parted her lips, her breath fanning his cheek.

'Woody?'

He could hear the apprehension in her tone and he wanted to reassure her, protect her, comfort her. For far too long, three long years, he'd wondered what it would be like to kiss her and right now he didn't care if a freak cyclone hit this very spot, nothing was going to stop him from following through on the urge that he could no longer deny.

'Shh.' He angled closer towards her until they were only a hairsbreadth apart. 'It's all right, Lore. This is meant to happen.'

'Meant to hap—?' She didn't even get to finish her sentence as Woody pressed his mouth firmly to her own.

CHAPTER SIX

LORELAI gasped, her eyelids fluttered closed, her breath slowly releasing the tension she'd been holding onto for far too long.

Woody was kissing her!

She'd dreamed of this moment and now it was happening. Actually happening. She didn't know what it meant. She had no rational thought to even figure it out and where that indecision, that inability to process would ordinarily scare her, right now she didn't want to think about anything other than wanting him closer, wanting his mouth on hers, wanting the sensations he was evoking deep within her to last for ever.

This was Woody. The man who had been such a rock to her during those initial hours after John's death. The man who had cared for and supported her throughout that first night, making her feel safe when she should have felt so vulnerable. Ever since then, whenever she'd felt at a loss, unable to cope with the emotions of what she'd lost, she would close her eyes and remember how protected she'd felt that night.

Since he'd arrived back in her life, her desire for him had only increased with each passing day. Her dreams were wild and vivid, the Technicolor moments

infusing what she felt for him with what she so desperately wanted—for him to tell her he would stay in
Oodnaminaby for ever.

Lorelai was looking for permanence, for a man she
could share her life with, and at this moment in time she
desperately wanted Woody to be that man. No other had
ever made her feel so alive, so cherished, so respected.
Surely, with such powerful sensations coursing between
them, he had to realise that this attraction they felt towards each other was only the tip of the iceberg, the
beginning of a whole new world?

He was in no apparent hurry to end the kiss, content
to savour her sensations and flavours, committing them
all to memory, and she basked in this knowledge, eager
to move at the pace he set, almost desperate not to do
anything wrong, lest he pull away. She wanted so much
to please him, to make him want to kiss her again and
again.

So perfect, so precious, so intoxicatingly pleasurable.
It was as though their mouths were meant to be, fitting
perfectly together, and as he leaned a little closer, wanting to slowly deepen the kiss, to share in the essence
of this incredible woman, he knew that giving in to his
weakness for her was going to cause him future pain.

But she'd been irresistible. Sitting in the messy bed,
wearing a borrowed nightshirt, her blonde hair loose
and tousled, making her look incredibly sexy. He was
sure she'd had no idea just how beautiful she was, no
idea what she did to him when she looked at him with
those wide blue eyes of hers, or the way her tilting
mouth made it impossible for him to resist kissing her.

He opened his lips a little wider and was more than
pleased when Lorelai seemed to match his intensity,

allowing him to lead her, to guide her through this storm of emotions that was creating havoc within both of them.

'Good morning,' he whispered against her lips, before indulging in a few more kisses.

He knew they should stop, knew he should pull back, put some distance between them, knew that the rest of the house would descend on them within a matter of minutes and that Lorelai might find it embarrassing to be caught kissing her colleague, but he couldn't help himself, needing just a few more quick kisses. Selfish, eager, desperate…addicted.

'I hear Hannah coming,' she murmured, pulling back and resting her forehead against his for a brief moment in an effort to control her breathing. She'd just leaned back against the pillows when Hannah came zooming around the corner and into the room, almost launching herself onto the bed. She was squealing with delight, quickly scrambling towards her mother, slipping between the rumpled bedclothes to hide from whoever was chasing her.

A moment later Steven, the second eldest, came into the room, pretending to growl like a monster. Hannah squealed and giggled and laughed, especially when a few more children came running in and followed her lead by slipping beneath the covers.

Lorelai looked at Woody, knowing the children were all too busy playing to even pick up on the undercurrents flowing between the two adults. There was no helping the embarrassment and uncomfortable sensations she was experiencing, especially when the children started tugging the covers from her. A moment later the covers slid from her legs. Little Martha was tugging at the sheet and Lorelai quickly pulled her nightshirt down as far as she could.

Woody smiled at the children's antics but Lorelai didn't miss the long, lingering look he gave her body. When he raised his gaze to meet hers, she could see, quite clearly, just how much he'd liked what he'd seen, his eyes glazed with a look of unveiled desire.

The realisation of such raw and unchecked emotion left her trembling.

'I'll go and see…' Woody pointed towards the doorway, trying to remember how to speak, but one glance at the incredibly sexy Lorelai and his words, as well as coherent thought, completely failed him. 'Er…someone.' With a nod, he quickly left the room, pushing both hands through his hair as though he was still trying to figure out what had just transpired between them.

Lorelai was everything he'd dreamed about—and more. Years ago, when he'd sat and watched her sleep through that long and painful night, he'd been attracted to her. Back then, he'd realised there was hope that one day he might be ready to move forward with his life, to leave the memory of his wife and daughter in the past.

Just now, having his mouth pressed against hers… had been heaven. She was an amazing woman and he could almost hear his sister's voice in his head telling him he'd chosen very well. Lorelai was a caring, thoughtful and giving woman and he should stop fighting the natural feelings he had for her. Perhaps it was time to move forward? To look towards some sort of future with Lorelai and Hannah?

His phone rang and he stopped in the hallway, absentmindedly extracting it from his trouser pocket. He was still pondering the way Lorelai's scent still floated around him, the way he could still feel the imprint of her mouth on his and the way he wanted nothing more than to do it again. He glanced at the caller ID, then froze.

Pacific Medical Aid.

He quickly pressed the button to ignore the call, his shoulders slumping a little as the reality of his world came crashing back over him. He wasn't free. For one brief second he'd forgotten his past, forgotten his commitment, forgotten the duty that would bind him for the rest of his life and had lived in the moment—the most glorious moment he'd had in far too long.

Woody closed his eyes. He shouldn't have kissed her. Kissing Lorelai only made things far more confusing than they already were. What had he been thinking? He hadn't. That was his main problem. He hadn't been thinking about his responsibilities. He hadn't been thinking about what he owed to Kalenia's family and their village in Tarparnii. He'd been selfish and he'd given in to the urge to press his mouth to Lorelai's.

He shook his head, completely unable to believe he'd actually followed through on his desire. The issue now was his difficulty in resisting the urge to head back in there, pull her into his arms and do it all over again.

Now he knew, now he understood, now he no longer needed to simply *dream* about kissing Lorelai because he'd experienced the *reality* of her luscious lips pressed against his. He'd discovered the answers to his questions about whether or not they'd be a compatible match. They were.

Surely now he had his answers he could move forward, put his infatuation with her behind him once and for all. He opened his eyes and exhaled harshly, rubbing his fingers to his temple, unable to believe his need for Lorelai appeared to have increased.

'Work.' The word propelled him into action and he proceeded along the hallway to Aidan's room. He'd used work to get him through worse times than this, although he had to admit that even though it had been wrong, kissing Lorelai had felt so right. Her divine mouth, the sweet bouquet of her scent winding itself about him, hypnotising him, drawing him closer. She had the ability to make him forget everything. He couldn't let that happen.

Too much was at stake. Too many lives hung in the balance, depending on him. He couldn't afford to lose his focus. It wasn't worth it. His own wants and desires were superfluous to the greater picture, the greater responsibility of caring for his extended Tarparniian family.

It was up to him. They were counting on him and he wasn't going to let them down.

Lorelai was able to find time to snatch a quick shower and as she turned her face into the spray of the soothing hot water she closed her eyes, remembering another night, over three years ago…the last time she'd been sent off to have a shower whilst Woody was under the same roof.

After they'd left the accident site, the pain in Lorelai's heart had been like a lead balloon, exceedingly heavy. Woody had been her rock. He'd driven them home to Edward's house where Edward's younger brother, Hamilton, had been looking after Hannah. They'd collected the baby and when Lorelai had protested she didn't need Woody to see them home, saying that she'd be all right, Woody had flatly ignored her, saying he didn't want her to be left alone.

'Not tonight, Lorelai.' His words had been calm yet firm and his tone had brooked no argument.

When they'd arrived at her home, he'd ordered her to go and have a shower and freshen up whilst he changed Hannah's nappy. By that stage she'd been too numb to argue and had headed to the bathroom, eager to wash away the grime of her past and her grief for John. Beneath the spray she'd tried to cry, she'd tried to feel something—*anything*—but she'd been too numb.

When she'd emerged, she'd entered her bedroom to find Woody standing by the window, baby Hannah cradled in his arms, humming a lullaby. He'd had a lovely voice, deep and smooth, relaxing and hypnotic. She could understand why Hannah had fallen asleep. It was what she'd wanted. To lie down, to sleep, to find some peace, and she'd been incredibly grateful for Woody's foresight in offering to stay.

He'd seemed to sense her presence and turned to face her. 'Into bed,' he'd said, his tone brooking no argument. Lorelai had done as he'd suggested and once she had lain down, he'd placed the sleeping Hannah into her arms. She'd shifted onto her side, facing her daughter—the one good thing in her world.

Then Woody had placed his large, warm hand at the top of her spine where she'd held all her tension. Initially the touch had startled her, a mass of tingles spreading throughout her body, but after a split second he'd applied slight pressure with his fingers and rubbed in slow, small circles, the sensations instantly releasing Lorelai's stress. Her eyelids had closed and she'd sighed with relief as peace and calmness she'd thought she'd never feel again washed over her…and that was all she'd remembered, sleeping peacefully for quite some time.

She'd woken quite a few hours later, initially concerned as Hannah had no longer been in her arms. When she'd sat up, she'd seen Woody, resting in the chair beside the bed, Hannah snuggled into his arms, an empty baby's bottle on the bedside dresser. Man and babe had both been dozing and she'd watched them for a few minutes, intrigued at how someone so big and strong and masculine could look so incredibly sexy cradling her baby girl.

Lorelai had relaxed back into the mattress, turning her head on the pillow so she could continue watching man and babe, her eyelids slowing growing heavy once more. Woody had been there to help and support her. Just knowing he had been in the room, watching over herself and Hannah, had calmed her breathing and made the future she'd had to face less frightening…at least for the moment.

Then she'd woken up to find him gone. Even now, the memory of the way he'd left town without even saying goodbye still hurt. For some reason she'd always thought they'd formed a special connection that night, a bond of some sort, and until this morning she'd always thought she'd been wrong.

Sure, ever since Woody had arrived back in town she'd been drawn to him and, sure, there may have been a few occasions where she'd realised he might have felt that same tug but when he'd leaned forward and pressed his mouth against hers, everything had been confirmed.

Woody was attracted to her. Woody was interested in her. Woody hadn't been able to stop himself from following through on the urges both of them had been desperate to push aside.

As she turned off the taps and stepped from the shower, towelling herself dry, she couldn't help but wonder if there *had* been more to his leaving town so suddenly all those years ago. She didn't deny he'd been called back to Tarparnii but surely he hadn't had to disappear as easily as a magician?

Lorelai had thought she'd done something wrong, that she'd been too clingy that night or perhaps she'd said something to upset him. Try as she might, she couldn't recall anything that seemed out of place, especially during such a mind-numbing night.

She finished towelling herself dry and quickly dressed, hoping that now Woody had kissed her, now that they'd broken down that barrier, she had some hope of discovering why he'd left so suddenly that long ago morning.

They stayed with Aidan until the ambulance came and once the transfer was complete, Lorelai, Hannah and Woody said goodbye to Martha and Neil and their children before heading back to Oodnaminaby.

Throughout the past few hours Woody had been professional and polite, not once giving her a knowing look or an accidental touch or a secret smile. As Lorelai concentrated on driving, she sneaked a glance over at Woody, wondering if he'd say something now they were alone. Hannah was dozing in her car-seat, having expended a lot of energy running around with the other children that morning.

'At least Aidan will make a full recovery, thanks to you,' Lorelai said as the ambulance turned one way, heading towards Tumut, and they turned the other. The sun was out today, which often made it even more difficult for driving as a lot of the snow had melted beneath the hot rays. Lorelai concentrated, watching closely for black ice, but couldn't resist the extremely brief glance at the man beside her. Usually, he was talkative and yet, since he'd kissed her that morning, he'd hardly spoken a word to her except in a professional capacity, asking procedural questions about Aidan's transfer.

'I was just doing my job,' he replied.

'I know but still it's nice to be thanked.'

'True.' He continued to look straight ahead at the road and Lorelai wasn't sure what else to say. Ever since he'd left the room after the kiss, he'd been rather reserved. Was it because of the phone call he'd received? After he'd left the room, she'd quickly pulled on her jeans and had just stepped into the hallway when she'd heard his phone ring. Wanting to give him privacy, she'd been about to turn away but then he'd cancelled the call. After that she'd watched as his shoulders had sagged with dejection and she desperately wanted to know what was bothering him so much that a simple phone call could affect him in such a way.

Should she ask him about the call? She hadn't meant to pry, hadn't meant to be watching him, it had all just sort of…happened. Had the call been from PMA again? Had something gone wrong in Tarparnii? She shook her head, deciding the calls he received were none of her business, but at the same time she wanted him to know she was here to support him. She could sense something was wrong but try as she might to rack her brain for another topic to get them chatting, the only thing on her mind was why he'd seemed so aloof since their kiss.

The bottom line was she wanted to know. She needed to know how he felt and now seemed like the perfect time to ask him. 'Woody?' She cleared her throat, surprised to hear a slight hesitancy in her tone.

'Yes?'

Lorelai swallowed and forced herself to say the words that were currently swirling around and around in her mind, never seeming to find any sort of answers. 'Do you…regret what happened this morning?'

'This morning?' Woody gave a mild shrug. 'A lot of things happened this morning.'

'Woody!' Lorelai's exasperation escalated. 'Don't be dense. You know I'm talking about the kiss.'

'Oh. Right. Are you sure you want to discuss this now? While you're driving? The road looks quite dangerous and I'd hate us to have an acc—'

'We're not going to have an accident,' she said firmly. 'I've driven on these roads many times, in far worse conditions. I've engaged the all-wheel-drive and as it isn't even raining or snowing, it's not going to be that difficult to concentrate and talk, although given your present attitude and the way you appear to be avoiding the discussion, I'm guessing you just want to forget the kiss ever happened. Am I right?'

Woody closed his eyes for a brief moment, then shifted a fraction in his seat so he could look at her. 'It's not that simple, Lore.' His words were tinged with a hint of sadness and regret. Was that regret for the kiss or the fact that it wasn't simple?

'Sure it is. You either regret it or you don't, and just for the record I don't. Naturally, I was a little embarrassed after the actual, you know, event but that doesn't change the fact that I'm not sorry it happened. This was a big step for me to take, to give myself permission to move forward. As much as I really like you, Woody, and whilst I'm not at all ashamed of the beautiful kisses we shared, I've been trying to fight my attraction for you since you first arrived back in town.

'You have?'

She lifted her chin with that hint of defiance he'd seen on other occasions and he couldn't help but admire her. 'Yes. You're going to leave Ood again when your contract here is completed. Last time you upped and left without a word and although it was quite stupid of me at the time, I was hurt by your cool dismissal of me.'

'Lore, it wasn't like that.'

She held up a hand. 'Spare me. That was then, this is now. The point is that you'll be leaving and I'll be left trying to explain to Hannah why her beloved Woody has left her. Why he never comes over any more. She's attached herself to you and that's a bad thing. You are not a permanent fixture in her life and it's my job to protect her, as best I can, from emotional and physical hurts.'

'And that's why you didn't want to kiss me?'

'Yes…or at least that's why I've been trying to steer clear of you.' She gave him a quirky smile. 'I didn't succeed very well.' Lorelai sighed and they drove along for a few minutes in silence. 'At the moment I just want to know where I stand. You have quite a few more weeks here before Honey and Edward return and I think it's best if we set down some sort of rules or guidelines or… something.'

'Or something,' he mumbled.

'Look, during my marriage to John I was too scared

to question him, to seek out the answers I so desperately wanted to know. I was weak and scared and I vowed to myself that if I ever found myself in a romantic situation again, I wouldn't be that way, I wouldn't allow myself to be the victim. If I wanted to know what was going on, I would ask…so I'm asking.'

'What do you want to know?'

'I want to know what the kiss meant to you. Did it mean *anything* to you? If you want to forget it, just say the word and I'll forget it. We can go back to being simply professional colleagues for the remainder of your time in town and then you can leave Ood and go and do…whatever it is you do.'

She turned off the main road and headed towards the Oodnaminaby medical clinic. She pulled the car into the car park, Woody not saying a word. His silence spoke volumes and she had a difficult time keeping her tears under control and her heart from hammering right through her chest.

'Right, then,' she remarked, her tone clipped, her walls once more being erected to protect and preserve. She needed to harden her heart, to keep herself and Hannah safe. She kept the car engine running. 'I guess your silence says it all. We'll forget the kiss ever happened. We'll ignore the attraction that sparks to life every time we're within cooee of each other and we'll simply be colleagues.' Hannah was starting to rouse in the back seat and Lorelai was almost desperate to have him out of her car.

'To that end, if you wouldn't mind doing the rest of the patients this morning, Dr Moon-Pie, I'll go and get Hannah organised. I'll do afternoon clinic so you can go and sleep or shower or do whatever it is that you want to do. It's certainly none of my business.'

'Lorelai—' he began.

'Out.'

'It's not that I don't want to—'

'Woody, I gave you the opportunity to say something. You didn't take it. Your silence said everything and I'd appreciate it if you'd get out of my car. Now!'

He closed his mouth and nodded. It was better this way…just so long as he didn't look at the pain and anguish he'd already glimpsed in her eyes. He opened the door and stepped from the car, Lorelai reversing away from him almost before he'd properly shut the door.

He stood there and watched as she drove away, knowing he was doing the right thing but unable to believe how much it was hurting him.

For the next two weeks Lorelai was adamant in keeping her distance from Woody. She would nod politely to him if she bumped into him during clinic. She'd sit calmly and discuss patients with him and she'd answer any questions he had in an efficient and direct manner.

Aidan had been monitored in Tumut hospital, was recovering well from his impromptu surgery and was back helping his father around the farm during the mid-year school break. The snow season was now in full swing, with many families flocking from all around the country for their winter vacations. The clinics were busy with cuts, sprains and the occasional broken limb. Lorelai was more than happy for work to be hectic because it meant she could focus on her patients during the day and her exhaustion during the evenings.

Hannah, however, was starting to exhibit a little bit

more attitude than usual and Lorelai wasn't sure why. 'Did you have a good day at Connie's?' she asked her daughter one evening as they walked towards their house, Hannah's purple and pink backpack in Lorelai's hand while her daughter stamped her way along the shovelled path, little puffs of steam coming from her mouth as she huffed.

'No. Tonnie got mad at me.'

Lorelai nodded, having already spoken to Connie about the incident, where Hannah had snatched a toy from one of the boys at the day-care centre, but she wanted Hannah to tell her about it.

'Why?' Her question was met with silence as they headed up their footpath. While Lorelai unlocked the door, Hannah picked up a handful of snow with her gloved hands and threw it at the garden gnome she'd decorated earlier that year as a Mother's Day present. The snowball hit the gnome fair in the face and Hannah nodded with satisfaction before heading inside, stamping the snow from her boots.

Inside, Lorelai bent down in the entryway and took off her gloves, helping an impatient Hannah to unbutton her coat. 'Hannah, what's really wrong, sweetheart? You can tell Mummy.'

Hannah angrily pulled off her gloves and beanie and threw them on the floor. Lorelai levelled her daughter a look that said she wasn't impressed with this behaviour. Hannah met her mother's gaze, held it for a fraction of a second as she tried to figure out just how far she could push her mother, then immediately bent and picked them up.

'What's made you so angry?' Lorelai asked, knowing something had been brewing for quite some time in the little girl's life. Hannah remained silent and Lorelai sighed, knowing she'd have to play twenty questions to drag the answer out of her. Hannah was as stubborn as her grandfather and some days Lorelai wanted to knock their heads together, hoping the stubbornness would fall out.

'Are you missing Aunty Honey and Uncle Edward? They sent you a postcard,' she said as she finished hanging their coats up in the drying cupboard before heading inside. Hannah followed but remained silent.

'Would you like me to ring Aunty Annabelle and ask her to bring the boys over so you can play with them?'

More silence, then a reluctant 'No'.

Lorelai shrugged as she sat down on the sofa and pulled Hannah onto her lap, the little girl instantly cuddling in. 'What's wrong, baby? Tell Mummy and I'll try to fix it.'

Hannah started crying and tears began to gather in Lorelai's eyes, wishing the little girl would tell her what was wrong.

'Wubduntlikeme,' Hannah mumbled, and Lorelai eased her back.

'What was that, sweetheart? I couldn't understand you.'

'Woody don't like me,' Hannah wailed, then really buried her face in her mother's neck and started to sob. At the mention of Woody, Lorelai tried not to stiffen.

'He…he…said we could read stories and he…he… don't do it, Mummy, and I *want* him to and Frankie said that Woody didn't like me.'

Lorelai rolled her eyes, realising that was the reason behind Hannah's bad behaviour that afternoon. 'Frankie is eight years old, Hannah, and eight-year-old boys often say things like that.'

'Woody don't like me,' Hannah wailed again as though she didn't really understand what the words meant but knew they weren't good.

'Of course Woody likes you,' Lorelai instantly soothed. 'Of course he does.' She held her little girl close and kissed her head.

'But he don't come over and read the stories to me.'

'He's been very busy at work, sweetheart,' Lorelai tried to explain, but when she looked into Hannah's eyes, seeing the utter misery in the blue depths, she knew there was only one thing to do. Like any loving parent, she was willing to sacrifice her own emotions in favour of her child. If she was honest with herself, she'd admit her own behaviour, desperately wanting Woody close but knowing she needed to keep him at a distance, didn't make any sense to her heart. The man was enigmatic and she wondered whether she'd ever understand him.

However, now, even though she knew Hannah's re-action was merely a taste of what was to come when Woody eventually left town, as he was still in the area and she could do something to fix Hannah's distress, perhaps she could bend the rules, just this once, and see if Woody was available to pop by for a visit. Purely for Hannah, she told herself quickly, but all the while know-ing she was lying. She simply didn't seem capable of self-control where Woody was concerned and neither, it seemed, was Hannah.

'I have a suggestion,' she said, forcing a smile into her words. 'Why don't we call him on the phone right now and ask him to come over and have some soup with us? Then, after you've eaten all your soup, you and Woody can sit and read before bedtime. Does that sound like a good idea?'

Hannah lifted her head and stared at her mother, hope lighting her little face. Then, as though by magic, the tears vanished and little blue eyes blinked brightly at her. 'Weally? I can speak to him on the phone?'

'Sure can.'

With a single bound Hannah was off Lorelai's lap and heading towards the phone, quickly bringing the cordless handset back to her mother. 'Call him now, Mummy. Call him *now*!'

'OK. Just…' Lorelai patted the sofa cushion next to her, trying to squash down her own nervousness. She'd been intent on keeping her distance from Woody, knowing it was better this way, to simply be colleagues with him rather than to give in to the memories of the powerful kiss they'd shared.

She'd worked hard to control her dreams, thankful the exhaustion from busy days helped her to sleep at night, but every morning, without fail, he was her first thought whenever she opened her eyes. In her dreams, he'd visited her, he'd held her, he'd kissed her more passionately, more intimately than he had before. He'd looked down into her face, caressing her cheeks, her lips, her neck with his soft fingers before covering the same path with small intoxicating butterfly kisses, turning her insides to mush and making her knees buckle.

The phone was ringing and Lorelai braced herself.

'Hello?' His deep, rich voice came down the line and her eyelids instantly fluttered closed, her heart beating even more rapidly than it had when his lips had been on hers.

She opened her mouth to say something but found the words stuck in her throat, her mouth as dry and as scratchy as sandpaper.

'Hello?' he said again, and she could hear the confusion in his tone. 'Crank calls in Oodnaminaby. Something I hadn't quite expected,' he continued.

'Mummy? Is he dere?' Hannah asked, her words earnest.

Woody must have heard her in the background because the next words out of his mouth were, 'Lore? Is that you?' His tone had gentled somewhat and Lorelai closed her eyes, allowing the sensation to wash over her for a split second before pulling herself together. Opening her eyes and clearing her throat, she nodded, even though he couldn't see her. 'What's wrong? Is something wrong?' he asked before she could get a word out. She could hear him moving around and a second later there was the sound of a door closing.

'No. Everything's fine,' she finally managed to grind out, forcing herself to swallow and her heart rate to settle. She had to breathe, to get herself under control. 'It's, uh…Hannah. She wants to talk to you.'

'Oh. Great. I've really missed her.' And he sounded as though he really meant it. Lorelai quickly gave the phone to her daughter, who took the receiver with both hands and brought it to her face so she could talk to him.

'Woody?'

'Hey, there, princess,' Lorelai heard him say. She shook her head and stood up, heading into the kitchen to put the kettle on. She needed a soothing cup of herbal tea, something to calm her nerves, to stop her world from spinning simply because she'd heard the caring urgency in Woody's voice when he'd assumed something was wrong.

She walked back towards Hannah, checking on her daughter and couldn't help the smile that touched her lips at the sight of the three-year-old lying back on the cushions, holding the receiver with one hand while she twirled her hair with the other, giggling into the phone. 'A glimpse of the future,' she murmured, and pleased her daughter was happy once more returned to the kitchen to make her tea and warm up the soup they were having for dinner.

No sooner had she placed the dish into the microwave than the doorbell rang. Frowning, she wiped her hands on a tea-towel and headed for the door, Hannah running ahead of her.

'He here. He here,' she said, the phone receiver still to her ear.

'Who's he—?' Lorelai didn't even get a chance to finish her sentence as she realised that Woody had been walking to her house whilst talking to Hannah on the phone. Who else would Hannah be referring to? No one!

'Hurry, Mummy.' Hannah demanded, jumping around beside the entryway door, excitement bursting from every part of her little body.

'All right. Just shift out the way and let me through.' Lorelai waited for her daughter to move, then opened the door. There they stood, staring over the threshold at each other, her heart instantly skipping a beat from one of his half-smiles aimed in her direction.

'Hi.' The word was soft yet deep and lovely and gorgeous, warming her through and through. He was dressed in his warm coat and scarf. He wore no gloves but still had his phone to his ear. He shifted his gaze to encompass Hannah. 'Hello, Miss Hannah.' His smile was a wide, beaming one that caused Lorelai to put a hand to the wall in order to steady herself.

'Woody!' Hannah thrust the phone receiver at her mother before launching herself at him. He bent down and scooped her up, slipping his own phone into his coat pocket. Lorelai simply stood behind the door as he entered, carrying her daughter in his arms, leaving her feeling very much like the third wheel.

CHAPTER SEVEN

AFTER dinner, and with Woody helping Hannah to finish up that last bit of soup in her bowl, the little girl began insisting it was time for her beloved Woody to read her some stories.

From the moment he'd walked through Lorelai's front door, Woody had been his usual self. Charming, funny and relaxed. The change in him from the man she'd been doing her best to avoid at the clinic was acute and she had to admit she enjoyed this version of him far more than the polite, professional one.

This was *her* Woody, the man she couldn't stop thinking about. It was all highly confusing and at times she found herself on edge, watching him closely, trying to decipher if there were hidden messages in his words and actions but she could find none.

She was almost desperate to relax in his presence, to find joy in his company as she had right up until that morning when they'd kissed. She'd glanced at him several times across the table, unable to believe the way one simple smile from him had had the ability to turn her body to mush. Did the man have any idea of the hold he had over her?

Lorelai still couldn't understand why he'd withdrawn

from her after that incredible kiss. Never before had something so simple, such as Woody's mouth against her own, rocked her world in such a way. Being with Woody, being in his arms, being so close to him, had felt so right. She still struggled with the pain and devastation at his rejection, confused about why he didn't feel the same way.

Even in those few moments afterwards, when she'd rested her head against his, the two of them breathing heavily, she'd felt a connection pass between them. She'd thought he'd felt it too. It was as though in that one moment time had stopped and their hearts had bonded. The odd sensation hadn't left her since but obviously she'd been wrong and Woody hadn't felt the connection after all.

'He was playing with you,' she'd told her reflection just that morning. Where she'd thought he wasn't like John, that he didn't need to have every woman he met fall in love with him, she was starting to think she'd been wrong. He certainly enjoyed the attention of women, continuing to be his charming, charismatic and chivalrous self towards every one he met. Even the men in town thought he was the 'bees knees', as one of her older patients had termed it.

However, she'd also noticed that his smile didn't hold as long, that the light didn't reach his eyes. He still provided excellent care to all their patients but something was missing and it had taken her a while to realise it was his natural spark. Somehow it had dimmed.

The nurturer within her had wanted to talk to him about it, to help him out, to offer to be a friend, to listen and support, but she knew that even if she'd offered, he'd have turned her down. He'd made his position clear on the drive back from Martha's farm when he'd remained quiet, withdrawing from her presence.

Tonight, however, he was as relaxed and at ease as the first time she'd met him. He paid close attention to Hannah and as she watched them interact, Lorelai was struck by a different train of thought. Perhaps the reason why he'd pulled back after their kiss had been because he'd thought he was being unfaithful to the memory of his wife.

Was that it? Was that why he'd withdrawn from her? When she'd been unable to stop staring at him while he'd stretched his limbs, he'd told her the last woman to look at him in such a way had been his wife. Was that a good thing?

She had to remember that *her* marriage hadn't been a happy one. Therefore, she was eager to move forward, to have new and exciting experiences. For Woody, moving forward might be more difficult. Her heart welled with concern for him and she shook her head, as though to clear her thoughts.

'Something wrong?' Woody asked, and she belatedly realised he'd been watching her. She met his gaze, desperate to ignore the way her heart hammered its momentarily uneven rhythm whenever his deep blue eyes stared at hers in such a fashion. She could hear the honest concern in his tone, could see it in his eyes, and it only succeeded in confusing her even more. He cared about her. That much was clear. He cared about Hannah, too, otherwise he wouldn't have bothered to come tonight. So if he cared about both of them, why was he erecting walls to keep them both at a distance?

'I'm fine.' Lorelai turned her attention to Hannah, who was carefully climbing down from her booster seat.

'Storwee time, storwee time,' she kept saying over and over, excitement in her tone.

'Go and get changed for bed first,' Lorelai instructed as Woody helped her carry the dirty dishes to the sink.

'But, Mummy! It's storwee time!' Hannah looked at her mother as though Lorelai was cuckoo.

'Yes, and story time is usually when you lie down in your bed and we read a book together. Do you need help getting out of your clothes?' She held her hands out towards her headstrong three-year-old.

Hannah stamped her foot and crossed her arms over her chest, clearly displeased with the scheduled programme of events. 'It's storwee time!'

'I'd watch your attitude, young lady,' Lorelai stated clearly, not breaking eye contact with her impertinent daughter. 'It would be a shame for Woody to have to leave early and without reading you one single story simply because you couldn't control your temper.'

Hannah's eyebrows rose at that and she quickly backed down. Woody couldn't help but admire Lorelai's way of handling her daughter, firm but fair. He put down on the bench the dishes he was carrying, then crouched down beside Hannah.

'I have an idea. Why don't you go and choose three stories for us to read? You bring them here to me and then while you're getting ready for bed and brushing your teeth, I'll get the kitchen all sorted out for Mummy. Then we can sit down and read stories. How about that?'

Hannah thought for a moment, tilting her head to the side, a very serious look on her face, and Lorelai quickly turned away, unable to keep a straight face due to the gorgeous posture of her thoughtful daughter. So adult. She glanced at Woody and saw he was having an equally difficult time to keep from chuckling at the three-year-old.

'Hmm… Otay.' With that, she ran off to her room in search of the story books. Woody stood and turned to face Lorelai.

'She's really becoming a handful, isn't she?' he asked rhetorically as he started rolling up his sleeves.

'She's three. No one ever tells you that the terrible twos start when they're about eighteen months old and the four-year-old's temper tantrums start when they're three.' She shrugged and sighed. 'There's not a day goes by that we don't have a disagreement about something. Peter and Annabelle keep telling me it's normal. Out of all of Edward's brothers, they're the only ones who have children. I would have been so lost without their help and support, even if it's just to hear the words "It's normal" or "She'll grow out of it".' She tried to laugh but it ended up coming out as a sigh.

Woody gave her a small, heartfelt smile. He wanted to put his hand on her shoulder, to reassure her, to encourage her, but he knew any physical contact with Lorelai would only result in him losing his self-control once again. 'Well, either way, you're doing a great job. You held firm, you didn't give in, and one day Hannah will respect you for letting your yes be yes and your no be no.'

'You sound as though you've had a lot of practice with children and yet you're not even an uncle yet. Honey's not due to have the baby for another few months.'

'I was raised in what some people would call a hippy commune, several different communes, in fact.'

'Oh, that's right. I forgot about that. Honey always said there were a lot of other children around.'

'Always, and a lot of the time, our parents were away protesting one thing or another.'

Lorelai moved around the kitchen, filling the kettle and switching it on, doing her best to avoid accidentally touching Woody. He began rinsing the dirty dishes.

'You don't have to do that,' she interjected. 'I can do them later.'

'It's fine, Lore. I'm more than used to pitching in. As you've just pointed out. I was raised in a commune where everyone pitched in with everything. Cooking, cleaning, dishes.'

'Even the children?'

'Especially the children. We did move around a lot. A new place every now and again depending on where my parents were protesting next. Honey and I went to a lot of different schools, as did all the other children in communes. Generally we stuck together, both at home and in the schoolyard.'

Lorelai smiled as she pulled two cups from the cupboard. She held one up towards him, silently asking him if he wanted tea. Woody nodded in agreement. 'Did you ever get into any fights?'

He looked at her and raised an eyebrow of surprise. 'With a surname like Moon-Pie? You are joking, right? Honey and I were teased at every school and, yes, I did have quite a few after-school fights but...' he held up his finger as though needing to making his point clear '...it was always in defence of others. Honey used to give me an earful whenever she cleaned up my scratches and grazes. She was quite the little doctor back then.' He shook his head as though bemused by the memory.

'And your parents? What did they say?'

'Nothing much. We'd been raised to fight for our rights, not necessarily with physical violence, but my dad was proud of me for defending my sister and the other kids in the commune.'

'Such a different way of life. Honey practically raising you and the other children in the commune and there you were, defending people's honour and making sure no one was picked on.'

Woody nodded as he finished rinsing the dinner dishes. 'It may have seemed strange to outsiders but it was a good life, even though it was probably more higgledy-piggledy than others.'

Lorelai smiled at his turn of phrase, then heard a light grunting coming from the direction of the hallway. She turned to find Hannah walking back into the room, almost crushed beneath the weight of three very large story books. Lorelai laughed as she took them off Hannah. 'Woody said *three* stories. Not three *volumes*.'

Relieved of her precious books and pausing only to draw in a rejuvenating breath, Hannah reached for Lorelai's hand. 'Tum on, Mummy. Hurry!'

Lorelai didn't want to go with her daughter, instead wanting to stay with Woody, to ask him more questions. He'd been quite open with her, talking to her as they had before the kiss. Perhaps there was some hope that even though he'd backed off on the romantic front, they'd be able to salvage some sort of friendship. Their worlds were going to be loosely linked anyway as Woody's sister was her best friend.

As she finished dressing Hannah in her nightie, slippers and dressing gown, she couldn't help but worry about her daughter's attachment to Woody. As soon as Honey and Edward returned, he would leave Oodnaminaby and go—wherever it was he was off to next. Hannah wouldn't have the luxury of simply calling him up on the phone and asking him to come over to read her stories and Lorelai wasn't quite sure how she was going to explain Woody's prolonged absence.

'Hurry, Mummy,' Hannah said as Lorelai tried to brush the little white teeth. 'Woody's waiting for me.'

'Then stop talking,' Lorelai grumbled, almost jealous of the fact that Hannah was right. Woody *was* waiting for her, more than content to give her daughter all the attention she deserved. So why couldn't he give *her* the same attention? Why had he backed off from the kiss?

As Hannah spat out the toothpaste and rinsed her mouth, before running from the room to no doubt launch herself at Woody, Lorelai realised that in order to silence the questions rolling around in her mind, she needed to find answers.

Perhaps when Hannah was in bed asleep, she'd be able to talk to him, to ask him once more what had happened. Why he'd gone from being so hot and sexy and flirty towards her to being ice-cold and withdrawn? If it was something to do with his wife, perhaps she could help him through it, help him to move forward. Maybe if she understood where he was coming from, she'd be able to let go of her own attraction towards him and move forward with *her* own life, treating Woody as nothing more than a family friend.

She tidied up and prepared Hannah's bed, hoping her daughter would fall asleep in Woody's arms while he read to her. At least that way Lorelai could avoid a tantrum about Hannah not being sleepy and not needing to go to bed.

When she eventually headed out, she found her kitchen to be spotless and a cup of tea waiting for her on the bench. She couldn't help the swell of appreciation at what he'd done for her. Something so small as making her a cup of tea, of tidying her kitchen—it was wonderful. As she collected her cup and walked into the lounge room, finding Hannah sitting on Woody's lap, completely engrossed in a story, it made her realise just how lonely her life had become.

Of course she had her father, who usually came around for dinner at least once a week, and she had Honey and Edward, as well as Peter and Annabelle and their children, plus countless of friends in Ood whom she loved dearly, but it wasn't the same as coming home to someone, sharing her thoughts, her hopes and dreams with someone special—someone like Woody.

She slid into the big armchair and watched him hold her daughter as though she were the most precious little thing in the world. It was the classic picture of domestic bliss, something she had hoped to find with John, but those dreams had been crushed.

Now her bundle of love, the apple of her eye for the past three and a quarter years, was starting to yawn, her eyelids beginning to become heavy as Woody continued reading to her, the brightly coloured hard-bound story book open before them.

Lorelai sipped her tea again and sighed into the chair, allowing his deep, relaxing tone to wash over her. Woody was so different from John. He was dependable, honest and hard-working. He was reliable and thoughtful. The way he was with Hannah, the way he gave her all his attention, was wonderful. As Hannah slumped further into Woody's arms, her eyes now closed, her breathing starting to even out into a deeper rhythm, Lorelai was overwhelmed with a sense of peace.

It was very rare she ever felt so at ease, so relaxed, as though it didn't matter what had happened in the past or what might happen in the future. Right here, right now, she was quite content. The last time she'd felt this way had been after John's accident when, distraught and confused, Woody had brought her home from the accident site. She didn't know what it was about him but whenever he was near, she couldn't help the sense of…completeness which seemed to surround her.

"'And then the prince looked down into the eyes of his beautiful princess and knew they would live happily ever after,'" Woody read, his tone soft and clear. 'Is Princess Hannah asleep, now, Lore?' he continued in the same voice, and Lorelai smiled.

'She is.'

Woody closed the book and placed it beside him before carefully shifting Hannah more comfortably into the cradle of his arms, the three-year-old moaning a little before settling into him, more than content.

'I'll just sit here a while to make sure she's really asleep,' he said softly. 'The last thing we want is for her to wake up the instant we put her into bed.'

Lorelai nodded. 'Thank you, Woody. You have such a deep, relaxing voice, I thought I was going to drop off as well.'

He shrugged one shoulder, images of a sleeping Lorelai flashing quickly into his mind. The last time he'd watched her sleep, he'd had a difficult time keeping himself under control. She'd looked so peaceful, so serene, so incredibly lovely. He'd felt her pain, her loss and he'd done his best to stand by her side, to protect her through the night. Whatever she had needed, he had been there on hand to help. When Hannah had started to awaken, he'd quickly removed the babe from her mother's arms, changed her, prepared a bottle for her and cuddled her back to sleep. The same beautiful little girl he was now cradling in his arms as she snuggled into him, sleeping peacefully once more. That night he'd felt a connection not only to Hannah but to Lorelai as well. She'd had a whole new life ahead of her and there was no way he could have been a part of it back then, just as he couldn't be a part of her life now. He had too many responsibilities.

'Feel free to drop off into slumberland, Lore. I'll cope with tucking Hannah into bed and seeing myself out.'

'Would you tuck me into bed, too?' The words were out of her mouth before she could stop them.

'Uh…Lore…um…' Woody's eyes widened at her question and he couldn't believe how he found himself so tongue-tied, such was the power she held over him. The more time he spent with her, the more he came to know her. And the more he came to know her, the more his feelings grew. 'I would definitely make sure you were comfortable enough to sleep through the night and ensure you didn't wake up with a crick in your neck,' he replied, after clearing his throat a few times.

Lorelai smiled. 'You're a good man, Woody, and, believe me, they're hard to find.' She put her cup down on the small table beside her chair and stretched her arms above her head, watching beneath hooded lashes as Woody seemed to follow her body's actions with great interest. His careful caress warmed her, giving her a touch of confidence.

'Woody? Why have you been…um…distant from

me? The real reason, please? I think you owe me at least that much.'

'Oh, Lore.' He closed his eyes for a moment and exhaled slowly before looking at her. 'My life is incredibly complicated and, despite how being with you makes me feel, I can't change it.'

Lorelai processed his words for a moment. 'How is it complicated? I'm presuming it has something to do with the death of your wife but surely I can help you in some way to deal with the pain of loss.' She angled her head to the side, a small sad smile touching her lips. 'I've unfortunately become quite an expert on dealing with the loss of loved ones.' She leaned forward in her chair, her hands clasped together, her words earnest.

'Please let me help you. Please allow me to be there for you, to listen to you, to support you. Becoming lost in grief can end up being a lonely road if you don't have caring people to tether yourself to. We can put on a brave face, we can nod and smile and make decisions. We can walk through our lives for years, the pain being shut away in some dusty corner of our mind, only to burst forth when we least expect it, unleashing the agony that's been festering and lurking there.'

Lorelai nodded slowly. 'I *do* know how you feel, Woody. How empty the loss can leave you, but not dealing with it isn't healthy.' She looked down at her hands. 'I know you have Honey, your parents and grandparents. I know you have countless friends you can rely on, and if you have someone who's helping you with this, then by all means tell me to back off and mind my own business, but…' She stopped again and sighed. 'I can see the emptiness you've tried so hard to hide for so long. I can only see it because I've felt it.'

Woody was silent for a moment, her words hanging in the air. He looked down at Hannah, now completely out to the world, off hopefully having lovely dreams of princes and princesses who always found their happily ever after, no matter who or what tried to prevent them. He had loved deeply and he had lost deeply. Now, being here with Lorelai, he was doing his best to ignore the way she made him feel, the way Hannah's innocence surrounded his heart, making him think about the child he'd lost, the child who would have by now been a little older than Hannah. So much pain. So much loss, a loss he'd never thought he'd be able to deal with, a loss that still bound him with responsibilities of honour and support.

He lifted his eyes to meet Lorelai's, the artificial glow of the lamps casting a halo around her, making him wonder if she wasn't some sort of angel sent from above to help him to let go of his past anguish and move forward into the light, into the land of the living.

'Who helped *you*?' His words were soft but he wanted to know. Lorelai was surrounded with people who loved her, who cared about her, who would always be there to support her, so who was the person she'd anchored herself to in order to deal with her husband's death.

'Who helped me? *You* did.'

CHAPTER EIGHT

'*ME?*'

Her words had astounded him.

'Yes. You were right beside me when I learned John was dead.'

'But...' He shifted in the chair, Hannah murmuring something inaudible as he moved. 'Oh.' Woody looked down at the sleeping child as though he'd momentarily forgotten she was there. 'Let me put Hannah into her bed,' he said, needing just a few minutes to process Lorelai's revelation.

Woody stood and carried Hannah to her room, tenderly laying the child on her waiting bed. Lorelai pulled up the covers and bent to kiss her daughter. 'Sleep sweet, princess,' she murmured, before the two of them headed back to the living room.

Woody stood, not wanting to sit, needing to move around in order to figure out just *how* he'd been able to help Lorelai. He shoved his hands into the pockets of his denim jeans as Lorelai went and fiddled with the heating controls.

'Lore,' he began when it appeared she wasn't going to elaborate. 'Please explain how I could possibly have been the person to help you through your grief? I left the day after the accident and I didn't see you for over three years. How could I have helped you?'

Lorelai sighed and smiled, a sense of calm washing over her. Woody appeared ready to talk, to finally open up to her, and she knew this was the next step in their burgeoning relationship.

'Hannah was born right here—in this room. Your sister delivered her.' Lorelai pointed to where Hannah's birth had taken place. 'John had told me earlier that night that he was leaving me, that I was useless as a wife and that he didn't want either me or the baby. If it hadn't been for Honey and Edward, and especially Hannah, I wouldn't have made it through that first fortnight.'

She tidied up the story books as she talked then turned to face him. 'Do you remember the first time we met? You'd just come to town and we had a big family dinner to meet you.' Lorelai smiled. 'You were tall and handsome and exuded joviality. We were quite a party for dinner that night, all of us filling Hannah's and Cameron's big house with rowdy laughter again.'

Woody nodded. 'It was a good night.'

'It was and through all the smiles and happiness and laughter, when you thought no one was looking, the smile would slip and your eyes would reflect such pain. The pain of loss. I only recognised it because after watching my mother die and then losing Edward's parents, it was something I'd learned to detect. Of course, I felt uncomfortable asking you about it because we'd only just met and, besides, I was largely preoccupied with a newborn and a heart filled with pain.'

'Yet you soldiered on.' He smiled. 'You're a strong

woman, Lorelai. I've always admired that about you and you've done a wonderful job of raising Hannah.'

'I've had great support.'

'Then how can you say *I* was the one to help you through your grief over John?'

'Because you made me feel secure. You made me feel protected. You made me feel as though I was still worthy as a person. When John rejected me, he destroyed more than our marriage. He destroyed my self-esteem.' Her voice cracked a little on the words and Woody's need to protect her kicked into overdrive.

'Before we met, Honey had told me what that oaf had done to you, what he'd said and how he'd treated you.' Woody clenched his hands into fists. 'I was as angry as the rest of the Goldmark clan, even though I'd never met the man. When we first met, I had just become a card-carrying member of the "protect Lorelai" brigade.'

She chuckled softly at his words. 'That was Peter's idea and it was a sweet gesture. It made me feel so loved by my family. But I noticed one other thing that night, something that astounded me.'

'What's that?'

'I found you very attractive.' She felt incredibly self-conscious in confessing such a thing and after looking into his surprised eyes she realised he might take her words the wrong way. 'Not that it was astounding I found you attractive,' she quickly clarified. 'Merely the fact that after everything that had happened to me, I was still able to *feel* that way again.'

'I understood your meaning and I'm…speechless.' He paused, unable to believe how warmed he felt at her words. 'Back then? Really? You were attracted to me?'

Lorelai nodded. 'My husband had left about a fortnight before, I'd given birth to a baby and yet, when I looked at you, I felt…feminine.' She shook her head and frowned, a small, shy smile on her lips. 'I can't explain it properly but feeling those emotions let me see there was more to life than what was presently taking place within my little world. It showed me the damage John had done wasn't permanent and that in time I would be able to move on, to one day open my heart again and love someone new.

'Then John died…' She trailed off, closing her eyes for a moment. 'I can still see him, trapped in that car. I can still hear you urging me to go home, but I couldn't.' She paused to control the emotion in her voice. 'That night, I'd just stood there, unable to move while you helped John. I was desperately waiting for someone else to come so that *you* could take me home—my knight in shining armour.'

Woody frowned. 'Armour? I'm no hero, Lore.'

'You were for me. I needed you that night and you stepped up to the plate, you helped me, supported me, cared for me. I didn't want to go home alone and you knew that. You refused to take no for an answer and you stayed with Hannah and me. You showed me compassion, you kept me safe, you gave me rest.'

Lorelai licked her dry lips and opened her eyes to look up at him. 'You brought us back here and all I really remember is you giving my neck and shoulders a rub as I lay on my bed, cuddling my baby girl, tears unable to fall.' She stepped forward, closing the distance between them, and reached out to touch her fingers to his cheek. He didn't flinch, didn't pull away, didn't move. Instead, he simply looked into her upturned face, a look of incredulity in his gaze at what she was saying.

'I also remember waking up and seeing you sleeping in the chair, Hannah in your arms. You cradled her as though she were the most precious little girl in the world.' She went to drop her hand back to her side but Woody quickly reached for it, lacing his fingers with hers. At the touch, she gasped. Her mind faltered, as it always did with one sweet touch from Woody.

'Your actions and your support gave me hope, even if it only was for a short time. I don't understand why you left so suddenly. For years I've kept thinking I must have done something wrong to drive you away, even though Honey assured me you left because you were needed in Tarparnii.'

Woody swallowed and Lorelai's gaze dipped to his lips, the warm atmosphere surrounding them becoming fraught with longing as he still desperately tried to fight his natural and instinctive reaction to this woman.

'You didn't do anything wrong, Lore.' He shook his head. 'It was all me. I was the one who had done something wrong.'

'But…how? Woody, I don't understand.'

'Lore, the reason I left that morning, why I hightailed it out of Oodnaminaby, was purely and simply because the emotions I felt towards you were…overwhelming.'

She blinked slowly as his words filtered through her mind. 'What!' It had been the last thing she'd expected him to say.

'From the moment we met, Lorelai, things haven't run smoothly. I can't explain it. I don't even understand it but at that first dinner, I was…aware of you, too. Ridiculous. Stupid.' He shrugged. 'Unexplainable. I'd come to town to see Honey, to spend time with my sister and check out this man she was obviously in love with, and instead I found myself interested in you...*drawn* to you. I was stunned at my reaction, not because you're not worthy of it,' he quickly clarified with a smile, 'but more because no other woman had ever drawn me in like that, except for my wife.' Woody paused for a moment, letting the words settle over them. 'The guilt swamped me. Guilt for remaining alive. Guilt for moving on with my life which, in turn, brings with it the guilt I've been carrying around for four years, ever since the death of my family.'

'Family?' Her eyes widened in shock. 'You had children?'

'One baby. A daughter.'

'Oh, Woody,' she breathed, empathy in her tone. 'What pain you must have suffered.'

Lorelai gave his hand a little squeeze, wanting to encourage him, wanting him to know she was there, she was happy to listen, to return the favour and support him in his time of need. She didn't rush him and waited patiently for him to continue.

'Kalenia and I met when I was in Tarparnii for my third stint with PMA only this time I wasn't there as a medical student but as a qualified surgeon. I was fresh out of medical school, this boy genius who was more of a novelty in Australia than anything else.'

'A novelty?'

'Honey never told you? I started medical school when I was seventeen and completed it in four years.'

'Four years?' Lorelai blinked one long blink. 'I mean, Honey's always called you a genius but I always thought that was more of a big-sister "I'm proud of you" type of thing. Wow. Four years! I take it you went into surgery after that?' While she spoke, Woody led them both to the sofa but made no effort to remove his hand from hers as they sat down.

'I did. They made an exception for me and again I completed the training quite quickly. By the age of twenty-four I was over working in Tarparnii. Honestly, Lore, that country is so beautiful. I'd love to show it to you one day.'

'I'd love to see it,' she replied, secretly delighted at the way he'd spoken of a future together.

'Kalenia spoke beautiful English and was often used by PMA as a translator. She travelled to a lot of very unsafe places with our teams as we worked to provide effective medical care. We fell in love and were married in the traditional Tarparnese festival, the *par'Mach,* which is a sort of big wedding. Kalenia became pregnant almost straight away but when she was only seven months gone, she gave birth to our daughter, Ja'tenya.'

'Oh, Woody. Was she…?'

'A fighter? She was. She may have been at a disadvantage but she was a fighter, my girl. Being in the jungle, it's difficult to look after neonate babies, but at that time Honey had come across for a visit and was able to bring her expertise to help me deal with what was going on. Ja'tenya started to put on weight. She started to feed more regularly and with increasing ease. She started to make little gurgling noises, to smile.'

A light touched his eyes, his face lighting with love as he spoke of his daughter, of the happiness she'd brought him. Then, just as quickly as it had come, the light began to fade and the smile disappeared from his lips.

'Then *Yellom Cigru* fever spread through the village.

It's a Tarparniian disease that acts like bad flu and unfortunately most babies are susceptible to it, especially neonates.' He rubbed his free hand over his face, then looked at her. 'Telling Kalenia that our eight-week-old baby girl had died was possibly the worst moment of my life.'

Lorelai couldn't believe the pain she felt, the way his anguish had somehow become her own. 'How did Kalenia take the news?'

'Badly. She'd already stopped coming out with our team as a translator when she'd become pregnant but she'd always been very active in her village. Not now. She didn't come out of our hut for well over a month. Then, one week, when I was off with a team doing a clinic in a village over a day's drive from where we lived, I received word that a carrier with the *clollifon* disease had been staying in the village.'

'What's that?'

'*Clollifon* is a Tarparniian disease that attacks the immune system of the natives. Usually if it's caught early enough a good course of antibiotics can kill it but if a person's already been ill, with flu-like symptoms, the outcome is far worse. There had been several outbreaks on the other side of the country but…' He stopped and collected his thoughts. 'Kalenia hadn't been eating properly since Ja'tenya's death and quickly contracted the disease.'

Woody closed his eyes and shook his head. 'By the time I returned to the village, she had hours left to live. Her father had been treating her, giving her natural remedies and a few of the Western medicines that were stored in the village, but none had worked.' When he opened his eyes, there were no filters on his soul and

Lorelai could see quite clearly the anguish he'd lived through.

'Things didn't improve after her death. Two of Kalenia's sisters contracted the disease and so did her father. We managed to save the girls but my father-in-law passed away a week later.' He trailed off and hung his head, covering his eyes with one hand.

'Woody.' Lorelai caressed his cheek, feeling his pain, unable to believe the loss he'd suffered. 'So many deaths together. No wonder you understood me so well that first night after John's death. No wonder you stayed and watched over me, taking Hannah when she grizzled so she didn't wake me. You knew how I felt.'

Woody dropped his hand and met her gaze once more. 'She blamed me, Lorelai. Kalenia blamed me for not being able to save our daughter. She was so angry with me, so distraught. My days were dark, my nights were darker, and the point is she was right. I *should* have done more to save Ja'tenya. I should have been vigilant, watched for the symptoms, been able to pre-empt the sickness.'

'You're a doctor, Woody. You're not a miracle worker. I know what it's like to lose someone you love but I cannot even begin to imagine the pain and heartbreak you must have felt at losing your child. I mean, if *anything* were to happen to Hannah, I'd...' Lorelai couldn't even say the words, tears welling in her eyes.

'I wouldn't wish it on anyone.' He cleared his throat and gently eased his hand from hers, rising to his feet. 'Hannah is a wonderful little girl, Lore, and you've done an amazing job of raising her. You should be proud, not only of her but of your own efforts.'

'Thank you, Woody.' She rose, too, knowing he was

about to take his leave, the walls having been erected once more. At least he'd taken them down long enough for her to glimpse the darkest moments he'd lived through all those years ago. She was honoured he'd chosen to confide in her.

'I'd best go,' he murmured, and headed towards the entryway closet to retrieve his coat, the mood between them quiet and melancholy. She waited for him to slip his arms into his coat, picking up his cherry-red scarf when it fell to the floor. It seemed so stark and overly bright against his thick woollen coat.

'This fabric is far too cheery right now,' he remarked as he wound the scarf about his neck.

Lorelai forced a smile and reached out to smooth down one side of the scarf that had rumpled. 'I think it suits you. It makes the blues of your irises stand out, highlights your chiselled jaw, your five-o'clock shadow, your manly shoulders.' She let her hand trail down the scarf to the end and was about to clasp her hands together when Woody took hers in his yet again.

'Thank you, Lore.' He raised her hand to his lips, pressing a gentle kiss to her skin. 'I do feel better for having talked some of this out with you.'

'I'm here to listen any time you need me.' She smiled brightly at him. 'That's what friends are for.'

'We *are* friends. Aren't we? I mean, *real* friends.' He shook his head, annoyed with himself for stumbling over the words.

'Good friends,' she agreed.

'Close friends,' he added, and she nodded.

'Yes.'

He looked down at her hand, still enclosed within his. Her light floral scent blending with the lingering aromas from dinner made Lorelai seem definitely good enough to eat. He clenched his jaw as his gaze dipped from her eyes to encompass her mouth, watching as her tongue slipped out to wet her pretty pink lips. Lips that tasted so good, lips that fitted so perfectly against his own, lips he'd dreamed of every night.

He knew how wonderful it had been to kiss another woman, to once again feel those first tingling sensations, the ones that seem to start in your fingertips, spreading up your arm before bursting forth like fireworks throughout your entire body. He knew how ardently she could respond to his touch, the sighing of her body as their souls danced seeming to fit so perfectly against one another.

The need to hold her now, to slip his arms about her waist, to draw her close, feel the warmth of her body next to his, was starting to become overwhelming. She'd somehow managed to get him to really open up and talk about his past. She hadn't offered bland platitudes, she hadn't brushed his feelings aside. Instead, she'd listened and she'd understood. She'd offered compassion and empathy and he felt a weight lift from his shoulders. The burden of carrying so much pain could easily destroy a man but tonight he'd been able to speak freely to a woman who somehow understood him, sometimes better than he understood himself.

'*Close* friends.' Lorelai edged a little closer, wanting the distance between them to vanish. 'Woody,' she whispered. 'I don't want to wreck this new-found friendship but…' she breathed out, her heart rate increasing as the essence of him wound its way around her '…I can't stop thinking about you. The attraction between us has only increased since that morning at Martha's farm and I…want you.'

She closed her eyes, unable to believe she was speaking these words out loud but at the same time feeling liberated in telling him how she truly felt. 'I want you to be around me, around Hannah, to spend time with us.' Opening her eyes, she looked directly into his, her voice strengthening with determination to make him see just what he'd come to mean to her. 'I want to get to know you even more than I do now, to support you in all aspects of your life.'

Woody put his hands on her shoulders, unsure whether to keep her at a distance or to draw her closer. He couldn't believe what she was saying and he knew he was fortunate to hear those words from her lips. It was clear she really did care about him, just as he cared about her. He, too, wanted to spend time with her, to come around more often, to read stories to Hannah, to simply sit and talk, all snuggly and warm by the heater on a cold and frosty night.

'Lorelai. You are an incredible woman.'

She tried not to show the pain that pierced her soul the instant he spoke those words. 'But you don't feel the same way.' She lowered her gaze and went to step back, to put some much-needed distance between them, but Woody's hold on her shoulder tightened a little, keeping her where she was.

'I didn't say that. You *are* an incredible woman. Full stop. There are no ifs, buts or maybes about that statement. It's completely true.

'Then what are you saying, Woody?' With a heavy sigh she spun on her heel, breaking his hold on her. 'I keep getting completely mixed signals from you. First you keep your distance, then you draw me in with your sexy eyes and irresistible mouth and make me feel like I haven't felt in—well, *for ever,* and then you kiss me before putting me back at arm's length and walking off again. I can't do this, Woody.'

'Lore, I—'

'I understand about your wife. I'm not asking you to forget her. I'm not asking you to confess undying love to me.' She stood in the middle of the room and held her arms out wide. 'I just want to know where I stand with you. I've told you how I feel. If you don't feel the same way, if all you've been doing with me the entire time you've been in town is messing with my mind, then…' Her voice broke on the last word and she couldn't believe she'd let herself get so worked up she felt like crying.

Woody crossed to her side and without hesitation took her into his arms. Lorelai buried her face in his chest, breathing in his scent and allowing his warmth to wash over her. 'I'm not usually so fragile,' she murmured, sniffing then blinking her eyes a few times in order to get herself under control. 'It's just with John cheating on me—and not just with the woman who was in the car crash with him but I've since found out there were several others before her. Ever since the first day we met, he'd always had another woman on the side. All through our engagement and our marriage. Do you have any idea how it feels? To be so betrayed by someone who professed to love, honour and cherish you?' She eased back, wishing he'd let her go.

'Lorelai. I can't stay in Oodnaminaby. I have—'

She sighed, closing her eyes and shaking her head. 'It's fine. You don't have to explain. I get the point. You can't get seriously involved with me because you're leaving Ood at the end of your contract. You might not be back for years and years because you have a completely different life to live from the one that I live here, in my sleepy little town with my headstrong little girl. I get it.'

She tried to control her voice as she spoke, tried to be strong and brave just as Woody thought she was, yet she couldn't help the little waver that quivered through her voice near the end. She wasn't strong. She didn't want him to go. Even having him here tonight, helping her with Hannah, doing her dishes, making her a cup of tea—all those little things meant so very much to her, especially when she was on her own. Day in, day out, it was just Hannah and herself, going through their daily grind. They'd been doing well, enjoying their life until Woody had come back to town and shown them what their lives were missing…they were missing *him*.

He belonged with them. She felt it to the very depths of her soul and yet here she was, telling him she understood, knowing that he had a different life somewhere else, living in a different place, travelling and helping and doing different things with different people—people who couldn't possibly understand him the way she did.

'Do you, Lore? Do you really get it? Do you understand that you drive me to distraction? Do you comprehend that I'm bad news for you? Do you really think I'd run the risk of hurting you again after what that creep did to you?' His words were vehement and coloured with confused pain. 'You deserve so much better, Lore. You deserve to be treated like a queen. Can you even begin to fathom how painful it is to stand here, holding you in my arms, desperately wanting to kiss you but knowing if I do, I could risk emotionally damaging both of us for ever?' He shook his head. 'Life isn't that simple, Lore.'

'I know, Woody. Don't you think I don't know that?' She wriggled in his arms. 'Let me go. Please let me go or…'

'Or what? Do something crazy? Crazy, like this?'

And with that Woody gave them both what they craved and pressed his lips firmly to hers.

CHAPTER NINE

His lips were soft and gentle on hers and she opened her mouth willingly, her need for him mounting with every passing second. Woody stroked his hands across her face, gently making their way around to the back of her neck where he gently pulled the band from her hair, allowing the blonde strands to fall loose around her face. Tingling with anticipation, his fingers sifted through her silky locks, loving the feel of them. Being this close to her, being allowed to touch her, to press butterfly kisses to her cheeks, to nuzzle her neck, to experience all those sensations he'd only fantasised about was better than any dream. The *real* Lorelai was literally taking his breath away.

When he broke his mouth free, she couldn't help but gasp in air, all the while wanting his mouth back on hers. He continued to wreak havoc on her emotions, flooding her body with wave after wave of goose-bumps and sparkles, with his tiny kisses to her neck, her ear, her cheek before returning to capture her lips with his once more.

This was no testing kiss, not like the first one they'd shared. This time he seemed intent on really delving into her being, to unlock the secrets she kept hidden deep down, almost desperate to know everything about her. Was that because there would never be a repeat of this moment? Was this the last time she'd ever have the opportunity to kiss him?

Desperation flared within her and she slid her hands beneath his coat, tightening her hold around his waist, wanting him to know that she never wanted these exquisite sensations to end. Her heart was bursting with joy and pain and power, so that when she decided to deepen the kiss even further, she was elated when he followed.

His masterful mouth continued to drug her senses. Emotions seemed to swamp her, one after the other, and she wanted them, she welcomed them. In his arms, with his lips firmly on hers, their torsos pressed together, she felt more alive than she'd ever felt before.

She slid her hands lightly over his polo shirt, edging down until she found the end of the material before boldly putting her hands beneath, instantly delighting not only as her fingertips made contact with the hard muscles of his back but also in the way Woody groaned with satisfaction. To know he was as much into her as she was into him gave her hope. Where she'd wondered whether he really felt the same way, his actions were now telling her loud and clear just how much he desired her.

Cherished. Feminine. Sexy.

Woody made her feel all those things and she loved it. No man had ever made her feel this way. No matter what might happen in the future, Woody was her one and only, her true love—for ever.

He broke his mouth free from hers, both of them panting wildly as he buried his face in her neck, breathing in the scent of her hair. It was so amazing to finally be able to give in to his desire to touch her this way. To have the silky strands of her hair brush lightly against his face as he nuzzled her neck.

'Lorelai,' he breathed, her name a caress upon his lips, her hands still splayed over the warm, firm muscles of his back. 'I shouldn't be doing this. I shouldn't be leading you on but you're just too hard to resist.'

'Then don't. Don't resist me,' she whispered against his mouth, pressing another kiss to his lips before he said anything else. 'I know there are obstacles in our way, Woody, but please let me have these moments. I'm going to need to have something to keep me warm on the long and lonely nights after you've left Ood.'

He opened his mouth to say something but she kissed him again. 'Shh. Later.' Closing her eyes, she held him near, resting her ear to his chest, sighing as she listened to the beat of his heart and how she had been the one to make it thump so wildly against his chest. At least she now knew he *did* find her attractive, that he *did* want her as much as she wanted him, and whilst she desperately needed to know what was holding him back, for now, in this one glorious moment, Lorelai felt content.

They stood there for a good five minutes, neither one speaking but both absorbing as much of each other as possible. 'We can't say here for ever,' Woody finally murmured.

'I wish we could,' she returned, but knew he was right. Closing her eyes, she breathed in his essence once more, desperate to commit every aspect of these moments to memory.

'So do I.' He breathed in, her scent firmly wrapped around him, and he loved it. 'I want things to be different, Lore. I really do,' he murmured, his deep tone rumbling through her. 'If you only knew how complicated my life is, perhaps you'd help me to keep my distance.'

Lorelai eased back and looked at him. 'Then tell me, Woody. Open up to me. Share with me this great burden that seems to be weighing you down so heavily that you feel there's absolutely no possible way we could ever be together. Tell me. Please?'

He closed his eyes. 'I can't tell you.'

'Why not?'

'You'll hate me.'

'Impossible.'

He laughed without humour. 'You've hated me before now.'

'No. Never hate, Woody. Perhaps I was annoyed that you wouldn't talk to me, that you felt you couldn't share things with me. We're so in tune with each other. Don't you feel it?'

'I do. I *do* feel it but—' He stopped. Could he do it? Could he tell her about the responsibilities of his world? Tell her of the burden he would have to continue to carry for goodness only knew how many years, to provide for Kalenia's family? How he couldn't leave them in the lurch? How doing his duty was stopping him from finding happiness with her? Could he do it? Would she truly understand?

'Lorelai.' He started to release her from his arms. 'Perhaps we should sit do—'

Lorelai's phone rang, cutting him off. She closed her eyes and hung her head for a moment, unable to believe the bad timing of whoever was phoning her. 'I need to get that,' she murmured, and he instantly dropped his arms, letting her go.

'Of course you do.'

She glanced at the clock on the wall, which read half past nine, as she headed for the phone. 'A call at this hour is never good news. Dr Rainbow,' she said after she'd connected the call. 'Hello?' she said a moment later, frowning as all she heard was deep, rasping breathing.

'What is it?' Woody asked, concern filling him.

'A heavy breather.'

'In Oodnaminaby? This place is wilder than I thought.'

'Hello?' she tried again.

'Lore?' Her name was squeezed out followed by a groan of pain but that one word was enough for her to identify the person on the other end of the phone. She felt the blood drain from her entire body.

'*Dad*?' His name was a horrified whisper.

'Lore?' BJ said again and this time she heard it more clearly, the inability to get air into his lungs.

'Lorelai?' Woody closed the distance between them and took the phone from her trembling hand. 'BJ?' His firm voice carried down the line.

'Woo—' BJ couldn't even finish his words.

'Where are you?' Woody asked. 'Are you at home?'

'Ye—'

He didn't even need to finish the word. 'I'm calling an ambulance. Lore and I will be there as fast as we can. Try and stay as still as possible, be calm. We're on our way, BJ. Hang in there.'

Woody disconnected the call, then looked at Lorelai who was standing there, clearly in a state of disbelief.

'Lore, who looks after Hannah when you have emergencies?' He was already tapping in the number for the paramedics at Tumut, hoping they weren't out on another call.

'Lorelai?' He snapped his fingers in front of her face, then put his hand on her shoulder and gave her a little shake. The way she looked was reminiscent of the night John had died and his heart instantly ached for her. She'd already lost so many people, so many who were close and important to her, and the thought that she might now lose her dad was more than her mind could process. 'Snap out of it, honey. I need you here with me. We need to go and save BJ. You and me. We can do this. We can save him.' His words were firm, imploring and filled with determination. 'Who looks after Hannah?'

He had no time to press her further as the paramedics answered his call and he quickly gave them the few details he had. When he'd disconnected, he hauled Lorelai close and pressed his mouth to hers in a swift, harsh kiss, hoping the firm action would be enough to snap her out of wherever she was. 'Lore?'

'Huh?' She blinked rapidly and shook her head, looking unseeingly at him for a brief moment before clarity began to return. 'Babysitter. Right. Edward and Honey are away, so that leaves Connie. I'll call her.' She accepted the phone, then pointed to her mobile phone on the table. 'Call Andrew Paddington. His number's in my phone. He's dad's closest neighbour. He can go around and sit with Dad until we get there. Also, my emergency bag is in the entryway cupboard. Give it the once-over and let me know if we need to stop at the clinic to get anything else.' She turned her attention to the phone as her friend answered. 'Connie? I've got an emergency and Hannah's asleep. Are you or Hank able to…?' A pause, then, 'Thanks. I'd appreciate it.'

Woody was on the phone with Andrew whilst checking her bag as Lorelai headed to her room to quickly change her clothes and put on some shoes, ready for the wintry night before them. She looked out the window and saw it had started to snow again. Her father's house was a good ten minutes from Ood and that was in fine weather. Still, if they took their time, letting the all-wheel-drive do its work, they should reach him in fifteen minutes. Staying calm and focused was of paramount importance. Thank goodness Woody was here, not only in town but with her. If she'd been alone when that call had come through, she might still be standing there in a complete daze.

Lorelai couldn't even begin to contemplate what might happen if they didn't get to her father in time. They had to. They just had to, that was all there was to it. Her dad. Her wonderful, brilliant, funny and fantastic father couldn't be taken from her. She wouldn't allow it.

Tiptoeing into Hannah's room, she bent and kissed her daughter on the forehead, brushing the fine blonde hair back with her fingers. 'I love you, Hannah Emily. Sleep sweet.' As she turned to head out, she saw Woody standing in the doorway, watching her with Hannah. Lorelai was both pleased and surprised when he, too, came quickly into the room and dropped a kiss to Hannah's sleepy head.

He straightened and turned to face her. 'Ready?' he asked, as both of them heard the front door opening, indicating Connie had arrived.

Lorelai nodded and Woody could see that firm determination in her eyes. 'Let's go and save my dad.'

Less than ten minutes after receiving BJ's call they were in their car and on their way to his place, Lorelai unable to sit still as she shifted and fidgeted her worry away. 'It's all well and good telling myself to be professional, to remain calm and collected because I know that's the best way to help my dad at the moment,' she told Woody as he drove her car, following her directions. 'But I'm completely freaking out!'

'That's understandable,' he replied. 'Quite natural, in fact, and perhaps admitting that to me will help you deal with the swirling multitude of emotions currently churning throughout your body and mind.'

'Perhaps.'

They'd stopped at the clinic on the way so Woody could collect a portable oxygen concentrator. 'If he's having trouble breathing, this is the one piece of equipment we'll most definitely need.'

'I just wish I knew what he'd done, why he can't breathe. Is he trapped under something heavy? Is he hurt in some way? How long has he been injured?' Lorelai thumped a fist to the dashboard. 'I hate not knowing my parameters.'

Woody did his best to reassure her whilst concentrating on roads that were now covered with slush and snow. He wanted to do everything he could to help Lorelai in any way possible. He was also surprised at just how concerned he was for her father. It wasn't surprising, given BJ had instantly welcomed him to Oodnaminaby. The man was the rock of the entire mixed Rainbow-Goldmark clan.

BJ had cared for his daughter when his wife had passed away, he'd held the Goldmark boys together after the deaths of their parents and he'd supported his daughter after the death of her husband. Tragedy had been a part of this man's life, a part of his daughter's life, and Woody knew he would do everything in his power to ensure BJ made it, but he could give Lorelai no guarantees.

The fact that Woody had definite feelings for the woman beside him, feelings that no matter how hard he tried to quell them, to push them away, to do everything he could *not* to give into them, meant this case was different from the usual ones he dealt with.

Woody had been in love with Kalenia and yet he'd been unable to save his own daughter. For years he'd carried his wife's harsh words with him, hearing her blaming him for Ja'tenya's death. *'You could have done more. You should have been watching for the signs. It's all your fault she's dead.'*

Once again, the pressure was high and he needed to be vigilant, to check and double-check, to pre-empt, to think quickly. He had no idea what they might find when they went inside the cabin but he fervently hoped his mind would remain sharp and focused.

He glanced across at Lorelai and quickly took her hand in his. 'How are you holding up?'

'Uh…I um…I don't know.'

'You'll be fine. You'll be able to focus. He's your dad. You love him and we're going to do everything we can, Lore. OK? I'm right here with you, working together. We work well together.'

His words, his deep rich voice was working its magic,

calming her down, helping her head to come out of the clouds. 'Yes. Yes, we do.'

'See? We'll get BJ sorted out.' He gave her hand one final squeeze before he turned the wheel, bringing the car to a stop outside the front of the small log cabin, which was situated on twenty acres. There were a few cars parked near the front of the house.

'That's Andrew's car. Good. He made it.' Relief crossed Lorelai's face. 'At least Dad's not alone.'

'Right. Let's move,' he said the instant he'd switched off the engine. 'Lore, you take the medical bag, I'll get the oxygen.' Not waiting for an answer, he opened the car door, eager to get their equipment out and into the house to find out exactly what was going on. Lights seemed to be on everywhere, blazing bright as they headed up the front steps into the house.

'Dad?' she called loudly. 'Andrew? Andrew, where is he?' Even as she spoke, Woody could hear the veiled panic in her tone.

'Through here. Kitchen,' Andrew called. 'I've just checked on the ambulance. They'll be here in ten minutes.'

'Oh, Dad!' Lorelai choked back a sob the instant she saw her father lying on the kitchen floor, rasping for breath, Andrew sitting beside him.

Woody brought the oxygen cylinder with him and quickly knelt down, placing the non-rebreather mask over BJ's mouth and nose before adjusting the dosage. 'There you go, mate. That's going to help.'

Lorelai was beside her father, and when he looked at her she could clearly see panic in his eyes. As she looked at him lying there, for one split second the world seemed to stop turning. When her mother had died, she had been young and there had been nothing she could do. With Hannah and Cameron Goldmark, they'd been cruelly taken from her by an avalanche. In that frozen moment Lorelai realised something—she had the power to save her father. The realisation gave her courage and cleared her mind from the fog surrounding it.

'It's OK, Dad. Everything's going to be fine.' Her words were firm, reassuring and filled with hope. She took out her stethoscope. 'I'm just going to listen to your chest.' She closed her eyes and concentrated on listening. A moment later she frowned. 'This isn't an asthma or panic attack, as I'd initially thought,' she stated, directing her words to Woody. 'There are no breath sounds on the right side. There's also increased hyper-resonance.'

'Pneumothorax?' Woody's eyes widened and he glanced up to look at Lorelai.

'But how? Dad, did you hurt yourself? Fall over? Hit yourself in the chest in some way?'

'Slipped on ice,' BJ gasped, his words intermittent. 'Hit chest on fence post.'

Lorelai rubbed her hands together, trying to warm them before putting them onto her father's chest, carefully checking his ribs. 'Why didn't you call and tell me earlier? Your lung is collapsing, Dad,' she told him. 'But don't you worry because we're going to sort you out. Isn't that right, Woody?'

'Absolutely. You're in luck, BJ, because after my many years working in the jungles of Tarparnii, I've become what the natives call a "bitsa" doctor, because I can do "bitsa this" and "bitsa that", and I've treated several collapsed-lung patients before.' While Woody spoke, he was pulling different things from the medical bag—tubing, a needle, a sterile bandage, a valve. 'Andrew,' he said, looking across at BJ's neighbour, 'I need a bottle with some water in it. Can you find one, please?'

'Wha—?' BJ asked from beneath the oxygen mask.

'What's happening?' Woody asked the question he could see in BJ's eyes. Lorelai was taking the tubing out of the protective wrapper and attaching the valve and needle as Woody spoke. 'BJ, it looks as though your lung has collapsed. That's why you can't breathe properly. There's a collection of air between the chest wall and the lung—the pleural cavity,' Woody said. 'When you fell and hit your chest, that caused a sort of puncture to your lung and now, whenever you breathe out, some of the air is going into the pleural cavity. That's why it hurts so much but, rest assured, we'll have you fixed in a jiffy.'

'That's right,' Lorelai continued. 'And once we've re-established the negative pressure within the cavity, the lung will expand again and everything will be…' She shrugged '… perfect.' She leaned forward and pressed a kiss to her father's forehead.

Andrew came back with the bottle of water, which Woody gratefully accepted. 'Sorry there's no time for an anaesthetic,' he said to BJ, 'but you'll feel better very soon.' He glanced up and met Lorelai's gaze as she handed him the scalpel. 'Are you OK?'

'Oh, yes. Let's save my dad.'

Woody smiled and nodded before making a small incision into the pleural space. He inserted the catheter through the second intercostal space, which would remove the air. The other end of the tube went down into the bottle of water, forming a water seal.

Once that was done, Lorelai assisted as they covered the wound with an airtight dressing. The pressure in BJ's lungs started to change, Lorelai pressing her stethoscope to her father's chest to confirm. 'Hyperresonance decreasing. Nice. That'll hold him until we can get him to Tumut hospital.'

BJ's breathing increased and Lorelai relaxed onto the floor beside her father, relief flooding through her. Her dad was going to be all right—thanks to Woody. She looked across at him to find him watching her closely.

'He's going to be just fine.' His words were sure and steadfast.

'Yes.' She smiled back, her heart filled with gratitude. Woody was a man who had proved himself time and again to be dependable, supportive and thoughtful. She wasn't sure what he'd been about to tell her before her father had rung through and right now she realised it didn't matter.

Her heart most certainly belonged to him.

When the ambulance arrived, Woody insisted that Lorelai ride alongside her father whilst he drove behind in her car. At Tumut hospital the night staff were astonished to learn of BJ's condition, all vowing to look after the State Emergency Services captain to the best of their abilities.

'Of course. Your dad would have worked with most of these people over the years,' Woody stated after the makeshift drain had been replaced. Lorelai sat by BJ's beside, holding his hand while he slept.

'He's certainly saved a lot of lives,' Lorelai agreed. 'And tonight you saved his.'

Feeling choked with emotion, she stood and crossed

to where he stood at the foot of the bed. Not caring who saw, she put her arms around his waist, holding him close. 'Thank you, Woody.' She buried her face in his chest. 'Thank you,' she said again, the words muffled against his shirt.

'Lore, you don't have to thank me.'

She eased back and looked at him. 'Oh, yes, I do. I now understand why patients often go on and on about thanking us for the work we do. Of course, being the calm, modest people we doctors are, we nod politely and smile, saying "It was nothing" or "It's my job" or "It's what I've been trained to do". However, I really mean this, Woody. From my heart. You've saved my father's life and I can never repay you or say thank you enough. You understood just how much my father meant to me and you used those clever hands of yours and that amazing intelligent brain to save his life.'

Woody tightened his hold on Lorelai, happy to have her in his arms once again. It felt so perfect to have her near, to have her close to his heart. He gathered her to him and closed his eyes as she rested her head against his chest. It felt right to be like this with her. His heart was beating out a rhythm that he knew was in sync with her own. They belonged together and he felt it with every fibre of his being—yet he knew it could never happen.

His world was different from the happy life filled with sunshine that Lorelai lived here in Ood with her daughter and the rest of her surrogate family. It wasn't that he didn't love Tarparnii and the people who needed him there, it was simply the fact that he didn't get to choose. His path had been carved out during tragedy and he was honour bound to fulfil it.

It was purely selfish of him to be holding Lorelai like this, selfish of him to want more, to have her lips pressed to his yet again, to feel the lightness only she could inject into his world. It would be best if he made a clean break, if he just told her the truth, confessed why he could never be with her, could never have a life with her and Hannah here in Oodnaminaby, and once he told her, she would understand why they needed to fight harder to keep their distance.

With a sigh filled with regret Woody eased back and looked down into Lorelai's upturned face. He wanted to tell her now but she'd already had enough to deal with tonight. Thankfully, BJ had managed to pull through and was now sleeping soundly, well on the way to making a full recovery.

What she needed now was not to bear his burdens but to head home and be with her daughter. He looked into her eyes, the pupils wide in the dim light, the blue of her irises rimming them. She was stunning. Gorgeous. Feminine. Utterly beautiful. *His* Lorelai. Although it was wrong, although he'd tried hard to fight it, there was no denying her importance to him.

His gaze dipped to encompass her lips and when her tongue slipped out to wet them, he couldn't help the groan that escaped from deep within.

'Woody?'

'Lore, you are…exquisite.'

'You're not so bad yourself.' Those tantalising lips of hers curved into an alluring smile, one he found impossible to resist. 'Kiss me, Woody,' she breathed. 'I need you.'

And heaven help him but he needed her, too. Without

another word he lowered his head and tenderly captured her mouth with his own.

There were no two ways about it. He knew he shouldn't be kissing Lorelai. He knew he should be keeping his distance not only from her but from her daughter as well. He knew all of this, he knew the logic behind the decision, but whenever he was close to her, he was finding it increasingly difficult to keep from touching her.

There was a connection of their hearts, their souls and their minds, so powerful and strong, drawing him to her, the need pulsing wildly between them. It didn't help his self-control when he knew her kisses were heavenly, intense and powerful. The real Lorelai soft and pliant in his arms, responding to his mouth on hers was infinitely better than a dream. It had been a long time since he'd felt so comfortable, so natural, so light-hearted around a woman that keeping his hands off her was becoming impossible. Lorelai was an incredible woman and he counted himself privileged at her response to his need.

Her want for him was evident and he didn't take it for granted, honoured by her attention. He knew he didn't deserve it, not when at some point in their near future he'd be forced to break not only her heart but her daughter's as well.

He was a man caught between two worlds and right at the moment, as Lorelai responded so ardently to his touch, to the way their mouths seemed to move in an uncanny synchronicity, he chose this world. Staying with Lorelai and Hannah, never having to leave them, never having to hurt them, was what he wanted more than anything.

Unfortunately, he knew it could never be. He was

honour bound elsewhere and would be for the rest of his life. He'd been raised to do what was right, what was honourable, and he would fulfil his duty at the expense of his own happiness.

'Lore?' he began, pulling his mouth from hers, needing to talk to her, to tell her the truth about his situation. Earlier in their friendship he hadn't felt it necessary to lay his problems at her feet, preferring to keep them a private matter between himself and those involved. Now, though, with the escalation of his desire for her and his apparent lack of self-control, Woody knew he owed her the truth. It was far better for her to hear it from him rather than someone else.

'Lore?' he tried again, but her answer was to draw his mouth back to hers, desperate to continue kissing him. If he didn't talk, if he simply kept on kissing her, then she wouldn't have to face the future. Right here, right now, in this one moment in time, she was happy. Her father was improving, her daughter was safe and the man of her dreams, the man she'd been waiting for her entire life, was holding her in his arms, cherishing her with his mouth, protecting her with his heart.

'Lore?' This time he leaned back. 'We need to talk, sweetheart.'

Lorelai shook her head and put her finger over his lips. 'Shh. I don't want to decipher this, Woody. I just want to feel and you most definitely make me *feel*.' She pressed her mouth to his once more, eager to capture his full attention. 'For too long I felt useless and unwanted and unloved but you've changed all that. You make me feel…fantastic and desirable and alive.' Her words were punctuated with kisses, her hands cupping his face ensuring he remained right where he was. 'There'll be time to talk…later.'

Woody knew he should argue, should make her see reason, but it was nigh impossible when he wanted exactly the same thing as her. He moaned in appreciation as he gathered her close, accepting her mouth, wanting to lose himself in her just as much as she wanted to lose herself within him. As the kiss began to intensify, their hearts continued to intertwine. There would be rocky times ahead but the memory of this time, of the two of them together, locked in mutual desire and need for each other, was what would get them through.

'That's a great sight to wake up to,' BJ murmured, and it was only then that Lorelai remembered their location. She slid her arms from Woody at the same time he released her, both of them crossing to BJ's bedside to check on their patient.

'How are you feeling, Dad?' she asked, taking BJ's hand in hers.

'Much better for seeing you with Woody,' he rasped, speaking slowly. 'It's about time you two kids realised how good you are together.'

Lorelai glanced across at Woody, feeling a little self-conscious at being caught by her father. Woody smiled but she noticed it didn't meet his eyes. Her stomach churned in knots as she realised her present happiness would be short-lived. Woody had something important he needed to discuss with her and whilst she didn't particularly want to hear it, she knew it was inevitable. For now, though, she turned her concentration towards her father and bent to kiss his cheek.

'Don't you ever scare me like that again, you hear?'

'Yes, darling. I won't be going anywhere, especially

if there's a big family event coming up.' He winked at her and Lorelai couldn't help the embarrassment she felt at his assumption.

'Well you rest.' She spoke quickly, trying to cover over her father's implication that she and Woody would be getting married soon. 'I'll bring Hannah in to see you tomorrow so you'd best be looking your dapper best.'

'Will do, love.'

Lorelai bent to kiss his cheek again. 'Sleep well and don't tease the nurses.' She pointed her finger at him in a stern manner, using her best 'mother' voice to discipline him.

BJ closed his eyes, showing how even a little exertion could tire him out. 'You spoil all my fun,' he murmured, before his breathing evened out.

Satisfied her father was now doing well, Lorelai turned to Woody. 'Ready to go?'

Woody held out her car keys. 'You go. Be with Hannah. I'm going to stay here a while longer and monitor your dad.'

Alarm instantly flooded Lorelai. 'Why? But…he's doing really well. I've read his chart.' She pointed to her dad. 'Is there something you're not telling me?'

Woody chuckled and cupped her face in his hands. 'Everything's fine. I just need to…stay. To watch over him. Make sure his progress continues.' He shrugged. 'That's all. Go and get some rest. Cuddle Hannah.'

Lorelai watched him for a moment, recalling something he'd said earlier that night…something about not being vigilant enough where his wife and daughter had been concerned. 'My dad's doing great and he's surrounded by staff who are not only highly trained but care for him on a personal level. He'll be fine.'

'I know. I would like to stay but I'll walk you to the car.'

Lorelai nodded and said goodnight to the staff before heading out. Woody slipped his arm about her waist as they walked side by side, needing her close.

'Woody, you don't need to punish yourself for not being able to save your daughter,' she said softly as they made their way through the quiet hospital. 'My dad will be fine, thanks to you.'

'Exactly, and he's going to stay that way. You've already lost far too many people, Lorelai, and I need to stay here, to be vigilant, to be one hundred per cent sure BJ's not going to develop any further complications. I've learned my lessons the hard way and I'm determined to protect the people I care about.'

Lorelai stopped just before the door and turned to face him. 'You care about me?'

'Oh, honey. I care about you so very much. It's why I need to stay.'

Lorelai reached up and stroked a hand down his determined jaw. 'Your daughter's death wasn't your fault, despite what your wife might have said. You can't keep punishing yourself, Woody.'

He nodded and captured her hand in his, bringing it to his lips. 'You're right. Logically I know Kalenia was only speaking from intense hurt and I *did* do everything possible to save my daughter.'

'Of course you did. Seeing you with Hannah has shown me just how caring and nurturing you are. You would have been an amazing father and I'm sure your baby felt your love.' She smiled at him. 'You're a dynamic man, Woody.'

'Lore.' He gathered her into his arms again and held

her. 'Why is it you know just what to say to get through to me?'

'We're connected,' she replied, before leaning up to brush a sweet kiss across his lips. 'I do appreciate you staying, though. Having you here, keeping watch over my dad, it does give me that extra level of security.'

Woody smiled and together they headed out, surprised to find snow had fallen again, making everything look fresh and brilliant and new. He held the door for Lorelai as she climbed into the vehicle, adjusting the seat. He kissed her once, twice before forcing himself to close the door and watch her drive away.

Finding happiness and peace in Lorelai's arms, finally taking those steps to look ahead rather than wishing for the past, had him yearning for a different future. One where he, Lorelai and Hannah made their own family.

He stood there in the snow for a few minutes, watching the flakes float quietly and gently to the ground. Fresh and brilliant and new. If only his life could be that way for ever—but he knew it was impossible.

CHAPTER TEN

'Aunty Honey!' Hannah squealed with delight, slipping from Woody's lap where the two of them had been sitting down, reading a story together. She ran towards the front door as Honey came inside, Edward not far behind as he hung up the coats.

Lorelai was equally surprised, watching as Honey bent down to welcome Hannah's cuddles.

'What are you doing back so early?' Woody asked as he came over to embrace his sister. 'You've only been gone for just on four weeks.' And those four weeks had been the most confusing and exciting he'd had in so very long. BJ was still in hospital, Woody demanding he stay for at least two days before venturing home. Thankfully, there had been no further complications and Lorelai's father would soon return to full health. The smile he'd seen on Lorelai's face earlier that day when they'd taken Hannah to see her grandfather had warmed his heart. Hannah, of course, had been duly concerned that her granddad was in the hospital but as soon as Lorelai had told the little girl that Woody was looking after granddad, Hannah's brow had cleared and a smile had beamed on her lips.

'Woody can fix him,' she'd stated firmly. 'Woody's

the best.' And with that glowing confidence in her beloved Woody, her world had righted itself. Woody had
been stunned to have both Lorelai and Hannah having
so much faith in him and he had to admit it was an incredible sensation to be so trusted.

Now he smiled as Hannah all but threw herself at her
Uncle Edward, his brother-in-law scooping the child up
and kissing her neck whilst tickling her. Hannah's giggles filled the room, the glorious sounds of happiness
washing over him, warming him all the way through.

'Woody and me was weading,' Hannah told Edward.
'We love weading storwees.' She wriggled from his
arms and ran to the sofa to collect the books and show
them to her aunt and uncle.

Lorelai embraced her friends, giving them a quick
update on her father's excellent progress before making
a pot of tea. It was great to have them back, everyone
talking at once, a jumble of laughter and happiness. She
hadn't realised just how much she'd missed her friends
and at the same time she was wary of Honey's natural
ability to see right into the heart of people.

Could Honey see that Lorelai was in love with
Woody? Was it obvious? Lorelai caught Woody's
glance, noting a hint of sadness in his gaze. What did
it mean? Now that Honey and Edward had returned, was
Woody planning on skipping town again? Leaving as
quietly as he had last time? Without even saying goodbye? Her heart began to ache at the thought of him
gone, of not seeing him, of not being able to bask in
the warmth of his presence, but now was not the time
to dwell on it. She pushed the emotions aside for now
and pasted on a happy smile.

Soon the four of them were watching as Hannah

eagerly unwrapped the cache of presents Honey and Edward had given her.

'We thought you would have been away for much longer,' Lorelai said as she sipped her tea.

'Not that we're not elated at having you home,' Woody added, conscious his sister was watching the interaction between himself and Lorelai very closely. They were sitting together on the sofa, his arm stretched out along the back cushions, Lorelai's body angled towards his, her legs crossed beneath her.

'The travelling became too tiresome,' Honey murmured as she rubbed her belly. 'I feel tired more often, frumpy—'

'You're not frumpy,' Edward quickly interjected, leaning over to kiss his wife.

'Besides, I missed everyone too much. Four weeks was long enough. I don't know why I ever thought I could stay away for longer.'

'Plus the nesting instinct has kicked in and the places we were staying at seemed to take offence when Honey would re-clean the room after the maid.'

Lorelai laughed and smiled at her friend. 'I remember that instinct. It became so strong with me that I actually vacuumed my cutlery drawer.'

Honey laughed. Edward smiled. Hannah oohed at the book she was looking at and Woody found himself wishing *he* had been Hannah's father. He closed his eyes for a moment, imagining a pregnant Lorelai walking around this house, tidying up Hannah's toys, *his* child growing inside her. She would smile at him, welcoming him into her arms. He would kiss her and then kiss her belly, already in love with his unborn child. Pain pierced his heart at the image and he quickly opened his eyes, astonished to find his sister watching him closely.

Honey knew him too well, had practically raised him, and he'd learned at a very young age that trying to hide things from her was plain ridiculous. He tuned his thoughts back into the conversation but only listened with half an ear as Edward recounted an amusing story from their travels.

'Well,' Honey said the moment Edward's tale had finished, 'I have an idea.' She wriggled out of the chair and stood, stretching her back muscles before looking at Hannah. 'How would you like to come and have a sleepover at our house tonight? Uncle Edward has missed your cuddles and kisses and reading you lots and lots of stories.'

Hannah scrambled to her feet and started jumping up and down, clapping her hands with delight. 'Yes. Yes. Yes.' She quickly ran to Lorelai and pleaded with earnest eyes. 'Please, Mummy? Oh, please?'

Lorelai put her cup down on the table and looked at Honey. 'Are you sure? You've only just got home and—'

'And we've both missed her so much, haven't we, Eddie?'

Edward blinked once, obviously having difficulty following his wife's train of thought. He looked into Honey's eyes for a second before his confusion cleared and he nodded. 'Yes. Absolutely. Missed you all but most especially our Hannah cuddles. Now that we're going to be parents soon, we need to get lots of practice cuddling yummy children.'

'Cuddle me. Cuddle me.' Hannah ran to Edward's side and begged to be picked up.

'Well…OK, then. If you're sure.' A little bemused, Lorelai stood. 'I'll go pack her a bag.'

'Tum on, Uncle Edward,' Hannah insisted. 'We choose the storwees.' She urged him to follow her mother and a moment later Woody was left alone with his sister.

'Neatly orchestrated,' he ventured, no stranger to his big sister's tactics of gentle manipulation.

'What's going on, Woody?'

'Why?'

'Because I received a call from K'nai in Tarparnii. Apparently Nilly's been trying desperately to get in contact with you.'

'I know.' Woody closed his eyes and shook his head. 'She wants me to come home for the *par'Mach*.'

Honey thought for a moment. 'That's in about four days' time! Why didn't you call me? Ask me to come back earlier? I thought one of Kalenia's sisters was taking part in the festival? As head of the clan, you need to be there for her.'

'Yes, but I did mention to Nilly before I left that I wasn't sure whether I'd make it back in time. She said she would get another elder to fill in the duties. She said she understood and that helping you was also an honourable cause.' He shook his head and raked a hand through his hair, confusion etched on his brow. 'But lately she's been sending more messages, urging me to come home.'

'Well, now that Eddie and I are back, you're free to go.'

'Free?' He laughed without humour. 'Yeah. I'm free to leave but never free to have the life I want.' His shoulders slumped and he shook his head. Honey watched him for a moment then gasped.

'You haven't told Lorelai?'

'I've told her most of it,' he defended, his hackles starting to rise.

'Woody!' There was censure in Honey's tone and Woody didn't like it. 'She's in love with you.'

'And I'm in love with her,' he replied, then stopped as though he hadn't expected to say those words out loud. He raised his eyebrows in surprise and stared at Honey, watching the slow smile spread over his sister's face. 'I'm in love with her!' he breathed with a hint of incredulity. 'Wow.'

'Oh, Woody.' Honey hugged her big little brother close. 'You're such a goose. You've always been so intent on protecting everyone else but yourself.' She smiled up at him. 'But I'm very glad to see you didn't protect your heart so fiercely that you locked it away for good. You deserved to be loved, and I can't think of anyone more deserving of you than Lorelai. You'll make a wonderful couple.'

He shrugged. 'No, we won't. We can't have a future together.'

Honey frowned. 'What? Why not?'

'Because of my responsibilities.' He took a step back and spread his arms wide, his tone imploring. 'It's not fair to Lore, Honey. She's been through so much over the years, lost so many people, experienced emotional hardship. I can't ask her to take on my problems. I'd never do that to her, or to Hannah. They both deserve better than I can give.'

'And that makes you sad. Poor Woody.' She smiled up at him, her eyes full of promise. 'As a word of advice, don't go giving up hope and predicting the end too soon. I thought I had no future with Eddie and now look at me.' She stared up into his face. 'I love you, Woody. You're a good man and you'll do what's right. You always do but please don't sell Lorelai short. She's incredible.'

He nodded as he hugged his sister. 'I know and that's the problem. She's so amazing, so great, so...' He exhaled harshly and raked a hand through his hair, knowing it was time to face the music. He'd been on the verge of telling her two nights ago before BJ's emergency. Since then, he hadn't wanted to burden Lorelai with his problems, especially when she was concerned about her dad. However, with Honey and Edward back, there really was no reason for him to miss the *par'Mach* festival and he knew Kalenia would want him to do honour to her sister as well as to her clan.

He nodded with determination. 'I'll talk to her.'

Honey smiled. 'I proud of you, Woody.'

Within another fifteen minutes he was alone in the house with Lorelai. She closed the front door, a look of bewilderment on her face. 'I have no idea what just happened.'

'Honey happened.' Woody shook his head. 'She just...*knows* things. She always has.' He stood by the heater and shoved his hands into his pockets. 'It made it difficult trying to keep her birthday presents a secret.'

Lorelai chuckled and crossed to his side. 'So what does Honey know that resulted in her kidnapping my daughter for the night?'

'She knows I haven't told you the truth.'

At his words Lorelai's mouth instantly went dry and her heart started to pound painfully against her chest.

'What? How can she know that?' And had Honey guessed about Lorelai's feelings for Woody? More than likely, as she was obviously giving them the opportunity to talk things out. Lorelai forced herself to breath calmly, to keep herself under control, even though it appeared Woody was about to tell her what she wasn't at all sure she wanted to hear. He was going to tell her why they could never be together and she didn't want to hear it.

Woody shook his head. 'I've stopped trying to figure out how she can read people, me especially, so easily and just accept that she can.'

Lorelai nodded gently, then closed her eyes, swallowing compulsively over her still dry throat. 'I don't know if I want you to tell me, Woody. I don't want to hear whatever it is you're going to say because I know it'll take you away from me, away from the incredible way you make me feel.' Her heart was hammering fiercely against her chest and her stomach was churning with fear.

'Why don't we sit down?' She could hear the uncertainty in his voice.

'No.' She opened her eyes and stared at him, brushing away a tear from her lashes. 'Just tell me. Blurt it out. Rip the plaster off.' She straightened her shoulders and lifted her chin with a hint of defiance.

Woody's heart pounded with love for the brave, courageous, beautiful woman before him. Her inner strength revealed itself right before his very eyes and he couldn't help but be enamoured by it. Even when faced with a situation she didn't want, she was still incredibly beautiful. His heart churned with love for her.

He exhaled slowly, then nodded. 'OK. Good. That's what I'll do.' He rubbed his hands together and clenched them tight. 'Well, as you know, I was married to Kalenia. She has three younger sisters and no brothers. When we were married, I became the only other male in the family besides her father. In Tarparnii, the males are responsible for providing for their greater clan. Her aunts and cousins live in the village and whilst there are other men around to help with the day-to-day needs, when Kalenia's father passed away, I became head of the clan, so to speak.'

Lorelai listened intently, processing his words carefully and slowly realisation started to sink in. 'You're responsible for them?'

'Yes, and I always will be.'

Her thoughts churned as she processed this information. 'That's why you spend so much time in Tarparnii. Why you're always working a few months here and there but always returning to Tarparnii.'

'Yes. I do love the country. I love the people. I love the beauty and simplicity of life, but travelling and working in other countries for short contracts gives me the opportunity to keep my skills up to date.' Woody paused and dropped his hands back to his sides. 'However, when Kalenia's father passed away, I was determined to do right by her mother and sisters, to accept the responsibility of provider and to be there for them in any way I could.'

'Do you have…?' She shrugged. 'I don't know, official duties of some kind? Rituals? Ceremonies?'

'Yes. I'm required to attend various ceremonies and

confer with the other elders in the village about any important decisions throughout the year.' He breathed out slowly. 'I have far too many people relying on me, sometimes waiting for my return so they can make decisions and move on with their lives.'

'How do you keep in contact with them?'

'Post. Satellite phone. An occasional email or phone call via PMA.'

'Ah…the phone calls you've been receiving. You've been called home?'

'Yes. There is a ceremony in a few days' time that I wasn't planning to attend. It had all been sorted out with one of the other elders in the village offering to fill in to complete my duties, but for some reason Kalenia's mother needs me home.' Woody moved away from Lorelai and started to pace.

Lorelai nodded. 'Then you should go.'

'I don't want to. For the first time ever I don't want to return to Tarparnii. These weeks I've been here in Oodnaminaby, spending time with you and Hannah, have been the happiest I've had in a very long time. *You* make me happy, Lore, and I don't want it to end, but—'

'But you already have another family,' Lorelai finished for him, then rubbed her hand across her forehead as she tried to process what he was saying.

'Yes. It's why I was desperate to try and keep my distance from you. Colleagues or friendship was fine but you…' Woody swallowed and stepped forward to take her hands in his. 'You've worked your way into my heart, Lore. Before I met you, I was more than happy to stay in Tarparnii for most of the year, to provide for Kalenia's people, to uphold my promises and respect their traditions. Now I don't want to leave you or Hannah but I must. I am duty bound elsewhere and to break from Kalenia's family now would bring disrespect to her entire clan. Her sisters would never be able to find worthy husbands and her mother would be shunned by others.'

Lorelai bit her lip, trying to control her tears as she realised Woody wasn't free. 'You're already tied to another family.'

'Yes.'

'That is so like you. You have such a strong sense of duty and honour, willing to sacrifice your own happiness for others. You're protecting them, just as you used to protect the other kids in the communes from being picked on in the schoolyard. Just as you protected me in my hour of need—my knight in shining armour.'

'I don't think my armour's all that shiny but on the helping scale, I think the feeling is mutual. You've helped me just as much, Lore. You've helped me let go of the guilt I've carried with me since Ja'tenya's death.' He reached out and brushed the back of his hand across her cheek, a small, sad smile on his lips. 'You're amazing, Lorelai. So strong and determined, so caring and kind.' His tone dropped and he cupped her face, stepping closer, his need for her doubling in that one moment. 'So beautiful and so incredibly sexy.'

Without another word Woody bent and claimed her lips, eager to show her just how much he loved her, how much he wished things were different and how he was incredibly proud of her for being so brave at such a painful time.

Tears ran down her face, their saltiness mingling with the sweet taste from his mouth as she kissed him back, putting all her love into the embrace, wanting to show him that her love for him would never die, no matter what.

When they broke apart, she rested her head against his chest, her tears wetting his shirt. 'You're not mine. You're not mine to have and to hold.' Even as she said the words she clung to him, desperate to somehow change their paths so they could always be together, but she knew it was impossible.

'Make it quick. Like last time,' Lorelai had pleaded. 'Don't say goodbye. It's too…'

'Final,' he'd finished for her before capturing her lips with his once more. As he passed through the jungle terrain, heading for Kalenia's village where his Tarparniian family was waiting for him, Woody closed his eyes, remembering the feel of Lorelai's mouth on his. They were a perfect fit both physically, mentally and emotionally. In the past, whenever he'd returned to Tarparnii, he'd always felt a sense of homecoming.

This time, though, he felt bound and shackled, even though Nilly and her daughters didn't deserve to be the reason for that sensation. If he left them now, if he selfishly walked away to pursue a life with Lorelai, he would leave them destitute and in disrespect. There would be no dowries, no opportunities, no promise of a future. Lorelai was right when she'd said he was a protector. He'd always been that way from a very young age and whilst he knew protecting Nilly and her daughters was the right thing to do, Lorelai and Hannah also needed protection.

'Hey. Wake up.' K'nai, his old friend, had brought the jungle Jeep to a stop. 'We are here.'

Woody opened his eyes and looked out at the village he'd called home for such a long time. It was the same. It would never change. Quite a few of the villagers came to welcome him home, speaking rapidly in Tarparnese as they embraced. Woody was happy to see them and forced a smile. He was doing what was right, even though his heart was broken.

'One day!'

Lorelai paced around her lounge room, Honey lying on the sofa with her feet up, Hannah sitting at the coffee table, colouring in.

'He's been gone one day and already I feel as if an enormous part of me is missing.' Lorelai pressed a hand to her heart. 'I can't breathe. I can't sleep. I can't think clearly.' She stopped pacing and spread her arms wide. 'How am I going to concentrate for clinic tomorrow? Poor Edward has returned from holidays and been dumped with weekend duty and a few house calls.'

Honey waved her words away. 'He doesn't mind. He was champing at the bit to get back and connect with his patients. You know Eddie. He loves this town and its people.'

'So do I. But...I love Woody more.'

'Me too,' Hannah piped up. When Woody had said goodbye to the little girl, he'd simply told her he had to go away for a trip, just like Aunty Honey and Uncle Edward had done. He hadn't said how long he'd be gone and Hannah had listened intently before nodding.

'And you'll bring me back lots of presents?' she'd checked. Woody had laughed and promised her a whole sackful of presents as he'd hugged the little girl close, the sight of the two of them piercing Lorelai's heart.

'He belongs with us,' Lorelai continued as she started to pace again. 'The three of us together. Him. Me. Hannah. A family. He had a family before and they were tragically taken from him.'

Honey smiled. 'I'm so glad he's told you about his past.'

Lorelai paused. 'That's right. I remember he said you were in Tarparnii when Ja'tenya was born, that you nursed her back to health.'

'I did what any doting aunt would do. She was gorgeous, Lore.' Honey sighed. 'I wish I could have said something to you about Woody's life, especially when I could see how perfectly the two of you were for each other, but I couldn't.' She shrugged. 'It wasn't my story to tell. I just had to trust that you and my genius brother would work it out in your own way.' Honey nodded with satisfaction. 'So now that you've realised you and Hannah belong with Woody, what are you going to do about it?'

Lorelai stopped and looked at her friend. 'What do you mean? I can't do anything about it.'

'Can't you?'

'Well, short of getting on a plane, flying to Tarparnii and demanding he admit we have some sort of future together—' Lorelai stopped in mid-tirade as her words slowly started to sink in. 'We have some sort of future together.' Her eyes widened as she stared at Honey. 'Why does it have to be all or nothing? Why can't he have both? Why can't *we* have both?' Lorelai started pacing again, although this time it was more thoughtful than frustrated. 'He loves Tarparnii, right?'

'Right.'

'He needs to provide for Kalenia's family, right?'

'Right.'

'So…why can't we provide for them together?'

'Exactly,' Honey remarked as she sat up a little straighter. 'Pass me the phone. We have some organising to do.'

Hannah was incredibly excited to be going on an aeroplane and with her purple and pink backpack proudly on her back, holding onto her mother's hand, they embarked on this new adventure together.

'We get Woody,' she'd told her granddad BJ before they'd left. 'We gonna bring him *home*. We *love* him, don't we, Mummy?'

'Yes,' Lorelai had agreed, sure and firm in her decision. When it had come time to board the plane for Tarparnii, though, she'd started to falter. Honey had convinced her it was best to surprise Woody and had organised for Woody's friend K'nai to meet them at the airport.

'It's all arranged,' she'd told Lorelai. 'Woody will go completely bug-eyed when he sees you and Hannah.' Honey had clutched her hands to her chest. 'Oh, I wish I could be there to see his face!'

Now Lorelai wasn't so sure. Perhaps Woody really wouldn't want them to encroach on his life in Tarparnii. Perhaps he wouldn't be happy to see them. Butterflies of doubt churned in her stomach and if it hadn't been for Hannah tugging her forward onto the plane, Lorelai might have chickened out.

'Think about Woody. About how much you love him. About how much he means to you,' she whispered to herself as the plane taxied. Hannah was busy looking out the window, oohing and ahhing at everything she saw, drinking in the experience and having a wonderful time. And why shouldn't she be happy? She was going to find her precious Woody. There was no doubt Woody would be pleased to see Hannah, he loved Hannah but what about her? Did he love her? *Really* love her?

Lorelai closed her eyes and tried to calm her thoughts. It was done now. They were on the plane, the adventure had begun. Whatever was going to happen was out of her hands and she'd do well to simply let the fear and trepidation leave her and join in Hannah's joy.

At the Tarparniian airport they were warmly welcomed by Woody's friend, K'nai, who somehow recognised them immediately.

'Not many people travel with children,' he said as he carried their luggage to his open-topped Jeep. 'Besides, I would have recognised you anyway. Woody described you perfectly.'

'Oh.' Lorelai smiled shyly and blushed a little, although secretly she was pleased Woody had spoken of her to his old friend. As they drove along, Lorelai gasped in delight at the lush green scenery spread before her. Everywhere she looked, there were trees.

'Look, Mummy!' Hannah had pointed as Lorelai held her firmly as the only 'seat-belt' was a piece of rope to hold you to the chair. 'A monkey.'

'That is called a *ne'quaha*,' K'nai informed her, and Hannah instantly repeated it, giggling at the sound of the foreign words on her tongue.

'She will be speaking like a native in no time at all.' K'nai laughed. As they drove to the village, they waved a greeting to every passing car. Sometimes K'nai would honk his horn if there was an animal near the edge of the road and it would quickly scuttle out of the way.

Twice they stopped to offer a lift to people and by the time they arrived in the village almost forty minutes later, Lorelai was already in love with the place.

'Everyone's so friendly and welcoming and...happy,' she remarked as K'nai helped Hannah from the Jeep. Lorelai bent to pick up Hannah's forgotten backpack. When she straightened, she looked directly into rich, blue eyes...eyes that were wide and bright with surprise.

'Need some help?' His deep, familiar tone washed over her and she felt as though she could breathe easy for the first time since he'd left.

'Woody!'

He held out his hand to help her from the Jeep and the moment she placed her hand in his, she was over-whelmed with a sense of homecoming. She was here. With Woody. *Her* Woody. The man who held her heart and always would.

Their gazes held, both of them drinking in the sight of each other as though it had been years since they'd seen each other rather than just a few days.

'You're here.'

'I'm here,' she repeated, and sighed.

'Why? Why are you here, Lore?'

'Don't you want me to be?' Confusion and panic started to rise within her before her held her close, wrapping his arms around her. She closed her eyes and breathed him in, wanting desperately so much for him to be with her for ever and hoping he'd accept her rea-soning for this impromptu trip.

'Oh, Lore.' He rested his chin on her head and breathed in the sweet, fresh scent he always equated with his darling Lorelai.

'I'm here too, Woody. Hug *me*,' Hannah demanded, as she tugged at his trouser leg.

Without releasing Lorelai, Woody bent and scooped Hannah up into his arms. 'Both my girls,' he whispered. 'I must be dreaming.'

Lorelai eased back and raised an eyebrow. 'Your girls?' she couldn't help tease, even though she still wasn't sure he was happy they'd come. Hope flared a moment later when he smiled, a wide beaming smile that for the first time in weeks met his twinkling eyes.

'Don't worry about me,' K'nai said. 'I'll just lug the bags to the hut,' he replied as he headed off.

'Yeah, thanks, mate,' Woody called after his friend. Hannah wriggled from his arms.

'I want to go with K'nai,' she demanded.

'Uh…well…um…' Lorelai looked to Woody for help. 'You know the place better than I do. Will she be all right?'

Woody blinked for a moment, surprised Lorelai was deferring to him as though he really *was* Hannah's father. 'She'll be fine. It's safe.'

Hannah cheered and clapped but Woody's voice held a warning.

'But you stay close to K'nai. OK, princess?'

'Yes, Woody,' Hannah dutifully replied, and within another moment had run off after her new friend.

'He'll watch her, introduce her to his children. She'll be fine,' he promised Lorelai.

'If you say so.'

'You trust me that much?'

'Of course I do.' Lorelai smiled brightly up at the man of her dreams. Woody adjusted his hold on Lorelai, slipping both arms about her waist.

'Why are you here, Lore?'

Lorelai wasn't quite sure how to answer that. Did she confess she was in love with him? Say that Hannah had missed him so much they'd just had to fly all the way to Tarparnii? Tell him she'd come to support him? That she'd only been half a person without him? That even though it had only been a few days since he'd left Oodnaminaby, it had been far too long? Or should she just say she refused to live the rest of her life without him?

Indecision warred through her and she decided the best thing she could do was to show him. Without another word she stood on tiptoe and pressed her mouth to his. Woody obviously approved of her answer as he moaned with delight before deepening the kiss.

Lorelai was here. She'd come after him. Surely that was a good sign? He hadn't been able to stay in Ood and so she'd followed him to Tarparnii. Lorelai was here. He had no idea why but right now he didn't really care. *Lorelai was here.*

The village was larger than she'd imagined, a line of huts with thatched roofs positioned around the edge of a big clearing, a well having pride of place in the centre. Children of all ages ran around the clearing, playing games and laughing. Goats were tethered to the side, eating anything they could.

Next to each hut was a small garden, some growing flowers, most growing vegetables. Women were scattered here and there, tending to the various tasks of food preparation, gardening and stringing long garlands of flowers together, no doubt for the *par'Mach* festival to be held tonight. Young boys were restocking a wood pile and helping with other chores. The whole place was a hive of activity and Lorelai couldn't help but drink it all in.

'It's a different world,' Lorelai breathed as Hannah ran up to them.

'I can run super-fast here in 'Parni,' she told them both. 'Watch me.' And off she ran again.

'Well, she's settled,' Lorelai murmured, and Woody smiled, holding her hand in his.

'Come. There's someone I want you to meet.'

'Who?'

'Nilly. Kalenia's mother. She was called away to the next village and has been gone for the past few days. She only arrived back just before you. I haven't had a proper chance to see her since I returned.'

'I hope every thing's all right,' Lorelai said as Woody directed them towards one of the huts. She stopped him short, just outside the door. 'Wait. Woody, should I be meeting her?'

'What's the problem?'

'Well…us. Whatever this is between us… I…um… don't want her to feel…threatened or something. That I'm trying to take you away from your responsibilities, because I'm not.'

Woody's answer was to squeeze her hand a little tighter. 'Relax. They understand the search for happiness. They're wonderful people, Lore, and I know they'll love you.'

And he was right. Nilly, Kalenia's mother, hugged her close and stroked her blonde hair. 'Shiny,' she replied. 'So beautiful. Your eyes are wise and yet…' She pressed her hand to Lorelai's cheek. 'You have known great sadness, child, just like Woody.'

Lorelai's eyes started to fill with tears at the maternal tone and she forced a smile. 'Thank you for your welcome. Hannah and I are very happy to be here.'

'As are we to have you and your daughter here.' Nilly looked to where Hannah was already joining in with the other children, running about, playing and laughing as though travelling to a different country was something she did every day.

Nilly returned her attention to Woody. 'I am sorry I was not here when you returned. There have been many final arrangements to be made but...' She sighed and smiled. 'They are done.' She smiled at Lorelai. 'We have a big festival tonight. The *par'Mach*. My daughter is to be bonded with her *par'machkai* and she is all...' Nilly paused, searching for a word.

'In a dither?' Lorelai provided, and Nilly nodded.

'Exactly. Now, there is other news I must tell Woody. It is the reason I was so insistent you return for the festival.'

'What's wrong, Nilly? Please tell me.' Woody placed a concerned hand on his mother-in-law's arm but she patted his hand. The smile that lit Nilly's dark eyes and tanned skin was beaming.

'Everything is perfect, my son.' Nilly clasped her hands together. 'A great friend has come to live in our village since you left. He lived in my village when I was a young girl and we were close friends. His name is Ka'nu and since he has come to be here, we have...' Nilly stopped and Lorelai could have sworn the other woman was blushing. 'I am also to take part in the bonding at the *par'Mach*. Ka'nu will be my *par'machkai*.' Nilly clutched her hands to her chest and Lorelai, even though she didn't completely understand what was happening, recognised the look of a woman in love.

'What's a *par*…?' Lorelai trailed off, not sure she could pronounce the word properly.

'It means romantic life partner. Or, in your language, husband.'

'That's beautiful.' Lorelai smiled at Nilly. 'Congratulations, Nilly.'

Woody was gobsmacked and she had to give him a little nudge to snap him out of it. 'Uh…Nilly!' He hugged the small woman close to his chest. 'I can see that this has made you very happy.'

'It has, my son. Ka'nu has never had a *par'machkai* before and he is most willing to take on all care of my daughters within the village. He has become a clear leader within the village and all that is left is your blessing.'

'My blessing?' He was humbled. 'Nilly, it's yours. If you have found love again, I am very happy for you.'

'As am I, for you,' Nilly remarked, looking over at Lorelai with a smile. She held out her hand, beckoning Lorelai towards her. 'A heart that loves with deep emotion is never lonely. Life is filled with colour.' She took Lorelai's hand in hers and then placed it in Woody's. She rested her hand on top. 'I bless your union. Fill it with colour.'

Woody replied to her in Tarparnese and then translated for Lorelai. 'We accept your blessing, Mother, and respect your wise ways.'

Nilly smiled, then looked outside her door. 'I hear the men returning from food gathering. Ka'nu is waiting with impatience to meet you, Woody. I shall collect him. Please wait. I will soon be back.' With a spring in her step Nilly headed out of her hut, pausing to slip on her shoes before crossing the large open area in the centre of the village.

Lorelai and Woody stood in silence for a moment, their hands still entwined as the reality of what Nilly had revealed started to sink in. 'She's getting married again.' Woody spoke slowly then turned to look at Lorelai. 'She's getting married again!'

'What does this mean?'

'It means my obligation to Nilly and her clan is… finished.'

Lorelai's eyes widened in surprise. 'You're no longer responsible for them?'

'No. I'll still love them, I'll still be a part of them and always will be, but…' He slowly exhaled as the truth of the situation hit him. 'I'm free.' He turned to face her, gathering her close. 'I'm free!' He pressed his lips to hers, then laughed out loud. 'I didn't realise what a weight had been on my shoulders.'

Lorelai smiled and rested her hands on those broad shoulders of his. 'But you carried that weight and far more around with you for so long. You're a wonderful man, Woody. So strong and dependable. So honest and caring. So protective and loving. When you left Ood, I couldn't bear it. I couldn't think, I couldn't sleep, I couldn't focus on anything except that you'd gone, you'd left me.'

'Never. I may not have been physically with you but my heart is forever yours, Lore.'

At his glorious words she kissed him again. 'Woody, the reason I came here, the reason Hannah and I needed to follow you, was because…I love you, Woody. With all my heart, and I didn't want you to feel you had to carry your burdens alone. I wanted to come and tell you that whatever you needed to do to support Nilly and her family, I would stand by you—always.'

Lorelai shook her head, her heart, her eyes, her words filled with love. 'We belong together. You. Me. Hannah. I love the way you care for Hannah, the way you adore your sister and the way you willingly stepped into the role of protector for Nilly and her clan in what was most probably a dark time for you all. I love you, Woody, and I would be honoured if you'd be my *par'machkai*.' She stared up at him, then bit her lip. 'Did I say it right?'

Woody looked at her with a mixed expression somewhere between surprise and elation but hidden in the depths was the smallest hint of doubt. 'You said it perfectly but, Lore, are you sure? Are you sure I'm the man you want?'

'Why wouldn't I want to spend the rest of my life with you, Woody?' There was no hesitation in her tone. She knew, even though he'd never said the words, that he loved both her and Hannah. He'd make the most wonderful father, of that she was sure. He was the man for her and she wasn't about to let any minor hint of doubt ruin that.

'Lore, I…' He shook his head. 'What if I mess things up? Near the end of her life, Kalenia was—'

'Depressed and not in her right mind. Her death, that of your child and your father-in-law were not your fault and I'm sure Nilly and everyone else here in this village would agree with me.' Lorelai clasped both his hands in hers and gave him a watery smile, her voice rich with emotion. 'I'm scared, too, Woody. I failed at my first marriage, remember?'

'You didn't fail. John failed you.'

'Either way, it wasn't a success but with you I know it will be different. Both of us felt that dynamic pull towards each other the first time we met. This—you and I—it's meant to be. I really want you to be my *par'machkai*, Woody. I'm excited to take part in the festival, to learn the customs of the Tarparniian people, to come back and visit Nilly and the rest of the village many times. They're a part of you and therefore they're a part of me. Please, please, say you'll be my *par'machkai*?'

Woody's answer was to bend down and brush a soft kiss across her lips. 'I'd be honoured. I love you, Lorelai. I have for quite some time but I kept thinking I'd lose you so didn't want to offer a commitment.'

'You're nuts.'

'Yes, yes, I am. I'm also crazy—crazy for you. Taking part in the festival tonight will be wonderful, declaring our love in the bonding ceremony.'

'And don't think this lets you off the hook of a bona fide proposal when we return to Australia,' she murmured against his mouth as he kissed her. 'I've proposed here in Tarparnii so it's up to you to propose to me for our Australian wedding.'

Woody smiled down into the face of the woman he loved, unable to believe how happy she made him. 'All right. I'll propose,' he murmured. 'But do you think you'll say yes?'

Lorelai's answer was to laugh before pressing her lips lovingly to his.

* * * * *

Read on for a sneak preview of Carol Marinelli's
PUTTING ALICE BACK TOGETHER!

Hugh hired bikes!

You know that saying: 'It's like riding a bike, you never forget'?

I'd never learnt in the first place.

I never got past training wheels.

'You've got limited upper-body strength?' He stopped and looked at me.

I had been explaining to him as I wobbled along and tried to stay up that I really had no centre of balance. I mean *really* had no centre of balance. And when we decided, fairly quickly, that a bike ride along the Yarra perhaps, after all, wasn't the best activity (he'd kept insisting I'd be fine once I was on, that you never forget), I threw in too my other disability. I told him about my limited upper-body strength, just in case he took me to an indoor rock-climbing centre next. I'd honestly forgotten he was a doctor, and he seemed worried, like I'd had a mini-stroke in the past or had mild cerebral palsy or something.

'God, Alice, I'm sorry—you should have said. What happened?'

And then I had had to tell him that it was a self

diagnosis. 'Well, I could never get up the ropes at the gym at school.' We were pushing our bikes back. 'I can't blow-dry the back of my hair…' He started laughing.

Not like Lisa who was laughing at me—he was just laughing and so was I. We got a full refund because we'd only been on our bikes ten minutes, but I hadn't failed. If anything, we were getting on better.

And better.

We went to St Kilda to the lovely bitty shops and I found these miniature Russian dolls. They were tiny, made of tin or something, the biggest no bigger than my thumbnail. Every time we opened them, there was another tiny one, and then another, all reds and yellows and greens.

They were divine.

We were facing each other, looking down at the palm of my hand, and our heads touched.

If I put my hand up now, I can feel where our heads touched.

I remember that moment.

I remember it a lot.

Our heads connected for a second and it was alchemic; it was as if our minds kissed hello.

I just have to touch my head, just there at the very spot and I can, whenever I want to, relive that moment.

So many times I do.

'Get them.' Hugh said, and I would have, except that little bit of tin cost more than a hundred dollars and, though that usually wouldn't have stopped me, I wasn't have my card declined in front of him.

m back.

ave him a smile. 'Gotta stop the impulse

spending.'

We had lunch.

Out on the pavement and I can't remember what we ate, I just remember being happy. Actually, I can remember: I had Caesar salad because it was the lowest carb thing I could find. We drank water and I *do* remember not giving it a thought.

I was just thirsty.

And happy.

He went to the loo and I chatted to a girl at the next table, just chatted away. Hugh was gone for ages and I was glad I hadn't demanded Dan from the universe, because I would have been worried about how long he was taking.

Do I go on about the universe too much? I don't know, but what I do know is that something *was* looking out for me, helping me to be my best, not to **** this up as I usually do. You see, we walked on the beach, we went for another coffee and by that time it was evening and we went home and he gave me a present.

Those Russian dolls.

I held them in my palm, and it was the nicest thing he could have done for me.

They are absolutely my favourite thing and I've just stopped to look at them now. I've just stopped to take them apart and then put them all back together again and I can still feel the wonder I felt on that day.

He was the only man who had bought something for me, I mean something truly special. Something beautiful, something thoughtful, something just for me.

© Carol Marinelli 2012

Available at millsandboon.co.uk

2 Free Books!

Join the Mills & Boon Book Club

Want to read more **Medical** books?
We're offering you **2 more**
absolutely **FREE!**

We'll also treat you to these fabulous extras:

 **Books up to 2 months ahead
of shops**

 FREE home delivery

 **Bonus books with our special
rewards scheme**

 **Exclusive offers and
much more!**

Get your free books now!

*Visit us
Online*

Find out more at
www.millsandboon.co.uk/freebookoffer

SUBS/ONLINE/M

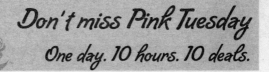

Don't miss Pink Tuesday
One day. 10 hours. 10 deals.

PINK TUESDAY
IS COMING!

10 hours...10 unmissable deals!

This Valentine's Day we will be bringing
you fantastic offers across a range of
our titles—each hour, on the hour!

Save up to 90%!

Pink Tuesday starts
9am Tuesday 14th February

Find out how to grab a Pink Tuesday deal—
register online at **www.millsandboon.co.uk**

Visit us Online

0212/PM/MB362

afin m R/

& 🌹 *A sneaky peek at next month...*

Medical Romance

CAPTIVATING MEDICAL DRAMA—WITH HEART

My wish list for next month's titles...

In stores from 2nd March 2012:

Visit us Online

You can buy our books online a month before they hit the shops! **www.millsandboon.co.uk**

0212/03